"Who are you?" Pasha whispered as he gaped at the cinder-smudged girl.

She stared at them for another moment. Then she spun on her heel and fled, a streak of red hair and gray dress dashing into the woods and disappearing into its shadowed depths.

But Nikolai didn't need her to tell them who she was. He already knew. He had never seen the girl before, but she had to be the one.

The other enchanter in the Game.

Also by Evelyn Skye
The Crown's Fate

THE
CROWN'S
GAME

EVELYN SKYE

BALZER + BRAY

An Imprint of HarperCollins*Publishers*

Balzer + Bray is an imprint of HarperCollins Publishers.

The Crown's Game
Copyright © 2016 by Evelyn Skye

www.epicreads.com

Library of Congress Control Number: 2015955181
ISBN 978-0-06-242259-0

Typography by Jenna Stempel
17 18 19 20 21   PC/LSCH   10 9 8 7 6 5 4 3 2 1

First paperback edition, 2017

For Reese—
You are the reason I believe in magic.

The Crown's Game is an old one, older than the tsardom itself. It began long ago, in the age of Rurik, Prince of Novgorod, when Russia was still a cluster of tribes, wild and lawless and young. As the country matured over the centuries, so, too, did the game. But always, always it retained its untamed fierceness.

For the winner of the game, there would be unimaginable power.

For the defeated, desolate oblivion.

The Crown's Game was not one to lose.

CHAPTER ONE
OCTOBER 1825

The smell of sugar and yeast welcomed Vika even before she stepped into the pumpkin-shaped shop on the main street of their little town. She resisted the urge to burst into Cinderella Bakery—her father had labored for sixteen years to teach her how to be demure—and she slipped into the shop and took her place quietly at the end of the line of middle-aged women.

One of them turned to greet her but shrank away when she saw it was Vika, as people always did. It was as if they suspected that what ran through her veins was not blood as in the rest of them, but something hotter and more volatile that might burn any who came too near. Her wild red hair with its streak of jet black down the center likely did nothing to settle the women either. The only thing "normal" about Vika was her dress, the pretty (albeit rumpled) green gown her father insisted she wear whenever she went into town—minus the dreadful yellow ribbon that cinched her waist too tightly, which she'd rather conveniently "lost" in

Preobrazhensky Creek.

Vika smiled at the woman, though it came out as half smirk. The woman huffed at Vika's impudence, then turned forward again in line.

Vika allowed herself a full smirk now.

When all the women in line had been served and had fled the bakery—*fled from* me, Vika thought with a shrug—Ludmila Fanina, the plump baker behind the counter, turned her attention to her.

"*Privet*, my darling Vee-kahhh," Ludmila said, drawing out her name in operatic song. She was the only one on Ovchinin Island—besides Vika's father—who met Vika's eyes when she saw her. The baker continued singing, "How are you this fine morning?"

Vika applauded, and Ludmila bobbed in an awkward curtsy. She bumped into a tray of *oreshki* cookies, and the caramel-walnut confections teetered on the edge of the counter. Typical Ludmila. Vika furtively charmed the tray to keep its balance.

"*Ochen kharasho, spasiba*," Vika said. *I'm very well, thank you.* She spoke in Russian, unlike the aristocrats in Saint Petersburg, who preferred the "more sophisticated" French. Her father might have been nobility (Baron Sergei Mikhailovich Andreyev, to be exact), but he wanted his daughter to grow up truly Russian—hiking through birch forests, playing the balalaika, and having an almost religious zeal for buckwheat kasha with mushrooms and fresh butter. It was why they lived on this rural island, rather than in the imperial capital, because Sergei swore that living on Ovchinin Island kept them closer to the heart of their country.

"And how are you?" Vika asked Ludmila.

"Oh, quite well, now that you've brought a ray of sunshine into my shop," the baker said in a normal voice. "The usual for Sergei?"

"But of course. It's the only thing Father will eat for breakfast."

Ludmila laughed as she fetched a Borodinsky loaf, the dense Russian black bread that was Sergei's daily staple. She wrapped the bread in brown paper, creased the corners, and tied it with cotton twine.

Vika paid and tucked the bread into her basket, which contained a few sausages from the butcher and a jar of dill pickles from the grocer two streets down, where she had stopped earlier. "Thank you," she said, already halfway outside. She adored Ludmila, but the bakery walls were too thick, and the air too humid, like sitting in a sauna for a few minutes too long. It was much better to be outdoors, where there were no boundaries placed on her. "See you tomorrow."

"Until then, Vee-kahhh," Ludmila sang, as the door to the bakery swung shut.

Vika stumbled as she hurried up the narrow dirt path that wound through the hills of Ovchinin Island and into the woods. She was supposed to maintain a practiced calm when she was out where people could see her, but it was difficult. Sergei said it was because Vika was like a jinni whose bottle was too small to contain her. *One day, I'll create a world where there are no bottles at all*, she thought.

For now, she wanted to get back to her father, and to the challenge he'd designed for her. As Vika crossed the perimeter of the forest, she leaned forward, muscles set yet relaxed, like a veteran racehorse on the starting line.

Two more years, she thought. *Two more years of training, and my magic will be powerful enough to serve the tsar and the empire.* Maybe then her figurative jinni bottle would finally be big enough.

Vika jumped over logs and wove through moss-covered rocks. As she hurdled over Preobrazhensky Creek, which burbled as if it had its own lesson to hurry to, she spotted her father, sitting on a log. His tunic and trousers were muddy from his morning spent digging up valerian root. There were leaves in his beard. And he was whittling a chunk of wood. Never had a baron looked so much like a peasant. Vika smiled.

"The bread smells delicious," Sergei said, angling his nose at Vika's basket.

She grinned. "Perhaps I'll let you have some in exchange for starting my lesson."

"Sixteen years, and still no patience." The laugh lines around her father's eyes deepened, as if his plow had gone straight from his vegetable fields onto his weathered brown skin.

"You confuse impatience with enthusiasm," Vika mock-scolded. "Just because I'm the only enchanter in the empire doesn't mean I'm going to rest on my laurels."

Her father dipped his head, conceding her point. "Have you put up the shield?"

"Of course." She'd had lessons for a decade now, ever since she was old enough to understand that enchanting was not only for fun, but also for serving Russia and the tsar. Casting an invisible barrier around the forest before starting a lesson was something she did automatically, without a thought.

Still, Vika glanced over her shoulder, to make sure a villager hadn't strayed into the woods. Her entire life, her father had hammered into her that people had been burned at the stake for much less than what she could do. And Vika didn't fancy a death engulfed in flames.

But no one was in the woods today. That was another reason they lived on this tiny forest of an island. There were but a few hundred people on Ovchinin Island, and they all lived on the flatlands, near the harbor. Up here in the hills, it was only Sergei, a mild-mannered scientist obsessed with medicinal herbs, and Vika, his doting (if not entirely obedient) daughter.

"All right," her father said. "I'd like you to create a lightning storm. No need for rain, just dry lightning. And aim for that tree." He pointed to a birch twenty feet away.

"Why?"

He shook his head, but there was a gleam in his eyes. "You know better than to ask why."

Which was true. He wasn't going to tell her what the lesson was. That would ruin the surprise. Besides, Vika liked surprises.

Behind her, something darted out of the shrubbery. Vika spun toward it, hands poised to freeze whatever it was. But it was only a pheasant dashing into another bush—nothing unusual, and certainly not the start of her lesson. She laughed, and her voice echoed through the wispy white trees. But when she turned back to the log where Sergei had been sitting, there was only empty space.

"Father?"

Huh. Where had he gone? Then again, this was not out of the ordinary. Sergei often removed himself from the scene

5

of the lesson so she could work things out herself. He was probably somewhere safely away from her impending lightning storm.

Speaking of which, the lightning wasn't going to summon itself.

Vika set down her basket, raised her arms, and focused on the invisible particles of electricity in the sky. They flitted around like sparks of static dust, content to whirl through the air by themselves. But that wasn't what she wanted. *Come together*, she willed them. *Come and play with me.*

The sky hummed, and then out of the clear blue came a deafening crack that split the silence. Vika covered her ears at the same time the lightning hit the birch tree twenty feet away and lit the trunk on fire.

As soon as the bolt struck, a silver wire flared. It had been camouflaged among the leaves, but now, as electricity blazed through it, Vika saw that the wire connected the first birch to a ring of fifty others. The initial fire spread so quickly, it was as if lightning had struck every single tree.

Her father might not have had much magic—he was a mentor, not an enchanter, so he could only manage small-scale conjuring and charms—but he was expert at setting elaborate traps. Vika was surrounded by flames and bitter smoke. The tree trunks teetered.

Vika smiled. *Here we go.*

As one of the trees began to fall, Vika shoved her hands outward to force the wind to push the tree back upright. It would have worked, if only one tree were falling. But there were fifty or so birches, all seething with fire and ash and toppling toward her at a speed too quick for her to reverse the motions of them all.

What to do, what to do . . .

The trees were nearly upon her.

Water! No, ice! Vika flung herself to the forest floor and waved her arm over her head, generating a dome of ice around her. She trembled as tree after tree slammed into her shield and sent icy shards stabbing into her neck and back. Crimson rivulets of blood trickled down the bodice of her dress. Vika squeezed her eyes shut.

The fiery assault seemed to last an eternity, and yet she held her position. Then, finally, the last trunk crashed into her ice shield, the earth shuddered, and the sky ceased to thunder.

Her smile burned even brighter.

CHAPTER TWO

Sergei sat on a nearby boulder the entire time Vika was crouched beneath her shield of ice. If he could, he would have helped her. But he couldn't. It was part of her training. She would face dangers greater than this when she became Imperial Enchanter.

At the end of five hours, Vika had charmed the last of the fifty fallen trees to rise off her shelter, and the ice melted. She emerged in a puddle, shivering.

She clucked her tongue at Sergei. "Father, you could have killed me."

"You know I would never do that. If I did, who would fetch my bread from the bakery every morning?"

"Well, the joke is on you, for it's well past noon now, and you left your bread with me." Vika winked as she reached into her basket and tossed him the icy loaf.

He defrosted it as it flew through the air, and it was toasty by the time he caught it. "You know I wouldn't do anything that could kill you, but the tsar isn't looking for someone to perform parlor tricks. Yes, there will be fancy balls and state dinners for which your aesthetic talents will be called upon. But there will also be politics and backstabbing and war."

A smile bloomed across Vika's face. "A little peril has never stopped me." She tipped her head toward the charred remains of the bonfire. "In fact, it makes me want to be Imperial Enchanter even more."

Sergei shook his head and laughed. "I know. You're fiery and you like things even better when they are challenging, just like your mother did. Nothing is too daunting for you, Vikochka."

She wrinkled her nose at the nickname. It was too cute for her now that she was grown, but Sergei couldn't help it. He still remembered when she was a baby, so small he could fit her in his cupped palms.

When she was younger, Vika had sometimes lamented not having other magical children with whom to play. But she quickly outgrew that, for Sergei had explained that it made her special, and not only in Russia. Most of the world had forgotten about magic, and so enchanters had grown rarer. It was rumored that Morocco had an enchanter, as their sultan was a patron of the old ways. But that was it, really, besides the tsar, who tried to keep his own belief in mysticism quiet. It was a political liability to believe in the "occult." Besides, concealing the fact that he had an Imperial Enchanter allowed the tsar a secret weapon against his enemies. Not that it was foolproof. Imperial Enchanters were still human, as evidenced by the unexpected death twenty years ago of the previous enchanter, Yakov Zinchenko, in the battle against Napoleon at Austerlitz.

Once, when Vika was six and just beginning her lessons, she had asked why Sergei wasn't the Imperial Enchanter.

"My magic is much too small," he'd answered, which was the truth, but only part of it. He'd swallowed the rest, a secret he kept for himself and hoped she'd never have to know.

"But my magic is big?" Vika had asked, oblivious.

"The biggest," Sergei had said. "And I will teach you as best I can to become the greatest enchanter there ever was."

Now, ten years later and a hundred times more powerful, Vika asked, "Are you worried I won't be ready to become Imperial Enchanter?"

Sergei sighed. "No . . . I didn't say that. I only meant . . . well, I want to keep you here on Ovchinin Island. For selfish reasons. I'd rather not share you with the tsar."

"Oh, Father. You're all gruff beard on the outside, but mush on the inside. Wonderful, sentimental mush." She smiled in that way she used to when she was small, eyes big and innocent. Well, as innocent as was possible for Vika.

Sergei crossed the muddy patch of forest between them and wrapped his arms around her. "I do not envy you. It is a burdensome calling, to be the tsar's enchanter. Promise me you'll remain my mischievous Vikochka, no matter what the future may bring."

"I swear it." Vika touched a finger to the basalt pendant around her neck. It was something she did for the most unbreakable of promises, because swearing on her dead mother's necklace seemed to lend solemnity to any commitment. It was also a tad theatrical, and Vika was fond of self-aware melodrama. Still, Sergei knew that the few

10

promises she'd ever made on the necklace were sworn in complete earnestness.

"But you know," Vika said as she pulled away from his embrace, "I wouldn't mind leaving the island once in a while. Or ever."

"I don't like Saint Petersburg," he said.

"What about Finland? It's not far."

"The Grand Duchy of Finland does not interest me at all."

"It might interest me."

"I am sure you will do plenty of traveling once you're Imperial Enchanter. But my time with you is limited. Humor an old man and stay on the island with me a bit longer. It's only seven more seasons until you turn eighteen."

Vika chewed on her lip. Sergei braced himself. He knew that glint in her eyes; when you had an enchantress as a daughter, disagreements often became more demonstrative than mere words.

Suddenly, the red and orange leaves around them fluttered to the forest floor, and autumn rushed away. Then a blast of snow set in on the bare branches. A moment later, the icicles melted, and flower buds shot out of the damp ground and blossomed in full perfume. They were quickly replaced by the lush greenery of summer. Then autumn again. And winter. And spring. All in less than a minute.

"Looks like seven seasons have passed," Vika said.

Sergei crossed his arms over his chest. "Vikochka."

"Oh, fine." She changed the season back to autumn, as it should be. The leaves on the birch trees were golden once again.

"Is it truly so unbearable to be here with me?"

"No, of course not, Father. I just—"

"I'll challenge you even more in your lessons."

Vika perked up. "Really?"

"As much as you'd like."

"I'd like to be a menace to anyone who dares to trouble Russia."

"You already are a menace."

Vika pecked Sergei on the cheek. "Then make me a bigger one."

CHAPTER THREE

Nikolai's pocket watch clicked as the hour struck two in the morning. He ought to have gone to bed long ago, but here he still was, standing in front of a tri-fold mirror in his bedroom as a measuring tape and several pins flew around him, designing a new frock coat. For a once pudgy orphan from the Kazakh steppe, Nikolai had grown up to be rather striking. His eyes were dark and fierce, his face and body all sharp planes, and yet there was an impossible fluidity to the way he moved—in fact, even in the way he stood—that was both incongruous with his trenchant edges and an inseparable part of his being. It was a brooding sort of elegance not often seen on a boy of eighteen.

The clothing he tailored was, of course, necessary for life in the heart of the capital. There was always an invitation to lunch or to play cards or to go to the countryside to hunt. But Nikolai had had to fend for himself in every one of these realms, for his mentor and benefactor, Countess Galina Zakrevskaya, was not about to spend a kopek on him for new boots or a proper rifle for shooting grouse, and certainly not for dance lessons, even though Galina's friends deemed it fashionable to invite her charity case to their balls.

And so Nikolai had learned to barter. He delivered packages for the tailors at Bissette & Sons in exchange for bolts of cloth. He sharpened swords for an army lieutenant in return for lessons. He served as an unpaid assistant to Madame Allard, the ballroom instructor to all the debutantes, and as a result, learned to dance in the company of the prettiest girls in the city. Nikolai knew he was worth at least the same as the noble-born boys in the capital, and he refused to give anyone an excuse to prove otherwise.

So while Nikolai might not have *belonged* to Saint Petersburg society, he was *in* it, in his own ill-fitting way. And all the while, Galina's daft admirers praised her for her *caritas* and her ability to polish a rough Kazakh stone into the semblance of a proper Petersburg jewel. Galina did not correct them.

Now Nikolai stood very still while his scissors hovered above a mahogany table on the other side of the room, cutting through a panel of black wool. He pointed at the scissors to slice a notch in the lapel.

Before they had a chance, though, Galina barged into his room—it was her house he lived in, after all—and halted the scissors in midair. *"Arrête."* She spoke French, just as she had the first time he met her, when he was a child and still living in a nomadic village on the Kazakh steppe. Then, French had been gibberish to him. But now the language was second nature, and Nikolai was rather proud that he spoke it without an accent. All the aristocracy in Saint Petersburg spoke French.

Nikolai shifted from his position in front of the mirrors, where the cloth tape was still busily flying about.

"No step in the lapels," Galina said.

"But I like them notched."

"For informal frock coats, that is acceptable. But this one ought to be formal. And make it double-breasted."

Nikolai bit the inside of his cheek. How utterly like Galina to deny him something as simple as notched lapels. But he swirled his hand in the air as he relayed new instructions to his scissors. They repositioned themselves and began snipping again.

"Actually, we don't have time for this." Galina clapped her hands three times, which made the jeweled bangles on her wrists jingle, and the wool and scissors vanished.

"Hey!"

"Get dressed to go out and meet me downstairs in five minutes. It's time for a lesson."

"It's two o'clock in the morning."

Galina shrugged and glided out of his room.

Nikolai sighed. Ever since her husband, the old war hero Count Mikhail Zakrevsky, had died six years ago, Galina had grown even more intractable than she'd been before. So it was no accident that Nikolai had turned out a touch morose. He'd endured Galina's lack of pity for a sum total of eleven years.

Nikolai eyed his bed. Without the project of his frock coat, a curtain of fatigue suddenly threatened to drop over him. His pillows crooned a siren song.

He could refuse Galina's command. It was inhumane to train at this hour.

But if he disobeyed, he would have to leave, because he

was only given a place in the Zakrevsky house as long as he was Galina's student. And he could not give that up, because studying with her was his ticket to becoming more than a no-name orphan. He could be Imperial Enchanter someday.

However, it wouldn't be as easy as knocking on the Winter Palace door and asking for the job. Well, it would have been, if Nikolai were the only enchanter in Russia, but it so happened that there had been two enchanters born after the last one perished. It was an anomaly, having more than one enchanter at a time, but not completely unprecedented. Like Mother Nature's occasional deviations from the norm, so Russia's magic sometimes gifted the empire with a pair of enchanters rather than only one.

But there was a solution for that. "It's a game," Galina had told Nikolai when she'd taken him under her tutelage. "The one with the best magic wins."

He'd been only seven when Galina came to the Kazakh steppe—the border between Asia and the Russian Empire— and she'd been unlike any woman Nikolai had ever seen. A dainty hat perched atop carefully coiffed brown curls. A voluminous gown made of iridescent purple fabric that shimmered in the sweltering midday sun. And preposterously high-heeled boots that looked like an accident waiting to happen on the uneven terrain of the grassy steppe.

An accident, that is, if the woman were actually walking. Nikolai twisted the hem of his tunic as he studied her. He focused on the space between the ground and the soles of her tiny feet and discovered that there was, indeed, a space between, if only inches. She levitated and merely moved her legs to create the illusion of walking. And she did so without seeming aware of it, as if the movement had been a part of her for decades. Nikolai grinned and puffed out his chest. The other children in the village wouldn't have noticed. They would simply have thought the woman was preternaturally graceful.

When she floated to a stop in front of him seconds later, she stooped—although still hovering—and asked, *"C'est toi que je cherche?"*

Nikolai tilted his head, and the fringe of his dark hair fell in his face. He could not understand the woman's language.

The woman muttered something to herself. Then she spoke again, this time in halting Russian, as if she had learned it by eavesdropping on others but not actually speaking it herself. *"Eto ti?"* Are you the one I'm looking for?

Nikolai screwed up his face at her pronunciation.

"I am the Countess Galina Zakrevskaya," she said, "and I have come for you. Where are your parents?"

"Mama died when I was born," Nikolai said without regret. He had not known her, so he had not had the opportunity to form an attachment. "And my father is also long gone."

Galina nodded, as if she had expected as much. "Then you are all alone?"

"I have the village." Nikolai pointed behind him at the cluster of colorful yurts, round tents decorated with brightly colored patterns woven in a rainbow of zigzags and stripes.

"I doubt they will mind one less mouth to feed," Galina said.

Which was true. The villagers had traded him to Galina all too easily, in exchange for two horses and two sheep. They'd been happy to be rid of the boy with powers they did not understand, that seemed to them to stem from the devil.

So now, even though Nikolai grumbled as he glanced at his pocket watch and at the empty space where his scissors and cloth had just been, he only half meant the curses he swore under his breath. *I didn't come all this way from the steppe only to revert to a sheepherder*, he thought. *And I certainly don't intend to continue as an errand boy.*

He commanded the ivory-inlaid doors of his armoire to open, and clothes flew out to meet him. He didn't know what Galina had planned, but he did know he needed to be more than presentable. She was very particular about appearances, which was ironic given that she'd never bought him so much as a handkerchief. It was as if she expected him to create something out of nothing.

Perhaps that was precisely the point.

Nikolai snapped his fingers, and a black cravat tied itself expertly around his neck. Next, a blue paisley waistcoat (which Nikolai had made last month) buttoned itself around him. Then, finally, a black frock coat enveloped him, although he smiled smugly as he chose one with notched lapels, because Galina be damned, it was two in the morning, and if there was any time that was informal enough for notched lapels, it was in these dead-eyed hours between twilight and dawn.

Oh, and a hat. He couldn't forget his top hat.

Having dressed, Nikolai flicked his fingers at the door to open it. He strode down the hall and, seeing no sign of Galina, slid down the curved wooden banister to the first floor. The grandfather clock at the base of the stairs showed four minutes past the hour. Nikolai hurried across the Persian rug in the drawing room, through the foyer—dark since the candles in the chandelier were dormant—and out the front door.

Galina was already tapping her high-heeled boot on what would be the cobblestones had her feet actually touched the ground. But of course they didn't. Galina had always thought the ground was both literally and figuratively beneath her.

She arched her brow as she took in Nikolai's notched lapels. Then, after just enough scrutiny to push him to the brink of cringing, she turned abruptly and started down the street, toward Ekaterinsky Canal, without giving any hint as to where she was headed, nor what she intended to do.

Nikolai swore under his breath again and hurried to follow.

CHAPTER FOUR

They wound through streets lit only by occasional lamps, their reflections shimmering on the damp cobblestones. Galina led Nikolai past grand mansions with pastel facades and ornate windows trimmed in white and gold, over the stone bridges that traversed the city's many canals—which had earned Saint Petersburg its nickname as the "Venice of the North"—and through grand squares empty of everything but bronze statues protecting the night. The dark closed in on Nikolai, and he pulled his coat tighter around himself. He thought again of his cozy bed. Where in the devil's name was Galina taking him?

Eventually, they arrived at the front door of the Imperial Public Library, on the corner of Nevsky Prospect—the wide, main boulevard of the city—and Sadovaya Street. The library was an immense stone building painted powder blue, with white statues flanked by white columns. It housed national and foreign treasures, like Voltaire's personal library, and since Galina had not wanted to pay for

Nikolai's enrollment at either a gymnasium or a military cadet school, Nikolai had educated himself in his scraps of free time within these very walls. The Imperial Public Library was one of his favorite places in the city. And now, at two thirty in the morning, the building somehow seemed even grander to him, looming like a shadow too colossal to be restrained.

"Please tell me you don't intend for me to break into the library?"

Galina looked down at him, for she was now hovering a foot in the air, since there was no one in the streets at this hour other than drunks, whose hungover morning stories would never be believed. (Which raised the question, again, of why Nikolai had to be dressed so neatly.)

"As if I would so disrespect a national institution!" Galina said. "No, I simply want you to reshelve some of the books inside. They have been misplaced."

"Reshelve them . . . now? From outside?"

"Of course now, and of course from outside." She threw her hands in the air. "Do you think we're out here because I wanted a walking companion?"

"I—"

"The Game will begin soon. You can feel it, can't you?"

Can I? Nikolai stuck out his tongue, as if he could taste the difference in the air. And in fact, he could. It was like . . . cinnamon. With a dash of death.

Nikolai's stomach, which was already unsettled from being denied sleep, sank to the bottom of his boots.

Galina carried on as if her announcement about the Game were ordinary news. "There are five books slotted into the wrong spaces on the shelves."

Nikolai took a deep breath. *Don't think about the Game yet. Focus on this single task.* Besides, he was probably wrong about the air, for who'd ever heard of magic tasting like cinnamon? And taste buds that detected death were not to be trusted. Death wasn't a flavor or even a scent.

"What are the titles of the books?" he asked Galina.

"You don't need them. This is about concentration, Nikolai, and working under pressure." She glanced up at the sky, and even though it was still pitch-black but for the streetlamps, she acted as if she could already see the sun's first rays. "Tick-tock. I estimate three hours, perhaps less, before the underlings of the city begin to scurry about on their errands and someone reports you to the Tsar's Guard."

Nikolai's stomach remained firmly splattered at the soles of his boots. There were hundreds of thousands, perhaps millions, of books in the library. And he had to find five that were out of order? In three hours? He sank onto the corner of the street and leaned back against a flickering lamp.

"Don't be pathetic," Galina said. "Oh, and don't let anyone catch you charming anything, of course."

Nikolai barely nodded. This had been drummed into him every time she gave him a lesson in a public place. He had to protect his identity. Galina was quite certain the other enchanter didn't know Nikolai existed, but just in case, he had to hide who he was. It would give him the advantage of surprise when the Game commenced.

Of course, Galina hadn't bothered telling him who the other enchanter was or how she knew in the first place. "I'm a mentor," she'd said by way of nonexplanatory explanation, invoking again her long bloodline of ancestors whose task it was to train enchanters. "And in any case, it isn't important who the other enchanter is. It will only distract you from focusing on what *is* important: making yourself the best enchanter you can be. Moreover, I'm quite sure my teaching is far superior to what the other mentor can offer. As long as you do as you're told, of course."

And so it went. Galina would make demands, and Nikolai would comply.

Now she drifted away from the library, down Nevsky Prospect, in the direction from which they had come.

"If only her lessons didn't take place in the middle of the night." But Nikolai took a deep breath and cracked his knuckles. Exhaustion could be overcome; he'd done it plenty of times before.

He tossed aside his self-pity and rose from where he'd sat against the streetlamp. He focused on the Imperial Library's impenetrable walls. *Imagine they are transparent,* he thought. *Imagine the walls are nothing but air.*

They held on to their solidness for a moment. And then the walls seemed to shimmer before evaporating from Nikolai's sight altogether, and he could see straight through them.

At first, everything seemed too airy, too insubstantial, as if he'd entered a dimension inhabited solely by ghosts. But slowly, the rooms began to fill in, first the tables and chairs, then the columns and shelves, and finally, the books themselves.

Nikolai gasped. Seeing the hundreds of thousands of books now, when he had an impossible task to accomplish, was so much more daunting than in the past when he had browsed the shelves. *I'll never be able to sort through all of them.* Even if he had been physically inside the library, it would take weeks, perhaps months, to check all the spines to ensure they were in the proper order.

If he were more powerful, he might have been able to command all the books in the library to fly off the shelves at once and direct them to reorder themselves correctly. But that was the sort of dream one had after too many glasses of wine followed by too many shots of cheap vodka.

In his mind, Nikolai walked through the inside of the library, from the more popular reading rooms full of newspapers and magazines, to the rare documents room, which required special permission—at least, permission was required for those who could not see through walls and peruse the holdings in the middle of the night.

If I can isolate the books that have been touched within the last twenty-four hours—maybe not even that long, since Galina likely visited near the end of the day to minimize the risk of the librarians undoing her work—then I can command those books to reshelve themselves in the right places.

He clasped his hands in front of him, as if in prayer, and concentrated on catching the attention of every last book in the library. *If you were moved yesterday, I command you to move again, now. Slide forward, pull yourself off the shelf.*

Nikolai held his breath. Some of the volumes quivered in place. *Slide forward, pull yourself off the shelf,* he willed again. A few books started to move, just an inch. He knit his brow. *Slide forward, pull yourself off the shelf!*

And then all at once, a few hundred books leaped off the shelves and came to a sudden halt, suspended in midair. Nikolai smiled.

Now go back to your places, he commanded the books.

They did nothing but hover.

Hmm. Nikolai twisted his mouth. It would not be as simple as he'd hoped, for his plan apparently didn't work if the books weren't told specifically where to go. Still, it was only a few hundred books. He could do that. He could check the numbers on the spines against the numbers of the adjacent books, push back the ones that belonged, and pluck out the ones that did not. *Unless a convention of anarchists visited the library yesterday, most books ought to be in their rightful spaces.*

And so Nikolai began the painstaking sorting. The first book was a Russian dictionary; the books on the shelf behind it were all labeled with the same classification number. *You may slide back.* It obeyed and slotted itself neatly in place. The next several books were similarly in their corresponding spaces. Apparently, they had just been taken off the shelves to be perused, but the patrons had put them back correctly.

After forty-five minutes, though, Nikolai had not found a single misplaced book. He rubbed the back of his neck. Perhaps this strategy wasn't any good. Perhaps the charm he'd cast on the books was faulty. But it was creeping toward four in the morning now, too close to when the city would wake, and Nikolai couldn't start all over. He had to press on before he was discovered.

The next book floating off its shelf was a manual on the cultivation of wheat. But it had been placed beside economic treatises, which was clearly wrong even without comparing the numbers on the spines. "Finally," he said aloud. Nikolai directed the wheat manual several aisles down to its brethren.

One down, four to go.

But a pair of voices sounded from around the corner of Sadovaya Street. Nikolai inhaled sharply, then darted around the other corner of the library and pressed himself against the wall.

It was a couple of fishermen staggering home—or perhaps to the docks on the banks of the Neva River—after a long night at a tavern. They stopped a mere foot from where Nikolai stood holding his breath and every muscle. One of the drunkards unfastened his trousers and relieved himself on the streetlamp. The other laughed and undid his trousers, too, but he aimed his stream at the other man's.

"You motherless bastard!" The first fisherman waved his own stream like a stuttering liquid saber at the other's. A urine duel commenced.

Deuces! Were they eight years old?

The fishermen convulsed with laughter as they "battled" with their stinking yellow swords. Nikolai plastered himself flatter against the wall as the second drunkard's aim grew even worse and came within inches of Nikolai's boots.

Finally, they finished and tottered on their merry, unfettered way. Only when their sloppy footfalls receded did Nikolai allow himself to exhale.

He worked at a quicker tempo thereafter and found three more books in the wrong sections. Only one misplaced title remained. But Nikolai was no longer the only person on the street. It was now a quarter after five, and others had begun trickling past. Nevsky Prospect was, after all, one of the busiest streets in the city. And those people had begun casting strange glances at the well-dressed young gentleman who stood as if in a trance on the corner of Nevsky Prospect and Sadovaya Street.

A flower girl across the street eyed him. She waved over a man carrying several crates of apples.

Now or never, Nikolai thought. There were only thirty or so books that needed to be checked. He was not powerful enough to handle the movement of an entire library of books, but surely he could handle thirty? He clasped his hands even tighter in front of him and murmured, almost to himself, "Return to your proper places! All of you!"

Inside the library, two dozen books shot straight back into their spaces. Five or six, on the other hand, whizzed through the air, a couple nearly colliding with each other, and weaved their way through the library, back to their correct rooms, correct aisles, correct shelves.

Nikolai dropped his arms to his sides and blinked when it was done. All he could do now was hope that the misfiled books he'd found included the five Galina had shuffled herself.

The apple man set down his crates and began to march toward Nikolai. Nikolai spun on his heels and hurried down the street. "You! Sir!" the apple man yelled, not at all polite despite his use of the word "sir."

Nikolai did not turn around. Instead, he careened around a corner and darted into an alleyway. He checked around him—left, right, up, down—to make sure no one was watching from a doorway or window. Then he passed his hand over the length of his body from head to toe and cast over himself the illusion that his gentlemanly clothes were actually those of a working man. Top hat to crushed bowler hat. Frock coat to suit of coarse flannel. Cravat to stained handkerchief. And so on, down to the frayed laces of his worn brown boots. When Nikolai emerged from the alley, the apple man ran right by him.

Nikolai exhaled for the thousandth time since Galina had dragged him out into the night.

And now, finally, he could go home and sleep. That is, if Galina did not have another surprise there waiting for him.

CHAPTER FIVE

Yuliana glided down the halls of the Winter Palace, past white columns and crystal chandeliers and all manner of gold gilt on the walls. If she were any other fifteen-year-old girl, she would run, but she was the grand princess of Russia, and royalty did not run. Well, actually, her older brother, Pavel Alexandrovich Romanov, was running down the hall ahead of her, even though it was unbecoming of a crown prince.

But Yuliana was not Pasha—that was what his family and closest friends called him—in almost every way. Yuliana cared about economics and politics (she was carrying an enormous, rolled-up map at this very moment), and Pasha cared about hunting and reading. He was quick to smile and chatty with all the servants, whereas she had the propriety to maintain the hierarchy of her royal rank. And his hair was always a mess! No, Yuliana was nothing like Pasha, and thank goodness for that. The Russian Empire needed at least one Romanov in this generation with her head screwed on straight.

Pasha waited for her at the heavy gold doors that marked the entrance to their father's study, not even out of breath. Two members of the Tsar's Guard stood at attention, one on either side. They had likely already bowed to Pasha—he *was* the tsesarevich, after all—but they bowed again when they saw Yuliana.

"Is Father occupied?" she asked one of the guards.

"He is meeting with the tsarina, Your Imperial Highness."

"Then we'll come back later," Pasha said.

"No, we won't." Yuliana shoved open the doors before her brother or the guards could protest. Not that they would. They'd long ago learned that it was better to allow Yuliana her own way than to suffer her wrath.

The tsarina jumped in her armchair at the sound of the doors flinging open, then burst into a fit of coughs. The tsar merely looked up from his desk and sighed. "Yuliana, how many times have I asked you to have the guards announce you properly? Look what you've done to your mother. Elizabeth," he said to the tsarina, "are you all right?"

Yuliana glanced at the tsarina. A pale-blue handkerchief was pressed to her even paler face, her elegant hands shaking as she convulsed. "My apologies, Mother. I didn't mean to frighten you." Yuliana turned back to the tsar. "But Pasha has just returned, and he has much to say about the Kazakh steppe. It's rather alarming."

Pasha came up laughing behind her. "Only slightly more alarming than the way you enter a room."

Yuliana shot him one of her famous scowls.

It only made him laugh more. *Ugh. Brothers.*

The tsar sat back in his chair, which, although simpler, seemed as much a throne as the one in the official throne room. "Your mother was in the middle of discussing plans for Pasha's upcoming birthday," he said. When he frowned, he looked a lot like Yuliana. Or Yuliana looked a lot like him. Severe blond statues, straight out of ancient Rome.

"It's all right," the tsarina said, having finally stopped coughing. She gathered her voluminous silver skirts and rose. "I was finished."

"Mother," Pasha said, "don't go. What I have to say can wait."

"It really can't," Yuliana said.

The tsarina smiled and kissed Yuliana on the top of her carefully coiffed ringlets, then stood on her tiptoes to peck Pasha on the cheek. "It's fine, love, talk to your father." The tsarina smiled at the tsar, too, and she departed the room.

Yuliana set her map—still rolled up, for now—against her father's desk and sat in the armchair her mother had vacated. It hadn't a trace of warmth, as if it were too much to ask the tsarina's tiny, sickly body to produce enough heat to warm the cushions. But Yuliana pushed that out of her head. What was important right now was the Kazakhs and getting the tsar to do something about them.

"Father, what I—"

The tsar put up a hand. "Yuliana, why don't you let Pasha speak? It's he who was on the steppe, was it not?"

"Yes, well . . ." But she gestured at Pasha, for this was why she'd dragged him here in the first place, even though he'd wanted to go out to see his friends as soon as he'd arrived back in Saint Petersburg.

"So," the tsar said to Pasha, "I received word that Qasim refused to sup with you?"

"Indeed, Father," Pasha said, raking a hand through his hair, tousling it in that casually defiant way that all the girls of the nobility seemed to love. "Like waves of gold," Yuliana had overheard Baroness Zorina's daughter say at a recent tea. Yuliana had wanted to punch her in her vapid face.

"Although I abolished their khanate," the tsar said, "the Kazakhs still look to Qasim as their leader. I sent you to dine with him for a reason, Pasha. I needed you to gather information for me, especially after the Kazakhs attacked our Cossack detachments earlier this year."

Pasha leaned against one of their father's bookcases, his elbows behind him as support. "But I learned what we needed to know, even without meeting with Qasim."

"How?" the tsar said.

"I have my ways." Pasha smiled.

The tsar rubbed his eyes with the heels of his hands. "I don't think I want to know your methods," he said.

"No, Father, trust me, you do not." Yuliana tried not to smile—in general, she did not believe in smiles—but she couldn't help it, because her brother brought them out of her. And Pasha had already told Yuliana the *how* of his espionage.

Pasha was notorious for slipping out of the palace in plain clothes, masquerading as one of the common people so he could waste his time playing cards with fishermen on the dock or frequenting taverns with his friend Nikolai Karimov. It was no different on the Kazakh steppe, where Pasha had left his officer's uniform at the army's camp and sneaked out in a plain tunic and trousers. Then he'd wandered through the main trading post, posing as an innocent traveler.

He passed stalls full of brightly colored caps, flat on top and intricately embroidered on the sides. There was a table that specialized in dried apricots. And another with sacks full of grain.

It was around the corner from the butcher's stall, however, that Pasha stopped and loitered. A cluster of men gathered around the butcher, who held a cleaver over a side of lamb. The butcher was the youngest among them—twenty-five at the most—but he seemed to hold court over the others. Perhaps it was his hatchet of a knife that did it.

"The Russians are a pestilence," one man said.

"Yes, a pestilence, a plague," another added. "They think they can draw arbitrary borders and forbid us from migrating across them. We will not stand for it."

"Patience," the butcher said. "The plans for revolt are underway. Qasim's men are prepared."

"I hope so," the first man said.

"Without a doubt," the butcher said. He raised the cleaver over his head. The blade fell swiftly onto the lamb with an earsplitting *thwack*. "We will crush the Russian plague."

"I heard the tsar sent his son here bearing gifts and empty promises," one of the men said.

The butcher swung his cleaver, and it again hit the meat with a resounding smack. "Bring the tsesarevich to me, and I'll show the tsar what we think of their gifts. I'll skin his son like a lamb and send his carcass back with a bow tied on top."

The men had whooped and roared. Then they had discovered Pasha, and he'd tried to convince them he wasn't a

Russian spy. When they didn't believe him, fisticuffs ensued (Yuliana had stopped listening as carefully when Pasha got into the gory and glorious details of his fight), followed by a mad dash through the trading post, and Pasha successfully evading the last of his pursuers to return safely to camp.

The Imperial Army had left the Kazakh steppe soon after that.

Now Pasha winked at Yuliana, then wiped the roguishness from his face and cleared his throat to address their father. "The Kazakhs are incredibly unhappy with our reforms. They do not like our officials or our attempts to give them land for farming; they're nomads and believe we are forcing our culture down their throats. No amount of promising that we wish to strengthen the empire with them as our partners will work, in my opinion. Qasim's men are preparing for revolt."

"You are certain?"

"Yes, Father. I heard it with my own ears, and my men, in their reconnaissance, confirmed."

"Well, then."

"You see?" Yuliana said. "I told you it was of the utmost importance—"

"Am I done here?" Pasha asked, looking to the door.

"No," Yuliana said, at the same time the tsar said, "Yes."

"Wonderful," Pasha said. "Then I'm off." He pushed away from the bookcase and opened the door.

"Don't forget the Imperial Council meeting this afternoon," the tsar said.

Pasha paused.

"You *will* be there, Pasha."

He turned back to face the tsar. The brightness that

34

usually danced in Pasha's eyes went out. "Right. Of course I will, Father."

Yuliana very much doubted Pasha would make an appearance. He'd been on the Kazakh steppe for over a month, which far exceeded her brother's capacity for official duty. Not that he wasn't responsible; he was. It was just that Pasha did not like doing things a tsesarevich was supposed to do. Especially in uniform. And under the tsar's command.

Pasha slipped out of the study to his freedom. The guards again shut the door.

Yuliana scooted to the edge of her chair and picked up the map of the Kazakh territories she'd brought with her. She began to unfurl it on the tsar's desk.

The tsar raised his hand. "That will be unnecessary."

Yuliana scrunched her nose. "All right." She rerolled the map. "Then what are you going to do?"

"I'll decide after Pasha's birthday."

She whacked the map on the edge of the desk. "Father! You can't sit around and wait. An uprising is brewing—"

"Yuliana." The tsar rose from behind the desk, slowly, purposefully. With every inch, the shadow on his face grew darker. Every second it took for him to reach his full height felt like a year. "You are not tsar. *I* am. And that means I am the one who knows best what to do for our empire."

But Yuliana met his steely glare with her own. "Perhaps you're right, Father. But let's suppose, for once, that the day comes when you are no longer tsar. At least prepare Russia for it. At least lay the groundwork to protect Pasha and me." She marched around to the tsar's side of the desk, then past him, to the corner of the blue-and-gold rug that covered most of the study's floor.

"What are you——?"

But the tsar stopped his question as Yuliana rolled up a yard or so of the rug. Beneath it lay a trapdoor in the wood floor. She pulled a couple of pins from her hair and picked the lock within moments. The trapdoor opened with a creak and a puff of stale air.

"Commence the Crown's Game," she said as she retrieved a small but heavy chest from the hidden compartment. It looked, amazingly, like it had been painted and lacquered yesterday, as if magic repelled dust from its shiny surface. In fact, it probably did. "Give Russia an Imperial Enchanter, Father, so we can fight if we need to. Do it for Pasha, for his birthday, even if he doesn't know."

The tsar gripped the armrests of his chair. "But how do *you* know about enchanters, let alone that there are two now? That information was closely guarded and limited to myself and those who practice magic themselves. How could you know about the Game?"

Yuliana crossed the rug and set the chest on the tsar's desk. Inside the chest, the ancient Russe Quill and Scroll lay dormant but ready to record the next Crown's Game when the need arose. She glanced at her father's throne-like chair.

"I know many things." She didn't tell him that when she was very little, she used to hide in the large cabinet behind his desk and eavesdrop on his conversations, including the ones he'd have with himself when he thought the rest of the palace was asleep, about subjects like enchanters and the Game and a mysterious "tsars' collection" (which Yuliana had deduced to be a library of ancient texts on magic—and presumably where her father had learned about enchanters and the Crown's Game in the first place—though she had never been able to locate this so-called "tsars' collection").

"Pasha may be heir," she said to her father, "but when you're gone—heaven forbid—he won't be able to rule Russia with charm alone. He'll need me. And he'll need an Imperial Enchanter."

"It's been peaceful in Russia for years."

"The peace we've known since Napoleon's end will soon be no more. Pasha's report is proof. And the Ottomans are rising again in the south. So will you do it? Will you declare the start of the Game?"

The tsar hesitated for a heavy minute.

"Do it for Pasha," Yuliana said. And she meant it. She loved her brother ferociously, as much as the tsar did. They'd both lay down their lives for him.

"How old are you again, Yuliana?"

"Fifteen, Father."

"But you act like you're—"

"Fifty. I know."

The tsar chuckled. "For Pasha, eh?" He touched his finger to the lid of the wooden chest. It was the one thing that Yuliana had never been able to pick open, and now she understood why: it was governed by magic that would unlock only at the tsar's touch.

The lid eased itself open, as if lifted by an invisible hand. A long, majestic black feather—plucked from the wing of a sea eagle centuries ago—and a yellowed parchment scroll floated into the air.

Yuliana gasped, for even though she knew *of* magic, she'd never actually witnessed it. "So does this mean you'll commence the Game?"

The tsar nodded.

She stared at the Russe Quill and Scroll. They spun lazily above the desk, the records of all past Games and so much of Russia's history, just hovering. "But we probably shouldn't tell Pasha," she said.

The tsar nodded again. "It's why I've never told you about the existence of enchanters and magic. I knew this generation would require a Game. And I didn't know if the two of you—Pasha, really—would be able to stomach its viciousness."

But Yuliana could. Her mouth curved up at the corners. Her smile was both a fierce and wistful thing.

CHAPTER SIX

Two days later, Nikolai sat on a palomino mare on Ovchinin Island. He had never been there before, even though it was only an hour's ferry ride from Saint Petersburg, but when Pasha had asked where they ought to hunt, "Ovchinin Island" had sprung from Nikolai's tongue before his mind could catch up with the idea. He had no inkling where it had come from.

But it turned out to be a grand decision. The sky was clear, the forest was dappled in red and gold, as it was wont to do in these early days of October, and the hounds were salivating for a chase. Nikolai watched as Pasha, smiling atop a white stallion, surveyed the land in front of him. The tsar had wanted Pasha to stay at the Winter Palace to listen to the mundane demands of farmers whose crops had been damaged by blight. But Pasha had escaped, and here, in the countryside, the tsesarevich rode wild and free from royal expectations.

"What are we hunting for today?" Pasha asked.

"I believe grouse, pheasants, and mink are all plentiful in this part of the country," Nikolai said. "Whatever Your Imperial Highness desires."

"'Your Imperial Highness'? Why are you being so formal?" Pasha glanced over his shoulder at the rest of the hunting party, the sons of barons and counts and other lesser nobility, all social-climbing buffoons, in Nikolai's opinion. "Don't do it on their account," Pasha said. "In fact, I rather wish you wouldn't."

Nikolai bowed his head. "As you wish, my heavenly sovereign, crown prince of all Russia."

Pasha laughed.

Nikolai couldn't maintain a straight face any longer, and he smiled. This was why they were friends, because Nikolai was the only one who didn't kowtow at the tsesarevich's feet.

They had met when Pasha was twelve and Nikolai thirteen. Nikolai had been crouched in the dirt in Sennaya Square, a sordid part of town, playing cards with a handful of other boys of questionable origin. He'd been betting money he didn't have, but he hadn't cared, for he'd long since mastered the ability to change the face of each card to whatever he wanted before the dealer flipped it from the deck. Nikolai lost often enough that the others didn't know better. It was just that when Nikolai won, he always made sure to win more than he'd given up before.

After a particularly horrendous hand of cards, in which Nikolai sacrificed a painful sum of rubles, an unfamiliar voice piped up from behind a nearby building. "Can I play?"

"Who are you?" Stanislav, the leader of the gang, said.

"Uh, my name is Pasha." There was a tremble as he

answered, but that wasn't uncommon around Stanislav, who at thirteen was already as stout as a dockworker.

The other boys turned to survey the new arrival. They looked him up and down, from the mess of his blond hair to the torn knees of his trousers. "It's pay to play," Stanislav said.

"I have some coins." Pasha produced a small pouch. It clinked heavily.

Satisfied by the sound, Stanislav waved him over and began to deal him in. But there was something oddly familiar about Pasha, like Nikolai had seen him before. He couldn't place him, though. Then he looked at Pasha's boots, which were covered by a thin layer of dust. . . .

Nikolai flicked his fingers, just barely, and a small puff of air blew the dust away.

Pasha's boots were shiny and completely unscuffed. And they weren't fashioned from cheap leather. No, they'd been master-crafted from sumptuous burgundy calfskin, the kind reserved for nobility. Nobility with a lot of money. This Nikolai knew from a short stint polishing shoes for a cobbler.

And from the gleam in Stanislav's eye, the extravagance of Pasha's boots hadn't slipped his notice either.

An hour later, Pasha had won a fair sum. "Thank you for the game," he said too politely. "But I'm afraid it's time for me to be going." He gathered up the coins and crumpled bills from the center of the circle into his pouch and stood to take his leave.

"Not so fast, pretty boy." Stanislav rose, and he towered over Pasha. "I think you cheated us."

"W-w-what?" Pasha reddened. He jammed his hands into his hair, tugging frantically on it, and in doing so, flattened the blond waves into something neater than they'd been when he arrived.

Oh, blazes! Nikolai thought as he put Pasha's fine-boned features together with the now-tamed hair. *Pasha is the nickname for Pavel. And Pavel is the name of the tsesarevich.* That was why he looked so familiar, despite the smudges of dirt on his face. Nikolai had seen Pasha with the rest of the imperial family in a parade only a week before. *What the devil was the tsesarevich doing out of the palace, trying to pass himself off as a commoner? And in Sennaya Square, of all places.*

Stanislav opened and closed a meaty fist. "I saw you slipping in your own cards," he said to Pasha. "What d'ya think I am, stupid, just 'cause I can't afford dainty shoes?"

"I—I don't know what you think you saw. But I didn't cheat." Pasha backed into the wall of the building behind him.

Nikolai stepped forward. "Give him all the money," he said to Pasha. "That'll appease him."

"Don't speak for me, *Kazakh*," Stanislav spat.

Nikolai's jaw tightened, but he didn't send Stanislav careening through the air like he wanted to. Instead, he held out his hand to Pasha, who dumped all his coins and bills into Nikolai's palm. Nikolai set them on the ground in front of Stanislav. Then Nikolai emptied out his own pockets of all his hard-earned cash (true, Nikolai *had* actually cheated, but it didn't mean he hadn't worked hard for it—it took a great deal of restraint to charm the cards in his favor only once every five or so hands) and added that to the pile of Pasha's money. "There, Stanislav, you can have my take, too, and consider the debt paid, all right? Besides, you don't want trouble with Pasha. If he has fancy shoes, you can bet he has fancy parents, too, with connections to the sorts of people you don't want poking around in your business."

Stanislav crossed his arms. He ran his tongue along the bottom edge of his teeth. And then he scooped up Nikolai's and Pasha's money. "Fine, Kazakh. But get out of my square, and don't either of you ever come back."

Pasha and Nikolai took off running. They didn't stop until Nikolai led them to the banks of the Neva River, to the Winter Palace, its green, gold, and white facade like a Russian version of Versailles.

Pasha gasped. "You know who I am." His face was flushed from exertion and his hair wild again.

Nikolai shrugged, still breathing heavily from running so hard and so far. "I won't tell anyone."

"I . . . thank you."

"Of course. But one piece of advice," Nikolai said as he glanced again at Pasha's too-shiny shoes. "If you're going to sneak out, you'll need better disguises. For one, your boots. And . . . well, to be honest, everything you're wearing is much too nice. Even the holes in your trousers are symmetrical. I could help, though. I know a thing or two about clothing. . . ."

They had been best friends ever since.

Now, on Ovchinin Island, Nikolai sensed his friend's same fatigue with the pomp and protocol of court life.

Pasha sighed. "Oh, I don't care what we hunt. Grouse, pheasants . . . Pick one and set the hounds off into the woods with the rest of them." He gestured a gloved hand at the preening noblemen and horses behind him. "Then you and I can go off in search of adventure."

Nikolai laughed. Pasha only participated in half the hunts

that were organized for him. The other half he spent wandering through unexplored forests, skipping rocks in rivers, and dozing to the music of rustling leaves. For Pasha's sake, Nikolai hoped the tsar lived forever. Pasha would wilt if he were ever locked behind the Winter Palace's doors, forced to actually live like the royal he was born to be.

"Hey-o!" Nikolai called behind him to Anatoly Golubin, son of one of the visiting barons from Moscow. "His Highness has decided we hunt for grouse today. He wishes your party to head for the north, while we shall head to the east. You can take the hounds."

Anatoly grunted unhappily from his horse. But the men bowed as Pasha dug his heels into his horse and took off toward the eastern woods. Nikolai followed.

They slowed the pace of their horses as they entered the woods, but soon the forest floor grew so dense with greenery and fallen trees that they had to dismount entirely. They secured their horses to a couple of sturdy maples and pushed forward on foot.

"Any idea where we're going?" Nikolai asked as he walked around a log in his path.

"None whatsoever," Pasha said. He made a show of balancing on the log Nikolai had sidestepped, then hurdled over a boulder.

Nikolai clapped in mock applause.

Pasha laughed. "You're just jealous that you weren't born as graceful as I."

"Oh, you want a demonstration of grace?" Nikolai hopped onto a jagged rock and leaped onto another, landing on one foot. Then he slipped off the mossy face of the rock and nearly twisted his ankle in the gravel.

Pasha hooted. Nikolai grimaced. Perhaps the Romanovs really were blessed with more grace. Or at the very least better balance.

"Don't pout, Nikolai. You can't be the best at everything." Pasha grinned as he pulled Nikolai off the ground.

I'm not, Nikolai thought. *Far from it.*

But it was impossible to sulk as they continued through the forest, which, like many that dotted the Russian countryside, was full of slender white birches with delicate leaves that glittered yellow in the autumnal sun. A creek burbled through the grass, and Nikolai was again struck by what a marvelous decision coming to Ovchinin Island had turned out to be.

A pheasant shot out of the bushes and into the air behind them. Nikolai's gun wasn't loaded, but he snatched a pebble from the ground and hurled it at the pheasant. It dropped out of the sky as if it had been hit by a bullet.

Pasha jogged over. "Did you just do what I think you did?"

"Er . . . yes?"

"*Incroyable*," Pasha breathed. "And you say you aren't good at everything. There are moments when I wonder if you aren't entirely human."

Nikolai flinched, although the comment shouldn't have bothered him, for he hadn't used any magic to hit the pheasant.

"I wish I could be you sometimes," Pasha said.

"No, trust me, you don't." Nikolai climbed through the shrubs, retrieved the bird, and stuffed it into a sack.

"I do, but I won't argue with you." Pasha inhaled deeply, then sank down onto a patch of dry moss, closed his eyes, and leaned his head back against a nearby log. "How glad I am to be out of the palace. I think when I inherit the throne, I shall abdicate immediately."

Nikolai perched on the log next to him. "You'd do no such thing, and you know it."

"Ah, but I can dream." Pasha opened his eyes. "The pressure is not only from my father these days. It's also my mother. She thinks it urgent that they find me a wife."

"I know more than a few who are willing." Nikolai nudged the prince with his boot. Every girl in the Russian Empire would sell her soul to be the tsesarevich's Cinderella.

Pasha responded by yanking Nikolai's boot straight off his foot.

"Hey!"

Pasha laughed and hurled the boot into the shrubbery. "You know I want more from a wife than a girl fawning at my feet."

"Well, all I want is a boot to *cover* my feet." Nikolai hobbled through the grass and rocks in the direction his shoe had disappeared.

Then the peace of the morning was shattered by a crash of thunder. It was so violent, it shook the leaves on the birches and vibrated through the ground. Nikolai and Pasha both leaped up.

Nikolai lurched through the bushes, struggling to pull on his boot while squinting at the sky. It was still bright blue, save for a black cloud above the easternmost side of the forest. A sharp bolt of lightning split the azure, and for a moment, Nikolai wondered whether it could ever be pieced back together again.

"We need to take cover," he yelled over the next crack of thunder.

Another bolt of lightning flashed, and this one struck a tree in the distance, black smoke instantly feathering into the sky. Then, in a brief period of quiet, a girl's scream carried from the east with the wind. Nikolai leaned in the direction from which it came. It did not sound like a call for help. It sounded like . . . a battle cry.

No sooner had her scream left the air than thunder and lightning stormed down in rapid succession. There was no rain, though, only fire, bursting from the lightning to the trees until the sky to the east was obscured by orange and yellow and black.

"The girl! We have to help her!" Pasha said.

"Stay here. I'll go." He couldn't let Pasha run straight into the center of a storm like that. What if something happened to him?

But Pasha was already running deeper into the woods.

"Damn it." Nikolai chased after him. But his boot was unlaced, and he tripped in a puddle of mud. Pasha hurtled onward and disappeared between the trees.

Nikolai glared at his laces, and they whipped into action and secured themselves in a double knot. Then he sprinted as fast as he could, weaving through bushes and leaping over fallen trees, pushing deeper into ash-thick air with every stride.

By the time he caught up, Pasha was already at a standstill, not a hundred feet from the edge of the flames.

"What *is* this?" Pasha pointed at the ring of blazing fallen trees before them, a perfect circle.

"I don't know," Nikolai said. But there was no way this

could have been an accident of nature. He spun around, searching. Something had done this on purpose. Some*one*. He could feel the otherness weighing on the air, thick and heavy. And again, that taste of cinnamon tinged with the portent of death. Nikolai swiped at his mouth as if that would obliterate the taste and foreboding.

The pile of fiery tree trunks began to move, lifting from the center. He and Pasha both staggered back and drew their hunting knives, and Nikolai positioned himself between Pasha and the inferno. He would not lose the future tsar of the Russian Empire without a fight, although what he was fighting, he hadn't a clue.

The fire grew hotter and burned at such reckless speed, the branches in the middle of the pile collapsed to embers the instant a flame licked them.

Then, as the blaze devoured the remaining length of the trees, lashing its way out to the edge of the circle, a small figure rose from the center, itself engulfed in flames.

"You see, Father," a girl's voice said calmly, almost cheerfully, "I told you I'd master it today. Fight fire with fire, not water or ice." Then she whistled a short tune, and the fire on her arms, her torso, her skirt, snuffed out. The only flames left were on top of her head, a wind-tossed mess of loose red curls, and one lock of black. She whistled again, and the fire on the fallen trees went out as well.

Pasha stepped backward onto a leaf. It crunched, ever so softly, but the girl whirled around. "Who's there?"

Nikolai and Pasha stood frozen, and not just metaphorically. She had iced their feet to the ground.

"Who are you?" Pasha whispered as he gaped at the cinder-smudged girl.

She stared at them for another moment. Then she spun on her heel and fled, a streak of red hair and gray dress dashing into the woods and disappearing into its shadowed depths.

But Nikolai didn't need her to tell them who she was. He already knew. He had never seen the girl before, but she had to be the one.

The other enchanter in the Game.

CHAPTER SEVEN

The tsar's message came to Sergei as the lightning storm in the forest ended. The note, on imperial stationery, was brief but clear:

> *Bring your enchanter to Bolshebnoie Duplo on 13 October.*
> *The Crown's Game will then commence.*

What? The Crown's Game? Sergei sagged onto the threshold of the cottage. It couldn't be. All this time, he'd assumed Vika was the only enchanter. He'd sent word to Galina when he discovered Vika's abilities, but she'd never informed him that she had an enchanter in her tutelage as well. He clenched his fists. So typical of his sister!

His anger was short-lived, though, for he did not have the energy to devote to it. Besides, what could be done about it now?

Because Galina had kept from Sergei that she, too, had a

student, there'd been no reason for Sergei to think another enchanter existed. It was the way it was supposed to be—when the Imperial Enchanter died, his or her magic returned to Russia's wellspring, and there it recharged and eventually sought out another vessel in which to grow. It was rare that more than a single enchanter existed at once. As far as Sergei knew, it had happened only a handful of times in the thousand years since Russia was born. And he'd immersed himself so completely in the small sphere of his and Vika's life here on Ovchinin Island that he hadn't paid attention to whether another enchanter's "otherness" lingered in Russia's air.

But now my Vikochka is not just one, but one of two, Sergei thought. And he knew how the Game always ended: there was only room enough for one Imperial Enchanter, for he or she needed access to the full force of Russia's magic. And therefore, the magic killed the loser of the Game.

Sergei sat paralyzed, his trousers covered in dirt. *How can this be? Especially when I thought I still had two years to train her, to spend with her. Now I have only three days. . . .*

And worse yet, how could he tell Vika, when he could hardly handle the truth himself?

He needed time to think. He looked to where the lightning storm had just abated. And he hiked into the woods in the opposite direction.

CHAPTER EIGHT

Nikolai stumbled into the kitchen at the Zakrevsky house immediately upon returning from Ovchinin Island. His eyes searched the room, but there was no one around. Perhaps Galina had decided to lunch at a restaurant with some of her society friends, as she often did, and the staff had been able to take a break. Thank goodness for all his mentor's ridiculous obligations.

Nikolai fumbled for a glass of water and drank it greedily. A good portion of its contents sloshed onto his woolen breeches. He filled another glass and gulped that down, too, before he dropped into the lone wooden chair in the corner.

A few minutes later, a servant girl walked into the kitchen with an armful of freshly laundered aprons. She started when she saw Nikolai and nearly dropped the aprons on the dusty stone floor. Then she tossed them onto the countertop and hurried to kneel at his side. "Nikolai, you're shaking! Are you all right? Did something happen on the hunt?"

Nikolai rubbed his face with both hands. He could tell Renata what he'd seen. Besides Galina, Renata was the only one who knew of his abilities. Not that he'd shared them with her purposely. Two years ago, he had forgotten to lock his bedroom door while he was reassembling a music box with his mind—these disassembly and rebuilding projects had begun when he was a child as lessons from Galina—and Renata had walked in with clean linens for his bed while the music box's cranks and gears were suspended in midair.

"Oh!" she had said. "Forgive me, Master Nikolai, I—I—"

The pieces of the music box had gone clattering onto the desk. He'd snatched them up and stuffed them into the pocket of his waistcoat. "It's not what it seems."

She looked down at the scuffed toes of her boots. "That they were floating of their own accord? Of course not, Master Nikolai."

"I could make you forget what you saw." He raised a finger to his temple.

She trembled. "No need, sir. I promise I won't tell a soul."

"How can I trust you?"

"I read tea leaves, Master Nikolai. I don't fear what you do."

Nikolai lowered his finger. "You read leaves?" He'd never met anyone who could do that. Or anyone who'd admit to it. The Russian Orthodox Church had quashed magic as superstition and heresy centuries ago.

"Yes," Renata said.

"Show me."

He followed her to the kitchen, and Renata poured him a cup of tea. When he drained it, she studied the gnarled black leaves that remained.

Then she shook her head so violently, her braids lashed across her face. "Perhaps it *would* be better if you made me forget what I saw in your room, sir."

Nikolai frowned, then looked from the teacup to Renata and back again. "No. There's something in those leaves that you're frightened to relay. Tell me. I won't hold it against you."

She swallowed hard.

"I give you my word." Which, to Nikolai, was a serious thing, because if your word could not be trusted, you were nothing as a gentleman, and that was its own dreadful shame.

Renata nodded. But she took another moment before she spoke, her voice shaky. "You see there is a cluster of leaves on the left, but a single one, isolated, on the right? It means . . . It means you're lonely." She hunched over the cup, as if waiting for Nikolai to cuff her. She had been hit on numerous occasions by Galina, for much lesser offenses.

But Nikolai only chewed his lip. "I see." It was an audacious thing for a servant girl to say, but it was nothing particularly remarkable. Any one of the servants could have made a similar observation; after all, Nikolai spent an inordinate amount of time in his room on his own, doing what, they did not know. "What about the jagged leaf along the bottom?" he asked.

Renata's eyes widened, and she shook her head, jangling her braids yet again.

"Tell me."

Nikolai restrained himself from reassuring her not to be afraid. He needed to know what the leaf meant.

"The jagged one represents . . . death. You were born of death, and . . ."

"And what?"

"And death will . . . it will follow you, always. The bottom leaf is the path of your life, and this one is a long and jagged blade."

Nikolai had shuddered then, and he'd felt as if his heart stopped for more than several beats. But he had been grateful that she was willing to tell him, despite her fear of reprisal. Perhaps the fact that beneath the elegant clothing and practiced airs he was a poor boy from nowhere gave her a reason to have faith in him. In truth, he was as much a nobody as she was. Nikolai had smiled sadly at how clumsily he fit into this life.

So began their friendship, and now they were huddled together in the kitchen once again, as they had been many times in the past.

"Nikolai." Renata pried his hands from his face. "Tell me. Did something happen on the hunt? Is the tsesarevich all right?"

Nikolai hunched forward, so close to Renata that his head almost rested on hers. "Pasha is fine."

She released the breath she'd been holding. "And you? Are you all right?"

"That, I do not know."

"Why not? What happened?"

"I saw her, Renata. I know who the other enchanter is." A tremor ran through him, although it was disconcertingly hot rather than cold. A true fever chill.

"Is she so formidable?"

"She rose from a bonfire all aflame, as if she were a phoenix."

Renata's grip on his hand tightened. "You're as pale as one of the countess's porcelain figurines."

Nikolai slumped farther into the hard wooden chair. How in blazes would he beat the girl when the day for the Game finally came? The girl need only cast one fiery lightning storm like the one on Ovchinin Island, and the tsar would declare it all over.

"Her magic is enchantment beyond my grasp," he said.

"It isn't," Renata said. "You wield fearsome power of another kind. You can see through walls, remember?"

"It's not the same."

Renata shook him. "Precisely. Perhaps her power is elemental because she lives on that island. But yours is commanding in a cosmopolitan way. You can manipulate an entire orchestra at the opera, instruments and all. You can rearrange the insides of a clock to make it a microscope. You've simply learned to use magic differently."

Nikolai buried his face in his hands. "I hope you're right."

"I hope so, too." Renata reached up and brushed her fingers through his hair. She had never been so bold before, and Nikolai did not know what to do with the gesture. She let her touch linger, then withdrew her hand and lowered her voice. "And I hope this is not where the jagged leaf in your cup comes to pass."

CHAPTER NINE

In the library on the far side of the Winter Palace, Pasha paced in front of a leather armchair, his footsteps so fervent, there was already a deep path carved in the burgundy carpet.

"Who was she?" he asked himself aloud. "*What* was she? Was she even real?" The girl on Ovchinin Island had fled as soon as she spotted Pasha and Nikolai, and the ice at their feet had melted instantly the moment she was gone. Then Nikolai had grabbed Pasha's arm and rushed them from the woods.

The rest of the hunting party had somehow *not* seen the lightning storm and fire. It was as if a drape of invisibility had been tossed over the small section of forest in which the flames were contained, and Pasha and Nikolai had happened to be close enough to be inside its folds.

And yet, Nikolai had refused to talk about it. At first, Pasha thought he'd imagined the girl entirely. But all the color had drained from Nikolai's face—which was how

Pasha knew that Nikolai had, in fact, witnessed the same miracle he had—and Nikolai hadn't uttered a syllable as they sprinted to their horses and galloped out of the forest. Then, once it became apparent that the remainder of the hunting party had seen nothing out of the ordinary, Pasha had been prevented from speaking up, because if he had, they would think he was prone to hallucinations, and that was not an acceptable reputation for a tsesarevich, even one who had no desire to one day be tsar.

Which was how Pasha ended up pacing alone in the palace library, working out the morning's events on his own. "There was lightning, a ring of fallen trees on fire. . . ."

Someone rapped on the open door. Yuliana peered inside the library. "Are you talking to yourself again?"

"Oh. Yuliana. I didn't hear you come in." Pasha ran his fingers through his hair, disheveling it even more than fleeing the forest had. It stuck up in dark-blond tufts, like peaks of torched meringue from one of their father's many banquets.

"You're muttering to yourself again." She tapped her sharp fingernails on the door frame. Yuliana was two years younger than Pasha, but most of the time, she seemed to think herself twice his age. "The servants could hear. You don't want them thinking the tsesarevich is a madman."

Pasha sighed. "I think they're rather accustomed to my mannerisms by now. If they don't already think me mad, they will not think it because of today."

Yuliana tilted her head. "Suit yourself. But at the very least close the door." She dipped in a perfunctory curtsy on her way out of the library, then reached for the heavy wooden door and shut it fast behind her. It plowed into the frame with a decisive thump.

Pasha shook his head as soon as she was gone. Sometimes, he wondered how the tsar could be his father, although it was obvious the tsar was Yuliana's. His sister and father were cast from the same steely resolve. And recently, Yuliana had even seemed the sterner of the two.

But back to the girl. Pasha began to pace the well-worn groove of the carpet again. "She rose as if the fire were nothing . . . no, as if she were *part* of the fire." He tugged on his hair again. The girl's appearance both unnerved and intrigued him. Had she already been there in the woods when the fire began? Or had she come out of the lightning, the cause of the very fire from which Pasha had sought to rescue her?

As quickly as he had begun, Pasha ceased his pacing and crossed the library to a towering bookshelf. The entire room was lined, floor to cathedral ceiling, with books—from old Church documents sealed in airtight cases to new treatises on politics and military strategy. What Pasha was looking for, though, was information on the occult. There would be no books on the subject in the Imperial Public Library, for the Church had ordered any materials on magic destroyed centuries ago. But the palace's private library was a different matter; if magic did, indeed, exist, and if there were books written about it, they would be here.

As Pasha climbed the ladder to the upper reaches of the wall, a giddiness fluttered within him. Perhaps investigating the girl and her magic was one thing he could do better than Nikolai, who excelled at pretty much everything else, from dancing to sharpshooting to understanding the intricacies of bridge building. Not that Pasha was jealous; he didn't begrudge Nikolai his talents at all, and in actuality admired him. But he could not help feeling the thrill of a little healthy competition, and Nikolai had seemed frightened of the girl, whereas Pasha had felt nothing but wonderment. Pasha grinned as he perused the highest shelves.

There were dusty spines of poetry from the last century, and novels from abroad in French, English, and German. How had he not seen these before? Out of habit, he reached for several. But he stopped short of pulling them out. This was not the time to lose himself in fiction and the study of foreign literature.

He pushed the ladder sideways, for it had wheels connected to a track on the top and bottom, until he found a row of books on Roman and Greek mythology, followed four shelves below by European fairy tales, and then on the fifth by Russian folklore. The last book on the fifth shelf was a thick leather volume titled *Russian Mystics and the Tsars*.

"*Et voilà,*" Pasha said to himself. He pulled the book from its place between *Vodyanoi, the Catfish King* and *The Death of Koschei the Immortal*, unleashing a flurry of dust possibly dating from earlier than the previous tsar. He waved the dust away and slid down the sides of the ladder, not bothering with the rungs. His feet landed on the carpet with a solid thump.

Pasha opened the book and sank into his favorite armchair at the same time, his movements easy and graceful, a subconscious compilation of all his experiences growing up in the imperial household, from participating in formal court functions to learning to fence, from watching ballet to being reprimanded when his own posture faltered.

He flipped to the table of contents. The page was yellow and crackled with age.

He stopped skimming when he saw the subject of chapter 15, the last one in the book: "Mysticism in Modern Times."

Pasha smiled so broadly, it was as if he'd discovered the secret to eternal life. This was the sort of book one ought to read in pieces, to properly appreciate and savor each bit. And yet he wanted to devour it whole. Messily and all at once.

But he didn't, because he was the tsesarevich, and crown princes had better manners than that, even when it came to tomes that promised to unveil an entire new world inside. *I should, however, at least have the luxury of reading out of order,* he thought.

And he thumbed his way to the last chapter, for although this book had been written ages ago, he figured this was the best place to try to understand the girl—what she did and what she was. Pasha hooked a leather ottoman with his foot and dragged it closer, then settled deep into his armchair for a long afternoon of reading.

But he did not admit to himself, either aloud or even quietly in his own head, that he was interested in the girl for more than just her magic.

CHAPTER TEN

They could be coming for me right now, Vika thought as she cast shields around the cottage. Father had warned her not to be seen using magic, and now she'd been caught, and those boys could be summoning a mob to burn her at the stake. She fortified the windows a third time, especially the ones in Sergei's bedroom. He didn't deserve to die for her indiscretion. He didn't deserve to die at all.

Where was he?

She ran outside again, for it was possible that he'd arrived while she was inside and been unable to get in, given how tightly she'd protected their home. She saw him emerge from the forest just as she crossed the threshold of the cottage.

"Father! You're all right." She lifted the edge of the shield around the front door to let him in. He stumbled into the entry.

"No, I'm not all right."

"Were you attacked?" Vika secured the protection

charm and rushed to his side. Sergei was a big man, but right now, he seemed . . . small. Not literally, but he didn't take up as much space in the entry as he normally did. On the contrary, it was as if the space pushed on *him* and shoved him inside himself. "I'm sorry," Vika said. "I didn't mean to be seen, but I got carried away, and—"

"You were seen?"

"Yes, and now they've come after you."

Her father laughed, but in a mirthless way. "Oh, Vikochka, don't worry about being seen. Because things are so much worse than that." He tromped away from her and into their tiny kitchen.

Vika rushed in on his heels. "What are you talking about?"

"You will have to meet my sister soon, as if that weren't bad enough."

"You have a sister?"

"In Saint Petersburg. It's all related to . . ." He sank into a chair at their small dining table. "I need some kvass first."

Vika brought a bottle of Sergei's homemade brew and poured him a mug. He downed it in a single gulp.

"We leave tomorrow for Bolshebnoie Duplo," he said.

"What?" *The Enchanted Hollow*. Vika knew the name like a pilgrim knew of Jerusalem. Every country—every country that still believed in the old ways, that is—had a physical, mystical heart from which its magic emanated, and Russia's heart was Bolshebnoie Duplo. Vika leaned across the table. "You know where Bolshebnoie Duplo is?" The name had always sounded to her captivating and wicked all at once.

"Yes. Knowing its location is part of my duty as your mentor."

"Your duty? Why exactly are we going there?"

"It is where you will take the oath for the Crown's Game."

"The Crown's Game." Vika did not even bother to inflect her tone upward this time, for everything now was a question mark. She was beyond using punctuation. "I don't know what that is."

"I didn't think there was a need for it. . . . I thought you were the only enchanter. But you're not, and that means there will be a . . . a test. A competition."

Vika wrapped her fingers tightly around her father's mug. The glaze on the ceramic heated at her touch. *There's another enchanter. And there will be a competition.*

Sergei didn't meet her eyes. He reached for a stale slice of bread on the table instead. "I'm in as much shock as you are. I had no clue my sister was mentoring an enchanter. I haven't heard from her since I left Saint Petersburg twenty-five years ago."

He tore the bread into pieces. And then into smaller and smaller pieces until it disintegrated into a pile of fine crumbs.

"What aren't you telling me, Father?"

He scooped all the crumbs into his hand and crushed them.

"Just say it."

He closed his eyes. "The tsar can have only one Imperial Enchanter. The enchanter who loses the Game dies."

"No . . . Why?" The mug in Vika's hands melted from pottery to clay.

"Each country's wellspring emits a finite amount of magic at any given time. It is not without limits. So the number of enchanters must be limited as well."

"But there have apparently been two of us all these years, not to mention you and your sister—"

"Yes, but the minor charms we conjure are relatively inconsequential," her father said. "As for you and the other enchanter, you've been splitting Bolshebnoie Duplo's magic between you. That's fine while you're training; in fact, it was likely better that you didn't have access to all of it while you were young and learning to control your powers. However, to serve the tsar—and to protect the empire from its enemies—the Imperial Enchanter will need *all* of Russia's magic, especially since Bolshebnoie Duplo is no longer as potent as it was when the people of our country still adhered to the old ways. The Imperial Enchanter must be the only major conduit of what magic remains. There cannot be any dilution."

It hadn't occurred to Vika that there might be an occasion when she couldn't execute an enchantment, for lack of magic. It had always been there when she needed it. But then again, she'd never attempted anything on as large a scale as Sergei was implying. She hadn't a clue how much power it might take to lead a war.

"I could steal Morocco's magic," Vika said. But the joke came out desperate and flat.

Her father scarcely pretended to smile. "Even Yakov Zinchenko wasn't powerful enough to steal magic from so far away. And magic is loyal to its countrymen, for it is those very countrymen whose belief sows it. Morocco's magic wouldn't answer to a Russian."

The kitchen grew colder. Vika hugged her arms around herself.

But why did death on the journey to becoming Imperial Enchanter shock her? Her father had warned her, hadn't he? There had even been a lesson when Vika was younger—a horrible lesson—in which he'd asked her to resurrect a stillborn wolverine pup. Vika had clenched her fists and gritted her teeth and mustered all the power she had to focus on the pup's heart, trying to feel if there were anything broken inside, anything she could move back together. She'd checked its muscles, its lungs, its stomach, liver, and every other organ, only to be met with silence. It turned out that had been the entire purpose of Sergei's lesson: to show her that death was real, and an inescapable part of the Imperial Enchanter's job.

So it should be no great revelation that dancing with death—defying death—could be part of the Imperial Enchanter's initiation.

Vika packed the clay from the former pitcher in her hands. It hardened into a ceramic cannonball. "I don't fancy dying."

Her father emptied the bottle of kvass. "Then the only option is, you cannot lose."

CHAPTER ELEVEN

After telling Renata about the girl in the bonfire, Nikolai had spent the early evening on a prolonged walk around Saint Petersburg. The brisk fall air and the tranquil *shush, shush, shush* of the water in the canals had helped calm his nerves a little; at least he'd managed to talk himself out of changing his appearance and fleeing to the steppe for the rest of his life.

When he came home and unlocked his bedroom door, however, his heart nearly burst out of his chest. There were animals everywhere—monkeys bouncing and shrieking on top of the armoire, vipers slithering across every inch of carpet, and a Siberian tiger on his bed. The tiger roared and leaped toward him.

"*Sacre bleu!*" Nikolai smashed the door shut from the outside and locked it tight. Then he snapped his fingers several times, and five new dead bolts appeared and slammed into place. The tiger rammed the other side of the door again and again. Nikolai's pulse pounded in his head to the same violent beat.

He was still plastered against the hallway wall, between a mirror and a portrait of an ancient Zakrevsky, when Galina appeared.

"Ah, Nikolai, you're home. I thought I heard you come in. You really ought to work on your stealth."

"Wh-what *is* that?" Nikolai pointed a shaky finger at his room.

"Do you like them? They're my pre-Game gift to you. You have no idea what I had to go through to have them shipped here. Which do you like most? The tiger? The snakes? Or the poisonous lorises? Good gracious, you prefer the painfully adorable lorises, don't you?"

Lorises. That was what they were. Not monkeys. Nikolai peeled himself off the wall. "Why are they in my room?" He enunciated each syllable, as if that would help Galina comprehend what he was asking.

She checked her reflection in the mirror and wiped away a small smudge of makeup. "The Game is beginning—well, it will as soon as you take the oath. And if you are to have a chance at winning, you need all the practice you can get."

The Game is beginning?

"You do want to win, don't you?"

"I—"

"Of course you do." She smiled, now that she knew her makeup was flawless. "If you win, you'll finally have wealth and respect. Well, respect in a warped sense, since no one can ever know *exactly* what we magical types do for the tsar. But regardless, they'll know you're an adviser of some sort, and besides, half his Imperial Council does nothing anyway. In any case, it's everything a poor orphan like you never had and could only, until now, dream hopelessly of."

Nikolai clenched his teeth. It was just like Galina to think he was so unoriginal that his fantasies would be the same as the dreams of any other common boy. Of course he wanted to be Imperial Enchanter. Nikolai's entire life—at least since he was seven—had been predicated on that one goal. He was an Imperial Enchanter-in-Training. There was nothing else he wanted to be. And he would certainly make a lousy sheepherder at this point.

But becoming Imperial Enchanter was about much more than wealth and power to him, unlike what Galina was suggesting. It was also about becoming closer to Pasha, who was like a younger brother to him, and closer to a family of some sort, even if it wasn't Nikolai's own. Because, needless to say, Nikolai had no real family. He was, and always had been, alone.

"What do *you* get if I win?" Nikolai asked. For surely there was something in this for Galina. She was not the self-sacrificing type. Not by any measure.

"I did it for our country," she said, "and I did it for the tsar. If you prevail, I have the honor of having been your mentor."

Nikolai arched a brow.

"And of beating my brother."

"You have . . . relatives?" Nikolai couldn't help that his jaw dropped. It seemed impossible that Galina came from an actual family. But of course she had mentioned before that she descended from a long bloodline of mentors. It made sense that if she had a brother, he'd be a mentor, too. And that besting him in a competition would motivate her.

"But enough about rewards," Galina snapped. "You need to secure victory first. We leave tomorrow for the site where you will take the oath to begin the Game. So what you need to be focused on is your last opportunity for training, and that begins with the tiger and snakes and lorises in your room." She clapped her hands, and one by one, the locks Nikolai had conjured began to unbolt. Only the last lock remained latched. She smiled viciously as she pushed him toward the door.

"But what am I to do with—"

"Kill them before they kill you. Do you want to know how you really win the Game? How you ensure it? You don't play nice, Nikolai. If you're smart, you'll think of the Game like a chess match. You *could* take your time, plotting moves to frustrate your opponent, prancing about the chessboard and showing off your abilities while trying to paint the other enchanter into a corner. Or . . ." Galina's smile grew sharper. "You could go straight for the king. The girl, in this case. Use your magic to kill her and end the Game yourself. Don't give the tsar the chance to choose anyone but you."

Nikolai's limbs liquefied. Or at least he felt as if they had. "I have to kill her?"

"Did you think the losing enchanter would simply get to live happily ever after?"

"I . . . Well, what else was I supposed to believe? You never even hinted at it before."

"Would you have continued your training if I had?"

Nikolai just stared at her.

"That's what I thought. The animals in your room are your final lesson. If you want any chance at winning the actual Game, you'd better get accustomed to blood on your soul."

And with that, Galina unlatched the last lock and shoved Nikolai to the dangerous side of his bedroom door.

CHAPTER TWELVE

Vika expected Bolshebnoie Duplo to be an enormous hollow of a tree, but there were no trees in this dusty place. In fact, there were no holes at all, only the sheer granite base of Tikho Mountain, the expansive, overcast sky, and the unnerving quiet of solitude. But after a three-day journey, her father swore this was where they needed to be.

Vika and Sergei had arrived at the mountain on horseback several hours ago, having spent the previous night at an inn in the nearby village of Oredezh. Galina and the other enchanter were nowhere to be seen. And the tsar, her father had explained, would be the last to arrive, for tsars did not wait for anyone.

If only Vika and Sergei could have evanesced here, it would have taken a lot less time. But Vika almost laughed aloud at herself for the thought. Evanescing took incredible amounts of power, energy, and concentration. You needed to dissolve yourself completely, then convince the wind to carry you to your destination—all while keeping the dissipated components of yourself in close proximity to one another—and finally, reassemble yourself and materialize. Vika had only ever succeeded in evanescing once, and she had moved a mere two feet before she panicked and put herself together again. She had spent the remainder of the day dead asleep on the banks of Preobrazhensky Creek.

Still, this journey to Bolshebnoie Duplo had been exhausting in its own way. Her father had insisted that Vika be shrouded from the minute they left the golden trees of Ovchinin Island, because they did not know at what point their path would cross that of his sister and her student. It was vital that Vika keep her identity from the other enchanter, for it would be harder for him or her to hurt Vika in the Game if the other enchanter didn't know who she was and, therefore, at whom to aim.

So a translucent haze surrounded Vika, shifting her appearance to whatever the onlooker expected to see. To the innkeeper at Oredezh, who had assumed the woman accompanying Sergei was his wife, she had looked like a middle-aged woman, with country clothes and rough features to match her husband. To the stable boy who saddled their horses, she had seemed to be a young man, an obedient son to a grumbling father. And to herself, when she had passed by a lake reflecting her image, she had appeared wild and feral, her outside as out of control as her inside. Or perhaps this was how she'd *actually* looked.

Her father, on the other hand, looked the same as ever, although the bags under his eyes were darker and more pronounced. He had refused to allow Vika to use her own strength to maintain the shroud, insisting she needed to preserve it for the Game. Thus, Sergei had been maintaining the field of energy around her for three days, which was a prodigious stress that pushed the very limits of his abilities. In the privacy of their room at the inn last night, Vika had finally forced him to let go of the shroud so he could get some rest. Only then had he relented. But he'd reinstated the shroud as soon as he'd woken that morning.

Now the oath drew near. What would her opponent see of her appearance? Did he or she have a similar shroud? And if so, what would Vika see?

An hour before the ceremony, a pale yellow carriage appeared on the horizon. It didn't bounce on the rocky soil leading up to Tikho Mountain, nor did it make any noise. As the carriage came closer, Vika noticed that its wheels didn't actually touch the ground, although the hooves of the horses did. There was no coachman.

The horses slowed to a walk, and the carriage came to a stop. A series of steps unfolded with a flutter, like an accordion made of paper. Would they be sturdy enough to hold the weight of the occupants as they emerged?

The door cracked open, and a dainty heeled boot issued forth. Like the carriage wheels, its owner did not feel the need to acknowledge gravity. She hovered above the paper steps and floated down. Even then, her feet did not meet the ground.

Vika screwed up her face. She could levitate, too, of course, but it had never occurred to her to do it all the time. It seemed rather vain. Or arrogant. Actually, both.

Upon catching sight of Sergei, the woman tilted her head, keeping her tiny hat perfectly perched on her chestnut curls. She lifted the hem of her voluminous dress and curtsied, albeit somewhat mockingly. "*Bonjour, mon frère*," she said. "I would say you haven't aged a day in the two and a half decades since I've seen you, but that would be a blatant lie, so I won't. You may say that of me, though, if you'd like."

Sergei stood with his arms folded across his chest, both feet firmly planted in the dirt. "Hello, Galina. You are, indeed, the same as ever, if not in looks, then at least in manner."

Behind Galina, a boy stepped out of the carriage. He had no real color, and, come to think of it, no real substance either. He was a shadow, but without a solid person to follow around. The boy did touch his shoes to the paper stairs as he descended, but since he was a mere silhouette, his weight hardly mattered. Remarkable. Vika could not tear her gaze from him.

He turned to Sergei first, removed his top hat, and bowed. Sergei grunted but bowed back, unable to justify rudeness to a boy he'd never before met. The shadow then pivoted to Vika and bowed to her as well.

She curtsied, but since he had no facial features, she couldn't tell whether he saw her curtsy through the shroud.

"Enchanter One," Sergei said to Vika, "meet Enchanter Two."

Galina clucked. "On the contrary. Mine is Enchanter One. Yours is Enchanter Two."

"Absolutely not. My daughter is One."

"Ah, but I am older than you, little brother, and I believe seniority merits my side being Enchanter One."

"Well, I—"

"This is ridiculous," Vika said. "I'll be Two, and he can be One." She pointed at the shadow boy. "What does it matter anyway?"

Galina grinned, baring her teeth. "Enchanter One gets the first move."

Vika scowled. "I know *that*. I simply meant it doesn't matter to me if I go first or not."

Galina frowned at Vika as if the girl were a pebble in her shoe. An inconsequential pebble, given that Galina's feet didn't even touch the ground. "A bit of ego on your student, eh, brother?"

No wonder Father doesn't like her. If I think highly of myself, it's because it's well deserved. Vika took a step toward Galina to say as much but stubbed the toe of her boot on a rock and tumbled forward.

The shadow boy caught her by the arm, his grip on her sleeve gentle but firm.

The instant he touched her, his shadow flickered, and his real self flashed through. Vika sucked in a breath.

Oh, mercy, he was handsome, all ebony hair and ink-black eyes and a face so precisely chiseled, Vika could almost picture the blade that had created him. And the sparks that danced through his magic! Goose bumps rose where his hand held her, even though there was a glove and a sleeve between them. Everything inside Vika quivered.

Half a second later, he released her arm, and he was shadow once again.

Vika blinked. *Did I imagine him?* she wondered, even as she still buzzed from his touch.

But no, he'd been too beautiful. Even Vika's vivid imagination wouldn't have been able to come up with *that*.

"Are you all right?" the boy asked her.

She couldn't find the correct words—which was, in itself, a miracle, for Vika was rarely without something to say—so she merely nodded.

The boy bowed and stepped back to his original place near Galina. It was as if he didn't realize what had happened when he and Vika touched. In fact, his retreat was so proper, it appeared to be more about decorum—not keeping his hand on Vika any longer than appropriate, ensuring she was uninjured—than about fear or competition.

Galina sniffed in Sergei's direction. "I don't see how you expect her to win if she can't even keep herself upright."

Sergei glared. "It's a marvel your student has such impeccable manners, given his teacher's complete lack thereof."

Galina shrugged.

They hadn't noticed the momentary falter in the shadow boy's facade. Or in Vika's composure.

In the distance, the rumble of hooves and carriage wheels announced the tsar's arrival. The ground shook as he approached. He was preceded, flanked, and trailed by dozens of his Guard.

No more time to dwell on the boy, Vika thought. *At least not on how he looks.* She did not acknowledge how he'd made her feel, all tremble and ache inside, for she couldn't. *It's about the Game now.*

The golden carriage came to a stop in front of them in a cloud of dust. Vika had thought Galina's coach was pretty, but this one was utterly magnificent. A painting of the Summer Palace adorned the door, with the handle the graceful stretch of a swan's neck. The tsar's coat of arms—a double-headed black eagle wearing imperial crowns and clutching a scepter and an orb and cross, the *globus cruciger*—ornamented the panels beside the door. Even the roof was trimmed in gold spirals and smaller versions of the double eagle. The coach's beauty was so extraordinary, Vika wondered if the last

Imperial Enchanter had conjured it.

The Tsar's Guard fell in around the carriage, poised to defend their tsar should it be necessary. *He doesn't trust us*, Vika thought. And it was the first time it truly sank in that the things she could do were not only fascinating, but also possibly deadly. She shivered at her own potential; if she were honest, a small part of her thrilled at it, too.

At the captain's signal, the coachman of the carriage leaped down from his seat, set down polished wooden steps, and opened the door.

Sergei and the shadow boy bowed low to the ground. Galina and Vika curtsied, as deeply as their skirts allowed. The four of them stayed genuflected as the tsar's heavy footsteps thumped on the stairs.

He paced slowly, pausing before each of them, as if memorizing the details of the bowed backs of their necks for future accounting, or as if contemplating slicing off all their heads right now. Vika shivered again, although this time, it was in reaction to the tsar's power, not her own.

The tsar lingered in front of Vika the longest. Was he confused by her shroud? She didn't know. But finally, after what seemed like several hours, he moved on, his boots crunching on the loose stones beneath him.

"Please rise," the tsar said. Sergei and Galina stood first, followed by Vika and the shadow boy. "Welcome, enchanters," the tsar said, the rich baritone of his voice echoing against the mountainside. "I am pleased to commence the first Crown's Game of the nineteenth century. I look forward to witnessing what you can do."

And with that, he walked straight into the wall of Tikho Mountain and disappeared.

CHAPTER THIRTEEN

Nikolai gasped as the tsar vanished into the rock. It was pure granite, as far as Nikolai could tell. How had the tsar done that? Did he have his own magic as well?

Galina smacked the back of Nikolai's head, and he had to lunge to catch his shadow top hat before it tumbled onto the dusty ground. "Close your mouth. You'll swallow an entire swarm of gnats if you keep gawking like that," she said. "What part of *bolshebnoie* do you not understand? It's the mountain that's enchanted, not the tsar. Now let's get on with it before the sun sets completely." She rolled her eyes and marched into the rock. She vanished, too.

The other enchanter—the girl—shrugged and plunged into the mountain, her father mere steps behind her.

Nikolai was left alone outside with the Tsar's Guard. Weren't they going to follow? But Nikolai looked from soldier to soldier, and every last one of them stood staring into the ether, their backs straight but their limbs loose, their expressions entirely blank. Their eyes didn't even blink.

The magic of Tikho Mountain had suspended them.

"I suppose it's just me, then," Nikolai mumbled. It made sense. The Guard was not privy to magic; they were ordinary folk, and Bolshebnoie Duplo needed to be hidden from them, just as everything Nikolai did (and the girl and Galina and her brother) needed to be, as well. Nikolai gave the inanimate army one last glance, then dived headlong into the granite.

He emerged on the other side in a cave, with not a scratch or speck of dirt on his shadow frame. His mouth fell open again, and this time, he didn't shut it. This was worth swallowing gnats for.

So this is why it's called the Enchanted Hollow. The inside of the mountain was not made of rock. It was carved entirely of wood. Smooth, polished, ancient wood, like the inside of a colossal, magical tree. *"Incroyable,"* he whispered as he hurried down a long tunnel to catch up with the others.

The cave walls might have been made of wood, but they gleamed as brightly as if they'd been composed of amber and agate. Wooden stalactites hung from the ceiling, dripping almost imperceptibly with mineral water, and stalagmites rose from the ground, like honey-colored warriors from a time long ago.

The heart of Russia's magic.

In fact, the air was so thick with it, Nikolai could hardly move. Although his own power was buoyed by being in Bolshebnoie Duplo—the magic that was always at his fingertips swelled as soon as he entered the Hollow—he was, paradoxically, also slowed by it. The others walked through the archaic magic undeterred, but Nikolai's shadow form struggled to push through matter as dense as himself. And his shadow top hat kept falling off.

The tsar led the way, descending into the caverns with nothing but a small oaken chest in his arms. *The magic here must protect him*, Nikolai thought. He'd never seen the tsar without his Guard.

Galina floated after the tsar, followed by her brother, and then Enchanter Two. Nikolai propelled himself through the fog of magic, trailing closely, but not too closely, behind the girl. She had a deception shroud around her, but its effect was lost on him, for he already knew who she was. Nikolai could see her clearly: her red hair, with its single black stripe, tumbling down her back in loose waves like a veil of smoke and flames; her slight shoulders, hunched forward as she ducked beneath a low ceiling in the cave; and her green satin dress, out of fashion by at least a decade but somehow endearing on her, not awkward in the slightest. It could have been improved, however, with a ribbon around its waist. Preferably in yellow.

If Nikolai hadn't been on Ovchinin Island and seen what this girl could do, he might have been deceived by her appearance. But like the poisonous lorises Galina had planted in his room three days ago, it was the smallest and most innocent-looking of creatures who were the most deadly.

The party descended deep into the caverns, twisting and winding their way until they reached a large cave. In it, there was a luminescent tree stump, a throne-like seat complete with wooden stalagmites that rose up to form its back and long flat branches that resembled armrests. Their edges were too gnarled to be man-made, yet too purposeful to be natural. Nikolai shook his head at the beauty of Bolshebnoie Duplo.

The tsar strode up to the throne and eased himself into it. The light in the cave brightened, shifting from dusty rose to a pearly pink. He gestured for the enchanters to step forward, and Nikolai and the girl obeyed. Galina and her brother, however, held back.

"I assume your mentors have informed you of the rules and format of the Game," the tsar said, "but I will repeat them again so they are clear. The Game is a display of skill and a demonstration of strategy and mettle. The goal is to show me your worthiness to become my Imperial Enchanter—my adviser for all things from war to peace and everything in between.

"The Game will take place in Saint Petersburg, and you will take turns executing enchantments. There is no restriction on the form of magic you choose, only that you do not alarm or harm the people of the city."

Right, Nikolai thought. *So no alligators swimming unchecked through the canals.*

"Each enchanter will have five turns, at the most," the tsar continued. "As the judge, I may declare a winner at any point in the Game, or I may wait until all ten plays have been made. Remember, your moves will reveal not only your power but also your character and your suitability to serve the empire. Impress me." He looked down at Nikolai and the girl from his glimmering throne. The tsar couldn't actually see through their facades, but his expectation pierced their shrouds nonetheless. Nikolai shrank a little inside his own shadow.

"To begin the Game," the tsar said, "we——"

"Pardon me, Your Imperial Majesty," the girl said. "I have a question."

Nikolai shifted in place. Was the girl really so bold that she would interrupt the tsar?

"What is it?" The tsar practically spat the question.

The girl was unfazed in her shroud. Bold indeed. "Why must the Game end in death? I understand that the Imperial Enchanter needs to be the sole conduit of magic, but why can't one enchanter win, and the other step aside?"

The tsar huffed. "And what would the other enchanter do? Retire to the countryside and promise never to use magic again? Or move abroad and have no access to Russia's wellspring? Would you be able to do that? Give up everything you are, in exchange for your life?"

The girl contemplated this for a moment. Then she looked up. "It would not be a life, Your Imperial Majesty, if I could not enchant."

"Precisely."

"So you just execute one of us in the end?"

Nikolai gaped. Was she really questioning the tsar again?

The girl stood with her arms crossed.

The tsar stared at the girl from his arboreal throne and shook his head as if unable to believe she was interrupting again, and doing so to ask about logistics, of all things. He rose from his throne and towered before them. "When I declare a winner, the Game's own magic will eliminate the other enchanter. Even if, for some reason, I did not declare a winner after you had each taken five turns, the Game would make the decision for me and extinguish one of you. Russia will have only one Imperial Enchanter to wield the full force of its magic. Understood?"

The girl seemed undisturbed. In fact, she pursed her lips, considering the tsar's answer. *It's as if she's contemplating the possibility that the tsar's word isn't absolute*, Nikolai thought. The girl was made of daring. Or recklessness.

"I see," she finally said. "Thank you, Your Imperial Majesty."

"If there is nothing else . . ." The tsar paused just long enough to glare at the girl, like a challenge to interrupt again. The message was clear that there would be consequences this time if she did.

She didn't.

"Fine. Then let us commence the oath." The tsar opened the oaken chest he had carried into the caverns. A yellowed scroll and a long black quill floated out. The scroll unfurled itself, and both Nikolai and the girl took a step back. The Game was its own living magic.

The parchment hovered beside the tsar, and he read its timeworn instructions. "Bolshebnoie Duplo has been imbued with ancient enchantments that will bind you to the Game and to Russia. Now, reveal your true selves to me."

Nikolai glanced at the girl. They would both have to maintain their shrouds but open up the enchantment so that only the tsar could see. He needed to know who his future enchanter was.

The girl looked at Nikolai, too.

Nikolai yanked his gaze away and faced forward. He focused on protecting his shadow veneer—he might know the girl's identity, but she did not know his—and allowed a pathway for the tsar to see him.

Would the tsar recognize him as Pasha's friend? Or not, given that the tsar gave hardly a whit about his son's social affairs? He cared only to engage Pasha on matters important to his training as tsesarevich.

The tsar squinted as he looked upon Nikolai, as if trying to place him. A moment later, it seemed to click in his head where he had seen Nikolai before, and he frowned.

"Interesting." The tsar drummed his fingers on the arm of his wooden throne. And then he cleared his throat and continued as if the presence of his son's best friend in the midst of a magical battle to the death were nothing extraordinary at all. Of course, it made sense that the tsar would appear unruffled at this turn of events. Certainly he had encountered much greater surprises in his career. Or perhaps the tsar truly didn't care that Nikolai was one of the enchanters. *After all, who am I but a common boy who happened to befriend his son?*

"Repeat after me," the tsar said to both Nikolai and Vika as he read from the Russe Scroll.

> *"I hereby swear my loyalty to the tsar,*
> *And promise to abide by the rules of the Game,*
> *A duel of enchantment, until a winner is declared.*
> *To this and all traditions here before established, I commit*
> * myself*
> *As an enchanter in the Crown's Game."*

Nikolai and Vika repeated the oath back to the tsar in unison. Nikolai kept his voice even, but hers carried and echoed throughout the cave, as if even in this inaugural moment of the Game, she was already trying to gain the upper hand.

But Nikolai had little time to think on that, for as soon as he uttered the last words of the oath, a searing heat bit into his skin, just below his left collarbone. "What the—!"

He stopped himself before he let out a string of obscenities in front of the tsar, but not quickly enough to save his dignity.

A pair of crossed wands branded themselves onto Nikolai's chest as if by an invisible iron. Even after the branding was over, the scar still glowed red-orange on his skin like live embers. Nikolai bit the inside of his cheek to stave off the pain.

The girl had not protested or screamed or made any sound other than a sharp inhale. Nikolai flushed, both at the heat of the fresh scar and at his weakness compared to this elfin girl.

"Who is Enchanter One?" the tsar asked.

"I am," Nikolai managed to answer through gritted teeth, the scar still faintly orange on his skin.

The tsar nodded. "The wands will burn until you have made your first move in the Game. Then they will go dormant as Enchanter Two takes her turn. They will reawaken on your skin once her turn has been taken. That is how you will know it is your move again.

"The wands will grow steadily hotter the longer you take to execute your turn. As days pass, the pain will become more unbearable. And if too much time elapses—if you dally or for some reason refuse to complete the Game—the scar will eventually ignite and consume you."

Nikolai shuddered. *Forfeiture by flame.*

"Is that how the Game ends?" the girl asked. The tsar didn't even bother to look surprised that she'd interrupted. It would be more of a surprise at this point if she didn't. "Does the losing enchanter combust?"

"Yes. The scar will incinerate the loser of the Game."

"It will be quick," her father said quietly. It occurred to Nikolai, though, that it was not the girl who needed assuring but rather the mentor himself.

The tsar nodded curtly. "Your mentors have taught you what they could, and now, as tradition dictates, and to ensure that your volleys in the Game are yours and yours alone, the mentors will be banished to the far reaches of the empire until a winner is declared. But first, they may give you a parting gift." The tsar turned to Galina and her brother. "You have a minute to say your good-byes."

The girl's father rocked his weight from his heels to his toes, as if he were contemplating moving toward the girl, but then he rocked back on his heels and stood firmly in place. "Practice every day it is not your turn," he said to her. "Get enough sleep and enough food to eat. Check our hiding place—you know where it is—if you need money . . ."

"Father—"

He held up his hand. "And wear this. Do not take it off." He yanked a braid of leather off his wrist and pushed it at her.

She slipped it onto her wrist, and it immediately tightened itself to fit. She winced. "What is it?"

"A good luck charm, of sorts." He turned his back to her, visibly swallowing back his emotions. "We will see each other again soon, my dearest."

The girl touched the necklace at her throat. "I promise."

Galina smirked in her brother's direction. Then she snapped her fingers, and a dagger in its sheath appeared in Nikolai's shadow hands. "The gift I leave you is a new knife," she said. "When you find the right occasion to use it, it will not miss its target. Remember all the practice you've received; killing is not so difficult and is the most direct way."

Nikolai knitted his brow, although no one could see him do so in his current shadow form. He could not bring himself to look at the girl.

"And don't take too long to win," Galina continued. "I don't fancy being trapped in limbo with my tiresome recluse of a brother. Oh, and try not to irritate the household staff while I'm away."

Nikolai sighed. He had always known, from the day Galina came for him on the steppe, that she would not be a mother to him, but still, he had hoped for a little more than this before she saw him off to the Game, and, perhaps, to his death. But she was already gliding away.

Her brother offered her his arm, and although Galina curled her lip in disdain, she took it.

"I hope it isn't too cold where we're going," she said.

"I hope you do not plan to complain the entire time," he retorted.

"Oh, if it bothers you, *mon frère*, I shall. Ceaselessly."

Dust began to swirl around them, first as individual particles, and then, picking up speed, as an opaque tornado. The storm swallowed the mentors inside itself, and Nikolai, being the closest to where the pair had stood, had to raise his hand to shield his eyes. The tornado grew taller and faster, and when it had almost reached the cavern ceiling, it shot out of the cave and into the labyrinth, the howling of the wind reverberating and deafening.

And then it was gone, out of Bolshebnoie Duplo and toward wherever mentors go to wait. Only silence remained.

"I have one more request," the tsar said, as if a magical

whirlwind had not just swooped away two entire people. "The tsesarevich's birthday is next week. I suggest you consider that your theme for the Game. Impress him to impress me."

Nikolai arched a shadow brow. Interesting. Perhaps the tsar cared more for Pasha than he let on, even to Pasha himself.

"Am I clear?" the tsar asked.

"Yes, Your Imperial Majesty," Nikolai and the girl said.

"Good." After a long pause, the tsar rose from his wooden throne. "Then let the Crown's Game begin."

CHAPTER FOURTEEN

Half a continent away, tall blades of grass trembled. The earth, still parched this early in the autumn, quaked in a cloud of dust. A fissure cleaved through the hard-packed dirt, and a shriveled hand punched its way to the surface, its sinewy muscle clinging to the bone like dried meat tethered to a brittle pole.

It didn't take long for the rest of Aizhana's body to emerge. During her many, many years underground, she had slowly, painstakingly stolen energy from worms and maggots to consolidate into a life force strong enough to resurrect herself. Now she climbed out of the earth and stretched, her limbs stiff from being dead—no, *nearly* dead—and she brushed the dirt off her withered skin.

She sucked in a breath between her teeth (what was left of her teeth, that is) and averted her eyes from the dry husk that hung from her body. *The skin is the least important*, she reminded herself. *What matters is that my insides are healed.*

But why now? Aizhana had been hoarding wisps of

energy for so long, but nothing until this moment had been able to pull her completely free from her decomposing half slumber. What was it that had shifted the balance in her world?

Aizhana drank in the endless brown horizon around her. She reached for the sky, cracked her joints, and rattled her aching bones.

Whatever it was that had woken her, she did not know.

But whatever you are, she thought, *I will find you.*

CHAPTER FIFTEEN

While the tsar was away on state business, Pasha slipped out of Saint Petersburg. He had read the entirety of *Russian Mystics and the Tsars*, twice, and he had it in his head that he'd go back to Ovchinin Island to track down the mysterious girl from the woods.

He had wanted to drag Nikolai into making the trip with him, despite his friend's reaction to their last encounter with the girl made of lightning, but when Pasha inquired at Countess Zakrevsky's home, a servant had informed him that Nikolai was out.

Which was how Pasha came to be on Ovchinin Island alone. If Nikolai couldn't accompany him, he didn't want anyone else. Perhaps it was all right this way, though. It gave Pasha more opportunity to investigate the lightning girl on his own.

But as Pasha stood on the docks of the island's small harbor, he had no idea where to look. Caught up in the adrenaline of finding the girl, he had failed to make any concrete plans beyond sneaking out of Saint Petersburg in disguise and unseen.

I suppose the forest is a good place to start, he thought. Although where in the forest? The same spot as the bonfire? If he could find it without a lightning storm directing the way. A different place, because she might not inhabit the same spot twice? But why wouldn't she? *Russian Mystics and the Tsars* did not cover the rules of rising out of magical flames. For all Pasha knew, there might be only a single location from which the lightning girl could emerge.

The other possibility was that she didn't come from the fire at all, but rather, the fire came from her. Or the fire came *at* her, from the lightning. Or . . . the lightning came *because* of her, like she was a magnet for firestorms. Pasha took off his hat and ran his fingers through his hair. There were so many possibilities.

The captain of the ferry Pasha had taken disembarked from his boat and walked past Pasha on the dock. He was several yards away when he turned back around. "Ahoy, boy. D'you need directions somewhere?"

Pasha crammed the hat back onto his head, even though the ferry captain had shown no sign of recognizing him, likely on account of Pasha's (temporary) mustache and sideburns. "No, sir. Well, actually, I'm looking for some*one*, rather than some*where*."

The old sailor snorted and jerked his thumb over his shoulder in the direction of a poorly paved street branching away from the harbor. "Then you'll wanna head up over thataway. Look for Cinderella Bakery. Ludmila Fanina, the baker, knows everybody as well as every piece of gossip in town. She also makes a hearty Borodinsky bread. That and a coupl'a pickled herring, and you'll be filled up for days."

Pasha dipped his head. "Thank you, sir. I suppose I'm off to the bakery, then."

"Last ferry to the mainland leaves at dusk." The captain waved and continued the other way toward a ramshackle dock building.

Pasha walked up the street the captain had pointed out, his boots kicking up the layer of dust on the road. This close to the harbor, there were few buildings, although the landscape was dotted here and there with *izbas*, small log houses, all very plain except for the detailed wood carvings of deer and fish around the windows and shutters. He strolled up the path, enjoying the cool morning air and the ability to walk in the open without fanfare and people bowing at his feet.

Once in town, the Cinderella Bakery was impossible to miss. For one thing, the whole of the village was only three streets long and two streets wide. For another, the bakery had no ordinary shop front, but, rather, an elaborate orange exterior shaped like a bulging pumpkin. That and the rich, tangy smell of rye and sourdough told Pasha he had arrived.

He opened the door and stepped inside, only to be greeted immediately by the curious stares of a half-dozen middle-aged women waiting in line.

He removed his hat and nodded his head. *"Bonjour, mesdames."*

The most elderly of the women performed a complicated curtsy, involving lifting the hem of her skirt and crisscrossing her legs several times, then bowing back and forth several more times, rather like a broken jack-in-the-box. Pasha's eyes widened. Was this some sort of country greeting? The other women in line tittered.

Or were they poking fun at him? Pasha frowned.

"Oh, leave the poor boy alone," a plump woman behind the counter said in Russian. "He can't help it if he was born with a silver spoon and a croissant in his mouth." She laughed, a robust laugh as rich as the *vatrushka* pastries on the shelf, but she winked at Pasha.

Ha! Fair enough. He had greeted them in French, clearly not the right language for the countryside. Pasha smiled good-naturedly back at the baker, and at the women around him, as well. Then he tried again, this time in Russian. *"Dobre dehn."* His accent was quite good; there was only a shred of French lace at the edges. (His German, Spanish, English, Finnish, and Swedish were excellent as well. Palace learning was good for something, after all.)

The woman behind the counter still had her broad smile plastered across her face. "You don't mind if I serve him first, do you?" she asked the other customers, although it really wasn't a question. "It's not every day Cinderella Bakery is honored by such a handsome young man. What can I do for you?"

"Are you Ludmila Fanina?" Pasha asked.

"I am."

"Then I need your assistance, if you please. I'm looking for a girl."

Ludmila puffed out her generous bosom and held a long loaf of bread suggestively. Mischief sparked in her eyes. "A girl? Why, I am a girl. I can be the one you seek."

The women burst into another fit of giggles.

Red flushed across Pasha's face, all the way to the tips of his ears. He didn't even have a hat on to hide it. If his

Guard were here, they would seize Ludmila and send her to the stocks for her insolence. No one would ever dare make such a salacious joke to the tsesarevich; no one would ever embarrass the tsesarevich. . . .

Ah. Right. They didn't know he was the tsesarevich. *I have to act like a normal boy. Or, rather, I have to act like myself, but the version of myself I would be if I weren't the tsesarevich.* And as soon as Pasha got that through his imperial head and let go of being offended, he grinned. He could play their game.

"But my lady," he said to Ludmila, who was wagging the loaf of bread at him, "although you are as beautiful as Aphrodite, and your way with words as poetic as Calliope's, I must regretfully decline your invitation. I would not want to anger your husband."

The women in the bakery hooted and cackled, the eldest one did a little jig, and Ludmila clutched her substantial middle, her entire body jiggling as she laughed. She slapped the counter a few times in her hysterics.

Finally, when she had almost caught her breath and the other women had settled down to only occasional giggles, Ludmila said, "Touché, Frenchie. Now, about the girl, who is she?"

The other women quieted completely and looked up at him for his reply.

"Well, you see, therein lies the problem," Pasha said. "I don't know."

"What does she look like?"

"She has red hair, like the most hypnotizing part of a flickering flame, and her voice is both melodic and unflinching."

The women sighed, and if he saw correctly, the eldest

95

one batted her eyelashes at him.

Ludmila smiled kindly, all jest in her expression gone. "Ah, to be young and in love."

Pasha shook his head. "No, you're mistaken. I don't love her. I hardly know her. I saw her once, and then she fled."

The women sighed again, but this time, they also nodded their heads at one another smugly.

"You don't love her *yet*," Ludmila said.

"I—"

She held up a spatula to shush him. "You're looking for Victoria. Although she prefers to be called Vika."

"Vika," Pasha repeated softly.

"*Da*, Vika. She lives with her father on the far side of the island, in a clearing in the birch forest. But she and her father left on a trip several days ago. They passed through the bakery before they went to the harbor. I'm sorry to disappoint."

The air leached out of Pasha's lungs. To have come so close, yet still be so far. "Oh, well . . . that's all right, Madame Fanina." The eldest woman snickered at his slip into French. He course-corrected to Russian. "I appreciate your assistance. May I compensate you for your time?" He reached for his coin purse.

"No, my handsome young Frenchie, the pleasure was all mine."

Pasha's cheeks pinked as he bowed slightly. "At least let me buy some of your famed Borodinsky bread."

Ludmila beamed. Then she grabbed a loaf of black bread and wrapped it in brown paper stamped with a picture of Cinderella's pumpkin. She tied the package neatly with a string.

Pasha placed a coin on the counter and tucked the still warm bread under his arm. *"Bolshoie spasiba,"* he said, thanking not only Ludmila, but all in the room.

And with that, he left town and caught the next ferry, where he spent the slow ride to the mainland chewing thoughtfully on his bread and contemplating the horizon beyond the Neva Bay. He murmured "Vika" to himself, more than once.

When Pasha returned to the palace, and after he'd calmed his Guard with an innocuous lie about where he'd been—he snuck out rather regularly, so they were accustomed to his disappearances, but still, the disappearances were alarming every time—he commissioned the imperial glassblower to create an enormous glass pumpkin to be sent as a gift to Madame Ludmila Fanina. It would be signed *From Frenchie.*

And then Pasha strode into the palace library and asked not to be disturbed, sank into his armchair, and read *Russian Mystics and the Tsars* for the third time.

CHAPTER SIXTEEN

Nikolai stared out his bedroom window onto Ekaterin-sky Canal while he twirled the knife Galina had given him. The inside of the Zakrevsky house was quiet without his mentor. There was no yelling, and the staff simply took care of their chores and stayed out of Nikolai's way. Outside the house, however, the city was riotous with preparations for Pasha's seventeenth birthday. Up and down the canal, boats hauled sections of the grandstands to be installed for the imperial family and other nobility. Food kiosks popped up all over the city, selling *blini* crepes and fizzy, malty kvass to the workers. And signs were posted on all the streetlamps, reminding everyone that the birthday celebrations would last through the week. It was only Sunday now.

The frenetic energy on the streets and canals matched the chaos in Nikolai's head. But while the people outside were driven by the promise of celebration, Nikolai was driven only by the specter of death.

There's no escaping death. Either I'll be defeated and therefore die, or I'll triumph but live with the guilt of sentencing the girl to her end. There is no such thing as a winner in the Game.

There was a soft knock on his door. Nikolai startled and dropped the dagger, which embedded itself in his windowsill. Who was it? He had ordered no one to disturb him unless it was time for a meal. . . .

He charmed his pocket watch out of his waistcoat. Oh. Two in the afternoon. It was, indeed, time for a meal.

He crossed the room and unlocked the door, opening it a crack. He expected one of the older women from the kitchen with a tray, but instead it was Renata. Nikolai almost smiled—smiles were hard to come by since the oath—and opened the door wider.

"I thought you might like some company while you eat," she said, slipping into his room with a tray laden with bouillon, chicken *à l'estragon*, and apple tarts. She shut the door behind her with her foot.

Nikolai furrowed his brow as he took the tray from her. "Are we expecting guests?" As Galina's "charitable project," Nikolai usually ate what the servants ate unless she had company. Only then did he get to take part in such lavish meals.

"I convinced Cook that you needed some cheering up, and that a nice lunch might do the trick."

"You're really too kind to me."

"I know." Renata smiled as she cleared a space on Nikolai's cluttered desk, which was littered with crumpled papers full of discarded ideas for the Game. She folded a tablecloth to fit on the small square of free space.

"Will you join me?" Nikolai asked.

"I already had my piroshki and cheese in the kitchen."

"I refuse to eat if you don't."

She wrinkled her nose and flattened a crease in the tablecloth on his desk. "Don't be difficult."

"I'm not. I'm being courteous."

"The countess would have my head if she found out I ate any of this food."

"The countess is indisposed. By a magical cyclone."

Renata smirked.

Nikolai set down the tray on the tablecloth. "After you, *mademoiselle*."

She hesitated.

"It's quite all right, Renata. I promise. You won't turn into a frog if you eat something."

"It's not that . . . it's . . . I've never eaten anything prepared so beautifully before. But you wouldn't understand."

"Believe me, I do." And he did. He still recalled his first formal dinner in this house after Galina had taken him from the steppe. Important-Someone-or-Other had been visiting from Moscow, and the Zakrevskys—the count had still been alive then—had served a feast of soups and oysters and roasted pheasant, so different from the sparse helpings of tough mutton Nikolai had grown up on. But what he remembered most was the *crème brûlée*, a decadent custard topped with a delicate pane of caramelized sugar "glass." It was the most heavenly thing Nikolai had ever seen, let alone tasted, at that point in his young life.

"Have dessert first," he said to Renata. "And eat it with your hands. Galina isn't around."

She smiled shyly, as if he had read in her mind exactly what she had been wanting to do. Then she picked up an apple tart and bit in.

Nikolai did not, though. He wasn't hungry. He hadn't been hungry since the oath. He'd eaten, of course, but only because he needed the energy to function, not because he found any pleasure in the consumption of his meals.

Instead, he walked back up to his window and unwedged Galina's knife from the sill. Then he charmed open his desk drawer, unlocked the enchanted hidden panel he'd constructed within, and secured the knife back inside.

He rubbed the back of his neck. It was something he'd done for as long as he could remember, whenever he was stressed. It helped him focus. Although it was questionable whether it was doing any good now.

"All I can think about is how ugly the city is," Nikolai said, "and how they ought to dress up the grandstands for Pasha's birthday, and how Nevsky Prospect, one of the supposed gems of Saint Petersburg, ought to have been repainted. I should be focusing on the Game, but my mind keeps wandering to stupid details about birthdays."

The scar beneath Nikolai's collarbone flared at the mention of the Game. It had been burning hotter every hour, as if impatient that Nikolai had already taken three days after the oath and not made his move. But this first play would set the tone for the entire Game, and he wanted to get it right.

"Aren't you supposed to do something for the tsesarevich's birthday?" Renata said. "You could repaint Nevsky Prospect as your move. You'd kill two birds with one stone."

"I'm not supposed to be killing birds. I'm supposed to be killing the girl."

"Her name is Vika."

"What?" Nikolai flinched.

"Her name is Vika. I overheard the countess saying it to herself in her rooms before you left for Bolshebnoie Duplo."

"I . . . I don't like the girl having a name." Nikolai shook his head, as if he could shake her name right out of his skull. It made it harder to hurt her if she had a name. He could only kill her if he forgot she was a person. Maybe. Because he knew where she lived, and she didn't know his identity. He could go to Ovchinin Island and find her house. Then when she least expected it, he could cause it to cave in on her. Or he could charm her pillow to smother her in her sleep. Impale her with a garden hoe.

The thoughts turned Nikolai a dismal shade of green.

Besides, it would never work. The girl would have cast protections on her home—if she hadn't already relocated to Saint Petersburg—and she had already displayed far greater skill than Nikolai. And that had been in the woods when she had thought no one was watching, when her life was not even at stake.

But at the same time, Nikolai did not intend to lie down and accept loss without a fight. He had endured Galina's tyranny in preparation for this. All that suffering needed to be worth it. If he won, he could finally be free of Galina, and he could finally have a place where he was respected and where he belonged. No more bartering for cloth or sharpening other people's swords. He would be the tsar's adviser.

Not to mention, Nikolai had no desire to die.

Renata put the remainder of the apple tart back on its plate and wiped her fingers on a cloth napkin. Then she walked back to Nikolai at the window. "You don't have it in you to hurt the other enchanter." She pulled his hands apart from each other. He hadn't realized he'd been scrubbing at

102

them again, still plagued by the memory of the tiger and the vipers and the lorises. So much blood.

"The Game ends when only one enchanter remains," he said.

"Or until one proves he is better than the other. You don't *have* to kill her. The Game will take care of that as long as there's a clear winner."

Nikolai retracted his hands from Renata's. He leaned against the windowsill. It was true he wasn't required to attack the other enchanter. But . . .

"I'll only have more turns in the Game if the girl doesn't kill me first." Nikolai shuddered as he imagined his body pierced by hundreds of fiery arrows. Or spontaneously bursting into flame. Which would also happen if her moves were simply better than his. "What do my tea leaves instruct me to do?"

"Tea leaves never give instructions. Only observations. And I haven't read your leaves since the time you forgot to lock your door."

The very corner of Nikolai's mouth smiled. But only the corner.

Renata reached up and brushed her finger against his dimple. She had always told him it looked like an accidental divot chipped out of the smooth planes of his face, for he only had one, not a matching pair. "There. I missed this dimple. This is a tiny bit of the Nikolai I know." Her finger stayed for an extra second before it dropped away.

Nikolai tried not to think about the way she lingered. Instead, he tugged at his collar, where the scar seemed to threaten to burn through his cravat.

He could reface all the buildings on Nevsky Prospect as

part of his move. Superficially, it would be a pretty gift to the city for Pasha's birthday, and hopefully the tsar would appreciate the effort it would take to execute such detailed splendor.

It had to be more than just beautiful buildings, though. But what? Something to help himself in the Game.

Nevsky Prospect was the main thoroughfare through Saint Petersburg. Nikolai didn't know where the girl was living, but surely she would make appearances on the street or in the shops there with relative frequency, wouldn't she? Most of Saint Petersburg did.

Gargoyles! he thought. He could install gargoyles or something else discreet on the buildings, and then *they* could take care of the girl. If stone soldiers did the dirty work, it wasn't really Nikolai killing her. Was it?

"Nikolai?" Renata asked.

He broke away from his planning. He'd forgotten Renata was still there.

"Yes?"

"You looked . . . like you'd been enveloped by a storm cloud."

"Sorry." He charmed an apple tart to float to him, and he ate it, although he didn't pay enough attention to taste it.

"So you're all right?"

Nikolai brushed a stray flake of pastry off his collar. "No, I'm not all right. I'm not sure I'll ever be. But I'll do what I have to. It's what I've always done."

CHAPTER SEVENTEEN

Vika dreamed that they were at Tikho Mountain, just outside Bolshebnoie Duplo again. It was hushed and hot outside, and so bright she could hardly see as she squinted in the white light. The tsar and his Guard had not yet arrived, so it was only Vika, Father, Galina, and the other enchanter. Vika stood in her shimmering shroud; her opponent was a silhouette, just as he had been before.

In the background, Galina had set up a small table, complete with lace cloth, several fine china dishes, and a set for tea. She nibbled on a croissant spread with strawberry jam.

Father pulled out a chair, its legs somehow squawking on the dirt of Tikho Mountain. He winked at Vika—the kind of wink that only worked in dreams—as if he knew the squawking would irk his sister. "I don't know how you can eat those *pastries*." He wrinkled his nose at his sister's croissant. "Have you any black bread?"

Galina cringed. "Honestly, why you insist on pretending you are ordinary country folk, I'll never understand."

"And why you insist on being so pretentious," Sergei said, "I will never understand."

Not far from Vika but out of Galina's earshot, the other enchanter chuckled quietly under his breath. His shoulders shook with laughter, and his shadow top hat tumbled onto the ground. It turned immediately from black to brown from the puff of dust.

How did dirt cling to a shadow, when the shadow wasn't really there?

Vika reached down to pick up the hat. It felt real in her hands, like silk and ribbon and rounded edges, and yet, it felt like nothing was there at all. It weighed as much as reality, and as little as fantasy.

She wondered what would happen if she put his hat on her head. Even just in her hands, his hat—his power—warmed her, like mulled cider on a winter's day.

And then she wondered what would happen if she touched the shadow boy himself. If she ran a finger along the sharp line of his jaw. If she touched the scar beneath his collarbone. If she pressed her mouth against his shadow lips . . .

She flushed hot at the thought. Much, much hotter than mulled cider.

And then Vika bolted awake. The sun had just begun its upward creep into the sky, but the scar throbbed against her skin as if only just branded inside the wooden caves of Bolshebnoie Duplo. Oh, thank goodness it was the heat of the wands, not the heat of blush and infatuation, that had seeped into her dream. She was not as silly as her subconscious would suggest.

And then she realized that if her scar was burning . . . the Game!

Vika leaped off the sofa on which she slept—after several days in Saint Petersburg, she was still not accustomed to the luxury of the mattress in the bedroom and much preferred the sofa—and scanned the third-floor flat she had rented on Nevsky Prospect. The scar flared again, which meant it was her turn. The other enchanter had made his move, and although Vika didn't know what it was, she was immediately on guard. Sergei had warned her that his sister's student was likely trained as a killer. He'd try to end the Game quickly.

Was the front door locked? Yes.

Any movement in the drawing room: in the corners, under the card table, behind the chaise longue? No.

Was there magic in the air?

Yes.

Vika's heart thundered in her chest, but she tried to breathe as quietly as she could.

She crept down the hallway toward the rest of the apartment. She'd used the money she found in Sergei's hiding spot (under the valerian root in his garden) to pay for the flat. It was small by Saint Petersburg standards, but twice the living space she and Sergei had at home. And it had seemed perfect when she found it, full of eccentric mementos from the owners' trips abroad, some so strange—like the taxidermied elk head wearing a Viking helmet or the garishly colored Venetian mask with mouths where the eye holes should be—that it seemed possible they were enchanted themselves.

But now, living in an apartment full of oddities didn't seem like such a good idea. Any one of them could harbor a trap. She tiptoed to the first bedroom. Were there signs of an intruder?

But the bed was perfectly made, its satin sheets shiny in the early morning rays. The hat rack stood guard on the other side of the room. The dressing table, with its gilded bronze mirror and dozens of bottles of perfumes left by the flat's owners, seemed as frivolous as ever.

The wands on Vika's chest throbbed again. She slunk down the hall to the other bedroom, but it also appeared undisturbed. She slipped into the kitchen, her eyes darting from the stove to the oven to the cabinets decorated with scenes from Russian fairy tales, but saw no one and nothing alarming, other than the feathered talons that served as the dining table's legs. Nothing, that is, except for the sense that there was magic other than her own floating about, as if the air were several particles heavier than it ought to be.

She flung open the windows in the kitchen. "Out!" she commanded the air, to cleanse it of anything dangerous her opponent might have planted. But instead, air even more enchanted tried to push in from outside.

"What? No!" Vika passed her hands over her head and up and down her body, fortifying the invisible shield she had cast around herself as she slept. She had protected the apartment from his enchantments, but his magic was trying to bully its way in. She doubled the charm around the window.

And then Vika saw the building across the street from her own. When she had gone to bed, that building had been a faded gray. Now it was a delicate powder blue, and its white trim, previously dull, had taken on a pearly tone.

If it had been only one home, she would have thought nothing of it. But she scanned the visible length of Nevsky Prospect, where the buildings, like many in the largest cities of Europe, were built right up against one another, and every single facade seemed a part of a candy wonderland. There were yellows soft as lemon cream, and greens like apples for pie. Purple like lavender marshmallow, and pink like rosewater taffy. Vika gasped. The buildings along the boulevard were the most breathtaking thing she had ever seen.

"This is his first move?" she said to herself. As if to confirm, the wands beneath her collarbone heated up, and she gasped again.

But the pain dissipated after a few seconds, and soon Vika's shoulders relaxed. She let down the shield around herself as well. If it was her turn now, she needn't worry about being attacked. And then it sank in that her opponent's first move had been a peaceful one for the tsesarevich's birthday. Vika's heart beat out of rhythm at the hope that the other enchanter was less bloodthirsty than Sergei had assumed.

Then she noticed the tiny statues on the buildings, and she immediately cast the shield back around herself. The statues were stone birds, so small they could easily be mistaken for real sparrows hopping on the ledges and rooftops every ten feet or so. They hadn't been there before, had they? Or was she just noticing them now because the entire boulevard had been brightened and was actually worth looking at?

She had to suspect the worst. As much as she'd wanted to believe that her opponent had laid down an amicable move, that someone as elegant as he wouldn't resort to violence, the Game would in fact end upon one of their deaths. *And there was something about the way he carried himself*, she thought. *Mesmerizing, but subtly perilous.* Perhaps the stone birds were enchanted to attack as soon as Vika appeared on the street. But would they be able to do that if her opponent didn't know who she was? She'd kept up her shroud diligently all the way home from Bolshebnoie Duplo. And Vika certainly wouldn't be able to charm something into tracking an unknown person.

Then again, the other enchanter could be exponentially more skilled than she. It was an unnerving possibility.

However, she couldn't remain in her apartment for the rest of the Game. She would have to go out and face the birds, whatever they were. Her father had prepared her well for this. He had taught her how to defend herself, from using the wind to blow dirt into a bear's eyes to creating ice barricades for protection from flaming trees.

So Vika fortified the shield around herself and left the flat, taking the stairs one slow step at a time. When she reached the first floor, she opened the building's door only a crack and poked her foot outside, like a tentative dancer testing the stage.

She waited. The stone birds did not fly off the ledges at her shoe. She slipped the rest of her body out the door, turning her head from left to right to take in all her potential avian assailants.

And then they attacked.

They dived from every direction—north, south, east, west—like shrapnel magnetized especially for her. The first ones slammed into Vika's invisible shield, and she shrieked upon their violent impact. But she held her shield steady, and they ricocheted off, shattering on the ground and against the building walls.

Then hundreds—no, thousands—more stone birds circled overhead, calculating, and Vika knew she wouldn't be able to hold the shield if they all came at her at once.

Heaven help me, I need my own birds.

She jammed her thumb and index finger in her mouth and whistled so shrilly, a dozen of the closest stone sparrows shattered. Their ranks, however, were quickly filled in by others.

Come on, come on, come on, Vika thought. *Where are my birds?* She fended off another wave of suicidal stone birds smashing into her shield. Each collision rattled through her magic and into her bones.

But a minute later, a dark cloud appeared in the sky, high above the misleadingly cheerful pastels of Nevsky Prospect. And then another minute later, the cloud revealed itself to be thousands of *real* birds—hooded crows with their gray-and-black feathers and wicked *caw-caw-caws,* chaffinches with brave, ruddy cheeks, and jackdaws, purplish-black and crying their hoarse battle cries as they careened down past rooftops and into the fray against the other enchanter's army.

"Yes!" Vika yelled. "Go get them!"

Her birds charged straight into the enemy. Just as fearless, the stone sparrows did not alter their flight. Real beaks gouged out jeweled eyes. Rock talons tore at soft feathers. And the waves of birds kept coming.

Vika clenched her fists as the blue sky exploded in red and black and purple feathers and shards of dark-gray stone. For every gargoyle sparrow dispatched, a real bird died. "Their lives are on his soul," she muttered through her teeth as the carnage grew around her. And yet, she knew that was only partially true. She could have come up with a different defense. Vika was the one who'd chosen live birds as her soldiers.

There's no way my birds can win a physical fight against

rock, she thought as her shield trembled under the nonstop attacks. *But we could win a psychological one.*

She whistled again and commanded her birds to form a barrier above her. They flew into defensive position, ten birds thick.

The stone sparrows regrouped even higher, near the clouds.

There was a moment of eerie peace.

"Come now," Vika said to the other enchanter's birds. "Isn't it tempting, seeing my flock lined up neatly, like targets waiting for you to knock them down?"

The stone sparrows seemed to come to the same conclusion as Vika taunted them. With shrieks as bloodcurdling as a thousand fingernails raking against blackboards, the gargoyle warriors plummeted as one, like a battering ram careening toward Vika's real birds.

Her army squawked as the monolith of stone came at them. But they held their positions. Then, at the last second, they darted aside. Vika also rolled out of the way.

The rock sparrows smashed into the ground and shattered into gravel and sand.

And then it was over, almost as quickly as the assault had begun. Death littered Nevsky Prospect, stone and feathered bodies, demolished. Vika's eyes watered.

But she didn't cry. She *wouldn't*. She summoned the wind instead and whisked away all the evidence of life—or lack thereof—so quickly that the early morning street sweeper who'd been gawking along the road suddenly questioned his own memory—or sanity, at having imagined such an improbably gruesome scene at all.

Only Vika knew for certain that it had been true. And she would get her revenge.

CHAPTER EIGHTEEN

The stone sparrow glided onto Nikolai's arm as he sat on the steps in front of the Zakrevsky house. He'd been watching the barges chug by on Ekaterinsky Canal and eavesdropping on passersby as they chattered about their morning errands on Nevsky Prospect. Most had been pleased that the once renowned boulevard had been restored to its former grandeur. And everyone assumed it was the doing of an overnight crew of painters hired by the tsar, despite the fact that no one knew a single painter in the city who'd worked on the street. Nikolai was unsurprised. For a people who were so religious, Russians had an awfully difficult time seeing the otherworldly even when it was laid out before their eyes.

"What do you have for me?" Nikolai asked the sparrow. He rested his hand on the tiny thing's head. Its feathers were rough from being cast of rock, but they were impressively realistic in appearance. At least, Nikolai thought, from a distance.

The bird cooed and nuzzled against his fingers. Nikolai

closed his eyes, and a stream of images rushed to him from the statue, as if Nikolai had been on Nevsky Prospect to see the series of bird's-eye views himself. It was a quiet picture, the undisturbed moments just after dawn. No shoppers carrying brown paper bundles out of the butcher shop or gentlemen emerging from Bissette & Sons, the tailors for whom Nikolai delivered packages. No one strolling out of the clockmaker's with a shiny new pocket watch dangling out of his waistcoat, or servant girls leaving the bakery with stacks of boxes full of cakes. Just a lone street sweeper and his thin, worn broom.

And then . . . there was the girl, leaving an apartment building.

His stone birds paused, high above her, all of them turning to her in sync. A moment later, they attacked.

Merde! Nikolai winced at the bloody, rocky battle that ensued.

"I'm sorry," he said to the sparrow, as if a statue could feel grief for his shattered friends. Or perhaps Nikolai was saying it for the actual birds who'd died. Or the girl herself. Regardless, he stroked the sparrow's stone wings.

It cooed, then flapped away, as light as if it were made of the breeze. Nikolai returned his gaze to the canals and barges floating by, although he might as well have been seeing the stone bird's images replaying again and again.

Nikolai sagged against the steps and exhaled.

The girl still lived. The Game continued.

But at least he wasn't a murderer today.

CHAPTER NINETEEN

The tsar sat on one side of the open-air carriage with the tsarina, while Pasha and Yuliana sat facing them on the opposite velvet bench. It was a fine autumn day, crisp and cool without a cloud in sight, and since it was mere days before Pasha's birthday, the tsarina had decided the city ought to have the benefit of admiring her son.

They had been parading around Saint Petersburg in their coach for nearly an hour now, and the crowds showed no signs of thinning.

"Pavel Alexandrovich! Happy birthday!"

"Your Imperial Highness, Your Imperial Highness, over here!"

"Best wishes, dear prince, to you and your family!"

Pasha beamed and waved to each and every person who called to him from the streets and the windows and balconies above. The tsar and the rest of the imperial family sat around him but did not steal the limelight. It was the tsesarevich's afternoon.

That did not stop Yuliana, however, from unrolling a map.

The tsar shook his head affectionately. Of course she'd brought a map.

"Missolonghi is at a crisis point," Yuliana said, attempting to update her brother on the recent meeting of the Imperial Council, which he had again skipped. "The Ottomans have besieged the city, and although the Greek rebels have managed to break the blockade several times for supplies, it is not long before the noose is tightened. And while the Ottomans are facing increasing political unrest from their subject states, it doesn't make them weaker. It only aggravates them and calls them to stronger arms, which in turn is a rising threat to Russia, for they're nipping at the land we took away from them. And . . . Pasha! Are you listening?"

Pasha turned from a mass of children who were giggling and shrieking his name. His smile carried over as he looked at Yuliana. "Of course. You were talking about . . . England?"

"Ugh!" Yuliana shot the tsar an exasperated glare, as if to say, *Why can't he be more like you and me?*

At that moment, a man in a tattered farmer's hat shoved his way through the crowd and charged at the carriage. "You sit on your gilded thrones while our people toil to their deaths in the fields!"

The Tsar's Guard pounced on the man before the tsar could even react. The man continued shouting as the Guard dragged him away. "You promised us equality! We fought side by side with your noblemen against Napoleon! But you lied! We died for you, and you lied!"

The tsar winced inside but did not show it. He knew

116

he'd reneged on his earlier promises. But it was better for Russia this way. The principles he'd once believed in his youth had been tempered by experience and age.

One of the guards hit the man with the butt of his rifle. The man went silent.

The tsarina stiffened beside the tsar. Across the coach, Yuliana looked with indifference at the man being taken away. Pasha, on the other hand, watched them, then waved a guard to the carriage.

"See to it that that man is given medical attention," Pasha instructed. "And then take him home. I'm pardoning him. Tell him I know we all get a little carried away sometimes on birthdays."

Yuliana frowned at her brother. The tsar did, too.

Pasha had too soft a touch. And with the empire fraying both at the edges—from the Ottomans and the Kazakhs—and within—from men like the fool who'd charged the coach, the tsar realized more than ever how right Yuliana had been. He needed an Imperial Enchanter. For the country and Pasha's sake.

CHAPTER TWENTY

The other enchanter wasn't the only one who could have spies. Vika had watched as the last stone sparrow flew away, and she'd sent a jackdaw after it. The jackdaw discovered where the other enchanter lived, and Vika had tailed him for the two days since he'd attacked her. It turned out the enchanter liked taking walks along the Neva River.

So now Vika stood at the granite embankments of the Neva, beside the enormous bronze statue of Peter the Great—the tsar who founded Saint Petersburg—atop his horse. It was a monument commissioned by Catherine the Great to pay tribute to Peter, and legend had it that as long as the statue stood guard, Saint Petersburg would never fall into enemy hands. It was only a legend, and most Russians dismissed it as such, or believed it out of superstition. But as she stood in such close proximity to the statue, Vika knew it was real. There was old magic—hefty, powerful magic— within the bronze.

As soon as the enchanter appeared for his afternoon

stroll, Vika would make her own move in the Game. Of course, she wouldn't kill him straightaway. He'd labored over the charming of Nevsky Prospect, and she wanted to outdo him first.

She planned to enchant the city's waterways.

This was a grandiose task, however. In addition to the Neva River, there were over a hundred other rivers, tributaries, and canals that ran through Saint Petersburg, totaling nearly two hundred miles in distance. There were more bridges in Petersburg than in Venice; water was the very essence, the life force, of the city. Even though Vika was skilled at manipulating natural elements—they were, after all, what was most abundant on Ovchinin Island and therefore what she had practiced most with—this move would require more energy and concentration than anything she had ever attempted.

After Vika had waited an hour, the other enchanter appeared. And despite wanting to hate him, she tingled at his presence. He was still some distance off, but it was unmistakably him. It was in the way his top hat was cocked on his head, jaunty and taunting at the same time, impossibly balanced by magic. The elegant yet razor-edged manner with which he slid through the crowd, cutting through but never jostling, and always, always smooth. And it was also the memory of his hand on her arm at Bolshebnoie Duplo and the flash of his angular face. . . .

No. Stop. Focus. *He tried to kill me. I have to get my turn underway before he draws too near.*

Vika planted both feet firmly into the ground. She closed her eyes. A strong breeze rippled through her hair, carrying with it the autumn cold from the Gulf of Finland from whence it came. She inhaled deeply, taking in the scent of the Neva River. It smelled . . . green. Fresh water tinged with algae. A hint of aspen, and what was that? Ah yes, alder wood, too.

Vika also listened to the sounds of the river. Ducks paddling on the surface. Sturgeon swimming, and eels slithering beneath. She had to, in a way, become the river, or at least understand it, before she could expect it to do her bidding. People walked by, but nobody paid her any notice, for, other than the steady rise and fall of her chest, she was as still as the statue beside her.

Finally, when she could almost feel the Neva's chilly waters coursing through her own veins, Vika opened her eyes and stretched her arms out in front of her. "This is my move," she whispered, so that the Russe Quill would know that *this* magic—and not other charms that she cast—was the one to be recorded on the Scroll. Then she focused on the center of the river and tapped her right hand upward, a slight movement, as if she were tossing a small ball. A stream of water leaped ten yards into the air and fell in an elegant arc back to the river's surface.

"*Prekrasno,*" she said to herself in satisfaction.

She tapped her left hand upward, and another stream of water mirrored the movement of the first. She followed with her right again, then left, alternating the height of the arcs as well as the speed, sometimes firing the streams in rapid succession, and other times slowing them languorously.

A crowd began to gather along the embankment, murmuring to one another and leaning out over the granite railings to get a better look. Still, no one noticed Vika. *They don't believe in magic,* she thought. *That's why they don't see that*

I'm the one controlling the river. One or two men did notice her, but they just laughed dismissively at the girl playing at copying the water's movements. Vika rolled her eyes.

She could also feel the other enchanter, near now. Watching. She didn't look for him, but his presence was there. He didn't try to hide it.

Vika continued on. She drew corkscrews in the air, and the river water twirled high into the sky like jeweled helixes, the droplets glinting in the morning sun like so many diamonds. The people on shore released a collective gasp. She clenched her fists, then slowly unfurled her fingers, and the Neva responded in kind, creating tight buds of water that then blossomed in waves of petals, like chrysanthemums blooming in fall. The onlookers oohed and aahed. What a rush to finally have her magic out in the open, seen and appreciated by so many, even if they couldn't possibly understand what it was. The years of hiding away her powers in the shielded forest of Ovchinin Island seemed a distant past.

Vika scooped handfuls of air and flipped them up, then puffed on them with her breath. In the river, spheres of water flew up to the clouds, then burst like transparent fireworks and sprinkled down like rain. The audience cheered.

The other enchanter stood close to the river's edge. Perfectly close for Vika's purposes. Too close for his own.

Just where I want you. She made a slithering motion in the air, and a stream of water climbed up the embankment and puddled around the enchanter's feet. It swirled around his right ankle and tightened itself like liquid rope. As he realized what was happening, she flicked her wrist, and the water yanked him into the Neva. *"Prekrasno,"* she said again as she grinned to herself.

A woman in the crowd screamed.

"Someone's fallen into the river!" a man yelled.

But the other enchanter didn't resurface.

Vika turned away from the water, even as she continued to direct it to hold her opponent down. Suddenly, she couldn't watch. But drowning him was a necessity, a part of the Game. If she didn't kill him, he'd kill her. And she wanted to be Imperial Enchanter; she'd wanted it all her life, to use her magic for the tsar.

And then there was Father . . . she had to see him again. If she lost the Game, she never would. It didn't make what she was doing any easier. But it made it possible. Unavoidable.

Vika held on to the watery rope as long as she could, and then she collapsed against the boulder at the base of the bronze statue.

People were still leaning over the embankment, searching for the drowned boy. Vika gasped for air, as badly as if she were the one underwater. Something inside her felt like it had drowned, too.

And then, behind her, shouts erupted. "There he is!"

"He's all right!"

"The damn boy gave us a scare, but he was just diving the whole time!"

Vika pulled herself up by the base of Peter's statue and looked out onto the Neva. Sure enough, out in the river, the enchanter floated on what looked like a raft of sea foam. He reached the shores of Vasilyevsky Island, on the other side of the Neva, before Vika could use the water to reel him back in.

Not that she had the stomach to do it again. Her

conscience was still waterlogged from the first attempt to drown him.

The crowd along shore realized the boy was all right and that the waterworks show was over. As they dispersed, they murmured their approval that the festivities for the tsesarev-ich were beginning ahead of schedule. They bounced as they walked, anticipating what other surprises the tsar had in store. And they wondered if the Neva Fountain would turn on again.

The Neva Fountain, eh? How nice that they've already given it a name. Vika smiled despite her morally dubious insides. Or perhaps she smiled because of them. She did not want to know which.

She looked again across the Neva to the other enchanter. He seemed to be staring straight back at her. And then he tipped his top hat, as if saying, *Nice try. Thank you for the amusement. Have a wonderful day.*

Why, that arrogant, insufferable . . . argh! "It's not like you managed to kill me either," Vika said, even though he couldn't hear her.

All right. So the other enchanter had survived. Vika had created the Neva Fountain, which, enchanted once, would now retain the charms in the water and be able to replicate the show on its own, every hour. But she'd set out to far better the other enchanter, and if she couldn't win outright, she would make sure her first turn shone exponentially brighter than his.

Vika's eyes fluttered shut, and she imagined all the canals flowing in and out and through the city. Then she thought of the colorful building fronts along Nevsky Pros-pect. As she stood there, bracing herself against the statue of

Peter the Great, the waterways throughout Saint Petersburg began to shift in hue.

First ruby red, then fire-opal orange. Golden citrine and emerald green. Sapphire blue, violet amethyst, then back to red to start the rainbow again. Even though the other enchanter had painted Nevsky Prospect first, Vika's colors were so vivid, it was as if his palette of pastels were merely a faded reflection of hers.

The canals were a jewel-toned taunt, really, at his move.

Vika finished charming the waterways enough to cycle through the colors on their own, then sank to the ground. The base of Peter the Great's statue was the only thing propping her up. But despite her exhaustion, Vika grinned.

The gleam in her eyes was one part gloat and ninety-nine parts mischief.

CHAPTER TWENTY-ONE

Late that night, something hard struck Nikolai's bedroom window on the second floor. Then another, and another, like hail hurling itself sideways at the pane. He peeked through a sliver in the curtains. Damn, how quickly the girl had played her turn! Even though it was his move, he was still wary of attack. She had tried to drown him in front of a crowd in broad daylight! Who knew what she'd do under the cover of moonlight?

Nikolai squinted out into the darkness. What in blazes was going on?

A pebble hit the window, right where Nikolai's nose was. *"Mon dieu!"* He cursed as he stumbled backward, halfway across his room.

Another pebble smacked against the glass. "Nikolai, open up!" a boy shouted from the street.

Was that . . . Pasha?

Nikolai tiptoed to the window. It could be a trick. He cracked open the curtains. A pebble hit the pane at the spot in front of his nose again.

It had to be Pasha. No one else had such impeccable aim, other than Nikolai.

He lifted the window. "Cease fire!"

Pasha laughed. "Nikolai, you devil of a fellow! You've been avoiding me."

"I have not." It was not a lie, exactly. Nikolai had simply been . . . preoccupied.

"You have, too," Pasha said. "It's been nearly a week since I've seen you. Have you not received my invitations to go hunting and watch polo matches?"

"You know full well you never actually do those things."

Pasha shrugged. "Technicalities. We would have had other grand adventures. But in any event, you admit to receiving the invitations, and yet not responding. You see, I was right. You *have* been avoiding me. Well, I have come to you, so there is no escape now."

Nikolai leaned against the windowsill. His eyes were now adjusted to the streetlamps outside. "Does your Guard know you've left the palace?"

"Do they ever?"

"I sincerely worry about their competence. I may need to request an audience with your father to discuss it."

"Or perhaps the answer is that I'm simply a brilliant escape artist. Now come on. Are you going to let me up? Or are we going to Romeo-and-Juliet the night away?" Pasha smirked.

Nikolai looked at his own position, like Juliet perched on her balcony, and then at Pasha on the street below. "Oh, be quiet. You're the one who came romancing at my window," he said, but he stood up and curtsied. "My room is a mess,

Romeo. Give me a minute, and I shall come down."

Nikolai closed his window and recast the charm to secure it. Then he glanced about his room for a frock coat. And his boots. And his top hat. If only everything weren't buried under canvas drop cloths and two dozen different jack-in-the-boxes, disassembled. Not to mention the marionettes sprawled across the bed. But it was all necessary. The other enchanter had far outdone him with her fountains in the Neva and the color in the canals. Nikolai had to counter-move by better showing off his skill—and that would be best done by focusing on his mechanical talent.

However, it did not solve the problem of his clothes being buried under all the cranks and gears.

"Oh, forget it." Nikolai snapped his fingers, and the frock coat waltzed out from under one of the drop cloths—spilling screws and springs in the process—his shoes tap-danced their way from under his bed, and the top hat spun out from the top of the armoire. "You don't have to be so flamboyant," he grumbled as he slipped his arms into the jacket and stepped into his boots. But the laces hung limp, as if pouting.

Nikolai sighed. "All right, if you must." Ever since the Crown's Game began, he'd been losing control over the small daily details he'd once easily managed. The shoelaces looped merrily and tied themselves in an elaborate bow.

The scar flared under his shirt. Nikolai sucked in a breath. He cast another glance around the chaos of his room. He ought to stay here. He ought to work on his next move, especially since the girl had executed such an impressively complex one, with an insult tacked on to boot. Damn her.

But he was still exhausted from nearly drowning in the

Neva. And now his head was full of fog and not much brain. He could not discern right from left, let alone how to make his next idea work.

What he needed was twenty-four straight hours of sleep. But Pasha was waiting for him on the street, and even though he was Nikolai's best friend, there were only so many times one could politely decline an invitation from the heir to the Russian throne.

Nikolai lifted his wool overcoat from its hanger in the armoire—at least that article of clothing was in its proper place—and stepped into the hall. He closed his door softly, so as not to wake the servants, although it was entirely possible that Pasha's rock throwing and Romeo taunting had already done the job. He charmed the locks on the door (after the tiger-viper-lorises incident, he had kept the five extra dead bolts installed), then set off down the stairs.

Pasha and Nikolai slipped in through the back door of the Magpie and the Fox. It was a tavern owned by Nursultan Bayzhanov, a brawny Kazakh fellow, with whom the boys had a long-standing arrangement for a booth in the dimmest corner. Pasha hovered in the shadow of a shelf of beer steins, while Nikolai went into the bar to find Nursultan. He returned a minute later.

"Nursultan is clearing the table," he said to Pasha.

"I feel rotten every time this happens, when he has to evict whoever is already sitting there."

"Don't feel bad. You're the shining future of Russia."

Pasha half smiled and half grimaced. "That's precisely why I feel bad."

Nikolai shrugged. They had had this conversation in

many different variations before. But the fact of the matter was, there was no other way for Pasha to patronize a place like this. Besides, if the men at the table knew it was the tsesarevich who was usurping their table, they would gladly relocate. That line of logic, however, had never appeased Pasha's guilt.

Nursultan charged around the corner and into the kitchen, where the boys stood. "Your table is ready. If you want beer, grab a mug yourselves." He pointed at the shelf beside them, then turned and disappeared back into the commotion of the tavern.

Pasha bounced on his toes. Nikolai almost smiled. When Nikolai had first spoken to Nursultan about bringing in an esteemed customer for whom anonymity was of the utmost importance, he had guaranteed that he would treat whoever it was in exactly the same manner as his other patrons (special booth notwithstanding). And Nursultan had followed through, every time, down to barking at them to bus their own tables. Pasha adored it. If he had his way, he would be at the Magpie and the Fox every night.

Nikolai paused. What if he hadn't come to the tavern? If he'd continued to ignore Pasha until the Game was done, would Pasha find himself a new friend? Someone else common and poor? Sometimes Nikolai wondered if that was the reason Pasha liked him, because he was different from everyone else in Pasha's blue-blooded world.

No, it's more than that, Nikolai thought. *Isn't it?*

"Are you coming?" Pasha asked, practically bounding in the direction of the table. He might as well have had springs in the soles of his boots.

"Not if you're going to call attention to yourself like that."

Pasha threw his arm around Nikolai's shoulder and winked, but the springs in his feet retracted. "Good point. I would be completely ungrounded without you."

And as easily as that, Nikolai's doubts about their friendship receded. For now.

They slunk into their booth in the back corner, steins in hand. Not a second later, Nursultan slid a pitcher of beer onto the table, its contents sloshing but not overflowing, along with two short glasses and an ice-cold bottle of vodka. With a thunk, he set down a cutting board filled with rye bread, smoked fish, and cucumber pickles. Then he grunted and stamped away.

Nikolai poured a shot of vodka for each of them, while Pasha filled their beer glasses. Then Nikolai raised his vodka and said, *"Tvoe zdarovye." To your health.* At a tavern like the Magpie and the Fox, one toasted in Russian, not French. The boys knocked back their shots and chased them with sips of beer. Pasha grinned and bit into a pickle.

"So are you going to tell me why you dragged me out of bed in the middle of the night?" Nikolai asked as he piled smoked sturgeon onto a slice of bread.

"You weren't sleeping."

"Perhaps I was."

"Not unless you sleep in a starched shirt, cravat, and waistcoat. I could see your clothes full well from the street."

"Damn you and your observations."

Pasha laughed. Then the jest fell away, and he leaned into the table. The flickering candlelight in the tavern cast harsh shadows across his face. "Things are happening, Nikolai."

Nikolai set down his bread and leaned away from the

table, pressing himself against the booth's wall. "What things?"

"The refacing of Nevsky Prospect. The Neva Fountain. The Canal of Colors."

Was that what the city's residents were calling their moves? Nikolai's scar flared at the reminder of the Game.

"Don't tell me you haven't noticed it," Pasha said. "Have you even left your room in the past week? Or are you keeping something from me?"

Nikolai poked at his bread. "Yes. And no. I mean to say, yes, I have left my room and even the house, and no, I'm not keeping anything from you."

"Hmm." Pasha scrutinized him. Nikolai charmed his own face so that Pasha wouldn't be able to see the falsehood on him.

"All right," Pasha said. "If you have, indeed, left the Zakrevsky prison, then you know what I'm talking about, yes?"

"The preparations for your birthday. Yes, I've seen them. The mechanics are impressive."

"*Chyort.*"

Nikolai arched a brow. Pasha rarely cursed, especially not in Russian. (Nikolai was also unconvinced that Pasha was saying it correctly, but what did they know? They spoke mainly French.)

Pasha was unapologetic for the profanity. "Mechanics? That's an utter lie, and you know it. This is *enchantment*, Nikolai. No one else recognizes it because they don't know it exists. Russia used to be full of magic, but then it faded away because people either started fearing it or stopped believing in it. For example, did you know that the forests and lakes used to be rife with faeries and nymphs? But they've died out from neglect and disbelief.

"And yet," he continued, "you saw that girl in the forest on Ovchinin Island, whether you'll admit it or not. Tell me you believe me, that magic is real. Tell me I'm not losing my mind."

Nikolai poured another shot of vodka for himself as he pondered whether to confirm or deny it.

He had actually considered confiding in Pasha many times before—both about his magical abilities and the related indignities heaped upon him by Galina—but he had always stopped short of confessing. For one, Nikolai knew Pasha looked up to him, as backward as it might be for the tsesarevich to admire a nobody from the steppe, and Nikolai was loath to have yet another thing that set him apart, for he wished to fit in with his friend, not stand out. On the flip side of that, Nikolai might work for Pasha someday, and he wanted to enjoy their friendship as it was for as long as possible, before that dynamic in their relationship shifted. And third, Nikolai did not want to tell Pasha about his abilities, when his magic was eventually going to be used to kill someone. Not that it wouldn't be revealed at some point, should Nikolai survive the Game. But he didn't want to think about that. That was a problem for the future, if that future existed.

Honesty, sometimes, was the worst policy.

Nikolai poured vodka for Pasha, too, but his friend shook his head. So Nikolai raised his own glass and muttered, "*Myevo zdarovye.*" *To* my *health*, and knocked back the shot. He washed it down with more than a sip of beer.

"Tell me I'm not losing my mind," Pasha said again.

Nikolai squeezed his eyes shut, then opened them. Pasha appeared to be tilting. Nikolai smacked himself on the cheek, and Pasha was righted. If anyone at the table was losing his mind, it was Nikolai. Especially now, since the alcohol had gone straight to his head. He hadn't eaten a thing since the afternoon.

"Fine. Magic is real," he said, before he could stop the declaration from trickling out. *Zut alors!* Why had he said that? What was this vodka made of?

Pasha sat up, his smile returned. "I knew it! But how do you know?"

"Uh . . ." Nikolai scrambled for a scrap of truth without revealing himself. "My mother was a faith healer."

"You had a mother?"

Nikolai crossed his arms. "Has a single shot of vodka completely shuttered your brain? Of course I had a mother. Everyone has a mother, at some point."

"My apologies. I didn't mean to offend. I simply meant, I didn't know you knew your mother."

"I don't. She died during childbirth."

Pasha looked down at the table, roundly chastened. Nikolai sighed. He hadn't intended to squelch his friend's enthusiasm. But alcohol made his words clumsy, like lumbering giants attempting to construct a glass dollhouse. There were bound to be accidents.

"I don't know anything about my mother, only that she was a faith healer, and the people in my tribe believed her abilities to be real."

Pasha glanced up. "Are you a faith healer?"

"No." At least Nikolai could say that without lying.

A few tables away, a chair fell over. Or rather, it had

been knocked over, as a man stood and thumped his fist on the tabletop. "We have rights!" he yelled. "The tsar must know he cannot continue to treat the people like vermin! We need a revolution!"

"Shut your trap or we'll all be tossed into prison!" one of his companions shouted.

Nikolai and Pasha watched as several men pinned down their friend, the mutineer.

"Should we report him?" Nikolai asked Pasha.

Pasha hesitated. He squinted to look at the man, and Nikolai wondered for a second if Pasha knew him. But then Pasha shook his head and sank back into the shadow of their booth. "He'll sleep it off and come to his senses. I don't want Nursultan in trouble for harboring traitors when he's only guilty of harboring fools."

"Present company excluded, of course."

"Of course," Pasha said. "But listen. I have an idea. Unrelated to that ruckus."

"Another drink?" Nikolai reached for the vodka.

Pasha waved him off. "I'm going to hold a ball for my birthday. Father will think I'm finally rising to the level of pomp expected of a tsesarevich, and Mother will be thrilled that I might find a wife."

"And your real purpose?"

"I'm going to invite the lightning girl."

The bottle of vodka slipped from Nikolai's hand, and he lunged to catch it and also charmed it at the same time so it would not crash and spill all over the food on the cutting board. But as soon as he snatched the bottle, his eyes darted up to Pasha's. Had he seen? Nikolai should not have done that. In his tipsiness, instinct had taken over.

Pasha looked at the bottle and Nikolai's hand for a few seconds. Then he shook his head and said, "Nimble catch, Juliet."

Nikolai exhaled.

"So . . . ," Pasha said, as he fiddled with the cutting board, "I went back to Ovchinin Island the other day. I discovered the girl's name."

Nikolai thumped the bottle of vodka onto the table. "You went to the island to look for her? Are you mad?" Perhaps Pasha *was* included in the fools whom Nursultan harbored.

"Are you afraid of her?" Pasha asked.

More than you'll ever know, Nikolai thought. Not only because the lightning girl could very well kill him, but also because her Canal of Colors had stirred something in Nikolai he hadn't known was there. Of course, her waterways were a swaggering jibe at his work on Nevsky Prospect. And yet, there was also something deeper there, something more untamed. All these years, Nikolai had been alone, with only Galina's minor magic keeping company with his own. But now there was suddenly another enchanter in his life, and he felt a paradoxical kinship with her. It dissolved the edges of his loneliness, like finding the path home after years of wandering the wilderness on his own.

And although it was arrogant how she'd changed the colors in the canals just to taunt him, Nikolai also admired that she wasn't afraid to do so.

Which made the girl all the more dangerous. She was the enemy. Nikolai could not afford to be drawn in.

He was also afraid that Pasha would fall for her, seeing as he had already gone far out of his way to track down her details on Ovchinin Island. How could Nikolai kill the girl if his best friend became infatuated with her?

Aloud, Nikolai said, "A rational person would be wary. A rational person would not go seeking to invite someone like that to a ball. Why invite her? To entertain your guests with feats of fire? You can hire the flame-eaters from the circus for that."

Pasha picked at the label on the vodka bottle. "Or perhaps I will ask her to dance."

"Pavel Alexandrovich."

"Don't call me that."

"Fine, then. Pasha."

"What?"

"You can't."

"Can't what?"

"Invite her. Dance with her. You're . . ." Nikolai lowered his voice to a whisper. "You're the tsesarevich of the Russian Empire."

"So?" Pasha threw up his arms. "Doesn't that mean I can do whatever I please?"

"You know it doesn't. Your mother has rules about whom you can even flirt with, let alone dance with."

"Guidelines."

"What?"

"Whom I can flirt with. They're guidelines, not rules."

"Pasha."

The tsesarevich slumped in the booth. He jammed his hands in his hair, and it rumpled to such an extent, it finally looked as if he were a patron of low enough birth and means to frequent this tavern. *Someone like me*, Nikolai thought. He, too, sank lower in the booth.

After a bit more wrenching, Pasha finally released his

abused locks and said, "You know, I've been reading a great deal about mystics and enchanters. They're not evil, contrary to popular belief. They're misunderstood. And the Church and the people's irrational fear of their powers have driven them underground, to hide their magic. How dreadful is that? Imagine how taxing it must be to hide your true self every minute of your entire life."

Nikolai bit his lip.

"I want her to know it's all right," Pasha said.

"To what?"

"To live in the open."

"Married to the heir to the throne?"

Pasha scowled. "That is not what I meant." He picked up the now-warm shot of vodka Nikolai had poured for him earlier, muttered a toast to the tsar's health, and gulped it down. His mouth puckered, but he didn't bother to chase the vodka with beer.

"She's not the type of girl you can send a glass slipper to and make into a princess," Nikolai said.

"You never know."

"She could turn out to be the wicked fairy godmother instead."

"Now you're conflating your fairy tales. The wicked fairy godmother is from *The Sleeping Beauty in the Wood*, not *Cinderella*. And why are you convinced the lightning girl is dangerous?"

So many reasons.

Nikolai rubbed the back of his neck. "We know nothing about her."

"Her name is Vika."

Nikolai's scar burned at the same time that the knot in

his chest—that foreboding sense of kismet that had begun when he saw the Canal of Colors—tightened.

"'Though she be but little, she is fierce.'"

"Quoting Shakespeare won't sway me, Nikolai."

"Then what can I do to dissuade you from searching for the girl again or inviting her to the ball?"

Pasha topped off their glasses. "You can't." Then he lifted his glass and toasted, "To the lightning girl. And all else that may come."

CHAPTER TWENTY-TWO

"Why hasn't he killed her yet?" Galina's teeth chattered, even though she was inside the cabin while the Siberian blizzard raged outside.

"Because I taught Vika well," Sergei said. He cast a look at the fireplace, and the flames expanded, filling the small cabin with more heat.

"Well, I also trained Nikolai well."

"It's been only five days since the oath."

Galina turned up her nose. "He ought to have dispatched her by now."

Sergei recoiled. But he quickly composed himself, for to show Galina that her comment had ruffled him would only encourage her to mention Vika's death more than she already did. He had learned this lesson from their youth, when Galina would torture him mercilessly with whatever made him most uncomfortable. Like murdering squirrels in the park with her glare and laughing when they fell out of the trees, their eyes already glassy and unseeing. And then laughing harder as Sergei mourned them through a curtain of snotty tears.

"We don't know what form the Game has taken," Sergei said. "You imagine an outright duel, but knowing Vika, I suspect it's something more subtle. She did not spend her entire life confined to a tiny island only to have her magic—her freedom—constricted to a few short days in the Game. She's going to savor the experience. Both you and your student would be gravely mistaken to take that as complacency or lack of skill."

Galina smirked and stalked over to the kitchen table. It had originally been constructed of coarse logs, but Galina had changed it into Italian marble. "You haven't grown too attached to the girl, I hope? Have you even told her you aren't her real father?"

Sergei furrowed his brow. "What are you implying?" He'd thought everyone believed she was his daughter. He certainly thought his sister, whom he hadn't seen in decades, would think so.

Galina conjured up a cup of steaming tea. "Honestly, Sergei, she looks nothing like you. And even though you did not care to check on me in Saint Petersburg all those years, I did check on you—actually, I paid someone to do it from time to time, because that sort of work is beneath me—and I know for a fact that you never married or had even a mistress. But it's fine if you want to pretend Vika is your daughter. It's . . . sweet, even." Galina's mouth puckered. "All right, *cloying* is more accurate. But that's your choice. All I want to know is, where did you find her?"

"I—I didn't—"

"Sergei."

"Fine." He knew if he didn't answer, she'd keep pestering him, and seeing as they were trapped in this cabin together, it was far less painful to relent now than to continue taking her abuse. Galina already knew the crux of the truth anyway. "I found Vika on the side of a volcano on the Kamchatka Peninsula, when I was there on a research mission studying winter herbs. Her mother, a volcano nymph, had abandoned her."

Galina sat back in her chair. "I thought nymphs were extinct."

"So did I."

"Huh." Galina contemplated the fact for a moment, then leaned forward again and said, "The girl really *isn't* your daughter, then."

How like his sister to be able to shrug off the existence of a magical creature in order to torment Sergei some more. He grumbled. "Blood determines nothing. Vika is my daughter, no matter what you say."

"For someone as surly-looking as you, you're disgustingly soft."

"It's better than being surly on both the outside *and* the inside like someone else in this room." Sergei reached over and helped himself to Galina's tea, ignoring her scowl. "I suppose you've remained cold and distant from your student, haven't you? You are so very talented at alienating people."

"Why would I form an attachment to a half-breed orphan from the steppe?" Galina scoffed. "I trained him because it was my duty to do so, and because I want to see my enchanter demolish yours. I like winning, you know."

Oh, yes, Sergei knew. Although more accurately, Galina

should have said she liked winning against *him*. It had always been about beating him, beginning when they were small children and she wanted more of their father's attention. She'd never outgrown her insecurity at being born a girl, even though their parents hadn't played favorites between them.

"It's a pity raising Nikolai didn't stir any maternal instinct in you. It would have been nice if Vika had grown up with a friend in the family to play with."

Galina plucked her teacup out of Sergei's hands. "Maternal instinct? Ha! You can't stir something that doesn't exist, thank goodness. And as for Vika having a friend, that is ridiculous, and you know it. They are enchanters, Sergei. They were always going to have to fight each other and die. They couldn't know who the other enchanter was, let alone be friends. Besides, you hate Saint Petersburg and would never have come to visit. I would never have visited you on that godforsaken island, either, because I hate . . . nature." She glared again at sheets of freezing, tumbling white outside the window.

"You honestly don't love Nikolai, then? After all those years, you can't say that even a single beat of your frigid heart belongs to the boy?"

Galina smiled, and her teeth gleamed at the points, as if she filed and polished them to appear that way. Except Sergei knew she'd always looked like that. She had always been a wolf.

"Every beat of my heart belongs to myself, *mon frère*. You'd do better if you kept yours to yourself, as well. We did our jobs as mentors, and that's that. No need for us to hurt unnecessarily when one of them dies, but that's exactly what will happen if you insist on remaining attached to your student."

Sergei snorted. As if he could so easily discard every memory of Vika—from watching her go from crawling to walking to leaping through trees, from teaching her the alphabet to how to conjure a doll to how to summon rain from a barren sky, from telling her she could grow up to be Imperial Enchanter to finally leading her to her fate at Bolshebnoie Duplo. No, it was impossible to extricate Vika's life from his; he wouldn't be who he was now without her.

Sergei plucked a slice of slightly burnt onion bread from the plate on the table. Even this reminded him of Vika, not only because she would have brought him a perfect loaf from Ludmila's bakery, but also because she would have shared it with him.

"Bread?" he said to Galina, a peace offering, of sorts. Or as close to peace as was possible for siblings in a cramped Siberian cottage.

She waved it away. "You know I don't eat peasant fare. Besides, why you insist on baking bread yourself when you can simply conjure it, I will never understand."

He wagged a finger at her. "Food is one thing magic does not do well. You know that. That's why you hire a cook at home. Although I can't imagine you in the kitchen, even if it were possible to conjure decent meals."

"I doubt magic could make bread much worse than what you bake."

Sergei shrugged, slathered butter on his burnt slice, and crammed the entire thing into his mouth.

"I'm going to die of hypothermia before they finish the Game," Galina said. "It's only October, for heaven's sake. It's downright indecent for there to be a blizzard in the middle of October."

Sergei chuckled and opened a book on the medicinal herbs of Siberia. He didn't mind the snow—he rather liked it, actually, especially when it fell so heavily that one forgot it was composed of individual snowflakes rather than a single blanket of fleece—and he enjoyed how much the blizzard upended his sister.

"A little precipitation never hurt anybody," he said. "Settle in, dear city girl. It may be a very long winter."

CHAPTER TWENTY-THREE

Aizhana rose with the sunset at her back, casting a long, barbed shadow on the dry earth. It had taken her much longer than she'd anticipated to traverse the distance from her grave, but now, finally, she'd reached the cluster of yurts she'd seen shortly upon resurrection. The brown grass snapped and whimpered under her feet.

She clomped her way to the fire pit, her left leg dragging a bit behind her right, for the left foot hadn't fully reanimated. The women who'd been tending the meat on the spit shrank back. Aizhana recognized a handful of them, their faces the same but for age-cursed wrinkles.

"Where is my child?" she asked Damira, who in her fifties was the eldest of the women.

Damira stared at her with unblinking eyes. Perhaps it was at how Aizhana looked. Her face was skeletal, with yellow-gray skin stretched taut in places and sagging in others. Her hair was missing in patches, and what she did possess hung limp and dirty like decaying fishing nets. Or perhaps it was how Aizhana smelled, as she had been dead for nearly two decades, and simply infusing a decaying body with new energy would not undo that unfortunate fact.

"Wh-what are you?" Damira asked. "What do you want?"

"I want my baby."

"I don't know who—"

"You don't recognize me?" Aizhana bared her yellowed teeth.

"Someone run to the pastures to summon help," Damira whispered to the other women.

"I would not advise it." Aizhana raised a fingernail in the air. It was as long and sharp as a blade.

The women remained obediently in place—or more accurately, they were too terrified to move. Aizhana limped to the edge of their fire. "I am going to tell you a story," she said as she settled herself on the ground. Damira, who was the closest, had enough sense not to wince at Aizhana's stench.

Aizhana took in a long breath. The smell of roasting meat filled her with a distant memory, and she fell swiftly into her tale.

Once, many years ago, there was a girl with golden eyes who lived happily among her people. She was renowned not only for her fleet-footed dancing and fine embroidery, but also for her extraordinary touch. She was a faith healer, and she could redirect energy from one part of an ill or wounded person to another part. From a strong stomach to a weak spleen, or from powerful lungs to an arrow wound. Because of that, she was one of the most valuable girls in the tribe, and as befit her position, she was betrothed to their leader's son.

But then, when she was sixteen, a regiment of Russian soldiers arrived near her village. Curious, she and the other girls snuck out to spy on them. They intended only to have a peek.

She did not expect one of the soldiers to spot her in the grasses. She did not expect to fall swiftly in love with his confidence and easy grace. She did not expect she would abandon her tribe to spend her nights in his bed, living hungrily on his love and his kisses.

She certainly did not expect to wake one morning to find him and his entire regiment gone.

The tribe took the girl back in, but she was disgraced, condemned to scrubbing laundry and hauling the manure of yaks. Eight lonely months crawled by. And on the nine-month anniversary of her first night in the soldier's bed, she gave birth to a baby boy. The umbilical cord wrapped like a noose around his neck.

"No!" The girl uncoiled it and touched the bruise already formed on his fragile skin.

Death stole into her yurt, reached out with its bony hands, and attempted to lift the boy away.

But the girl snatched the baby back. "You cannot have him." She hugged the child, the only thing she had, and heard his pulse fluttering like a dragonfly, trying to escape. "Shh . . . ," she said. "Shh. I am a healer. I will save you."

And then she thought of all the times she'd healed a wound or nursed an ache. It was simply a matter of moving energy, of shifting the patient's strength from one place in a body to another. She looked at the gasping baby in her arms. What is stopping me from channeling my energy to him? *Nothing. It would either work, or it wouldn't.*

She focused on the place where the baby's skin touched hers. Then she felt her own energy flowing hot with the fear of losing him. She directed her remaining strength into his veins.

The boy cried, so loudly it shook the walls of her yurt.

Death cocked its head and moved to take the girl, who lay weak on the dirt floor. "But I'm not dead," she whispered.

Death paused. And then, instead of picking her up, it knelt and passed its skeletal fingers over her eyes to shut them. Because she was brave enough not only to face and defy Death, and also to outsmart it, she was rewarded with sleep in ante-death, the space between the living realm and the dead.

But she would not stay in ante-death forever. She swore with her last breath that when she was strong enough, she would rise again.

The women around the fire pit quivered.

"Do you remember me now?" Aizhana smiled in a way that once would have been sweet, but now was nothing but rotting gums and disdain.

"You rose from the dead," Damira said, scrambling away. She did not go far, though, before she bumped into the other women.

"No. Were you not listening? I was never dead. I was merely not living. But I have returned, and I want my boy. Where is he? Is he out shepherding or hunting with the men?"

"He . . ."

"Is he out shepherding or hunting with the men?" Aizhana asked again, the screech of her voice rising.

Damira's eyes widened. "I . . . We haven't seen him in eleven years. He left the village."

Aizhana scraped her fingernails against her papery temple. They rasped like claws against molted snakeskin. "He could not have left on his own at age seven. What did you do?"

Damira sniveled. The other women held one another, as if something so simple would protect them.

"Where is he? What did you do?" Aizhana snarled.

"A Russian aristocrat came. She wanted him. You have to understand, he was too much for us. We didn't know what to do with his power—"

"You lived with me among you all those years. How could a boy be any different?"

"He was. He *was* different!" Damira said. "You were a healer. You made people better. You were a force of good. He was . . ."

"Like a demon," another woman, Tazagul, said. Her face glowed in the light of the fire. "He had too much power. It came from somewhere other than the people who needed to be healed. He wasn't like you."

"My son is not a demon!" Aizhana howled, and her shriek nearly drew blood from the women's ears.

But if he wasn't a healer, then what was he? Could he be an enchanter? It would make sense, the way Damira and Tazagul described him. Healers utilized small magic, and the energy came from their patients. But enchanters could use greater magic.

"Whatever he was, we did not know what to do with him," Damira said. "And the Russian woman offered two horses and two sheep to take him away to train—"

"You *sold* my son? For four animals?"

"No, we—"

But that was all Damira got out before Aizhana pounced on her and slashed her throat with her wicked nails. Thick, hot red spurted everywhere. Aizhana grinned. Then she siphoned off the energy as Damira's life left her body.

"What have you done?" Tazagul said, trembling. She and the other women still kneeled on the ground, too paralyzed to flee. They gaped at their dead kinswoman.

"Even if I was disgraced, my son was innocent, and you were supposed to mother him in my stead," Aizhana said, her voice now a low growl. "That is how a village works. But you left him without a mother, and now I will leave all *your* children without theirs."

She lunged at the women. She shredded them with her nails, ten merciless blades compelled by vengeance. And as she killed them, she absorbed their energy, just as she'd done to the worms and the maggots in the ground.

She was now so full of both life and death that it would take more than a mere bullet to kill her. And her left foot seemed almost awake. Which was good. For apparently she had a long journey ahead.

Nikolai, she thought. *I am coming for you.*

CHAPTER TWENTY-FOUR

The following morning, Vika's apartment brimmed with the smells she had so missed: the sour tang of the Borodinsky bread starter in its pot in the kitchen corner, the sweet richness of farmer's cheese for the *vatrushka* pastry filling, and the brightness of fresh pears cooking down into jam. Ludmila had arrived last night at Vika's invitation—Vika had lived with her father her entire life, and being alone in an unfamiliar city, especially after the attack of the stone birds, felt too exposed—and the older woman had wasted no time taking over the flat's kitchen as her own and laying out plans for opening a temporary Cinderella stall in Saint Petersburg.

When Vika walked into the kitchen, she found Ludmila with icing all over her face and apron, like a cake frosted by a flurry of euphoric five-year-olds. Ludmila swayed around the tiny kitchen, her hips nearly touching from countertop to stove, humming a folk song.

Vika sighed happily. How she loved folk songs. Her

father sang them all the time.

She sat down on one of the dining chairs. Its red lacquer was buried under a light dusting of flour snow. A Ludmila pastry storm.

"You're a mess with the ingredients," Vika said, "but you're a magician with the oven and stove."

Ludmila beamed as she flourished a wooden spoon in the air. "Thank you, my sunshine. But what I do is merely good chemistry. Butter and flour and water, combined with just the right amount of heat . . . The true magic is out there." She pointed her spoon at the window, to Nevsky Prospect and beyond.

Vika smiled. "Yes, the tsar's city planners and engineers are quite talented."

"Oh, no, it isn't engineers who managed that river fountain. It's real magic. I know. And so do you and your father." Ludmila winked.

Vika's smile faded away.

"Don't worry, dear, I haven't told a soul. I may be the island gossip, but I know when it's wise to keep my mouth shut. Not everyone would think so kindly of your abilities. It's the reason Sergei taught you to hide them."

"I . . . But . . . How do you know?"

"I grew up in a circus, my dear."

"You did?" Vika perked up in her chair. When she was younger, she'd longed to be part of a circus, moving from place to place and seeing the country. It seemed to be a place where the performers could be themselves in front of entire audiences, no matter how outlandish their talents might be. They had no need to hide in remote island forests.

"Indeed," Ludmila said. "And when you grow up in a

circus, you learn early on how to distinguish what is real and what is made of smoke and mirrors. I'll tell you that most feats in the circus are pure trickery. But you and your father have something about you that cannot be hidden from those who know there is more to this world than what we see."

Incredible. Vika shook her head. She'd gone her entire life concealing who she and her father were, when right in front of her, every single day, someone else had known. She and Father hadn't even bothered to cast shields around themselves when they weren't actively using magic; they'd assumed no one would be the wiser.

Ludmila crossed the kitchen and wrapped Vika in her arms. "I know it's quite a lot to take in, dear. And I'm sorry I said nothing earlier, but I didn't think you or Sergei wanted your true natures known. Now, however . . . well, you've decided to put your magic on display for all to see. And with Sergei absent, wherever it is he's gone, I thought you might need a mother. Or a friend." Ludmila kissed the top of Vika's hair. "I am lucky to have you, sunshine."

But Vika only patted Ludmila on the back. Maternal affection was unfamiliar territory.

After a minute, Ludmila released her, smiling from icing-covered ear to icing-covered ear. She hadn't seemed to notice that Vika had been hesitant to return her embrace. "The facades on the buildings outside are lovely," Ludmila said.

Vika laughed. She loved that her magic was being seen by others, but she couldn't take credit for something that wasn't hers. "It's true that I'm an enchantress. But the paint on Nevsky Prospect is not my doing."

Ludmila tapped her spoon against her chin, leaving sticky

jam prints on her skin. "Really? There is yet another . . . what did you call yourself? Enchanter? How fascinating."

Vika nodded, and now she wanted to hug Ludmila. What a gift it was to have someone else know what Vika was, and what she could do.

And then it occurred to her: she could tell Ludmila about the Crown's Game. She would not have to bear it on her own.

But no. One glance at the baker's jolly mood and she dismissed the idea. Vika couldn't burden Ludmila with the knowledge that she was walking a tightrope to her death. And why spoil what she'd only now acquired, a confidante for her magic?

No, she would not tell Ludmila about the Game. Having her here, knowing that she knew what Vika could do, was enough.

So instead, Vika stood and walked over to the counter. Ludmila had brought a glass pumpkin with her from the island, and Vika picked it up and turned the iridescent sculpture in her hands. "Well then, since you know what I can do, it makes setting up your new bakery a great deal more fun. How do you feel about selling pastries from another enormous pumpkin?"

That afternoon, a team of men wheeled two large boxes—both a yard long on each side—into Palace Square. One of the boxes was plain red with a large metal crank sticking out of its side. The other was royal purple and decorated with scenes of ballet dancers on every face. There was no explanation given for the appearances of the boxes, nor did the crew that brought them know any more than the crowds that gathered around them.

An albino rat scampered onto Vika's kitchen windowsill. She recognized him as the rat she'd fed a piece of *blini* to the other day, on her way back from the river. Vika circled her pinkie over its head to translate its chattering.

"Two boxes in front of the Winter Palace?" Vika asked. The rat's red eyes glowed brighter in confirmation. "I wonder what he's up to."

"Your mystery enchanter?" Ludmila said. "We should go right away."

Vika sat at the windowsill and fed a few scraps of leftover pastry to the rat, who tore at them greedily. The boxes could be a trap. Instead of cheese to snare a rat, it would be boxes that served as bait to catch an enchantress. Palace Square was immense, and her opponent could hide in the crowds. If Vika went, he could attack and kill her unseen.

Ludmila wiped her hands on her apron and tossed it onto the counter. "What are you waiting for? This is why I came to the city, because it's more exciting than the routine at home."

Vika tried to smile. But if she died in Ludmila's arms, or worse, if Ludmila died in Vika's arms, it would not be exciting at all.

Ludmila stood by the door of the kitchen, icing still smearing her cheek. "You know I'm going, with or without you, don't you?"

"Well, if you put it like that . . ."

There was no way Vika would let Ludmila around the other enchanter without her.

Besides, Vika refused to be the type of girl who hid from danger. And she needed to see what her opponent's move was, so she could best him again. Because if he didn't kill her outright, the tsar always could. Her death sentence was as simple as the tsar declaring her opponent the victor. It didn't matter that she technically still had four turns.

Vika walked over to wipe the smudges of frosting from Ludmila's face. Then she tossed the rat one more scrap of pastry before she grabbed her shawl and wrapped it around her shoulders, casting a shield around herself and Ludmila at the same time.

"All right."

"Hurrah, an adventure!" Ludmila said as she launched herself through the apartment's front door.

Yes, an adventure. But hopefully not a fatal one.

Even though Vika had walked by the Winter Palace every evening since she'd arrived in Saint Petersburg, its grandeur hadn't ceased to amaze her. It was a pale-green-and-white Baroque masterpiece, its three stories lined with proud columns and arches and almost two thousand gilded windows. On one side of the palace was the Neva River—she hoped the imperial family had a clear view of her fountain, her first "gift" to the tsesarevich for his birthday—and on the other, Palace Square, where the two peculiar boxes sat and a crowd of several hundred now gathered.

Ludmila fought her way to the front, using her girth and her elbows to clear a path for Vika to follow. A short fence of sorts had been erected quite some distance from the boxes, but instead of wood, the fence was constructed of woven silver ribbon, each piece as wide as Vika's hand. There were no posts that supported it, and yet the ribbon remained cordoned in place, as if set through invisible stakes.

Having made it to the ribbon, Vika scanned the square for obvious danger. Nothing, other than a larger-than-usual contingent of the Tsar's Guard, likely owing to the sudden appearance of the boxes. And there, bobbing along the top of the palace roof, was the albino rat. He had very quick feet for a creature with such tiny legs. If he ever came back to her, she would give him a name. Perhaps *Poslannik*. Messenger.

A figure moved in the window directly below Poslannik. No! Vika jumped in front of Ludmila and held both hands in defense in front of them. A transparent shield enveloped them, and the people behind them stepped away as though they had been nudged, although there was no evidence they had been touched at all.

But the figure in the window didn't attack. He didn't even seem to see Vika. He tilted his head, leaning it against the windowpane, as if he, too, were waiting to see what the boxes would do.

"Everything all right?" Ludmila asked.

Vika nodded and stepped to the side, so that she was no longer in front of Ludmila. But she held on to their protective sphere, on top of the spell she'd cast before they left the flat, just in case.

Behind them, the crowd grew to at least a thousand. Vika had worried that the other enchanter could hide in the masses and attack her. But he wouldn't try to kill her in front of all these people, would he? The tsar had warned them at Bolshebnoie Duplo not to frighten anyone, and here they were, ordinary, nonmagical folk, filling Palace Square to its very edges. It was not like Nevsky Prospect at dawn, empty but for the lone street sweeper. It wasn't even like her fountain in the Neva, where it was easy to make it look as if her opponent had slipped. Here, there would be too many witnesses.

In the distance, a bell tower chimed six o'clock, and the crank on the plain red box began to move, winding in slow circles to a tinny, playful scale. *Do, re, mi, fa, sol, la, ti, do.* The music progressed from C-major to the next scale, G-major. *Do, re, mi, fa, sol, la, ti, do.* And then the next, D-major, and then the next, A-major, the pace of each scale faster than the previous one, with the crank speeding up to match its pace. By the time the box reached the twelfth scale, the crank turned at a frenetic pace. *Do, re, mi, fa, sol, la, ti*—

The top of the box exploded open on the final *do!* and out leaped a life-size jack-in-the box. Vika and the rest of the crowd gasped and jumped back.

But the Jack—who was no longer in the box, and who had legs where his accordion body ought to be—stood still in front of his box, wavering slightly back and forth as if he were still on his springs. Vika watched him carefully. There was something devious about his wooden grin.

Beside him, a tinkling version of the music from the ballet *Zéphire et Flore* began to play from the purple box. But unlike the red one, the lid of the purple box started to open as soon as the song began. As it lifted, a life-size ballerina doll, wearing a periwinkle-blue dress and fairy wings, rose on a spinning platform, as if she were part of a music box. Now Vika had two dolls to track.

As the song came to an end, so did the ballerina's twirling. It was then that the Jack came back to life. He bowed to the ballerina, one toy to another, then danced to her box and offered her his hand. "Don't take it," Vika whispered. "Don't trust him."

But the ballerina placed her delicate porcelain fingers in his wooden ones and pranced down to the cobblestones in the square. Vika shook her head.

Ludmila pressed up to the ribbon fence, and because they shared an invisible bubble, Vika found herself pulled to the edge of the makeshift stage as well. The figure in the palace window likewise leaned forward as far as he could. Was it the tsar, keeping track of the Game? Or the tsesarevich, watching the show put on for his birthday?

A melody pealed out from the purple box again, this time for a pas de deux. The Jack led the ballerina to the center of their cobblestone stage, where they bowed once again to each other. Then he set his hands gently about her waist, and she lifted onto the points of her shoe, both arms arched overhead, and spun as ethereally as a fairy.

They danced as the music played. The ballerina spun. The Jack leaped. And when together, he lifted her, light as the doll that she was. Then the music began to soar, and their dancing did as well, with the ballerina and the Jack whirling together so quickly they began to levitate into the sky.

"How are they doing that?" someone behind Vika asked, as if he had forgotten they were not real people.

"There must be strings," another person said.

But next to Vika, Ludmila said, "They're like puppets manipulated by masters they cannot see."

Too true. Vika knew the ballerina represented her, and the Jack the other enchanter. Like the puppets, she and her opponent had never had a choice: their destiny was a pas de deux, a splendor and a torment fated for the two of them.

And yet, there was something about the other enchanter, about the magic he chose, that drew her to him, as if the bond between them was not an altogether evil thing. It was more like a tenuous thread attempting to reconnect two halves of a whole.

And although Vika hated to admit it, she'd dreamed of him more than once. Each time, he would appear as a shadow boy, but each morning, just before she woke, she would catch a glimpse of his real face. . . .

The bubble around Vika quivered.

I am tied irretrievably to my enemy, she realized.

The Jack and ballerina continued to twirl around the sky. The music soared louder and louder. It crescendoed to a furious trill. And then it suddenly broke off into silence.

Every muscle in Vika's body tensed. The Jack and ballerina halted their dance, as if they, too, were startled.

The crowd gasped then and pointed at the ballerina's chest. Although she hadn't heard Vika's earlier warning, the ballerina heard the audience now. She looked down at the bodice of her dress. A red silk handkerchief blossomed from where her porcelain heart ought to be.

"I knew she couldn't trust him," Vika said.

The ballerina's painted mouth formed a devastated O. She glanced at the Jack. He looked not at her, but at a cloud near his feet, his wooden mouth set in a grim straight line.

Then the ballerina went limp and plummeted from the sky into her box. The Jack hung his head. The ballerina's lid lowered and latched with a click.

Palace Square burst into deafening applause. Everyone clapped and howled.

Everyone except Vika, for something had begun to press

on her from above, forcing her to her knees. *What? How? I have a shield—*

But then she saw them, thousands of tiny needles protruding from the cobblestones at her feet. They must have appeared while she was busy watching the Jack and ballerina. The needles bowed in unison, as if they knew she'd finally seen them, before they retracted into the ground.

Those impertinent needles punctured and destroyed my shield! Vika hadn't even known it was possible. But perhaps that was the problem. She couldn't properly protect herself from something of which she was unaware.

She pushed her hands upward and tried to stand, but the pressure of whatever was pushing on her was too strong. Vika flung herself forward to escape, but smashed into an unseen wall.

She spun to the left. Trapped.

To the right. Blocked off.

Backward. Another wall.

It was as if she was inside the ballerina's music box.

"No!"

The invisible cube kept shrinking, and Vika's lungs burned as the air grew thin. She was nearly at a crouch.

In front of her, Ludmila cheered, oblivious to what was happening. Could nobody see Vika? The enchanter must have cast a deception shroud around her. And the invisible box was now almost the same size as she was, with little room to spare. Vika pressed outward with her palms one more time and kicked with her feet. She rammed the top of the box with her head.

If I stay inside, I'll die, and I'll never see Father again, never become Imperial Enchanter, never have a chance to become who I was meant to be.

As the sides of the cube squeezed out the last of the air, Vika felt all its edges against her. She pushed up, down, in every direction again, rebounding like a marble rattling in a box too small. The corners pressed inward. The walls crushed against the sides of Vika's ribs.

Oh, mercy. She winced at the pressure that she knew would soon turn into pain.

But what if they weren't walls? What if they weren't solid, but vapor instead?

"Steam," she gasped.

The inside of the box began to grow hot and humid.

Vika hovered on the brink of a faint. *Just a little more . . .*

She ran her fingers along the sides of the box and imagined them transforming from glass—or whatever they were—into steam. *Please, please, turn into steam.*

The walls of her near coffin exploded. Vika tumbled out of the stifling mist. She wheezed as air rushed to fill her empty lungs.

And then, from somewhere on the other side of Palace Square, came a voice. It was quiet, yet it cut through the noise of the still-applauding crowd.

"Bravo," it said, and Vika knew the compliment was for her, not for the Jack and ballerina's show. "Your move, Enchanter Two."

CHAPTER TWENTY-FIVE

She was still alive. He was still alive. Nikolai was glad, but he wasn't. Because now it was the girl's move, and every time she had another move meant another time Nikolai might die.

The next evening, just as an audience formed in Palace Square to wait for the Jack and ballerina to dance again, the sky darkened. It went from pale blue to storm gray in the time it took the nearby clock tower to chime six times. Nikolai looked up, along with everyone else in the square.

There were no clouds. But the sun was gone, and a diaphanous drizzle began.

The would-be audience murmured. The men were glad they had hats on their heads, and the women found scarves in their bags with which to cover their hair.

"It's just a passing sprinkle," a thin man said to his even thinner wife.

"It must be. The fishmonger this morning predicted sunshine all day."

The jack-in-the-box's crank began to turn, and its tinny scales started to play once again. Everyone in the crowd returned their focus to the boxes. Everyone except Nikolai, who kept his gaze planted firmly upward. *What are you playing at, lightning girl?*

A second later, her namesake lightning splintered the sky into shards, and a flood of rain gushed out from its cracks. It drenched the crowd and drowned out the sound of the Jack's music. People ran for cover, their once-sufficient hats now tumbling onto the cobblestones upside down and full of water, their scarves no more than sopping rags plastered onto their heads.

All around Nikolai, the crowd stampeded out of the open square. The storm kept coming, like Zeus himself out for revenge in one of Pasha's favorite myths. Nikolai rubbed the back of his dry neck—he'd conjured a waterproof shield over both himself and the Jack's and ballerina's boxes at the first hint of rain—and sighed. The girl had made quite a display of commanding the weather. The immensity of her power was impressive indeed.

Nikolai snapped his fingers, and the crank and music from the Jack's box stopped. He could hardly hear it anyway. There would be no show tonight.

A bolt of lightning slammed into the cobblestones mere feet away from him.

"Merde!" Nikolai leaped back from the pulverized pavement.

Another bolt slammed into the ground behind him. He jumped again, but this time he cast the strongest shield he could conjure and sprinted for cover.

The Winter Palace. If only he could make it across the square—

The path in front of him burst in an explosion of electricity and mortar and stone.

"The tsar won't be happy if you demolish his square while you try to kill me!" Nikolai yelled as he continued to run. "And I doubt this qualifies as something impressive for the tsesarevich's birthday!" He didn't know where the girl was, but she had to be near if she was directing the lightning straight at him.

She responded by whipping the rain into his face, aiming a thousand stinging needles at him all at once. They bounced off his shield.

"You'll have to try harder!" He was almost at the palace. Only ten more seconds and he'd be at a door.

The girl unleashed the lightning again. Several bolts ruptured the sky, ferocious veins of searing white in the darkness, and they convened on one target: Nikolai's shield.

The crack blew all sound out of his ears, and he was thrown to the ground as the lightning shattered the invisible layer protecting him. The palace was still too far. It was Nikolai against the weather now.

The sky crackled and popped again. Recharging, readying for attack.

He remembered the girl rising out of the fire on Ovchinin Island. He didn't think he could fight that. Not without a shield.

But if Nikolai was going to die, he was going to do it with dignity. He reached for his top hat, which had skittered away on the cobblestones and finally gotten wet. He brushed it off and rose to his feet.

Then he turned to face the ballerina's purple box in the center of the square. He wasn't sure where the girl was, but he could address the puppet he'd created in her stead. He took a deep breath and stood as still and as serenely as he could, given the circumstances of thunder bellowing all around him.

Electricity buzzed in the air. Nikolai tried to conjure another shield, but it sputtered out.

"I don't blame you." He tipped his hat in the ballerina's direction, but unlike the time he did so after the other enchanter had tried to drown him, there was nothing mocking in his gesture now. "I don't blame you if this is the end."

Then the sparks in the sky extinguished themselves, and the gray clouds blew away with a hiss. Not a trace of violence—or even rain—remained.

And the scar at Nikolai's collarbone warmed.

She'd ended her turn. Nikolai exhaled. She had spared his life. He let his posture slide.

Whether the girl was actually showing him mercy or simply toying with him to draw out the chase, Nikolai would take it. He would live to play another day.

CHAPTER TWENTY-SIX

It was the fortitude in his voice. And the grace in his poise. *That's why I wasn't able to kill him*, Vika tried to convince herself.

But in reality, it was his eyes. There was a sadness in them, a deep pool of it, which she could see even from where she hid inside the ballerina's box. The lid was cracked open just an inch, but it had been enough for her to falter.

There's always next time, she thought as she curled up next to the limp ballerina with the red handkerchief spilling from her porcelain heart. Vika had thought she would relish the irony of her opponent trying to kill her in a box, only to turn it on him and kill him *from* the box. But it hadn't worked out for either of them.

It's all right, she told herself. *I still have three more turns. I'll kill him the next time.*

CHAPTER TWENTY-SEVEN

The next morning, Pasha was once again in the palace library, although this time, instead of reading *Russian Mystics and the Tsars*, he was poring over reports from the Imperial Council. He had fallen asleep during yesterday's meeting—he had, at least, attended it, as he'd promised his father—but afterward, Yuliana had shoved into his arms these stacks of paper on topics ranging from the state of the corn and sunflower harvests to the worsening siege in Missolonghi.

"The ministers are thorough, I'll give them that," Pasha said aloud to himself as he flipped through yet another pile of papers. He yawned and tapped his pen on the top page, which was filled with tables of data on wheat yields. Surely there must be a better way to rule a country than to read reports from afar.

And yet, what other way was there, when the country was so vast? The tsar could not be in all places at once.

Pasha yawned again. He was just about to skip the

wheat tables to read an account of the current situation in the Crimea when Gavriil, the captain of his Guard, poked his head into the library.

"Your Imperial Highness, please forgive the disturbance, but you asked to be informed of any, er, important developments."

Pasha threw the report onto the table and sat up straighter. "Yes?"

"Well, Your Imperial Highness, a, uh, giant glass pumpkin has appeared along the Ekaterinsky Canal."

Pasha grinned. "Excellent." Because he hadn't wanted to miss a thing, Pasha had ordered his Guard to inform him of any new happenings around the city, especially if they seemed . . . unusual. He disliked reducing his Guard to messengers and gossipmongers—he suspected they resented it—but it gave them something productive to do instead of the typical routine of losing track of him and panicking before his return.

Pasha rose from his armchair, no longer seeing the Imperial Council reports stacked before him. "Inform the stables to ready my carriage. I'll go to the pumpkin at once."

The guard knitted his brow.

"Is there something unclear about my instructions, Gavriil?"

"No, Your Imperial Highness. It's just . . . I was confused because you informed me of your intended whereabouts rather than . . ." He trailed off.

"Rather than sneaking out?" Pasha grinned even more brightly. "It's only because I have greater roguishness planned."

Pasha could see the line stretching from the bakery kiosk before he saw the pumpkin itself. Word had spread quickly about Madame Fanina's incredible confections, and the carriage had to stop a block away because the crowd was too thick to pass through.

A handful of his guards dismounted their horses while Pasha disembarked from the carriage.

"Make way for His Imperial Highness, the Tsesarevich Pavel Alexandrovich Romanov!" Gavriil called.

Pasha flushed. "I could have waited in line," he muttered.

But it was too late for that, for everyone on the street had turned to catch a glimpse of the crown prince. And then the entire queue bowed low, like a line of dominoes tumbling onto its knees. The Ekaterinsky Canal glittered red, orange, yellow, green, blue, and violet beside them.

As Pasha walked past, men and women rose and reached to kiss his hand. He smiled kindly as they declared their love for him and prayed for his health, and his heart swelled to span the far reaches of the empire. He loved it, not because they kissed his hand, but because the people of his country were infinitely more real in the flesh than in Imperial Council meetings and reports.

Halfway through the line, the pumpkin rose into view. Pasha bounced in his boots. *I knew it!* It was the glass pumpkin he'd had commissioned for the baker on Ovchinin Island! Well, a very enlarged version of it. Pasha recognized the crystalline curl of the green vines around the stem, and the ripples the imperial glassblower had chosen to incorporate into the pumpkin's orange ribs. The only modifications that had been made to the pumpkin—other than its size—were a window cut out of it and a counter tiled with enormous pumpkin seeds from which to serve Ludmila's patrons.

Pasha could hardly wait to reach the kiosk. He had to force himself to slow down and not plow through the men and women who still wanted to kiss his hand.

Eventually, his guards led the way to the counter, and Gavriil once again announced, "His Imperial Highness, the Tsesarevich Pavel Alexandrovich Romanov!" Pasha grimaced.

Inside the pumpkin, Ludmila and a dark-haired girl were already curtseying. Had they been in that position since he was announced when the carriage arrived? He hoped not. That had been fifteen minutes ago.

"*Bonjour, mesdames,*" he said, remembering how he had greeted the women in the island bakery not too long ago. "Please rise."

Ludmila perked up immediately at the sound of his voice, and when she stood, her face exploded in a gap-toothed grin. "It's you!" But just as quickly, her mouth contorted. "Oh, heaven forgive me, Your Imperial Highness, the things I said the last time . . . I didn't know . . . your appearance was so different . . . I—"

"Madame Fanina, I take no offense," Pasha said in Russian. He reached across the counter and patted her hand. "It is I who deceived you. You are not at all to blame."

The other girl in the pumpkin gaped at Pasha. He turned to her. She seemed familiar. "Are you one of the girls who works in the Zakrevsky household?" Pasha glanced down the street, where he could just make out the corner of the building in which Nikolai lived.

"Yes, Your Imperial Highness. My name is Renata

Galygina." She looked at her feet as she spoke. "When I saw Madame Fanina's kiosk here, I, um, thought I could earn some additional wages. I have some free time, as Countess Zakrevskaya is away, and my services are not in high demand."

Pasha nodded. This, he knew. Countess Zakrevskaya had declared a sudden trip abroad, and no one knew when she would return. It was not at all out of character, for she was rather . . . *eccentric*, to put it politely. Pasha hoped, for Nikolai's sake, that the countess was gone a very long while.

"Well, it's a lovely surprise to see you here," Pasha said to Renata.

She curtsied.

"What may I get Your Imperial Highness this morning?" Ludmila asked.

"I liked it better when you called me Frenchie."

"I will do no such thing, Your *French* Highness." She winked.

Pasha laughed.

"You may have anything you see." Ludmila spread her arms wide, showcasing not only the Russian staples—honey poppy-seed rolls, Tula gingerbread, walnut-shaped *oreshki* cookies filled with caramel—but also a special glass case behind her.

"You've outdone yourself, Madame Fanina."

She curtsied, although it appeared more like an amiable bear bobbing than a proper curtsy. "I admit I had some help from another girl," she said. "I made all the components, but the assembly . . . let's say that girl has a magic touch."

Pasha stood taller. "Magic touch, you say? Show me everything you have."

Renata scooted out of the way, and Ludmila began to describe the confections on each shelf. "Here," she said, pointing at the bottom row, "we have chocolate truffles filled not with ganache, but with steaming-hot cocoa that doesn't cool until it touches your tongue."

"Incredible."

She dipped her head in gratitude. "Next, we have a pear pie, but as you can see, it's no ordinary pie, for the pastry is shaped like the fruit itself."

"Exquisite." The pie was not merely shaped with pear-like curved edges. It looked truly like a three-dimensional pear, round and tall and narrowing at the stem, the kind you could pick off a tree and bite into. The large crystals of sugar on its "peel" even approximated morning dew. Magic, indeed. The laws of gravity would not allow such a pie to bake without falling.

"And finally"—Ludmila pointed at the top shelf—"we have cream puffs light as air."

Pasha gasped because they were indeed as light as air, or even lighter, for the puffs floated and had to be tied to the shelf with colorful strings, like mini *pâte à choux* balloons.

"If I may, I would like one of those," Pasha said. Ludmila nodded so emphatically, all her chins wobbled. Renata opened the glass case and retrieved one on a violet ribbon and passed it to Pasha. He couldn't stop smiling as he held the tiny balloon's string between his fingers.

"Would Your Imperial Highness like something else?"

Pasha glanced at his guards, who stood at attention nearby, and at the line behind him. "I would like to buy something for every man, woman, and child here." He motioned to Gavriil, who retrieved a stack of ruble notes from a hidden pocket and quietly passed it over the counter to Ludmila.

"You are too generous, Your Imperial Highness."

"Well, I would like to ask another favor as well."

"Anything."

"There is to be a ball tomorrow evening in my honor. A masquerade, because, as you know, I'm rather fond of disguises. Invitations have been sent to all noblewomen in Saint Petersburg, but the problem is, I cannot seem to locate the one girl I wish to have attend. I thought you might be able to assist me in that endeavor."

Ludmila touched her heart. "You're still searching for Vika."

"Yes."

Renata's eyes grew even wider than when Pasha had first made his appearance at the kiosk. *Does she know about Vika?* he thought. *Has Nikolai talked about her?*

Ludmila ushered her to take pastry orders from the tsesarevich's guards. Renata hurried out of the pumpkin.

"In the excitement of my arrival in the city," Ludmila said to Pasha, "I'd forgotten all about telling Vika that a mysterious, handsome Frenchie was inquiring after her."

"So you could deliver my invitation to her?"

"Absolutely. I'm staying in her flat on Nevsky Prospect."

"She's here?" No wonder his messenger had returned from Ovchinin Island with Vika's invitation, undeliverable.

He turned to Gavriil, who was stuffing his face with a pear-shaped pie. "See to it that the invitation for Vika . . ."

"Andreyeva," Ludmila said. "Vika Andreyeva. Her father is Baron Sergei Andreyev."

"Is that so?" Pasha brightened even more than his usual self. So Vika was nobility. There, at least, was one of Nikolai's objections struck down. It was not in violation of his mother's rules for Pasha to dance with an unbetrothed girl who belonged to the aristocracy.

He pivoted back to Gavriil, who had, in the meantime, wiped clean the pear smudges from his mouth. "See to it that the invitation for Mademoiselle Andreyeva is delivered this afternoon. Madame Fanina will ensure its conveyance to its recipient."

"Yes, Your Imperial Highness," Gavriil and Ludmila said at the same time.

Pasha looked at the cream puff in his hand once more. "Absolutely stunning," he said, then popped it into his mouth. The pastry and vanilla cream burst as if the little balloon had been punctured with a needle.

"I will hold that compliment dearly for the rest of my humble life," Ludmila said. "How else may I be of service?"

"You have done more than most. I hope I will see you soon, perhaps as Mademoiselle Andreyeva's escort to the ball?" He smiled, in a way that he knew was both infectious and persuasive.

Ludmila grinned and nodded. Her chins waggled again.

"Good." With Ludmila by Vika's side, it would be much easier for Pasha to identify her. He had not quite thought it through when he informed his mother that the ball would be a masquerade. Only after the invitations had gone out had he realized it would be that much more difficult to identify *any* girl when she was in costume, but especially an enchantress, who could surely put to shame any other attendee's disguise.

"Thank you again, Madame Fanina. I will see you very soon."

She curtsied. It was a wonder she didn't knock over her trays of tarts and cookies in the process. In fact, it seemed to Pasha that she did tip over one pan much too far, but against all laws of physics, it righted itself before any cookies fell.

Vika. Her magic wasn't only in the pastries.

Pasha smiled and turned to leave. His guards fell into formation and awaited his command. But he paused by the canal. Perhaps he would stop by Nikolai's to boast of his victory in inviting the lightning girl. After all, Nikolai lived only a five minutes' walk away.

But what if Vika decided not to attend? It was unlikely, given that Pasha had personally invited her (well, personally through Ludmila). But if any girl in the empire was bold enough to decline an invitation from the tsesarevich, it would likely be the lightning girl.

No, Pasha thought, *better to wait until the ball itself to gloat. I'll just have to make sure that Nikolai shows.*

CHAPTER TWENTY-EIGHT

Nikolai was sitting in the center of the carpet in his bedroom, staring at a blood spot on the ceiling—left over from the slaughter of the poisonous lorises—when Renata yelled at him through his door.

"Nikolai? Let me in!"

He shook his bleak musings out of his head. Had Renata discovered something at the pumpkin bakery? He'd sent her there for information. Nikolai leaped to his feet and flicked his fingers to unlock the dead bolts. The handle to the door turned itself.

Renata tumbled into his room. He grabbed her by both arms to steady her. "What happened? Are you all right?"

"I . . . I'm fine." She stopped to catch her breath. "I'm fine. But the tsesarevich. He invited her to the ball."

Oh. Was that all? Nikolai released Renata's arms.

"Did you hear me?" she said.

"Yes." Nikolai dropped down into the center of his carpet again. "But I already knew."

"How could you? It happened just now. He didn't stop here at the house. I watched him leave in his carriage. We are talking about the same thing, aren't we? The tsesarevich invited Vika to his birthday ball."

"Mm-hmm." Nikolai refocused on the bloodstain on the ceiling. "Pasha said he was going to, so I knew he would, despite my attempts to convince him otherwise."

Renata collapsed into Nikolai's desk chair and caught her breath. "Then *you* will not go to the ball, will you?"

"Pasha invited me. I must. He's the tsesarevich."

"But it could be dangerous."

"Even if Pasha weren't the crown prince, I would go. He's my friend. I won't leave him alone with her."

"But you could die." Renata's voice was strained thin. "Nikolai, please. Don't go."

He tore his gaze away from the ceiling and looked at Renata, although it was more like he looked straight through her. "Thank you for the news of my friend's ill-advised infatuation. Now if you'll kindly leave me, I have some work to do."

That evening, two massive oak armoires were delivered to different parts of the city. The first went to Bissette & Sons, Fine Tailors. A note accompanying the armoire read:

Masquerade Box. Insert the article of clothing you wish to exchange, shut the doors, and a new one shall appear in its place. Twenty-four hours only.

The second armoire went to a third-floor flat on Nevsky Prospect, registered to a certain V. Andreyeva. A portly woman answered the door, and the movers attempted to wheel the armoire inside, but it did not seem to fit through the entryway, despite all three of them taking measurements of the chest and finding it significantly smaller than the door frame.

Finally, the woman instructed them to leave the armoire in the hall. The movers pointed out that she would have difficulty moving it if (1) it would not fit through the door, and (2) she did not have the wheeled platform—which they would have to take when they left—for the armoire was incredibly heavy. It felt as if it contained an entire elephant.

But the woman shrugged, and she signed the invoice and dismissed the movers. And they left the strange chest in the middle of the third-floor hallway.

CHAPTER TWENTY-NINE

There was a long queue outside Bissette & Sons, Fine Tailors, full of the types of women who did not usually frequent queues but, rather, sent their servants to wait in their stead.

"Pardon me," Vika said to a woman in a fuchsia dress and matching hat. "What is the line for?"

"The Masquerade Box. You stuff in your old hats and gowns and shoes, shut the door, and a few minutes later, you reopen the door, and a new outfit appears. But not just any clothes—a costume for the tsesarevich's ball."

"Oh. How . . . fascinating." Vika craned her neck. "Uh, do you know how it works?"

"Rumor is there's a hidden compartment in the bottom of the armoire. When you put in your unfashionable rags, they're retrieved by the tsar's men in the basement and replaced with the new costume."

The woman in line behind her—this one dressed in a gown the color of brick—leaned in and added, "I hear it's because the tsarina is looking to find a wife for the tsesarev-ich. This way, all the eligible ladies will be impressively attired. I'm hoping for a particularly stunning costume for my daughter." She looked toward the front of the queue to gauge how much longer she would have to wait.

"Ah, I see. Thank you," Vika said. She left, shaking her head. People would go through such incredible mental gymnastics to explain away the existence of magic.

She was still laughing at the nonbelievers when she stepped into her apartment building and climbed up all three flights of stairs, and because of that distraction, she didn't recognize there was other magic nearby. She felt it, but she thought it was the remnants of the Nevsky Prospect charm following her in from outside. That is, until she turned the corner into her hall and almost walked straight into an armoire, a near duplicate of the Masquerade Box at Bissette & Sons.

Vika gasped and frantically cast a shield around herself. Her heart pounded like a tympani, rattling her bones.

Inside the flat, Ludmila banged pots and pans, singing a song from her favorite opera, *Magician, Fortune-Teller, and Match-Maker*. Vika shook herself out of her stupor and reinforced the protections she'd cast on their front door.

She tiptoed around the armoire, inspecting it for traps. Like the chest at Bissette & Sons, it was made of oak, with two large doors that would open outward if she tugged on the handles. However, unlike the one at Bissette & Sons, which had a carving of a masquerade ball etched onto its panels, this one was very plain.

There was nothing obviously wicked about it. If Vika hadn't seen the other armoire at the tailors', and if she weren't on guard because she was in the middle of a magical duel, she might have thought it a rather ordinary closet.

After she had circled the chest several times, an envelope revealed itself, materializing in front of her.

She shrank away from it. "As if I would touch that."

But she didn't need to. Her opponent had predicted her caution and had taken the liberty of charming the envelope for her. It opened, and a heavy sheet of cream paper slipped out from within. It unfolded itself in the air.

The handwriting was neat, the angles of the letters precisely aligned. The loops in the cursive were modest but still bold. The tail of each word ended in a flourish.

*My thanks for your mercy
from the lightning storm.
Please accept this Imagination Box
as a token of my appreciation.
—Nikolai*

"A token of appreciation. Right. It's probably full of snakes." Vika collapsed her hand into a fist, and the note followed suit and crumpled itself.

But wait. He'd signed his name. She opened her hand, and the sheet of paper smoothed itself out again.

"Nikolai," she whispered.

The combination of her voice and his name together for the first time whipped the wind outside. "His name is Nikolai."

She reached out toward the armoire. Through her shields, she could feel his magic, strong yet airy. Carefully, she touched her fingertips to the wood, and words began to

carve themselves into the wardrobe's doors. It was the same
script as on Nikolai's note.

Imagine, and it shall be.
There are no limits.

Imagine?

Nikolai's words faded from the doors, and in their place,
the question *Imagine?* etched into the wood as if straight
from Vika's thoughts.

"Are you reading my mind?" she said aloud.

The armoire changed again, and *Are you reading my*
mind? appeared on its face.

Vika jumped back.

But snakes did not leap out of the armoire. Her fingers
did not fall off her hand. Nikolai did not take over her brain.

She took one step, then two, back to the so-called Imagination Box. But she didn't touch it.

She did, however, begin to imagine something else:
her dresser at home, the one her father had built with the
carving of a snow-capped volcano on it. Vika's mother had
studied volcanoes; in fact, that was how she'd died—she'd
perished during an unexpected eruption while researching
lava flows. When Vika was young, she liked to pretend that
her mother had somehow survived and was living inside the
volcano, just waiting for her daughter to be old enough and
strong enough to visit. Which was why Vika had always
been fond of that dresser.

But now, nothing happened. *Are you reading my mind?*
remained on the wardrobe.

Huh. She must have to physically touch the door. The

question was, was it wise to do so?

But Vika had never been the overly cautious sort, much to her father's chagrin, and now curiosity got the best of her. She reached for the armoire again, and as soon as she made contact, the doors wiped themselves clean and began to replicate the image she had in her head. It was a perfect copy, down to the way Sergei had gouged the curlicues of smoke deeper into the wood than the rest of the volcano.

Vika traced the lines of smoke, touching the smooth edges of the carving and the natural knots in the wood. If she closed her eyes, she could, for a second, imagine she was home in their cozy cottage, where Sergei tromped outside in the garden and she made buckwheat porridge at the stove.

When she opened her eyes, she saw that the scene on the armoire had changed yet again, this time to an etching of her kitchen, with a pot of steaming kasha on the burner and a bottle of milk and a bowl of raisins set to the side. Vika's mouth watered.

But then she forced her mind to go blank, and the doors to the Imagination Box followed suit. She tore her hands away from the wood.

As soon as she lost contact, her fingers stretched for the armoire again. Nikolai's magic. She wanted to be closer to it. *Needed* to be closer.

"Stop," she said aloud to herself. "He's the enemy, remember?" And she conjured a wall of ice in front of the Imagination Box so she couldn't touch it, no matter how much she yearned to.

The Game was not about friendship. After all, Nikolai had tried to kill her. Twice.

No, this Imagination Box—this "token of appreciation"— was not to be trusted. Nothing was. Vika couldn't even trust herself.

As soon as Vika walked in the front door, Ludmila pounced on her.

"Veee-kahhh! Where have you been? Oh my word, I have so much to tell you! The armoire, it won't fit! The prince, he says you must come! The pumpkin, oh, the lines! He was looking for you, on the island, I forgot to mention. . . ."

Vika hung her coat on a hook. "Slow down. I cannot keep up."

Ludmila waved a spatula, still dripping with whatever she'd been stirring in the kitchen a few seconds ago. "Oh, where to begin?"

"At the beginning?"

"Of time?"

"How about the beginning of today?"

"Oh, yes, today, that's a good place to start." Ludmila sniffed at the air. "But do you mind if we talk in the kitchen? I don't want the caramel to burn."

Ludmila led the way, weaving around a sofa and dodging the outstretched paw of a stuffed polar bear. The bear was wearing a fur hat and a saddle. But after experiencing the enchantments of the past few days, neither Ludmila nor Vika even registered anymore the peculiarity of the decorations in the apartment.

Once in the kitchen, Ludmila stirred the pot of caramel and recounted how well sales in the pumpkin kiosk had gone, and how word had spread so quickly, the tsesarevich came to call.

"The tsesarevich?"

"Yes! Can you believe it? And he was still searching for you."

Vika had been picking through a plate of broken shortbread, but now she dropped the cookie she'd been considering. "What do you mean, *still* searching?"

"You see, this is why I wanted to start my story *before* today. . . . A week ago, the tsesarevich came to Cinderella—the pumpkin on the island, not the kiosk here, of course—asking about a girl with hair like flame, only he was in disguise, so I didn't know it was him, and I was going to tell you the next time you came into the bakery, but it was around when you left the island to come here, so I never had a chance. But he seemed rather smitten, the first time around, and then today, he called to inquire about you again—and to buy a cream puff balloon, he liked that the best, probably because he had a feeling you had a hand in its creation—and anyway, his messenger came by the flat this afternoon and delivered—"

"The armoire?"

"Huh?" Ludmila paused in her stirring. "Oh, no, the armoire is a different story altogether. I'll get to that. No, the tsesarevich sent you an invitation to the ball!"

Vika frowned. "But why would he invite me?"

"Because he's smitten."

"I've never met him before."

"He seems to have met you. Or at least seen you from afar."

"But when would he have . . . Oh."

"Oh?"

Vika nodded. He had known to look for her on the island, which meant . . . he had been one of the boys. The day she'd succeeded in escaping her father's firestorm. The tsesarevich must have been one of the two boys she'd frozen before she fled the woods.

Oh, devil take her, she had frozen the tsesarevich.

Ludmila removed the caramel from the heat and wiped her sticky hands on a towel. Then she retrieved a card from her apron pocket and laid it on the counter. It was light blue and deckle-edged, with the gold double eagles of the tsar's coat of arms embossed on the top.

The pleasure of your presence is requested at
A MASQUERADE BALL
In honor of Pavel Alexandrovich Romanov,
Tsesarevich of all Russia
EIGHT O'CLOCK IN THE EVENING
SATURDAY, 22ND OF OCTOBER
WINTER PALACE

Vika blinked at the card. "This is real?"

"Quite real."

Then the tsesarevich could not have been too offended that Vika had frozen him. Unless he meant to arrest her at the ball. Would he do that? On his birthday?

"He's a sweet thing, that boy," Ludmila said as she began working on assembling macarons filled with pistachio curd and fig jam.

All right, so perhaps he wouldn't arrest her at the ball, if he was as sweet as Ludmila thought.

"And you would make an excellent princess."

Vika burst out laughing. "Me, a wild girl from the woods, a princess? And can you imagine Father, in his tunics and rough trousers, living in the halls of the Winter Palace? No, I don't think princess-hood, or whatever it's called, would suit me at all. Besides, I highly doubt that's what the tsesarevich is after."

"I'm willing to wager a hundred chocolate truffles that that is exactly what His Highness is after."

But Vika wasn't listening, since it occurred to her that perhaps the tsesarevich wanted to meet her because of the Game. Perhaps his father had informed him of it. And surely the tsar himself would be at the ball. Vika would need to be at her best.

"We'll have to decide on our costumes." Ludmila held two green macarons over her eyes.

Vika groaned. "Not that. You look like a murky-eyed frog."

"Then what will we wear?" She lowered the macarons. "Can you conjure costumes for us?"

"I could. . . ." Which was true. But Vika had never been any good at tailoring clothes. It was part of the reason why her dresses were not up to the standard of the gowns worn by Saint Petersburg girls. Perhaps it was because cloth was not a living thing, which made it more difficult for her to manipulate. Or perhaps it was because she had never much cared what she wore. She was very much like Sergei in that way. But no matter what the reason, Vika had only ever mastered making the simplest of clothes.

Yet there was another option: the armoire. Assuming it functioned like the one at Bissette & Sons, she and Ludmila could throw in old garments and *voilà!* New costumes would appear. Vika had seen a woman at Bissette & Sons leave with a dress made of white swan feathers and a black-and-white mask to match. Another left with a gown that was red at the hem but orange and pink near the bodice, with a yellow veil for her face like the rising sun. It would be easy to use the armoire.

It would also mean trusting her opponent.

"What are you thinking about?" Ludmila asked.

"The armoire."

"It's still in the hall."

"I know."

"It wouldn't fit through the front door."

"That's because I have protections on the flat." Vika had cast double protections, actually, ever since the day Nikolai's Nevsky Prospect magic almost seeped in. "The armoire is enchanted. My charms wouldn't let it in."

"Ah . . . that makes so much sense. We measured and remeasured, and the dimensions seemed as if it ought to easily fit, so we couldn't figure out what was wrong." Ludmila finished assembling the last of the macarons. She offered one to Vika. Vika declined. "So the armoire from the other enchanter? What does it do?"

"If it is anything like the other one at the tailor shop down the street, you fill it with old clothes, and it changes them into something new. But not something ordinary. Something extravagant, for the masquerade."

Ludmila clapped her hands, and cookie crumbs sprinkled down from them. "So we should use it."

If only they could. If only Vika could give in and trust her opponent, enjoy his magic as a complement to her own. If only the Game did not exist. But no. She had allowed herself the pleasure of enjoying the wardrobe's wood carvings, but only with her shields intact. Using it to clothe themselves

189

was a more intimate matter. A dangerous matter.

"No," she said to Ludmila. "We cannot use it."

"Why not? It would save you some work."

But that was another reason Vika couldn't allow herself to utilize the armoire. She didn't want to depend on the other enchanter. She didn't need his help.

This couldn't be explained adequately to Ludmila, though, without telling her about the Game.

Instead, she said, "I'm not the sort of girl who likes to be dressed by a man, as if I were his doll. I think it would be best if the costumes we wore were our own."

CHAPTER THIRTY

At thirty minutes past eight on Saturday evening, Niko-lai arrived at the Winter Palace. He had enough pride not to arrive at the very beginning of the masquerade but also enough awareness that, despite being Pasha's friend, he was enough of a nobody to require appearing before the real nobility arrived.

At the threshold of the ballroom, Nikolai adjusted his mask over his eyes. It had red and black diamonds in a harlequin pattern, which matched his waistcoat and also matched the jack-in-the-box outside in Palace Square. Other than this small splash of color, however, his clothing was unremarkable—a starched white shirt, a black cravat, char-coal trousers, white gloves, and a formal dress coat. He did not feel like being particularly visible. Besides, it would be lovely to blend in for once. Tonight, he didn't have to be Galina's "charitable project," the poor orphan she'd refined into a gentleman and paraded around at her friends' balls. He could be anyone.

The majordomo announced his presence—simply "Harlequin," for at a masquerade there were no real names—and he smiled to himself as he proceeded down the carpeted steps.

The tsarina had had the ballroom decorated lavishly. The ceilings were draped with richly hued fabrics, deep burgundy and midnight blue, giving the effect of being inside a sumptuous tent. The chandeliers were adorned with wreaths of tiger lilies and red dahlias, and the walls were hung thickly with curtains and garlands of peacock feathers. Divans with deep cushions sat around the edges of the room, a departure from the staid chairs that usually lined the perimeter, and one corner of the ballroom had been transformed into a miniature café, complete with quiches and petits fours and coffee and tea from an army of copper samovars.

Many guests had already arrived, and a veritable menagerie whirled around the dance floor. A tuxedoed brown bear soared to the string ensemble with a butterfly. A rhinoceros wearing a bowler hat waltzed with a bejeweled mouse. And a white tigress prowled the ballroom with a tottering dodo bird in tow. Nikolai shuddered at the memory of the tiger he'd had to slaughter.

Of course, Pasha and the rest of the imperial family had not yet appeared. They would wait until nine o'clock, or even later. Then again, it being a masquerade, they could very well be hidden among the guests. Nikolai scanned the room again. No, it was impossible that Yuliana or the tsar or tsarina would do such a thing. It was highly likely, however, that Pasha would.

Nikolai smirked. How easy would it be to pick Pasha out of the crowd?

The majordomo announced General Sergei Volkonsky, a hero of the Napoleonic Wars, and his wife, Maria. *I did arrive just in time*, Nikolai thought. *Indeed, only seconds before the real nobility.*

Behind Nikolai, a man whispered, "I hear Volkonsky is not as loyal to the imperial family as the tsar believes. Some say he is in league with Pavel Pestel."

"Pestel?" another man said. "The agitator who has been calling for democracy?"

"The very one."

"*Mon dieu!* What a state Russia is in these days."

Nikolai turned around, curious as to the identities of the speakers. But both the men were masked, and one of them, upon seeing Nikolai, said, "Let's not discuss this tonight," before he herded his friend away.

If only they knew about magic and the Game, Nikolai thought wryly. *Then they'd truly wonder at the state of Russia these days.*

Nikolai brushed aside the men's talk—it was not only Galina's set that liked to whisper about gossip and scandal—and began to scan the crowd again in search of Pasha. Surely he was here in disguise.

But before Nikolai had looked at an eighth of the room, a familiar swirl of braids caught his attention. She wore the same gray tunic as the rest of the servants, although she shouldn't have, for she did not work in the Winter Palace. She did not belong here at all. Nikolai strode across the ballroom and caught her arm.

"What are you doing here, Renata?"

"Nikolai!"

"What are you doing here?" he repeated.

Renata wrenched free of his grip and maneuvered so

that a divan stood between them. "What do you think?"

"If the girl tried to make a move in the Game tonight, there would be nothing you could do to stop her."

"I could try."

"By doing what? Distracting her by reading her tea leaves?"

Renata's face crumpled, and she looked away.

Damn it. Again with the clumsy words. And this time he didn't have vodka to blame. Nikolai reached across the divan and put his hand on Renata's arm, gentler this time. In the background, the waltz and its music came to a close. "I'm sorry. I didn't mean to belittle your abilities."

"It's all right." She rested her hand on his. "I know you're under a great deal of pressure. I thought I could help by coming and keeping watch on her."

"Vika will be in costume. It will be hard to keep watch on anybody tonight."

Renata inhaled sharply. "Since when did you start saying her name?"

Nikolai dropped his hand from Renata's arm and stepped back. Had he said the girl's name? He hadn't meant to. Until now, it was a boundary he hadn't crossed. The Game would have been easier if she were unnamed, if she remained a stranger.

But it was already too late for that. From the moment she'd charmed the canals, it was too late. And then she had spared him from the lightning storm, and he'd made her the Imagination Box. . . . Yes, it was much too late. In more ways than one.

Renata stood on the other side of the divan, awaiting his reply.

He cleared his throat. "How did you get into the palace in the first place?"

She gave a melancholy laugh. "Servants are interchangeable. They don't keep track of us. I slipped in through a service entrance and picked up a tray, and they pointed me in the direction of the uniforms without even looking at my face."

Nikolai frowned. It wasn't that long ago that he'd been mistaken for a servant at one of Galina's fetes, back when he wore whatever rags she scrounged up for him, before he learned to make his own clothes. And if Galina had never plucked him off the steppe, he could have been someone in a gray tunic, permanently. So it seemed patently unfair to Nikolai that he could be here, on one side of the ball, while Renata, his loyal confidante, could be on the other, wiping up spills and serving tea.

"Come with me." He had an idea. Perhaps not a wise one, given his suspicions of how Renata felt about him, but he could not let her spend the evening slaving away when she had come for his sake.

"Where are we going?"

"Nowhere, and at the same time, somewhere better than this faux café."

He came around the divan and led Renata farther into the corner. Then he raised his arm above them both and cast a shroud, such that if anyone looked in their direction, they would see only the curtains.

"What are you doing?" she asked, but her voice was steady, her eyes large and curious rather than afraid.

Nikolai untied a peacock feather from one of the garlands and gave it to Renata. "Hold this."

She clutched it to her chest, and he pointed his fingertips at it, then lifted his right hand up and pressed his left, down, as if stretching the feather to Renata's full length.

"If you are going to be here at the ball, you might as well enjoy it," he said.

Renata looked down. "Oh, Nikolai!" Her plain tunic had metamorphosed into a green lace bodice and a skirt composed entirely of peacock feathers. Her shoes were patterned to match.

"And of course you'll need gloves and a mask." He clasped his hands, and when they opened, white gloves and a mask of green, gold, and blue glitter appeared.

She picked them up as if they would vanish if she handled them too roughly. She slipped on the gloves, and Nikolai helped her fit the mask on her face.

He bowed and offered her his arm. "May I have the honor of dancing with you?"

"I—I don't know how."

"I will show you."

The shroud covering them faded away, and the harlequin led the peacock to the center of the ballroom, where the floor manager was filling the next set of dancers for a waltz. They took their places, and Nikolai rested Renata's left hand on his right shoulder and wrapped his arm around her. With his other hand, he clasped hers and pulled her close. She held her breath.

"The beat is one-two-three," he said quietly. "But don't worry. All you have to do is follow me."

As the orchestra began, Nikolai led Renata forward, sideways, backward, whispering, "One-two-three, one-two-three," for the first few counts. She caught on quickly, and as they glided around and across the room, he dropped the count. "You're dancing beautifully."

Renata blushed.

They rose and fell with the music, whirling up and down and all around, and when the song ended, Renata asked, "Can we do that again?"

Nikolai shook his head. "Not immediately. It would be terrible etiquette if I monopolized your attention."

"Besides," a boy's voice said behind him, "I would like a turn with the beautiful peacock."

Ah, there he was. Nikolai knew it was Pasha without even looking. For all of Pasha's claims that he wasn't any good at planning ahead, he was masterful at it when it involved sneaking out, or, in this case, sneaking in. "I knew you would come early," Nikolai said.

"I had to, before you stole the hearts of all the pretty girls."

Renata blushed again.

Pasha stepped up from behind Nikolai to join them. He was an angel—white dress coat, white waistcoat, white shirt, white cravat, white trousers, white shoes, white gloves, white mask. The only things not white were his silver wings and the gold halo nestled in his hair.

"Renata, may I introduce—"

"Dmitri," Pasha said. He winked at Nikolai. "Dmitri Petrov."

Nikolai tilted his head in a question. But then again, why not? It was a masquerade, after all, and tonight was the one night Pasha could truly get away with being someone else. Just like Renata could be more than a servant girl.

Dmitri the Angel bowed, offered her his arm, and whisked her back to the dance floor. Nikolai watched them go. Then he retreated back to the edges of the ballroom, to wait for the real reason he had come.

CHAPTER THIRTY-ONE

When angelic Dmitri finished his dance with Renata, he led her off the floor, where she was immediately swept up by a pirate. The angel stayed a minute to confirm she was amenable to the pirate's attentions, and then, having ensured that she was, Pasha took advantage of his disguise and invited another young lady to dance. And after that, another. And another, and another. Because as the tsesarevich, he never got to do this with such freedom, but as Dmitri the Angel, he could. Perhaps this would be the first ball ever at which he would dance with more girls than Nikolai did.

Eventually, the orchestra needed a break, and Pasha, flushed but content, decided to seek out Nikolai again. But his friend seemed to have disappeared from the ballroom.

What's gotten into him lately? he thought as he made another pass by the dance floor, the refreshment station, and all the divans around the room. Nikolai couldn't have left. It seemed unlikely that there would be another event tonight more compelling than the masquerade, and even more unlikely that Nikolai would have abandoned Pasha on the night of his birthday. Could he have? Pasha scanned the ballroom again.

However, his search was halted by the majordomo banging his staff at the entryway. The servants ceased their clearing of plates in the café area, and the guests around the dance floor stopped their chattering to turn to the entry of the ballroom.

"The Grand Princess Yuliana Alexandrovna Romanova!" the majordomo announced.

"What?" Pasha said. Beside him, a mermaid and a clown frowned.

Right. He shouldn't disrespect his sister. And since he was in costume, the mermaid and clown didn't know Yuliana was his sister. But he could not be here when she arrived.

The entire room stood rapt as they awaited the grand princess's arrival. Only Pasha ignored the announcement and slipped out a side door.

He ducked in and out of the service passageways, deftly avoiding the servants carrying trays of sandwiches and fresh coffee to the ballroom, and reemerged through another service door into a small chamber his mother occasionally used for holding audiences with those who wished to speak to her.

The room was simple by Winter Palace standards—a cherrywood desk and a few cushioned chairs, lilac-painted walls, and cream drapes held back from the floor-to-ceiling windows by gold tasseled rope. It was unfussy and very much his mother's style, and Pasha could breathe here, so he paused for a moment and tried to shake the tension from his shoulders. Then he continued onward, out the door and into a proper hallway, until he'd circled back around to the entrance outside the ballroom.

His father and mother stood there, tall and proud, her hand on his arm. Yuliana must have already entered, and the majordomo was giving her due time to enjoy the guests' attentions before he announced the tsar and tsarina. Upon hearing Pasha's footsteps, they turned.

"Oh, darling, thank goodness you're here. They are about to announce us." His mother wore a deep ruby gown brocaded in gold, with glittering diamonds and sapphires on her ears, neck, and wrists, and a crown studded with diamonds and pearls on the blond ringlets atop her head. She waved a jeweled red-and-gold mask on a baton, holding it as regally as if it were a scepter. She looked every bit the role of tsarina. If it weren't for the cough that racked her body every few seconds, Pasha would have smiled. She had had the cough for months now, and it was not getting any better. Worse, actually.

"Are you sure you're well enough to attend the ball?" he asked. "Perhaps you ought to rest instead."

"It is your birthday, my love. I wouldn't miss it if it killed me."

"Mother."

"Darling, don't fret. It won't kill me. I promise." She released the tsar's arm and glided over to smooth Pasha's hair, which must have gotten unruly from the dances he had snuck in.

"Where have you been?" the tsar asked. Unlike the tsarina, he did not move to greet his son. He had also made no effort to change his usual attire for the masquerade; he'd donned his ceremonial military uniform as always. "Your

Guard has been frantic, yet again, and frankly, I am weary of it."

Pasha bowed low to the ground. "My apologies, Father. I required some time to myself before the festivities. I do not have your natural ease at being in the public eye."

The tsarina patted Pasha's arm. "It will come with time, my dear."

"He turns seventeen tonight," the tsar scoffed. "The time to grow into his position has long since come and gone." He turned to Pasha. "You have already been inside the ballroom, haven't you?" He scowled at Pasha's hair. That traitorous, traitorous hair.

Pasha looked at the floor, in part to avoid his father's glare, but mostly to avoid the disappointment he was sure had settled on his mother's face. The scene of horses and soldiers woven into the carpet had never seemed so interesting before.

"You do realize how inappropriate your actions are, do you not?" The volume of the tsar's voice remained low and steady, but the tone had picked up a bitingly sharp edge.

"Yes, Father."

"Even the lowest-ranking nobility must be announced."

"Yes, Father."

"There are rules governing with whom you interact and how. Your sister has never had a problem comprehending this. And yet, after seventeen years, it has somehow still not been impressed upon you that the conventions and ceremony of the tsardom matter. You are the tsesarevich of all Russia. I suggest you start acting like it."

"Yes, Father."

"Now go upstairs and change."

Pasha looked up from the carpet. "What? Why?"

"For a multitude of reasons, the foremost being that you have already been seen in that ridiculous costume, so if you march in as an angel now, the whole of Saint Petersburg's nobility will know that you had previously slunk among them, unannounced, like a gutter rat. And also, your costume is unbecoming for a man of your station."

"But it's a masquerade. . . ." Pasha's voice wilted. There was no fighting the will of the tsar, and he knew it. He had always known it, which was why he tried to live so much of his life when his father was not looking.

"It is a masquerade for all of them." The tsar flung his hand in the direction of the ballroom doors. "But it is an imperial state function for *you*."

CHAPTER THIRTY-TWO

Nikolai had seen Pasha slip out a service door, but he had not anticipated such a long delay between the announcement of the tsar and tsarina and the official announcement of Pasha's arrival. But when he saw his friend come down the marble steps, he understood the reason why: he was no longer the playful angel Dmitri but was instead the staid heir to the throne, complete with a forced smile and formal military uniform. No mask.

"The Tsesarevich, Pavel Alexandrovich Romanov!" the majordomo shouted.

Poor Pasha.

After he descended the stairs, Pasha turned and bowed to the tsar and tsarina, who were sitting in a balcony above the rest of the ballroom, not unlike a box at the opera, well separated from the ordinary people. Yuliana hurried to Pasha's side, her movements somehow graceful and grace-less at the same time, and he kissed her hand. And then half the guests abandoned their current conversations and rushed to give their birthday wishes to the tsesarevich, no longer caring whether their masks fell and their true identities were revealed. In fact, many of them purposely ripped their masks off their faces, the better for the tsesarevich to recognize them and take note of their show of loyalty.

If only they knew that Pasha was likely not keeping track.

Nikolai let his shroud fade away, and he appeared once more against the backdrop of the curtains. Renata quickly found him.

"I was beginning to wonder whether the tsesarevich would come to his own birthday ball," she said, watching the queue of people lined up for the possibility of a few words from Pasha. "But it's a shame that he hates it."

"Hates what?"

"Being the tsesarevich."

"How do you mean?"

Renata shrugged, as if the observation were obvious. Then again, she was disarmingly good at seeing through to the truth of people. Most of the time. "He winced when the majordomo announced him."

Nikolai also watched Pasha. Now that he had come down from the steps and was able to interact with the guests one on one, Pasha's smile had grown more relaxed. "No, you're wrong. He doesn't hate the position itself. He hates the formality of it. But he has great respect for the tsardom and the people of the empire. He only wishes it came with less pomp and ceremony."

As if to emphasize Nikolai's point, Pasha tossed back his head in laughter in response to something the pirate, Renata's former dance partner, was saying. The pirate beamed.

"Ah, all right, I see what you mean," Renata said. "It's a pity, though, that he won't get to enjoy the costume aspects of his own masquerade."

Nikolai nodded. Pasha would also lament that his other goal for the ball—meeting Vika—had not yet come to fruition. It was already half past nine. Would she make an appearance at all?

Nikolai absentmindedly pressed his hand to the spot where his scar lay beneath his cravat. The wands didn't burn; because he'd built the Masquerade and Imagination Boxes, it was currently Vika's move. He half hoped she would appear and cast something stunning. He half feared she would, too. He'd even considered wearing Galina's knife tonight, but then left it behind when he realized it would be confiscated at the door. No one could have weaponry at the tsesarevich's ball.

"Do you think she'll come?" Renata asked, her eyes on the placement of Nikolai's hand on his scar.

He dropped it down to his side. "I don't know."

She wrinkled her forehead, studying him. "Do you want her to come?"

Nikolai charmed his face to smooth out the emotion so Renata couldn't read him. "I don't know that, either."

But it didn't matter what he wanted or how he felt, for in the same heartbeat as Nikolai uttered those words, Vika appeared in the entry.

A hush blew through the ballroom until even the couple bowing to Pasha rose to see the cause of the quiet. Pasha turned. All eyes were on the girl on the stairs.

Her ordinarily red hair was pale blue tonight, and the black streak had been transformed to silver, like a sliver of mercury. On her face, she wore a mask made of birch wood, rough white with flecks of gray. But it was the gown that had triggered the silence, for it was unlike anything the guests had ever seen. The bodice appeared to be carved from white ice, reflecting the light from the chandeliers on its polished surface, and yet it hugged the curves of her frame and moved with her as if made of water. The skirt was similarly frosty, an endless eddy of snowflakes, like a blizzard erupting from the ice above. Even the air seemed to chill around her. This was not from Nikolai's Masquerade Box. This was far beyond his tailoring and imagination.

She was a diamond in a quarry full of quartz.

Even the majordomo stood agog. It was a good minute before he gathered himself and inquired the girl's masquerade name. And that of her chaperone, a lady dressed in a rich brown dress that, from Nikolai's vantage point, seemed to be made of actual chocolate, and that would usually have elicited awe and admiration had it not been upstaged by Vika's gown.

"Madame Chocolat . . . and Lady Snow," the majordomo yelled, and it was arguable whether he had announced the tsesarevich or Vika with more reverence.

"Good gracious." Renata trembled beside Nikolai. "No wonder you feared her the first time you saw her."

But fear no longer described how Nikolai felt. As soon as Vika floated into the ballroom, he'd felt her pull. She was the sun, and he was a mere rock, drawn in by her gravity. He needed to be closer, to feel her magic, to touch . . . her. He trembled at the thought. And he took a step in her direction.

Renata reached out and placed her hand on his shoulder. "Be careful. . . ."

And then she let go. For even she knew there was only so much one could do to protect a winter moth drawn to an icy flame.

CHAPTER THIRTY-THREE

Vika paused at the top of the ballroom stairs, not because she wanted everyone's attention, but because she had no idea what to do or where to go next. She was already self-conscious that they were so late—creating the gowns for Ludmila and herself had taken a great deal longer than she had hoped it would—and now it was evident that they had arrived well after the imperial family. Even a country girl who knew nothing of the rules of Saint Petersburg society could deduce that that was an insult. *Please, please don't let the tsar hold it against me.* She did not want him to declare a winner—and loser—tonight.

"I think we should pay our respects to the imperial family," Ludmila whispered. "And smile."

Vika tensed but forced up the corners of her mouth. She and Ludmila were only halfway down the stairs when the tsesarevich began to come up. Vika stood paralyzed. She had disrespected him once by freezing him in the forest. Now she had offended him by arriving late to his birthday ball. Although she couldn't be sure he knew she was the girl from the woods, she suspected her icy dress gave her away. It had been part of the point of her costume. Perhaps an arrogant and foolish point. *Please let the tsesarevich be as kind as Ludmila thinks he is. Please don't let him take offense.*

Ludmila curtsied on the steps. Vika not so much curtsied as fell to her knees in as low a genuflection as she could manage without sitting down. Her skirt spread across the stairs like an avalanche cascading over the sides of a mountain.

The tsesarevich stopped in front of her. "Please rise, Lady Snow." He offered his hand.

Vika was aware that all eyes and ears in the ballroom were on them. What she said and did next could seal her fate. She took his hand and kissed it.

His laugh echoed through the entire room. He didn't sound cruel, but then again, the worst kinds of cruelty come in the guise of kindness.

"Take my hand, Lady."

She glanced up briefly and laid her gloved fingers in his. He pulled her up from the steps, but she kept her head bowed. When she was standing again, she said quietly, "Your Imperial Highness, please forgive us for our late arrival. It is entirely my fault, and I assume full responsibility. I did not mean any offense. I owe you my deepest apologies."

This time, the tsesarevich lifted *her* hand to his mouth and kissed it. "You are forgiven."

Vika startled and met his gaze. The blue in his eyes sparkled with his smile.

"May I have the honor of dancing with you?" he asked.

Vika nodded, unable to utter a word.

The tsesarevich turned to Ludmila. "Would that be all right, Madame Chocolat?"

Ludmila giggled. "Oh, yes, quite so, Your Imperial Highness."

He bowed slightly to her, then offered his arm to Vika and led her down the remaining stairs.

The grand princess awaited them at the bottom. She had dark-blond hair that matched the tsesarevich's, and broad shoulders like his, too. Her gown was made of violet velvet and tulle, and her neck was adorned with an entire treasure chest of jewelry. *It's a minor miracle*, Vika thought, *that she can stand beneath the weight*. Like the rest of the imperial family, the grand princess wore no mask.

She eyed Vika, then turned up her nose at her (which was quite a feat, since the grand princess's nose was already upturned in shape). She said to her brother, "Don't tell me you were going to take her to dance without introducing her first."

"I wouldn't dream of it," the tsesarevich said, although from the barely concealed smirk on his face, Vika suspected he'd at least considered it. He turned to Vika. "This is my sister, the Grand Princess Yuliana Alexandrovna Romanova. And this," he said to the grand princess, "is Lady Snow."

Again, Vika curtsied low to the ground. The grand princess also curtsied, although barely. "I gather you two have met before," she said. There was a thinly veiled hint at impropriety in her tone.

Against her better judgment, Vika scowled. She also flushed, which only made her scowl more that she'd let the grand princess get to her.

The tsesarevich simply waved off his sister's implication.

"In fact, we have not." Which, technically, was true, as Vika had fled when she last saw the tsesarevich rather than properly paying her respects. He turned to Vika. "Please ignore my sister. She's a bit protective of me."

"With good reason," the grand princess said. But she dipped her head at Vika to indicate that she was dismissed, and Vika tried not to bristle. Not visibly, anyhow.

The orchestra had begun to play again, and the other guests pretended to return to their conversations all while keeping their focus on the newcomer monopolizing the tsesarevich's attention. He led Vika past the now-broken queue of people who had been waiting to wish him well, until they arrived in front of the balcony where the tsar and tsarina presided.

Vika held a very long breath.

"Father, Mother, may I present to you Lady Snow."

Vika smiled as if she had never met the tsar before, and she curtsied to the floor again.

"That is an impressive gown," the tsarina said when Vika had risen. "The shimmering fabric gives the illusion of the snowstorm being real. Wherever did you have it made?"

"I tailored it myself, Your Imperial Majesty. I am very grateful that it pleases you." Vika cringed at her own words. She sounded like such a sycophant. But what was the appropriate thing to say when the tsarina complimented your magic, without knowing it was magic? There was certainly no etiquette manual to cover that.

"Take care not to become too enamored of the tsesarevich," the tsar said. "It will require more than a showy gown to be worthy."

Vika's hand fluttered to her collarbone. She had charmed

her scar to be invisible tonight, but it still burned. And even though the tsar was commenting ostensibly on her dress, his warning was clear: he was not impressed by the enchantments recently cast over the city by her and the other enchanter, Nikolai. They would have to do more to win the right to advise him.

But at least it seemed that he would not end the Game tonight. He would give them more chances to prove themselves. A little of the tension leached from Vika's shoulders.

"Yes, Your Imperial Majesty," she said. "I understand completely."

The tsar grunted. The tsarina nodded and said, "Enjoy the ball."

As the tsesarevich led Vika across the ballroom, he said, "Now it's my turn to apologize. I'm sorry my family are so . . . dreadful."

Vika shook her head violently. "Oh, no, Your Imperial Highness, they're not—"

He grinned, and it appeared more the expression of an impish boy than that of the heir to an empire. "Please, call me Pasha. And it's true, they are dreadful. Well, not my mother. But Father and Yuliana can be. Father is an awfully good tsar, though. And Yuliana can't help being dour; she was born that way."

Vika didn't know anything appropriate to say. *How to respond when the crown prince pokes fun at his family* would also not be in the etiquette manual. She could respond with something clever or snide—*I never thought kindness was a prerequisite for world domination anyway*—but Vika didn't fancy being arrested tonight for treason. So she kept her mouth shut.

As they approached the center of the ballroom, a bald man in white uniform—not a military one, but something with silver tassels and epaulettes nonetheless—scurried up to the tsesarevich.

"Your Imperial Highness, would you like the entire floor to yourself?"

The tsesarevich scrunched his nose. "Goodness, no, Fyodor. And ask the orchestra to play a waltz, please."

Fyodor, whom Vika deduced must be a dance manager of some sort, scuttled away and began waving urgently at the costumed men and women around the room. As Vika and the tsesarevich took their place, the dance floor around them began to fill with other couples. Nearby, a peacock and a young man in a harlequin mask caught her eye.

The tsesarevich took her hand and rested his other behind her opposite shoulder.

"Oh! I, uh . . . I've never waltzed before, Your Imperial Highness. Actually, I must confess I have never danced any sort of dance."

He blinked at her. "*Any* dance?"

"Folk dances. But not proper ballroom ones, Your Imperial Highness."

The tsesarevich lifted her left hand and placed it on his shoulder. "Will you please call me Pasha?"

"I—"

"I will call you Vika, if that makes it a fairer trade."

"I . . . Wait." A tiny laugh escaped her. "You do know who I am."

"The gown was a clever clue. My boots are still cold from that day. I'm very glad you accepted the invitation. My

214

apologies for its last-minute nature. You're a difficult girl to track down."

Now Vika truly laughed.

"So you will call me Pasha?" He tilted his head, and he looked like a little boy asking for something as simple as ice cream. As if calling the heir to an entire empire by his nickname were such a simple matter.

But why not? He was a person, just as Vika was. "All right then. Pasha."

"Thank you." He smiled, and the delight lit him from within. Those around them on the dance floor smiled, too, as if his joy were contagious.

He could smile like that and have anyone agree with him, about anything, she thought. It wasn't magic, but it was close.

The orchestra began a gentle rhythm, and Pasha squeezed Vika's hand. "Just follow my lead."

At first, she concentrated on her steps. It would be best not to make a complete fool of herself, since everyone was watching. Thank goodness for the mask. Although it would not save her from the tsar. He already knew who she was.

They spun around the floor, and Vika tried not to step on Pasha's toes. Soon, however, she figured out that they danced in the shape of a box, and she was able to release some of her focus and let him guide her.

"Thank you for what you've done to the city," he said close to her ear.

"What I've done?"

"You know: Nevsky Prospect, the Neva Fountain, the Canal of Colors, the music box pas de deux, the pumpkin kiosk, the Masquerade Box . . ."

"I'm not sure what you mean."

Pasha whirled her around easily. "I think you do. By the way, you dance exquisitely."

Vika's stomach fluttered, and she had to charm her face to conceal her surprise. "I assure you, any ability I have in this waltz is all on account of you."

"But the city . . ."

"Was not all my doing."

Pasha missed a step. When he recovered, he said, "You're not the only enchanter?"

Now it was Vika who stumbled. Had she really confessed she was an enchanter and revealed that there was more than one, all in a single breath? Pasha had complimented her on her dancing, and because of a few honeyed words, she'd let down her guard? The snowflakes on her gown blustered.

"I didn't say I was an enchanter."

Pasha smiled. "But I did. And you haven't denied it."

She glanced over her shoulder. No one was close enough to hear their conversation, although she could swear that the harlequin was paying more attention to *them* than to the peacock with whom he danced. Vika lowered her voice. "Being an enchanter is much more complicated than charming a few things to look pretty."

"My apologies. I didn't mean to imply that it wasn't."

The waltz ended, and across the floor, the dancers all bowed and curtsied to one another. The floor manager hustled to Pasha's side.

"Does Your Imperial Highness have any requests for the next dance?"

"A mazurka, please, Fyodor. I feel rather energized after that last one."

"A mazurka it shall be, Your Imperial Highness." He ran off to inform the orchestra.

Pasha offered Vika his arm. "Would you care to dance again?"

The harlequin slipped beside him, the peacock close behind. "It would be poor form to keep Lady Snow all to yourself," the harlequin said. "Even if you are the tsesarevich, and it's your birthday."

Vika stared at him, her mouth open.

"Ought I have his head for his impudence?" Pasha asked her. But then he burst out laughing. Pasha seemed always to be smiling or laughing. "Yes, it would indeed be poor form to keep such a beguiling lady to myself. I suppose you've come to steal her from me, Nikolai?"

The harlequin inclined his head.

Vika swallowed.

He was here. It was Nikolai.

CHAPTER THIRTY-FOUR

Vika gaped at Nikolai, unblinking. The harlequin pattern on his mask matched the harlequin outfit of the Jack. It was really him.

But she hadn't even felt his magic, his otherness, despite his proximity during the last dance. He must have cast a barrier shield as part of his disguise.

"I will, indeed, steal her," Nikolai said to Pasha.

"You forget I outrank you," Pasha said.

"A bit of an unfair fight from the outset, I'd say. But you underestimate the demand for me on the dance floor." Nikolai's brows arched over the top of his mask.

Pasha laughed again. "Believe me, I do not. Your skills are legendary. But you underestimate my charm."

"I remain steadfast in my intention to steal her from you."

Vika wrinkled her nose. Were they still talking about her? Yes, they were. As if she were an inanimate object. Especially Nikolai, who spoke of "stealing" her. Did he think he'd be able to carry her off like a prize without consulting her? If so, she would show him—

"But only if *mademoiselle* consents, of course." Nikolai turned to Vika. "Lady Snow, may I have the honor of dancing the next mazurka with you?" He bowed.

Oh. Well, then. He had manners, so . . . Right.

The girl in the peacock gown reached out toward Nikolai as if she wanted to stop him from dancing with Vika. But when Vika looked at her, the peacock girl backed away. Who was she?

"I know even less how to dance a mazurka than I do a waltz," Vika said as she took several steps back. She surreptitiously checked her own shields.

"I have no doubt you will dazzle the room," Nikolai said.

Pasha bowed to her. "Thank you for the lovely waltz."

Vika curtsied. "The pleasure was all mine. Happy birthday."

Pasha lingered a moment longer than he needed to before he turned to the peacock girl. "May I have the honor of dancing with you?" The girl blushed and accepted. He offered her his arm, and after she cast one last look at Nikolai, they drifted away.

When they'd gone, Nikolai pointed at Vika's gown and said, "You didn't use my Imagination Box." He allowed her to maintain the several steps of space between them.

Vika touched the ice on her dress. "No."

"Why not?"

"I didn't trust you. Should I have?"

Nikolai smiled, and there was both shyness and mischief in it. "No, I suppose you shouldn't have. After all, I must look after myself. The armoire would have made you a beautiful gown, though."

"Which would have squeezed me to death?"

His smile fell away, as if off a cliff. "Am I so obvious?"

"The corseting would have been convenient. Would the dress really have killed me?"

Nikolai rubbed the back of his neck. "Only if I had commanded it to."

"Clever."

"Not clever enough. You didn't fall for it." Nikolai offered her his arm.

Vika didn't take it.

"There is no charm on my arm, I promise. You can test it."

She hovered her hand over his sleeve. There was no hint of magic, not even anything residual on the cloth.

"The coat is an ordinary one from Bissette and Sons," Nikolai said. "A gift last Christmas from the tsesarevich. But if you leave me standing here like this and don't take my arm, I'll never hear the end of it from him. Spare me his teasing, will you?"

She pursed her lips and nodded. Then she slipped her arm through his, although carefully.

But she didn't die when her white glove met his black sleeve. Instead, every one of his turns in the Game flashed back in an instant. She gasped. It was like the shock of touching Nikolai at Bolshebnoie Duplo, when she had suddenly seen him so clearly. Except this time, rather than seeing his face, she saw and understood his magic. Quiet euphoria coursed through her as she relived the first moment she saw that breathtaking, powder-blue building on Nevsky Prospect, and all the other candy pastel buildings that followed.

Then she recalled the Jack and ballerina's bittersweet duet, and the tugging began again at her chest. Oh, and that feeling when she'd placed her hands on the Imagination Box and it carved everything she longed for . . .

It was as if the attempts to kill her faded into the background, and now she saw the truth at the core of it all: Nikolai's magic was gorgeous and powerful and . . . and . . .

Her lungs faltered. Even the mere memory of his magic was so strong. And touching Nikolai, even through her gloves and his sleeve, was like being pummeled by a stampede of wild horses. No, wild unicorns. Beautiful, wild unicorns.

Vika stumbled.

Nikolai reached to brace her. His breath also stuttered.

Had he felt their connection, too?

Their eyes locked. They didn't move.

The orchestra began to play in the background.

After a very long moment, Nikolai cleared his throat and asked, in a hoarse whisper, "The mazurka?"

She nodded slowly. "Yes. The mazurka." She merely repeated his words without processing them. A mazurka could have meant a death drop into the ocean, and Vika would have agreed to follow him. Nikolai led her in a daze to the far end of the ballroom.

But the orchestra's upbeat, chirpy tune soon roused her. Vika suddenly remembered she did not know the dance.

She gripped Nikolai's hand tighter. "I don't know how—"

"Will you trust me now?"

"To do what?"

"To dance for you?"

She didn't know what that meant. But the other couples around them had begun to trot, and from across the ballroom, the tsar seemed to frown at her. And the grand princess watched her as if just waiting, *hoping* for Vika to fail. Vika and Nikolai needed to dance, or they would create chaos in the carefully planned set.

Yet what had she whispered to the ballerina in Palace Square when the Jack had offered his hand? *Don't trust him*.

Vika touched the basalt necklace at her throat. "No. I still don't trust you."

Nikolai shrugged. "No matter. I'm not giving you a choice."

Magic rushed around her like the floodgates of a dam had been released, and Vika levitated several inches off the floor on its flow. "Oh!" He must have released the shield he'd used earlier to contain his power. It nearly swept her away.

Nikolai smiled, and this time it was different from the first. There was no mischief. It was purely a blush in smile form. "I'm sorry. But I really want to dance with you."

A part of Vika—the nonrational part of her—melted.

And the rational side of her was too shocked to fight back. She'd never encountered magic that surged and glowed like this before. It wrapped around her like silk, and she found herself reveling in its warm elegance. Nikolai charmed her feet and her arms, and immediately, they joined in on the lively mazurka. Without needing to think, Vika glided and spun with him, as perfectly synchronized as if they had been dancing together forever. He twirled her out, and like the other men, he knelt, and Vika and the other ladies pranced around them. Then he rose and drew her back in, and they were a couple again, stamping and whirling together.

There was, of course, another irony: Vika was now Nikolai's puppet, his ballerina in a music box. But Vika also knew that if she wanted him to release her strings, she could force him to. She had magic, too. Only, she didn't want him to stop.

They didn't speak, but, rather, let the music carry them. They swiveled and sidestepped, came apart and back together again, each time united with Nikolai's hand resting gently on Vika's waist and the snow on her skirt flurrying fiercely. To counter the chill, she threw her arm out toward the fireplace behind the orchestra, and the flames blazed and warmed the room. He smiled at her small enchantment.

Then he spun Vika quickly, and she was a blur, blur, blur, and they danced as if lifted by the wind. He commanded the instruments and their musicians to match their blistering tempo, and the mazurka accelerated faster and faster and faster.

All around them, couples attempted to keep up. They stepped and twirled. They tripped and stumbled. When the song finally ended, one dancer fainted, and her chaperone and a gaggle of others hurried to her side. The orchestra declared a break. And despite the fire in the fireplace, the servants rushed to serve hot tea and warm cakes to their shivering guests.

Only Vika and Nikolai stood in the center of the floor. Their chests rose and fell in rapid, synchronized rhythm. He released the mazurka charm he had cast.

"Let's dance again," he whispered.

"It would be poor form," she quipped.

He smiled his blush of a smile. If only she could capture

it and keep it in a bottle.

"Then probably for the best that we don't," he said. "I believe we'll have an uprising if I do not relinquish you soon." Nikolai gestured behind her, and Vika shifted to see a line of knights and devils and gentlemen tigers waiting their turn to ask her to dance. They were apparently unfazed by the speed of her last performance.

"My two left feet will be revealed."

"Not while I am here." Nikolai waved his hand over her heeled boots, and she floated imperceptibly off the ground. "Do you trust me?"

The question seemed altogether different now than before the mazurka. Nikolai no longer seemed like the enemy. He was that tugging. That tenuous thread. He was her other half on the end of the string.

And yet she would be a fool to trust him.

But they could have a détente, at least for tonight. Vika looked up at him and tapped her mask. It went transparent, although only for him, and only for a few seconds.

He nodded, as if he understood exactly what she meant, and he mirrored her movement. His mask went invisible for a moment as well.

Oh. Heaven help her. Nikolai was more striking than she remembered, and the darkness in his eyes was more dangerous than she recalled. He was a poisonous autumn crocus: deadly beautiful with no antidote.

She wanted the flower anyway.

And Vika remembered the dreams of him she'd had, when she'd wondered what it would feel like to run her hand along the sharp line of his jaw, to touch her fingertips to the scar beneath his collarbone, to press her lips against his mouth. He was so close. She could put to rest all those questions now. And he wasn't even a shadow in a dream. He was real.

But Nikolai was a gentleman, and there was no possibility that he'd kiss her in the middle of the ballroom, in front of the tsar and tsarina and the rest of Saint Petersburg's nobility, even if he felt the pull as strongly as Vika did. Instead, he offered her his arm and led her off the dance floor. Then he bowed before he gave her up to the knight rattling in his armor.

"I hope to see you again, Lady Snow," Nikolai said softly.

Vika gathered herself—stashed away her dream thoughts and dream wants—and curtsied. "I am sure you will, Harlequin." She let her eyes linger on Nikolai for another moment. Then she turned and allowed the knight to take her back to where the floor manager was assembling the next set.

She danced a quadrille with the knight, a polonaise with the devil, and a cotillion and a gavotte and countless other steps. Pasha managed to squeeze in another waltz, and during one set, just for ladies, she even danced with the peacock girl. The dances were all at ordinary speed.

Nikolai did not invite Vika onto the floor again. He stayed on the fringes, near the drapes and the café, and closed his eyes, as if both listening to and channeling the music. He might not have been there with Vika, but his magic was with her for every step. When the violins swelled, she would feel a surge of energy in her boots; when the woodwinds crooned, her feet would glide with equal gentility. It was as if each dance was a dance with him.

And with each quadrille and cotillion and gavotte, the warmth of Nikolai's magic grew brighter. Like Vika's own power, Nikolai's pushed at the boundaries that contained it, yearning to burst like starlight and wash over everyone and everything with its glow. She wanted again to hold on to him, and have him hold on to her, so they could whirl together through the cosmos like galaxies that could not—and would not—be confined.

If only he weren't the other enchanter in the Game.

Forget about it, Vika told herself. *Just for tonight*.

But the longer the ball went on, and the longer she allowed Nikolai to dance for her, the more undeniable the horror of her reality became. *This one night is a farce*, she thought. *The Game hasn't actually gone away*.

Her gown grew suddenly heavier. The swirling flurries of snow in her skirt began to melt, and the snowflakes transformed to icy raindrops. Vika shivered as her gown shifted from blizzard to sleet, soaking through her petticoats. Weighing her down. Chilling her through and through.

At the end of the next song, she curtsied hastily to her partner and rushed off the dance floor, retreating to the side of the ballroom into the curtains. "Off," Vika said as she ran her hands frantically over her gown. "Get off." She could feel Nikolai's magic on her, fine invisible threads everywhere, as if she were covered in cobwebs. "No more dances. I can't. I can't do this. Get off."

His magic tangled and clung to her. She slapped and swiped at it. It was too much. He was too strong.

And then her fingers found a loose tendril, and another and another. His enchantment's edge.

Oh, thank goodness.

Knowing where it began and ended, Vika could push it away. She gathered the threads of Nikolai's charm and flung them all aside. Her feet were free. She recast her own shield. And she hurried off to find Ludmila.

"We have to leave," Vika said, pulling Ludmila away from a conversation with a tuxedoed brown bear. Out of the corner of her eye, Vika could see Nikolai rising from where he'd been sitting in the café. There was concern on his face. Or so she thought. Was it possible to read his emotion even though he wore a mask? Regardless, Vika didn't want concern.

"Why do we have to go?" Ludmila asked.

"We just do." Vika flew up the stairs and out the doors of the ballroom, with Ludmila panting to catch up behind her. Vika didn't even bid farewell to the imperial family. She certainly did not look back at Nikolai.

For it was too cruel of life to bring him to her now, only to remind her that one of them would soon be taken away.

CHAPTER THIRTY-FIVE

"What in the tsar's name is wrong with you?" Galina asked, as she brought a steaming bowl of borscht to Sergei's bedside. He lay on the mattress with his eyelids barely open, his book on medicinal herbs splayed on the pillow next to him but untouched in the last day.

"I'm . . . tired."

"You had better not have a contagious disease while I'm locked up in this cabin with you." Galina helped prop her brother up against the wall. It was like lifting two hundred pounds of deadweight. If it weren't for her magic, she would not have been able to manage. "Here, at least eat something." She scooped up a spoonful of the dark-red borscht and lifted it to his mouth.

Sergei opened and swallowed the soup. He screwed up his face. "What is *that*?"

"Borscht."

"It absolutely is not."

"Well, I tried my best!" Since Sergei had been in bed the

last two days, Galina had had to do the cooking, which was a near-impossible task, seeing as she had a full kitchen staff at home and had never lifted a paring knife in her life. Add in the fact that most of her meals were French in nature, so she had forgotten what a proper Russian beet soup ought to taste like. She had attempted to make the borscht herself, but she couldn't figure out how to get the hairy little roots off the beets, and the beets stained her hands and rolled off the cutting board onto the floor. In a huff, she had finally resorted to conjuring the dish, even though she knew Sergei despised conjured food. Still, she had made an effort.

Sergei pushed her hand and the bowl away and slumped back onto the mattress. His bare wrist hung off the edge of the bed.

That was when Galina remembered the leather bracelet that had been there at the oath. "*Mon frere* . . . what exactly did you give Vika that day in Bolshebnoie Duplo?"

"A bracelet," he muttered.

"But not any bracelet. It was charmed, wasn't it?"

"Of course it was. I'm sure the dagger you gave Nikolai was also enchanted."

Galina set the soup bowl on the nightstand. "I would be a fool if it wasn't. But the bracelet is the problem. It must be. What is it? What is it doing to you?"

Sergei grumbled and turned away from her to face the wall.

"Sergei!"

He rolled back and scowled. "What does it matter?"

"Because I need to know how to help my brother." Whether he knew it or not, she did actually care about him. She remembered how much it pained her when they were children, when she watched him trying to keep his pet chin-chilla alive and suffering with each failure. It died at least five times, surviving a month in their home only because Sergei kept half succeeding in resurrecting it by siphoning some of his own energy into it. The chinchilla just had not had much will to live. Finally, after the sixth death, their father had ordered the chinchilla be left in peace, partly in pity for the poor beast, but mostly because every resurrec-tion left Sergei weakened and susceptible to pneumonia or other illness. He had always been so attached to animals.

Which was precisely the problem now, wasn't it? Sergei was too attached to Vika. Because she'd come into his life as a helpless baby, she must have seemed more like one of his gentle forest animals than the preening people of Saint Petersburg society he so despised. And his current fatigued state must have very much to do with that bracelet he'd given his adopted daughter.

"You're giving her your energy, aren't you? The bracelet is a magical conduit you've created?"

Sergei sighed. "She's strong, but this way, she'll have even more stamina."

"Oh, Sergei. Is there a limit?"

"No."

Galina sank to her brother's bedside. "So if the Game continues for much longer, she could drain your entire life away."

Sergei shrugged. "If she wins, it will have been worth it." His eyelids drooped, and he buried his face into the rough pillow.

"But the problem is, she won't win."

Sergei didn't answer. Instead, he sang himself a wistful

lullaby that their mother had sung to them when they were children.

> *Na ulitse dozhdik,*
> *S vedra polivaet,*
> *S vedra polivaet,*
> *Zemlyu pribivaet.*

> *It is raining, outdoors,*
> *As if from a bucket.*
> *Pouring from a bucket,*
> *Rain is settling dirt down.*

Galina stirred the borscht, around and around, with no intention of eating it. She stayed by her brother's bed until he fell asleep.

The fact was, she did not care a mite about the girl. Nikolai, whom she had trained to be a fighter, would ultimately prevail. But for Sergei's sake, she hoped the Game ended sooner rather than later.

The snow kept falling endlessly outside.

CHAPTER THIRTY-SIX

Nikolai slept the entire day after the masquerade. When he woke thirty or so hours later, he was groggy and felt as if he could sleep another day more. But his scar throbbed, and the realization that he was still in the Game—that the dance with Vika had changed everything and yet changed nothing at all—catapulted him out of bed.

He had thought, during the mazurka, that they'd had something. Their touch had both frenzied and frozen the ballroom. Their breathing had synchronized, heatedly. And then they'd had all the dances afterward, where she'd let him charm her feet and he'd felt as if they'd spent the entire evening wrapped around each other, the warm silk of his magic against the strangely comforting chill of her dress, their magic and their bodies moving as one.

But then she'd suddenly run away without so much as a "Thank you for the dances" or even "I'll see you again in the Game." It was as if the mazurka had never happened at all.

And now Nikolai's scar burned again. She had already

made her move. *But how? How could she have the energy to play the Game after the exhausting night at the ball?* He splashed cold water on his face. Of course, it had been *his* powers used during her dances, but conjuring those two dresses—the blizzard and the chocolate gowns—would have been enough to take Nikolai out completely. How had she managed not only to create them, but also to appear so fresh-faced at the ball, full of wit and vibrance? And then to follow it up with a move in the Game? He shook his head at his reflection in the mirror.

He was getting dressed when Renata knocked and said through the door, "You have a message from the tsesarevich."

Nikolai hopped into his trousers, unbolted the locks, and flung open the door without even tucking in his shirttail.

Renata stood in the hall, her hair neatly braided, as always. She seemed to have grown an inch, and grown prettier, since the ball. But he didn't have time to dwell on that.

"What does he say?"

"I didn't open it." She held out the envelope in her hands.

Nikolai took it and tore it open. "Why didn't you wake me?"

"I tried, but you didn't answer. I've been pounding on your door off and on for the last hour."

"Oh." Nikolai glanced at her and had the decency to look sheepish. "Sorry."

She stepped into the room and leaned over his arm so she could see as he unfolded the heavy stationery.

N—
Come quickly. There is a new island in the bay.
—P

"What?" Renata said.

"Vika's third move."

"But—"

"I have to go."

Nikolai ran to his wardrobe and threw on a waistcoat, shoved his feet into his boots, and snatched a frock coat that didn't match. Then he slid down the banister and was out the front door before he realized that, like Vika the night before, he'd run off without saying good-bye.

Nikolai saw Pasha pacing the dock before he even saw the new island. Not that the island was far from the shores of Saint Petersburg. But Pasha's pacing was so frenetic, it was hard to focus on anything else. From the looks of his hair, Pasha had been pacing for quite some time. There was probably a path already worn onto the wood planks beneath him.

Pasha glanced up and caught sight of Nikolai. "Gavriil!" he hollered to the captain of his Guard. "Ready the ferry." Then he bounded down the pier to meet Nikolai.

"What took you so long?" Pasha asked when he reached his friend.

"It's not even eight o'clock in the morning. I was asleep."

"How could you sleep when a new island has cropped up in the middle of the night?"

Nikolai twisted his mouth. "Because in my slumber, I was unaware that a new island had cropped up in the middle of the night."

Pasha laughed and slapped him on the back. "Fair enough. Besides, you're here now. I was about to give up on you, although I vastly prefer doing this together." He started down the dock. "Come on. I forbade anyone to land on the island before we had a chance to explore it."

Nikolai hung back. "Are you sure it's wise for you to be the first? We know nothing of this island." Which was true. It could very well be dangerous. But it was also true that a selfish part of Nikolai wanted Vika's magic to himself, even though she'd left him at the ball. He didn't want the experience of her new island spoiled by anyone else, even if it was Pasha.

"I doubt that the enchanter, whichever one it is, would be so bold as to build a trap for me. It would be suicide to harm the tsesarevich." Pasha grinned, as if he were amused with himself for actually admitting that he was the heir to the throne.

But Nikolai hardly heard the last part of what Pasha had said. "Did you say 'the enchanter, whichever one it is'?"

"Indeed. Can you believe it? The lightning girl is not the only one. She didn't mean for it to slip out, but I caught it. I gather enchanters are rather protective of their identities." Pasha hopped onto the ferry.

Nikolai bit on his knuckle. Then he followed Pasha, although Nikolai didn't hop. He almost tripped on a rope snaking across the deck. One of Pasha's guards caught him and helped him onto the ferry. The rest of the guards clambered on right behind him.

So Pasha knew there was another enchanter. But he didn't seem to suspect Nikolai at all. Still, Nikolai's stomach lurched, and he leaned over the railing. Damn seasickness. Except Nikolai never got seasick. And they hadn't even left the dock. Which meant it was the guilt of lying to his best friend that was making him feel this way. Splendid.

A few minutes later, the ferry pushed off from shore,

leaving behind the throngs already amassed along the embankment, gawking both at the island (they'd managed to convince themselves that it was an artificial one, installed overnight as a birthday gift from the King of Sweden) and at the sight of the tsesarevich in their midst. They didn't know Pasha often walked among them in disguise. To the people of Saint Petersburg, Pasha was a rare snow leopard who kept to his gilded cage in the palace.

Pasha waved jauntily as he and Nikolai sailed into the bay, and a few onlookers waved and blew kisses back. Then he strode to the ferry's bow.

Nikolai took several deep breaths and pulled himself together. He took one more breath for good measure—what he'd do if the river tried to rope him in and drown him again, he didn't know—then he followed Pasha, and the two watched the new island as they approached.

The island was a small one, perhaps a half mile squared or a little more, but what it lacked in size, it made up for in appearance. Its banks were composed not of sand, but of low granite ridges, sparkling in the sun. Bright flowers freckled the shoreline, and trees reached halfway up to the clouds. It was also very green with all those trees. *Unnaturally green for this time of year*, Nikolai thought, *when the leaves ought to be turning shades of red and gold.*

"It reminds me of the Summer Garden," Pasha said.

Nikolai nodded. "Except the summer here is eternal." He wondered if the island, like the Summer Garden in the city, was also full of rare flowers and plants and marble statues and fountains. But regardless . . . Vika had created an *entire island*. Nikolai's chest tightened as their ferry sailed closer.

They arrived not long afterward. However, the ferry master could not find a place to bring the boat to shore. Nikolai frowned. It would have been easy for Vika to create a natural dock, an extension of land or an outcropping of rock. It wasn't as if she were unfamiliar with ferries and ports; she lived on an island herself.

Unless she did it intentionally, to make it harder to approach. But why? Why would she go to all the effort of conjuring something as magnificent as an island, only to make it difficult for anyone to come ashore?

"You're already building it, aren't you?" Pasha asked.

Nikolai jumped. "What?"

"I wager you're already mentally calculating how to construct a dock or a bridge to the main part of Petersburg," Pasha asked.

"Oh, right." Nikolai forced a smile. "Yes, it would be possible to erect an iron bridge, perhaps like the one in Coalbrookdale in England. Although more recently there has been talk among engineers of truss systems, such as the Gaunless Bridge that was just finished, also in England . . . Why are you laughing?"

Pasha shook his head. "I don't understand that brain of yours. It's unfair, really. How is it possible for one person to know so much?"

Nikolai shrugged. "I just like bridges."

"All right, well, if you ever find you don't need all that genius for yourself, I'm happy to take some off your hands. And when it comes time to build a bridge, I'll be sure our corps of engineers consults with you. But for now"—Pasha turned to the ferry master—"we'll take the skiff." He pointed to the small vessel kept on board as a lifeboat.

"Yes, Your Imperial Highness." The ferry master shouted to his crew to prepare the boat. "One of my men will row you to shore."

"That will not be necessary, thank you. Nikolai and I will manage on our own." He glanced at his Guard, who had gathered nearby. Gavriil cleared his throat. "No, Gavriil, I am not going to allow you to explore the island first. I'm quite sure it's harmless."

"I am sure it is as well, Your Imperial Highness. The tsar ordered a regiment to ensure its safety shortly after sunrise this morning. The island is small enough that they were able to scour it from coast to coast. I was merely about to suggest that I accompany you to shore, just in case."

Pasha scowled. Nikolai knew he didn't like that his father's men had beaten him to the island, especially since Pasha had declared it off-limits. And even more so, Pasha hated that his father could anticipate that he would come to the island first thing. Pasha didn't like to think himself so predictable.

"All right, Gavriil, you can come with us—but only you. The skiff will capsize if there are more than three of us in it."

Gavriil boarded the skiff first to verify that it was sturdy—Pasha scowled again at being handled so gently—and once its fitness for the tsesarevich was confirmed, Pasha and Nikolai were permitted to climb aboard. The boat rocked with the weight of all three of them, but once they were settled in, it was stable. The ferry's crew lowered the skiff into the water.

"I can row," Nikolai said.

"I'll do it," Pasha said.

"Your Imperial Highness," Gavriil said, "either Nikolai or I can—"

"No." Pasha grabbed the oars. "I said, *I'll* do it."

Nikolai relented. Pasha was much better at sea than he was, anyway. After all, Pasha had been on ships to Stockholm and Amsterdam, not to mention he'd sailed on the Sea of Azov. And where had Nikolai been all his life? On the ground, following yaks on the steppe, or delivering packages on the streets of Saint Petersburg. Nikolai sighed. It wasn't even a contest.

Nikolai leaned back and focused on conjuring a shield around their little boat, in case the Neva decided to grow violent again.

Pasha's strokes were long and strong, pushing and pulling the water in a steady rhythm. *Swish, swash. Swish, swash. Swish, swash.* The cadence almost hypnotized Nikolai back to sleep. He was still so tired from creating the Masquerade and Imagination Boxes, and from staying up all night at the ball.

He didn't get the chance to doze off, though, for he needed to keep the shield intact, and a few minutes later, they were at the island.

As soon as the skiff pulled close to the rocky shore, Gavriil jumped out to tie the boat to a maple on the coast. The tree was fully leafed and green. Eternal summer, indeed.

Pasha climbed out next, and finally, Nikolai. All three of them stood with mouths agape as they took in the scenery.

It was, as Nikolai had guessed, very much like the Summer Garden in Saint Petersburg. The breeze from the bay rustled through trees and pink flowering bushes. The burbling of water indicated fountains or waterfalls in the distance.

Warblers chirped and ducks quacked.

And everywhere in the air was her magic.

Nikolai closed his eyes and felt the tingle of it on his skin, like a sprinkle of rain or a dusting of snow. Her enchantment pulsed in the ground beneath his boots. And he could smell it in the wind, the scent of honeysuckle mixed with cinnamon, the same fragrance that wafted from Vika's hair when she danced. He felt hot and cold again, found and lost, like he'd felt with her in his arms at the ball.

"Are you asleep again, Nikolai?"

His eyes fluttered open, and Pasha stood in front of him, grinning. How long had he been there? Nikolai really had lost track of space and time.

"Gavriil has gone off to inspect and secure the coast. But I thought we might head inside." Pasha pointed at the wide gravel path that led into the park. It was a long promenade lined with oaks and shaded overhead by their leaves.

"Yes, of course," Nikolai said. "Lead the way."

They followed the path and entered the boulevard of trees. Everywhere they looked, there were larks and wrens, peeping a melody that sounded almost like an old Russian folk song. If Nikolai listened too closely, the song disintegrated into random notes, but if he softened his focus, the tune came back together again, like the whistling of pan-pipes and the strumming of a balalaika.

"This is a wonderland," Pasha said.

Nikolai could only nod, for he did not have the words to express how true a statement that was. For every leaf that Pasha saw, Nikolai also saw every stem and vein on that leaf. For every pond that Pasha marveled at, Nikolai sensed every droplet of water that filled it. A boulder was not merely a boulder, but a rock face full of detailed crags and slivers of crystal. None of it was as simple as it seemed, and it had all been conjured out of nothing.

"This island is the best enchantment yet," Pasha said.

Nikolai suppressed a grimace. Ever since dancing with Vika, it had been harder to think of the Game as a competition. But here was proof once more that it was, and she had bested him yet again.

The boys walked deeper into the park. It was easy to maintain their bearings; like the Summer Garden, the island was laid out geometrically, with paths running parallel and perpendicular. Unlike the Summer Garden, however, Nikolai noticed an absence of statues and fountains. In fact, there was nothing resembling the man-made here—no benches, no sculptures, no columns and iron-grille fences. Perhaps because that was not Vika's strength.

But it was his.

Nikolai's scar seared against his skin, and it suddenly occurred to him that the lack of a dock and the dearth of statuary were deliberate. It was an open invitation for him to play. This island was not Vika's alone; it could also be Nikolai's.

He looked overhead to the canopy of leaves and smiled.

But then his smile faded. Had she created this island for them to collaborate? Or was it a trap, waiting to be sprung? Nikolai might have forgotten about the Game the other night at the ball, but it was possible she had not.

No, it was *likely* she had not.

Pasha waved to him from an outcropping that overlooked the Neva Bay to Saint Petersburg. Beside him rose a pillar of rock shaped like an enormous candle.

"Hey-o, Nikolai, come see the view."

Nikolai sighed. "I'll be right there."

He trudged over to where Pasha stood. But he did not take in the bay or Saint Petersburg. All he could focus on was the pillar of rock.

It looked just like a candle that had been snuffed out.

CHAPTER THIRTY-SEVEN

Since work at the Zakrevsky household had slowed to a tortoise's crawl, Renata was permitted to set up a tea stall next to Ludmila's pumpkin kiosk to make some extra money. Her station consisted of a simple table and several large copper samovars and a set of barely chipped cups and saucers Renata had salvaged when the countess declared them wanting. For a few kopecks, Renata would sell Ludmila's customers a cup of tea to go with their pastry. For a few more coins, she would read their leaves.

As soon as she opened her stall, the first customer arrived. "I understand you read leaves," she said.

Renata gaped at her. It was the lightning girl, Lady Snow, the other enchanter in Nikolai's Game. She tried to look Vika in the eyes but had to turn away. There was something too vibrant about them. Too green. Too intense. "Y-yes, miss. I read leaves." She fumbled with setting up the samovar.

"Will you read mine?"

"Uh . . ." She could not seem to form a coherent sentence. Although she and Vika were close to the same age, Vika's confidence and the way she carried herself made her infinitely more formidable than Renata could ever be.

"You were the girl at the ball with Nikolai, were you not? In the peacock gown. I recognize your braids. They're very intricate."

"Yes, that was me."

Vika reached over to help Renata with the stubborn spigot on the samovar. "There. That ought to be better."

"Thank you. Your dress was, er, exquisite."

Vika beamed. "Thank you. I was lucky to have such a gown. Now, if I may inquire about the tea?"

"Oh, yes. I . . ." Renata could think of no excuse for not serving Vika. It also seemed unwise to defy her. She grabbed one of the clean cups and a saucer and filled it with tea.

"Come join me." Vika glanced behind her as if to confirm there was no one else waiting for Renata's services. Renata instinctively looked down the street, toward the Zakrevsky house, as if Nikolai could come to her rescue. But he couldn't. He was on the new island with the tsesarevich. She followed Vika to one of the tables by the canal that Ludmila had set up for her patrons. Renata waited until Vika was seated before she herself sat.

"I'm Vika Andreyeva, by the way."

Renata stood up again and curtsied.

"I hardly think that's necessary. It's not as if I'm the grand princess. What is your name?"

"Renata. Renata Galygina."

"It's nice to meet you, Renata. Please do sit."

She obeyed.

"Are you . . ." Vika spun her cup back and forth on the saucer. "Are you Nikolai's betrothed?"

Renata's eyes widened. "Me? Oh, no! I wish I . . . I mean, no, miss. He's my friend, but I'm a servant in the Zakrevsky household. Nikolai would never marry someone like me."

"I'm not so sure of that." Vika tilted her head, as if to get a better, deeper look at Renata. "He seems rather fond of you. He took you to the ball." Her voice lifted at the end, almost like a question tinged with the hope that Renata would deny it.

Which, of course, she had to, not only because it was the truth, but also because Renata was trained to speak honestly to her superiors. "No, miss," she said. "I came to the ball on my own. I wanted to . . ." The words drained away, along with the color in Renata's face.

Vika seemed to relax into her chair. "Let me guess. Keep an eye on me?" She smiled kindly.

Renata stared at the table and focused on the floral pattern of the tablecloth.

"You know about the Game," Vika said.

Renata considered hiding under her table. She had promised Nikolai she wouldn't tell anyone about the Game. Of course, her promise probably did not cover telling the other enchanter, since Vika already knew, but as Renata nodded, she still felt she had breached her word.

"I understand if you don't want to read my leaves," Vika said.

"I think I already know what they will say. I think you do, too."

"That either Nikolai or I will die in the Game." She cast her eyes downward to the table.

"Yes."

"I suppose I was hoping this Game would be different from the ones in the past. That perhaps the tsar somehow wouldn't have to choose only one of us." Vika looked back up. "I was hoping for a miracle."

Renata was, as well. She wanted so badly to read Vika's leaves, and yet, what was the point? If she already knew what they would say . . .

But morbid curiosity latched onto her, and she reached across the table to take Vika's cup. This would be her only chance to see into Nikolai's future again. He had refused to let her read his leaves after she'd read so much darkness in them the last time. Perhaps Vika's cup would shed some light.

The leaves were grouped in three small clusters. Three separate but related prophecies. At the top of the cup were two curved leaves that almost formed a heart, but for a third leaf that jutted into it. It represented love—possibly from a lover, but possibly from parents, siblings, or friends—and it foretold that love for Vika would always come with suffering. But Renata didn't tell her so. It seemed cruel. And, selfishly, Renata didn't want to say anything about love. She didn't want Vika to think about the word "love" when she was asking about the Game and Nikolai.

So Renata skipped those leaves and went to the next cluster, three arched leaves, one right after another. "This could mean movement."

"Like a journey?"

"Yes. Or emotional movement, internal change. I don't know. It's a bit vague."

"I see." Vika bit her lip. "And what about that one?"

Renata swallowed. The leaf she'd indicated was a sharp line with a jagged edge. There was another short leaf across the top, like a hilt. "A knife. Death."

"Oh." Vika sagged in her chair.

"The crookedness means it is not as expected."

"But one of us will still die."

"One of you will still die." Renata clutched the sides of the cup tightly. Both she and Vika stared at the leaves, as if they could will them to move and prophesy something else instead. In that moment, it seemed that the canal next to them turned black. But when Renata looked again, the water was purple.

And there was something else in the leaves, although Renata didn't say it, for she suddenly felt as if she'd revealed too much.

But Vika stared at her. "What is it?"

"What is what?"

"The thing you're keeping from me."

"I'm not—"

"Renata." Vika curled her fingers. Was it a threat? What would she do to Renata if she didn't tell her what was in the cup? Or worse, what would she do to Nikolai?

Renata's heart rose into her throat. "The knife," she blurted in her panic over Nikolai. "The leaves that form the knife are close to the inner circle—the bottom—of the cup."

"Which means?" Vika's fingers tensed.

"It means death is coming soon."

CHAPTER THIRTY-EIGHT

Beneath one of the bridges that traversed Ekaterinsky Canal, a hooded figure loitered, listening. She kept her distance from the girls discussing their tea leaves, for the woman stank of rot, like scraps of meat left out in the garbage on a midsummer day. But because there was no one else at the pumpkin bakery at this early hour, she was still close enough to hear.

After the steppe, Aizhana had traveled to Moscow. There, she lurked outside restaurants and horse races and anywhere she could find nobility, hoping for a glimpse of her son. Of course, she did not know what he looked like. So she'd done the only thing she could think of—stalk the aristocracy and hope she would recognize her boy, if only because she was his mother.

But then word reached Moscow of the wonders springing forth in the capital city, and Aizhana knew the source must be Nikolai. From the stories her village had told of his powers, it had to be him.

Aizhana rushed to Saint Petersburg then, her putrefied heart swelling with pride. She tracked him down to a house along Ekaterinsky Canal, and it was here that she had hidden, hoping for a glimpse of her son.

But now, as she eavesdropped on the girls, a different horror set in. For it was apparent Nikolai was involved in a game of sorts, a competition, from which only one enchanter could emerge victorious. And the tsar would choose the winner.

Aizhana had to lean against the walls of the dank underpass for support as her weak leg crumpled beneath her. Her son could die when she had only just found him. Was this the purpose for which the noblewoman had purchased Nikolai from the tribe? To enter him as a pawn in a game for the tsar's amusement?

Aizhana's blood boiled, threatening to rupture her brittle veins.

But then her rage settled at a simmer. *It is because of me that he was lost in the first place. I was not strong enough. I nearly let Death take me. Nikolai's misfortunes stem from my failure as his mother.*

She pulled herself deeper into the shadows beneath the bridge. She was not worthy of meeting her son now.

It did not mean, however, that she could not make herself so.

As flies began to swarm around her, attracted to her stench, Aizhana adjusted the hood around her face and smiled a rotten, gap-toothed smile.

I will find you again, Nikolai. As soon as I redeem myself as your mother.

And she had a plan. She would kill the tsar.

CHAPTER THIRTY-NINE

The next day, Pasha stood in the archery yard with a bow and a quiver of arrows. The weaponry master, Maxim, had cleared not only the archery range, but also the entire practice arena where the Tsar's Guard ordinarily trained and sparred, because Pasha's aim was so accurate, he needed twice the normal distance in which to practice.

"Ready?" Maxim hollered.

"Ready," Pasha said.

"I don't want to hurt you, Your Imperial Highness."

"So little faith in me, Maxim." Pasha grinned. "I said I'm ready. Now shoot."

Maxim shook his head but lifted his bow. He pulled an arrow from the quiver on his back. He aimed it straight at Pasha. "All right, Your Imperial Highness. Ready?"

"Yes! Shoot!"

"I pray to the Lord you know what you're doing." Maxim aimed again, making sure his line was directly to Pasha's chest, took a deep breath, and let an arrow fly.

Pasha drew back his own arrow and shot it straight at the incoming one. He knocked Maxim's out of the air, and the arrows clattered to the dirt below.

Maxim's jaw dropped so far, his gray beard met the armor on his chest.

"Again," Pasha said, grinning even harder than before. "I like this trick."

"Your Imperial Highness, I can't. If I strike you, the tsar will have my head."

At that moment, Yuliana appeared on the gravel path leading to the archery range. "What nonsense are you up to that would cause Maxim to lose his head?" The way she moved always appeared elegant but sounded like an angry stampede of wildebeests, even when she wasn't angry or irritated—which, to be honest, was rare. But she wasn't upset now; although her footsteps were vehement, the tone of her question was woven through with genuine curiosity. Pasha's archery practice was one of the few settings where he and his sister were both consistently pleasant.

Well, Pasha was *always* pleasant. But yes, watching him shoot arrows somehow soothed Yuliana's ruffled edges.

Maxim bowed to Yuliana.

Pasha wiped the sweat off his brow. "Oh, nothing. Maxim's being overly cautious. He refuses to shoot any more arrows at me."

"I'd say that Maxim is the wiser of the two of you, although that's nothing we don't already know."

Pasha laughed.

"Maxim, I believe you're finished here. Pasha and I will shoot at something safer. A stationary, nonhuman target." She gestured at the bull's-eyes that were set up a hundred fifty feet away, at the end of what was the *normal* archery range, not Pasha's extended one.

"Yes, Your Imperial Highness." Maxim bowed to both Pasha and Yuliana, hung his bow and quiver on the weaponry rack, and left the field.

"You're no fun," Pasha said through a smile.

"But I'm rather good at keeping my brother alive," Yuliana said.

Pasha set down his bow for a second to roll his sleeves to his elbows. After an hour of shooting—much of it involving running while hitting moving targets that Maxim threw in the air—Pasha was hot, and the muscles in his forearms were taut from the exertion. But if Yuliana wanted to shoot with him, he'd press on. There was no holding back anyway when it came to target practice, for it was one thing for certain in which Pasha was better than Nikolai, and he wouldn't cede that ground. Even if archery was a completely useless hobby.

"What are you musing on?" Yuliana asked.

"What do you mean?"

"You come out here when you need to think. Something's on your mind."

Pasha laughed. He actually hadn't realized that he came to the archery range to think, but now that his sister mentioned it, he found that it was true. The library and the range were solace to him.

"Nothing slips your notice," he said.

"As a general rule, no," Yuliana said. "So what is it that's preoccupying you?"

Pasha picked up his bow again and drew an arrow from his quiver. "Do you think she likes me?" he asked Yuliana.

"Who?"

"The girl from the ball." Pasha's stomach somersaulted just thinking about her.

"Which girl? You danced with half the room."

Pasha lowered his bow and cast a wry smile at his sister. "You know the one. Lady Snow. She was, as far as I'm concerned, the *only* girl in the room."

Yuliana walked—or rather, stomped—her way to the weapons rack and lifted a small bow. She strapped on a quiver, too, then returned to Pasha's side. "Well, if she's the one you're pining after, I'd say you ought to move on."

"And why's that?" Pasha aimed at the target again.

"She's not at all your equal."

Pasha let three arrows fly in rapid succession. Two of them hit their marks, but the third landed far awry with a *thwack* in the outer ring. He sighed. "I know. She'd probably like Nikolai better than me."

Yuliana rolled her eyes at him. "I didn't mean that she's *above* you! You're the tsesarevich. You have few equals, if any at all." She sighted her arrow and shot. It hit two rings off center. "And Nikolai is no competition. He's a commoner. At best, he can aspire to work for you someday."

Pasha laughed. Nikolai, working for him! He could only imagine what that would be like, having Nikolai in his Guard. He could probably slay an entire enemy army with a single scowl. "I cannot picture Nikolai taking orders from me."

"It's your future," Yuliana said. "Not necessarily Nikolai, but people in general. You have to get used to the idea that you're better than everyone else."

"That sounds horrible and lonely."

She shrugged. "It's not so bad, being horrible."

"Yuliana . . ."

She glide-stomped over and stood up on her toes. She pecked him on the cheek. "Oh, don't worry about me, brother. It's I who ought to worry about you. You haven't a horrid bone in your body, which means you'll make a wretched tsar."

Pasha smiled down at her. She was chilly, to be sure, but it was impossible for him not to respect her. His sister knew what she wanted, and she knew how to get it. That certainly couldn't be said of himself.

"So do you think she likes me, even though I'm destined to be a disaster of a tsar with no friends and sadly un-horrible bones?"

Yuliana sighed, but there was a light in her eyes. "Pasha, if you want her to like you, she'll like you. You're the tsesarevich. It's time you got that into your pretty little head."

CHAPTER FORTY

Nikolai landed on the Stygian-black shore of the new island at half past ten. He had "borrowed" a rowboat from the dock and charmed it to sail across the bay. The waters were savage at this late hour, a combination of the wind and the tide, and if it weren't for the enchantment to smooth the way, the boat would have ended up capsized or smashed against the rocks.

Once on solid ground, Nikolai unpacked a bundle of balsa wood and sandpaper from his satchel. He was quite sure now that the island wasn't a trap, as it hadn't tried to swallow him whole or otherwise kill him the last time he was here; perhaps the ball had changed something after all. What he wasn't sure of was what that meant for the Game.

But the scar beneath his collarbone still burned, insisting that Nikolai play. If he didn't, he would burn slowly, painfully, to his death. And so self-preservation plunged him forward with his turn, even though he no longer knew how he wanted the Game to end.

First, he intended to build the island a proper dock. This place—this magic—was something the people of Saint Petersburg should have the chance to see, even if they couldn't understand it.

Nikolai slashed his index finger through the air, slicing the wood boards into sticks. He charmed notches in the wood where the pieces could fit snugly together. He enchanted the sandpaper and set it about evening out the rough edges, before he commanded the pieces to fit themselves together. *Just like being a child again.* A simple project, like the ones Nikolai had mastered when he was only a boy, when Galina had taught him the physics of construction and architecture by drilling him with kit after kit of model bridges and towers and masted ships.

When the miniature dock was finished, Nikolai leaned over the rocky edge of the island and dropped the model pier into the water. Now was where the effort came in. He gritted his teeth and focused all his energy on the dock, and it began to expand, growing larger and larger until it was wide enough and long enough for a ferry to anchor itself at the end.

Sweat trickled down the back of Nikolai's neck. His jaw cramped as he pressed onward, fighting the hostility of the waves and extending the dock's posts into the floor of the bay. Finally, he embedded them deep in the sandy bottom.

Then he collapsed on the shore and lay on his back, panting.

But there was no time to rest. There was so much more to do before daybreak. Nikolai gave himself another moment to catch his breath and then climbed back to his feet, picked up his bag, and dragged himself to the center of the island.

Now for another enchantment.

Wire. Nikolai snapped his fingers.

And paper. He snapped again. And there, in the midst of all the trees, a spool of wire and a large sheet of crepe paper appeared in the air.

Nikolai began to hum a snake-charming song, an eerie, hollow tune. The wire unfurled and twisted up in wide spirals, as if it were a cobra at Nikolai's command. When it was round and full, like the circular ribs inside a globe, Nikolai halted his melody.

The crepe paper came next. With a flick of his wrist, the white paper wrapped itself around the wire and instantly, the metal frame turned into a paper lantern. Nikolai tapped the top of the lantern, and it lit up, despite having no candle inside.

"Now I need about a thousand more."

The lantern leaped to action and flew straight up into the sky. There, it began to multiply. Two, four, eight, sixteen, on and on until they had doubled ten times and reached a thousand and twenty-four. Nikolai pointed in every direction, and that sent each of them zipping to a different part of the garden, the island now lit up by a seemingly endless string of glowing paper orbs.

"*Voilà*," he whispered. He hardly had enough energy to speak.

And yet, he produced a tiny bench from the satchel, purchased as part of a dollhouse set, and put it on the ground. Then he blew on the bench, and where there had been one, there were suddenly ten. Nikolai flung his arm outward, and the benches shot off and planted themselves along the main promenade, each bench equidistant from the next. There, they began to enlarge, like the model dock and the jack-in-the-box and ballerina had done before.

When the benches had grown to full size, Nikolai fell to his knees, all his muscles shaking. His shirt was drenched with sweat, his hair damp against his forehead. He wanted to lie down right there, melt into the gravel, and sleep for days. He could use his overcoat as a blanket. The waves slamming against the shore would be a fitting, violent lullaby.

But it was already past midnight, and there was still so much, *too much*, to be done before the sun rose in seven hours. At least the next part of his turn could be accomplished in his sleep. It would be a fitful sleep, but Nikolai would be able to recover a little while he worked. In theory.

He scraped himself off the ground and staggered to the nearest bench. There, he shrugged off his overcoat and laid it on top of the seat, then lay down and stretched out his legs, thankful he'd decided to make the benches extra long. He pulled his satchel under his head, like a pillow, and closed his eyes to sleep. But before he drifted off, he reached over and drummed his fingers several times on the armrest, and he whispered to the bench, "Moscow. This one is Moscow."

And then his entire body relaxed, and he fell into a dream.

CHAPTER FORTY-ONE

At dawn, Vika's scar flared, and she knew that Nikolai's move had been made. She was also certain it was on the island, as sure as she knew that her hair was red. What Vika didn't know was how Nikolai had interpreted her island. She didn't even know herself whether she'd intended it as a means to cooperate or merely the next step in one-upmanship. Had she ruined their connection by fleeing the masquerade? Was Nikolai still merely an opponent? Or was he something more? Vika both feared and hoped for the latter option.

She climbed out of bed and peeked out of her curtains. It was barely light outside. And yet, she couldn't wait several more hours until the ferries began to run and someone could be convinced to take her to the island. She could, of course, go down to the dock and commandeer a boat for herself. But even that seemed too slow. If only she could evanesce.

But why not try? Ever since the Game began—ever since she'd moved to Saint Petersburg—Vika had felt stronger. Maybe it was being close to Nikolai, their magic magnifying against each other. Or maybe the challenge of the Game simply pushed her to be better. But whatever it was, it allowed her to perform enchantments greater than she'd ever created before and to get by on almost no sleep, even after conjuring an entire island.

Of course, in the past, she'd only been able to evanesce a few feet, and it would be a few miles to the island. But it was worth an attempt. If it didn't work, there was always a boat to steal.

Vika closed her eyes. She imagined herself disappearing and reappearing again on the new island.

Do it.

Do it.

Go . . .

She squeezed her eyes shut tighter. Nothing happened except everything got blacker.

Vika huffed and opened her eyes. Perhaps she *would* have to steal a boat.

Except I don't want to, she thought. She really, really wanted to evanesce. In fact, this intensity of wanting reminded her of the same spark she used to feel right before she mastered a new skill, like mending a fox's sprained ankle or beckoning the snow. It was a combination of pure will and the right moment that had allowed her to do those things. And now, with this increased power, with all this new energy from the Game . . . this was the moment. Vika *knew* this would be the moment she would learn to evanesce. It had to be.

Perhaps she needed to approach it differently. Rather than jumping from one place to the next, perhaps Vika needed to *feel* the sensation of evanescing, in order to coax it to happen. Provide her body with actual instructions, so to speak.

She closed her eyes again. But this time, instead of commanding her body to disappear and simply reappear, Vika first envisioned her body, whole, and then, when she could see every detail of herself, she began to think of her body not as one, but as an infinity of tiny pieces.

I am no longer Vika Andreyeva, she thought. *I am composed of minuscule bubbles.*

She felt herself begin to disintegrate.

And then she really did become those bubbles. *I am effervescent!* It made so much sense now. Vika was a master of the elements, and now she had become an element herself. She'd become a fizzy, magical rain.

The wind heard her desire to evanesce, and it whooshed through her window and blew her away.

The island, her thoughts whispered, and the wind obeyed, whisking her like champagne raindrops over Nevsky Prospect, past the colorful canals, and across the Neva River and bay. It carried her over the island and swirled down to the gardens. Then it deposited her dissolved quintessence at the foot of the main promenade.

Vika's sense of self was nebulous; if she'd had a head, it would have felt full of clouds. But although she was not much more than sparkling fog, she retained the impression that she used to be something more. *Come back together*, she thought, although she was not sure what it was that she was supposed to be.

The tiny bubbles, however, knew. She'd shepherded them all safely to the island, and one by one, they reunited.

She blinked, for a moment staring at her hands and feet as if she'd never seen them before. Then the memory of being human rushed back, and she laughed and wiggled her fingers and toes.

"I did it." Vika touched her arms and legs and neck and head, and yes, every single piece of her was there. She laughed again. She stretched and she spun, and she found that her body worked exactly as it should. "I did it!" She wasn't tired at all.

After another minute, she remembered to look around her, because she'd come to the island not for the experience of evanescing, but to uncover Nikolai's move. She stood at the beginning of the promenade in the middle of the island's gardens, and as she took in her surroundings, she gasped. Where there had been only a canopy of leaves when she'd left yesterday, golden globes now ornamented the branches, suspended by invisible string and floating in the breeze. The soft glow of the lanterns complemented the orange light of the rising sun.

Across the path from her was a new bench. Although Vika was not tired from the evanescing, her breath was a bit unsteady, as if her newly reconstituted lungs were still relearning how to breathe. So she walked over to the bench. It looked ordinary enough, except for a brass plaque on its seat back that said *Moscow* in both Russian and French. And magic wafted off the bench in a mist of pale-blue vapor.

Will this kill me if I sit?

No one answered except the larks and wrens she'd put in the trees, singing her favorite folk songs.

But Nikolai's magic reached out, the pale-blue mist curling in wisps around her. The tugging began again in the center of her chest.

So she took a deep breath and dropped down onto the bench. It was reckless, but Vika had done plenty of reckless things before, and for a great deal less in return.

As soon as she made contact with the wooden slats, her chest swelled with warmth as it had at the masquerade. At the same time, the park around her began to fade. Then, like a watercolor, a new scene filled in. She stood along the Arbat, the main thoroughfare of Moscow, surrounded by opulence. Corinthian columns and intricate mahogany veneers adorned the houses, and women in fashionable gowns strolled arm in arm along the street. The entire city had been rebuilt after its citizens had burned it down to prevent Napoleon from pillaging it, and here Moscow was, shiny and proud and new.

It was like being in a dream. Vika could scrape her boots against the dirt, feel the autumn chill upon her skin, even take in the rich smell of mushroom and meat pies wafting in the air. And yet, for all the reality of the scene, the people on the Arbat couldn't see her. When she said hello, they did not greet her.

She strolled away from the Arbat and continued walking until she came to Red Square. She marveled at the white Kremlin walls and paused to admire the red brick and the cupolas of St. Basil's Cathedral, built to resemble a bonfire rising to the sky. Vika had never been to Moscow, but it was beautiful to behold.

After a while, she had gotten her fill of churches and monuments and squares. She was ready to leave Moscow except . . . how? It was not as if Nikolai had provided an obvious exit. Her heart pounded faster. She looked all around her, at the people who could not see her and the city that was too fake to be real but too real to be feigned.

Oh, the devil, it was a trap. He'd finally caught her. Her stupid curiosity had led her here, and now she'd be stuck in Moscow forever. It was even worse than being confined, as Sergei used to say, to the jinni bottle that was Ovchinin Island. Now she was literally trapped on a bench in a dream.

A never-ending, lonely dream.

But wait. Dreams could be woken from. Right? Yes, please, please, please, be right.

Vika shook her head from side to side and yawned. She stretched her arms above her head and opened her eyes wide. A few seconds later, Moscow began to fade away, and reality and the island came into view again. She exhaled.

She was free.

And even better, it had not been a trick. Nikolai had not tried to hurt her, just as she had not tried to hurt him with this island. She sighed and leaned back against the bench.

Then it dawned on her how incredible it was what Nikolai had created.

There were other benches along the promenade. If this first one had been such a glorious rendition of Moscow, what else had he done? She stood and hurried across the gravel path—the benches zigzagged across the promenade, each fifty or so yards from the next—and wandered to the next bench.

A subtle fog hung over this one, too. Sea green, rather than blue. It also had a brass plaque on it, but instead of Moscow, it was labeled *Kostroma*. Kostroma was a small city at the junction of the Volga and Kostroma Rivers, and famous for the venerable Ipatievsky Monastery and the Trinity Cathedral, both beloved by the tsars. Had Nikolai been to all these places? A prick of jealousy twinged inside her.

She wanted to sit on the Kostroma bench, but she was still a little skittish from panicking inside Moscow. So she ran down the gravel path to look at the next one instead. *Kazan.* The largest city in the land of the Tatars, where mosques and Orthodox churches coexisted, and where the tsar had recently founded the Kazan Imperial University.

After Kazan came Samara, then Nizhny Novgorod, seat of the medieval princes, followed by Yekaterinburg on the Ural Mountains, the border of the European and Asian sides of the empire.

Vika spun in a circle in the middle of the promenade, looking at all the benches behind and in front of and around her, each with a different plaque and a different, subtle mist about it. "It's a dream tour of the wonders of Russia," she said aloud.

The next bench was Kizhi Island, known for its twenty-two-dome church constructed entirely of shimmering silver-brown wood, each piece painstakingly interlocked at the corners with round notches or dovetail joints. Legend had it that the builder used only one ax to construct the entire church, and when finished, tossed the ax into the nearby lake and declared that there would never be another ax like it.

Now that one, she would sit on. Maybe after she'd seen all the others. Vika was sure she could spend hours on Kizhi Island.

Next came benches for the crystal clear waters at Lake Baikal in Siberia, the glacier-capped Mount Elbrus in the Caucasus Mountains, and the Valley of Geysers on the Kamchatka Peninsula.

The second-to-last bench was not a historically significant location. It was not a particularly populous one, either. It was not as stunning as Lake Baikal or Mount Elbrus or the Kamchatka Peninsula, and hardly anyone knew it existed. But these were Nikolai's benches; he was the final arbiter of what qualified as a wonder of Russia. And he had decided this would be the penultimate one.

"Oh . . ." Vika pressed her hand to her necklace. A golden mist shimmered around the bench, as if swathing it in autumn sunset. It was Ovchinin Island.

She reached out and traced the brass plaque with her finger, following each engraved letter from beginning to end. She did this twice, and then she lowered herself onto the bench. All apprehension from the Moscow bench disappeared at the anticipation of this next dream.

As soon as she sat, the garden once again faded away. And when the fog burned off, a birch forest encircled her, and wolverines and foxes and pheasants cavorted at her feet.

"Home," she whispered.

She hiked through the woods, to a break in the trees, and looked out over the Neva Bay. Nikolai had captured the view of Saint Petersburg from Ovchinin Island flawlessly. He had also included her new island, a small isle of green in the middle of the deep-blue bay. She smiled but knitted her brow at the same time. It was an odd sensation, to know that she was actually on that island, and yet to feel that she was somewhere else, on the outside looking in.

She continued hiking, pushing her way through overgrown shrubbery and crossing a log over Preobrazhensky Creek. She came to the clearing where she'd emerged from the fire, where Nikolai and Pasha had first seen her. In

Nikolai's dream version, the trees still smoldered, and thin plumes of smoke trailed from the singed trunks into the sky.

There were also two patches of ice on the forest floor, with two pairs of footprints embedded in them, still fresh as if the boys standing there had recently fled. Vika laughed. How funny, the details he'd included just for her!

But what she wanted to see most was her house. Now that she was back on Ovchinin Island—or the daydream of the island—the yearning for home that she had been suppressing bubbled to the surface and propelled her toward the last hill of the forest. She began to run, as fast as she could.

As she ascended the hill, however, her vision started to blur. She tried to push onward, but the haziness continued, and although her feet moved, the setting remained the same and her progress halted. It was as if she ran the same spot on the hill over and over again.

Ah . . . this was the edge of Nikolai's knowledge, the perimeter of the Ovchinin Island he'd created. He had never been to her cottage, so he couldn't include it in his dream. All he could conjure was what he had personally seen and what he could embellish from his experience.

Vika stood another minute longer at the base of the hill, then shook herself awake and out of the scene before too much disappointment could set in. It was still a marvel what Nikolai had created; she couldn't fault him for failing to include her home. And perhaps it was better that her house remained absent, for soon the people of Saint Petersburg would be here on the island, sitting on these benches and walking through these same dreams. She wouldn't want them opening the cabinets and drawers in her house, even if they were imaginary.

There was only one more bench left on the promenade. Vika rose and approached it slowly, even considering
whether she ought to go back to the beginning and sit on
each of the other benches before she came to the end. But
she was already here. She sped up to discover what the final
bench held.

She stopped short when she saw it.

"No!"

Nikolai lay limp across the final bench, one arm falling off
the seat and dragging on the ground, and Vika dashed over,
visions of her tea leaves flashing through her head. *Death
is coming soon*, Renata had said. But Vika hadn't thought it
would be this soon.

She shook him, but he didn't react, and his chest didn't
rise and fall as it should have. There was no breath puffing
out into the chilly morning air. His dark hair fell in disarray
across his face.

How much energy had it taken him to create the dream-
state benches? All of it?

"Nikolai . . ." She touched her hand to his cold cheek.

But then his eyelashes fluttered.

And Vika gasped as she was towed into another dream.

CHAPTER FORTY-TWO

Nikolai was watching a golden eagle fly across a vast
plain when Vika appeared beside him.

"Nikolai!"

He turned and blinked at her. Her voice seemed too
loud in the quiet of the savanna. He took several steps back.
"Vika? How are you here?"

"The bench . . . I thought you were dead. I touched you,
and it brought me."

"I'm not dead."

She exhaled and touched her scar. "Thank goodness."

The walls he'd erected around his heart crumbled a little. He tried to remind himself that she was his opponent,
but it was difficult when she was right there. "I'm definitely
not dead. But I think I'm still asleep."

She looked around her and took in the surroundings.
"You're creating these benches in your sleep?"

He nodded.

"Amazing . . . Then this is a dream, too. Where are we?"

"The Kazakh steppe."

"It's beautiful."

His walls crumbled further. Nikolai knew he was being foolish, but like at the masquerade, he felt no desire to rebuild them. She was here. She'd been worried he was dead. He shoved aside the warnings blaring in his head.

"See the eagle?" He pointed upward at the stately bird soaring across the sky with its golden-brown wings outspread. "This is a special type of falconry. If you look carefully, you can see the eagle's master, the *berkutchi*, on his horse near the base of the mountain."

Vika squinted in the direction Nikolai was pointing. She nodded when she saw the stout man on horseback. "Yes, I see. I can barely make him out, but he's there."

The eagle glided above them without a sound. It flapped its wings on occasion but mostly used the wind to carry it across the clouds.

"There are many animals on the island where I live," Vika said. "They bring me their stomachaches and broken bones."

"To heal?"

Vika nodded, eyes still on the eagle in the sky. "I can do it if it's not too complicated a wound. A clean break or a straight cut."

Nikolai shook his head. "I didn't know enchanters could also be faith healers. I'm impressed."

She shrugged. "I don't think I'm a faith healer. They work with shifting energy, right? But what I do is different, and certainly based in magic. I imagine it's a bit like sewing. Matching up the fabric and the threads. Lining up the flesh and the veins. Although I'm wretched at creating clothes."

"Your masquerade gown was not wretched."

"It also wasn't fabric." She smiled.

Nikolai had to concede that she was right.

They watched the eagle as it soared farther across the plains. Vika turned her head to follow it. "I like this dream. The eagle hunting is stunning. This bench may be your best one."

"Thank you. There's actually an old Kazakh proverb that says, 'There are three things a real man should have: a fast horse, a hound, and a golden eagle.'"

Vika wrinkled her nose. "And what about a real woman?"

Nikolai laughed. "A real woman should have those things, too."

She watched as the eagle continued to glide over the steppe. "How do you know all this? How did you create all those benches? Surely you haven't traveled to each of the places you conjured. Unless you can evanesce there?" Her eyes widened.

Nikolai began to walk through the long, dry grass, and Vika followed. "No, I can't evanesce at all. I've tried. However, I have spent a great deal of time in libraries over the years, and I've also heard many stories from Pasha of his and his father's travels both abroad and within the empire. I gleaned all these details from them. Yet I cannot claim that my dream depictions are entirely accurate; I admit to taking a fair amount of artistic license, for much of what I have to base things on are paintings. But there are a few places I have actually been: Moscow, your island, and here."

"You've been to the steppe? But how? It's so far from Saint Petersburg."

Nikolai pulled on a strand of hair, which was neatly

combed, in contrast to the tired mess on his head on the other side of this dream. "Can you not tell from the near black of my hair? Or the shape of my eyes? The steppe is where I was born."

"You're Kazakh?"

"My mother was. She was a faith healer in one of the tribes. But she died when I was born."

"And your father?"

"Russian. But I never knew him."

Vika turned her eyes back up into the sky. "I never knew my mother."

Nikolai stopped and looked at Vika. "I'm sorry."

"Thank you. But it's all right. I've had my whole life to get used to it."

"I understand." And he did. Entirely.

She began to walk again. Nikolai watched as her dress swayed with each step, brushing against the tall grass, the brittle blades so high they rose almost to her hip. There were few girls he knew in Petersburg society who would traipse through the savanna without complaining about the burrs snagging their skirts or the dry wind mussing up their hair. But those thoughts didn't even seem to occur to Vika. She was a mythological creature among ordinary humankind.

She turned around to wait for him. "Is there more?"

"More what?"

"More of this dream?"

He nodded.

She held out her gloved hand. "Show me."

A smile began to spread across Nikolai's face, but he tamped it down. She was tempting—too tempting—and that was dangerous. He could enjoy her company, for now, but he had to remember this was part of the Game. Still, he jogged to catch up, and when he reached her, he took her outstretched hand.

He momentarily forgot how to breathe.

Her touch, even through their gloves, resonated to that ethereal part of his core he could only describe as his soul. He suspected that even his real body, asleep on the bench, warmed as her hand clasped his.

She blushed and looked at their entwined fingers. But she didn't unlace them.

"Come this way," he said, when he'd gathered himself.

Nikolai led her farther into the grassland, creating more of the dream as they trekked. He hadn't planned to expand this setting beyond watching the eagle hunting for prey, but then again, he hadn't accounted for Vika appearing in the dream with him and wanting to know more about his past. So now, as they walked, he filled out the landscape, not only stretching the barren plains and the mountains in the background, but also generating a yurt village in the near distance.

As they approached, a herd of sheep came into view, as well as a smaller herd of yaks some men on horseback were bringing home from pasture. There were boys there, too, about Nikolai's age, and for a second, longing flared inside him, desiring their simple existence. But then he remembered the reality of his life on the steppe, the looks of disdain—and fear—from the members of his tribe, and even the outright pretending he did not exist. No, Nikolai could never have been one of them.

He and Vika passed the animals unseen, although they could see and smell and hear everything around them, from the pungent scent of the livestock to the *zhauburek* kabobs roasting over the fire. A group of boys marched past, each carrying a younger boy on his shoulders and singing, *"Ak sandyk, kok sandyk . . ."* Nikolai almost started humming along before he caught himself.

"Are these memories from your childhood?" Vika asked.

"Yes."

"Do you miss it?"

Nikolai shrugged. "I think I see the past more kindly than it treated me."

She quirked a brow. "How do you mean?"

"I mean, when I was here, they didn't know what to do with me. Although my mother had some abilities as a faith healer, they were very different from the things I could do. And without a proper teacher to show me how to hone my skills and to discipline me, all I did was wreak havoc on the village."

"How?"

"All sorts of nonsense. I'd mute the *dombras*—they're guitar-like instruments—while the men tried to play music, or I'd turn the other children's suppers from rice into sand. Things like that."

Vika laughed. "It sounds amusing."

"Yes, well, the villagers didn't think so. They tried to beat the magic—the *demons*—out of me. They were glad when Galina came and took me away. What I have here in this dream, however, are the good parts I recall."

They walked into the center of the village, past yurts with elaborate wooden crowns and walls covered in bright embroidered fabric. There were lions and tigers and garudas stitched on the yurts, symbols of power, as well as pictures of fire, water, and earth, the elements of the universe. The village was a riot of colors and patterns.

"I understand why you think fondly of this place," Vika said as they neared a group of women cooking skewered meat over a fire. "Even if they didn't know what to make of you."

The wood crackled, and a log broke, sending up a plume of smoke. It smelled like charred memories. Then the wind blew the smoke away and left behind only the glowing embers.

"But I'm also glad the countess found you," Vika said.

Nikolai blushed, but it receded quickly. It was possible Vika didn't mean it the way he'd first interpreted. And that was why he was supposed to keep up the walls to protect himself.

She stopped walking. "Are you glad for the Game?" she asked.

Nikolai stumbled. Vika gripped him tighter and held him up so he wouldn't fall. Like when they'd met at Bolshebnoie Duplo, only with their roles reversed.

Nikolai wished, for a moment, that he could keep falling, and she could keep catching him.

But they couldn't. He stood, and she released his hand so he could brush the dirt off his trousers.

"Thank you," he said.

She nodded. But she did not reach for him again. Rather, she looked at him as if she expected something else.

All he wanted was her hand again, that quickening of his pulse when she touched him. But he answered her question instead. "No, I am not at all glad for the Game. Are you?"

Vika chewed on her lip as she considered. Finally, she

said, "Yes. I'm glad for it. I both love it and hate it. Which, I think, means I both love and hate myself. I *am* the Game, and the Game is me. This is what my whole life has led up to, and this will determine the rest of it."

Nikolai sighed. He knew she was right, despite these fleeting moments of peace they seemed to have. They would both continue to play the Game to win. His entire existence had been built upon fighting for this, fighting against powerlessness, fighting to be somebody who couldn't be ignored, and he wouldn't give it up so easily. He suspected Vika felt the same way. If only he'd never started calling her by her name.

But who was he kidding? He would've been drawn to her whether he'd said her name or not. Their enchantments might be pitted against each other, but they were also part of the same magic. Part of the same whole. It would make winning so much more bittersweet.

At that thought, the dream around them vanished suddenly. Nikolai found himself crumpled on the bench, with Vika kneeling at his side.

"What happened?" she asked.

"I . . . nothing. I just . . . I lost my grip." Nikolai pushed himself upright, but unlike in the dreamworld, fatigue saturated him, and he could hardly keep his eyes open.

"The benches have taken a great deal out of you," Vika said.

Why didn't creating the island do that to you? he wanted to ask, but he was so thoroughly exhausted, his mouth couldn't form the words.

"You should rest," Vika said.

"I'll sleep on the bench," Nikolai managed to whisper.

"No, people will be coming to the island soon. After all, you made a dock that invited them. You should rest in your own bed."

"It's too far."

"Not as far as you think." She laid her hand on his arm, and again he warmed at her touch. "Sleep well, Nikolai. You deserve it."

"I—"

But he didn't get the chance to finish, because she pushed him gently, and he exploded and imploded all at once. His eyes flew open as the world went completely white, and for an instant, he thought she had finally killed him.

But she had turned him into . . . bubbles?

He rematerialized a few seconds later, and his vision pieced itself together. He was standing at the steps outside the Zakrevskys' house.

"Vika?"

It took a minute for Nikolai to realize what had happened. He had been a person. And then he'd dissolved. Then come back together again.

"*Mon dieu!* She evanesced me." He shook his head and stumbled. His reconstructed hand shook as he tried to charm open the front door.

She was so powerful, she had evanesced him all the way home.

CHAPTER FORTY-THREE

Curtain rings scraped along their metal rod. Drapes parted, and the midday sun blazed into Nikolai's room, straight into his face. Renata stood over his bed.

"Argh, what are you doing?" He buried his face in his pillow.

"You need to get up."

"What time is it?"

"It's almost three in the afternoon."

"But how did you get in here?"

"You forgot to lock the door."

"What?" Nikolai rolled over and stared at his bedroom door. The five locks were indeed undone. How had he forgotten? He never forgot, even when it was only a single lock, not since Renata had discovered him in the midst of magic two years ago.

Then he remembered the island, and the benches, and it made some sense that he'd drowsed asleep without flipping the dead bolts. He flopped back onto his pillow.

"You're falling to pieces, Nikolai."

"Am I? I appear to be rather intact." He held out his arm to prove it. Which, however, reminded him of Vika evanescing him, and he drew his arm back close to his body, for perhaps he had fallen to pieces after all. Only, she had put him back together. This time.

"You know what I mean." Renata set a tray on the table by his bed. On it was a pot of tea, a section of baguette next to a dish of butter and jam, and a tiny pastry shaped like a swan. The swan swam in a dish of butterscotch. It literally swam.

"What is this?"

"Ludmila gave it to me. I mentioned you were ill, and she sent me home to nurse you, with this as medicine. Of course, that was hours ago. Lucky the swan isn't real. Its poor legs would have broken off from exhaustion by now."

Nikolai jolted up in bed. "How could you bring this here?"

Renata frowned. "What do you mean? It's only breakfast, well, afternoon tea, now. And I . . . Oh. Oh no." Her eyes grew wide.

"Precisely."

"It was enchanted by Vika. So I shouldn't have been able to bring it past the front door."

"Let alone into my room."

"What happened to your protections?"

Nikolai fell back against his pillows. "I fear I'm too weak to keep them up."

"But the Game! If you're not strong enough . . ." Renata stared at him, her mouth downturned.

He sensed the conversation was about to take a sad turn.

But Nikolai didn't want to talk about dying. Not again. "Could I have some tea?"

"Of course." Renata poured a cup for him.

"You won't read the leaves?"

"I won't read the leaves."

Nikolai nodded, although he did not drain the cup, just in case.

"Do you want the swan?" Renata asked. "Or should I decapitate it or something?"

The edge of Nikolai's mouth turned up, a hint of a smile. "No need for violence. But I . . . I can't eat it. I shouldn't. Who knows what would happen if I ingested her magic?" Yet there was a warmth in the pit of his stomach, a visceral desire to taste Vika's magic even if it poisoned him. He picked up the baguette and took a bite of it to smother the yearning.

Renata pushed the swan farther away. "Nikolai . . . There is something I need to tell you. I read her leaves two days ago."

"You what?" He sat up on the edge of his bed and almost knocked over the entire tray. He tossed the rest of the baguette onto its plate. "When? Why didn't you tell me?"

"I haven't had a chance to. You've either been asleep or gone. Vika paid a visit to the pumpkin and asked me to."

"What did they say? Or . . . do I not want to know?"

Renata stared at the carpet. "Oh, Nikolai. There was a knife in the inner circle. Death is coming for one of you soon." She flung herself at him and buried her face against his neck. So much for not talking about dying.

He wrapped his arms around Renata to soothe her. But he looked at the slim drawer of his desk, where the knife

Galina had given him rested, biding its time. The dagger that would not miss.

"I don't want either of you to die," Renata said into his collarbone, her breath hot right above his scar. "But especially not you." She held him tighter. "I love you."

Nikolai pulled back. Renata's bottom lip quivered as she held her arms out, not quite releasing their embrace even though he'd already broken away.

"I . . . Renata, you mean so much to me, but—"

"But what?"

"You shouldn't love me. It isn't wise."

"There's no wisdom in love." She watched him, her eyes rimmed with red. "But you love *her*, don't you?"

Nikolai said nothing.

"You've loved her since the first time you saw her."

"No." For that could not be true. Falling in love with Vika would mean a complete loss of control, and Nikolai did not lose control. It would also mean he'd given in to someone else, and he would not and *could* not trust someone else so entirely. It had always been himself, on his own; no one else was dependable. No one else would put his interests first. "Renata, you're one of my best friends." Nikolai reached for her. But she stood from the bed and backed away. "I'm sorry," he said.

She gathered his tray. "You don't need to apologize. It was silly of me to hope. I knew it all along."

"It's better for you not to love me. I'm doomed whether I live or die. You don't need to be a part of that."

"It doesn't matter, Nikolai. You're a part of me, whatever the outcome. If you die, a part of me dies. If you live but suffer over guilt from the Game, then I suffer as well."

"I am very sorry for that."

She shook her head. "I'm not." She took the tray of dirty dishes and strode to the door. "I don't regret loving you, Nikolai. It's always been in my leaves, and I wouldn't trade it for another cup." She opened the door and slipped out to the hall.

Nikolai looked after her long after she had gone. He did not relock his door.

CHAPTER FORTY-FOUR

The tsarina had been unwell for quite some time. This Pasha knew, as he had heard his mother muffling coughs into handkerchiefs at supper, seen her retire earlier and earlier from state functions, and watched her once-regal presence wilt into a near nonexistent one. Yuliana had commented on the tsarina's wan complexion as well, and Pasha himself had caught her once when she fainted during a stroll in the gardens.

Now Pasha strode into the small chamber his mother used for conducting business—the same room through which he'd sneaked the night of the ball—having been summoned by the tsarina in the middle of his meeting with the Spanish ambassador.

"You wished to see me, Mother?" Pasha asked as he strode up to the tsarina's desk. He took her gloved hand and kissed it.

"Yes, darling." There was no one else in the room but some of her attendants, and she waved them out. "I apologize for interrupting your meeting. This may be the only moment I have free before I leave."

"No apology necessary. The Spanish ambassador is a pompous bore, and Father had me meet with him only to keep the Spaniards out of his own hair. But did you say you're leaving? Where to? Are you sure you're fit to travel?" Pasha dragged a chair from the opposite side of the desk and set it next to his mother's. When he sat down, he took her hands and clasped them in his lap.

"The doctor has deemed it advisable to move me to warmer weather, now that October is ending and the chill has arrived. Your father and I shall depart for the South in two days' time."

"Forty-eight hours' notice? Why the rush?"

She frowned. "Your father has urgent business to which he must attend in the Crimea."

"Trouble with the Ottoman Empire."

"Yes, the situation is worsening." The wrinkles on her forehead pinched, making her look even more worn down. "He wants to see it for himself. You'll take care of the city and your sister while we're gone, will you not?"

"Yuliana does not need taking care of."

The tsarina laughed then, and her wrinkles unpinched. But her laughter was punctuated with hacking coughs.

Pasha winced.

She waved off his concern with her handkerchief. "I shall see you soon, all right?"

"All right." Pasha kissed his mother's hand again. For what could he say? She was his mother, but she was also the tsarina, and other than the tsar, the tsarina had the final word.

"Now if you will help me up, I need to check on how the staff is handling my luggage."

He stood and pulled her up. She needed a second to steady herself, and then he led her out of the room, into the hall. She clung to him for support the entire way to her rooms.

Pasha rowed toward the island with long, even strokes. It was not hard to know where to go; the island was lit with twinkling lanterns, luminescent against the black sky. He had been back to the island only once—the tsar had been trying his hardest to keep Pasha occupied—but unlike the first time, Pasha's second visit had been crowded, since the new dock allowed the rest of Saint Petersburg access.

And everyone had known he was the tsesarevich, for his Guard had accompanied him. It was impossible to enjoy the Dream Benches when he knew everyone would watch him, and besides that, Gavriil had refused to allow the tsesarevich to "fall under the influence of hallucinatory drugs." Pasha shook his head. As if the benches could be explained so simply! But the people of Saint Petersburg had convinced themselves that the colorful mists surrounding each bench were hallucinogens, and then they'd shown a surprising willingness to throw themselves into the experience anyway. *That in itself*, thought Pasha, *could be construed as magic*. He laughed aloud at the memory of the crowds of ordinarily staid Petersburgers, packing themselves ten people to a bench.

But at least now, in the middle of the night, Pasha would have the island to himself.

Or so he thought. When he rowed up to the dock, there

was something else tied to the pier. It was not a boat, per se. But rather, a leaf. A yellow birch leaf with its edges turned up, enlarged to the size of a small boat.

"Vika," he whispered.

He leaped out of his own skiff and secured it to the pier. Of course, it could be the other enchanter who was here, but Pasha had a feeling it was Vika. It was a birch leaf at the dock, and Vika came from an island covered in birches. It had to be her.

He ran toward the main path, leaving his dignity at the dock, the gravel crunching under his boots as he approached the promenade. The lanterns appeared to dance with the leaves in the breeze, the moonlight somehow not detracting from their brilliance, but adding to it. Pasha emerged from the trees to the center of the island, and it was there that he stopped short, on the walkway lined with benches.

Vika sat on the bench for Ovchinin Island.

Pasha slowed as he walked toward her so that he would not startle her with his presence. But she didn't look up, even though his boots seemed to pound on the path no matter how lightly he tried to tread, and he knew she must be immersed in a dream.

He hovered. He could sit next to her, and perhaps join her. He didn't know if each person had their own separate dream, or if you shared the same vision on the same bench. Of course, if he sat down, it might surprise her, and he had been attempting to avoid that all along.

"It's a tad eerie of you to stand there and watch me sleep," Vika said, her eyes still closed.

Pasha jumped. Ironic that *he* had been the one trying not to startle *her*.

She opened her eyes and smiled.

Pasha recovered himself and bowed. "It's a pleasure to see you again, Vika."

"And you as well, Pasha."

He straightened. "How did you know I was here?"

"I have a knack for sensing anomalies in my magic."

"Ah. So I am an anomaly. And the benches are yours, not the other enchanter's."

She laughed. "Oh, goodness, no to both. You're an anomaly only to the extent that you are *not* my magic, and thus, I can feel when you—or anyone—is there, if I so choose. And the benches are not mine. The island, yes. But the benches . . . I couldn't create something so magnificent."

"I would venture to say the island itself is quite magnificent."

"Thank you." Vika stood and straightened her skirt. "I'm rather pleased with it myself."

"Is that your leaf at the dock?" Pasha pointed in the direction from which he'd come.

"Yes, I've been experimenting with different modes of transportation. Do you like it?"

"Very much."

"I could make one for you."

"I think Gavriil would die of fright."

Vika tilted her head. "Gavriil?"

"The captain of my Guard. He doesn't like it when I try new things. A boat made of a leaf, I think, may push him to the limits of his tolerance."

"You may assure him it is entirely safe."

"I have no doubt. Perhaps I ought to send him out on the leaf first, to prove its sturdiness."

Vika laughed, and Pasha did, too. She sparkled like the lanterns under the moonlight.

"Have you tried the benches?" she asked.

"No. Gavriil wouldn't let me when so many people were around during the day. Have you been through all the dreams?"

"Yes, and some more than once. They are all astounding."

Pasha glanced over his shoulder at the benches he had passed on his way to Vika. "Which is your favorite? Besides the obvious?" He dipped his head toward the Ovchinin Island bench on which she sat.

"The steppe," she said without pause.

"Interesting. I have a friend who is originally from the steppe. You met him, actually, at the ball. Nikolai. He was the harlequin."

Vika paused, and for a moment she seemed as frozen as her dress had been that night. But then she was herself again. "Right. The harlequin. I think I remember him. Remarkable dancer."

"Indeed. He is always popular with the girls at balls." Pasha watched her closely for her reaction.

"Is he?" Vika's expression remained even and bland. It was as if she were neither impressed nor unimpressed, as if Nikolai wasn't memorable to her at all. Pasha exhaled.

"But enough about Nikolai. Could we sit on the bench with the steppe dream? Would you show me around?"

Vika furrowed her brow. "Actually . . . if you don't mind, I was rather fancying a walk. I've been sitting here for a while. Or if you'd rather have some time alone with the benches—"

"No. A walk sounds perfect." Pasha offered her his arm, and she linked hers through his.

They strolled down the rest of the promenade, past the last bench, the one that contained the dream of the steppe, and turned left onto another path.

"Why did you come to the island in the middle of the night?" Vika asked. "To experience it without Gavriil watching? And how *did* you escape his watch? I would think a tsesarevich would be closely guarded."

"They try, but I know secret passageways in and out of the palace of which they are unaware. In general, they don't report my absences, for at best they would appear to be fools, and at worst they would be disgraced and lose their positions. So in exchange for them 'forgetting' on many occasions to inform my father when they lose track of me, I return unscathed each time."

"A risky bargain, but I suppose I understand. You haven't answered my other question, though. Why are you here?"

"I may ask the same of you."

"I couldn't sleep."

"Nor could I."

They walked on for a while without speaking. Vika looked up at the lanterns, while Pasha took pleasure in the weight of her arm against his. There were many layers of cloth that separated them, but he swore his skin tingled at her touch anyway. His pulse definitely thrummed faster. It was a welcome distraction from worrying about his mother.

When they turned onto another path—this one, Pasha recalled, led to a grove of maple trees—Vika said, "You have a great deal on your mind."

Pasha started. It was the second time she had surprised him in half an hour. "Are you also a mind reader?"

"No. I hate to tell you, but your face gives everything away. There's so much tension in your jaw, and you have a groove chiseled into your forehead. Not to mention your hair. Do you always pull it when you worry?"

Pasha shook his head. "You are remarkable."

"Merely observant."

He sighed as they stepped into the maple grove. "It's just that my mother is very ill," Pasha said. "It has been one thing after another, and the doctors are at their wits' end. Their last hope is to send her to the South in hopes the warmer weather will do her good. I love her dearly, so I, too, hope it is the cure, but the truth is, I doubt it. Her problems began long before autumn arrived."

Pasha released Vika's arm and began to pace along the path. He thought of his mother's life; it had not been easy to live in the Winter Palace with his father. The tsar had had many well-known affairs. Other children, borne by other women. The tsarina could have left and taken Yuliana with her, but Pasha would have had to remain behind as official heir to the throne. As such, his mother had stayed and abided a mountain of insult and indignity for the love of her son.

"I wish there were some miracle that could heal her."

"Are you asking me to use magic on her?" Vika asked.

Pasha stopped his pacing. Hope caught in his throat. "Can you?"

Vika exhaled slowly and rubbed a spot just under the collar of her coat. She took several more breaths before she replied. "I can heal cuts and broken bones, but what ails your mother sounds much deeper. I think I'd do her more harm than good."

"Oh."

"I'm sorry. Magic is not always the answer. It's old and very complicated, and comes tied with many strings. Even this"—she tapped the knot of the maple tree, which began to pour amber liquid into a bucket below—"one of Ludmila's innocent ideas, has consequences greater than syrup."

"What do you mean?"

Vika pointed up at the branches of the maple. The green leaves that swayed in the wind began to blur, then vanish. They were replaced by dead limbs.

"What . . . how did you do that?"

"The leaves are a mirage. These trees have actually been drained completely of life."

"In order to create one thing, you had to sacrifice another."

"Yes. Sometimes, magic is deadly." She frowned.

Pasha eyed her. "Are you telling me you're dangerous?"

Vika's frown vanished, and she laughed, almost too wildly given what they'd just been talking about. "Quite so. But I'm no danger to you."

The moon shifted then, and its light slivered through the bare maple branches and landed in pale stripes on Vika's face. It highlighted her delicate cheekbones. It emphasized her otherness. Pasha couldn't resist stepping closer to her. He reached out to touch her face.

"Please don't," she whispered.

"I'm sorry, I just—"

She didn't move away as his fingers hovered next to her cheek, aching to brush against her skin. But she said, "I mean, you don't want this."

"What if I do?" He wanted to kiss her. And not just her lips, although he wanted that, badly. He also wanted to kiss her neck, to peel away her coat and touch his mouth to her pale shoulders. He wanted to feel the softness and warmth of her skin. Pasha leaned closer.

This time, Vika backed away. "Trust me, you don't. I'm too complicated. I am bound by too much not in my control."

Pasha sighed. He, too, was bound. By his father. By duty. By the people of an entire empire. He wondered what trappings hindered Vika.

"There's no such thing as simplicity," he said.

She took off her glove and ran a finger through the trickle of maple syrup, frowning at the crystallized lumps in it. "I'm beginning to fully comprehend that."

"I like you," he said. "More than like you."

She shook her head slightly, but more to herself than to him. "I don't want to like you."

"But you *do*?" Pasha went to run his hand through his hair, but caught himself before he gave his nerves away.

"Doesn't everyone?"

"I'm only asking about you."

Vika focused on a deformed crystal of syrup on her thumb. "I'm not in a position to fall in love. With you, or with anyone else."

If he could, Pasha would have sucked the sugar off her finger. But it wasn't appropriate, and she'd made it clear she wasn't interested, so he settled for removing his glove and wiping the sugar crystal off her fingertip, lingering for a second as their hands touched. Even that sent sparks through every one of Pasha's nerves.

"Will you tell me if that ever changes?" he said, his voice a touch hoarse.

She frowned. "I doubt it will."

"But if it does?"

She looked up at Pasha, and it took everything in him not to bend down and steal a kiss. "Yes," she said. "If it changes, I will tell you."

He sighed again.

"You have a lot weighing on you," Vika said. "I'll leave you to enjoy the island and sort through your troubles. I hope for the best for your mother."

"You don't have to go—"

But she had already vanished. How? Now Pasha allowed his hand to run through his hair. It was the third time in an hour she had startled him.

He dashed to the other end of the island to the pier, and there she was, already halfway across the bay on her leaf. He watched her all the way until she made it to the opposite shore.

She was unlike any girl he had ever known. And likely would ever know. His nerves were still on edge from their encounter.

He started to head back toward the main promenade, perhaps to sit on the steppe bench or the Ovchinin Island one. Vika was right. Pasha did have a great deal to ponder. But as he walked, he turned to look at the water one last time. She was gone, but her presence was not.

Tied to the dock was a gift. His own enchanted leaf.

CHAPTER FORTY-FIVE

In his study, the tsar pored over his maps of the Crimea, as well as his generals' most recent reports on the activities of the Ottomans. It was as Yuliana had warned. He should have made this trip south a while ago.

There was a gentle knock from the hall. Followed by a cough, weaker yet louder than the knock. The tsar hurried to open the door.

The tsarina smiled and coughed again into her handkerchief.

"Elizabeth, my dear," the tsar said, offering his arm and leading her to the armchair by his desk. "Why are you here? It's late. You ought to be in bed."

She wore a white dressing gown with lace at the collar and sleeves. Her hair was swept up in a loose bun. When younger, she'd been known as one of the most beautiful women in Europe. But even now, older and ill, she was arresting. "I just wanted to see you, love," she said.

The tsar kissed her on the top of her head. He had

disregarded her for decades; they had married too young, when he was fifteen and she only fourteen, and the tsar had openly had many affairs. But age had worn him down—as had politics and too many wars—and in the end, it was Elizabeth he wanted. She had been regal and patient through everything, and when he came back to her, she forgave him his trespasses right away. The tsar was not so kind to himself.

"I am looking forward to the Sea of Azov with you," he said.

"As am I, love. You deserve the rest."

"There is no rest for the tsar. But at least I will be with you."

Elizabeth nodded. But then she coughed into her handkerchief again.

"Are you all right?"

"Yes . . ." She wheezed as she drew in a shallow breath and devolved into another fit of coughing so deep, blood sputtered from her throat.

"You need the doctors—"

"No." Elizabeth waved her handkerchief at him. "I'll be fine. I only need you and the sun in the South." She leaned her cheek on the tsar's arm. "Will you help me to my room, love?" Her voice frayed at the edges.

He softened. "Of course, dear." He pulled her up to her feet, but she stumbled and collapsed against him.

"I'm sorry," she whispered.

The tsar shook his head. Then he wrapped one arm around her shoulders and slipped the other behind her knees. She had lost so much weight, he lifted her as easily as if she weren't even there.

What a wicked twist of fate that Elizabeth might be ripped away from him when he had only now begun to appreciate her. He needed to get her to the South as soon as possible. It was the only hope of saving her.

As he carried her out of the study and into the hall, the captain of his Guard fell in line behind him. The tsar didn't even look at him as he gave his order: "Get me Nikolai Karimov and Vika Andreyeva. Immediately."

CHAPTER FORTY-SIX

The guard led Vika through the Winter Palace, past all the paintings and mirrors and wall upon wall of windows, all dark at this hour of night, until they reached a door flanked by more guards. They nodded at the soldier who escorted her, and he opened the doors and let her in.

Vika's stomach had been in knots since the moment the guard appeared at her flat, and she'd hardly breathed the entire carriage ride here. The streets of Saint Petersburg had passed in a blur of nondescript night, and all she could think was that the Game was over. Either she or Nikolai was done. The tsar would declare a winner and a loser tonight.

But as she stepped into the room in the palace, some of the tension in her body eased. For this was no stern throne room. With its peach silk drapes and pale-yellow furniture and the scent of roses perfuming the air, it seemed completely opposite of a place from which the tsar would sentence one of the enchanters to die.

"You may sit until the others arrive," the guard said.

Vika didn't feel like sitting. Although the surroundings placated her a little, her nerves still jangled. But she sat on a daffodil-colored settee, because the guard wore a sword on his hip that she was quite certain he would use should she prove to be anything other than compliant.

Vika listened to the small clock in the nearby cabinet tick.

Tick.

Tick.

Tock.

Tick.

Tick.

Tock.

Three hundred and fifty-two excruciating ticks and tocks later, Nikolai arrived.

"Vika," he said as the guard who'd escorted him closed the door to the room. Nikolai's face was composed, elegant as ever, but the slight quaver in his voice betrayed him.

"Fancy seeing you here," Vika said, trying to lighten the sense of impending doom before it crushed them both. "You manage to dress impeccably, even in the middle of the night. Although I can't say I'm surprised."

His carefully controlled rigidity cracked, and he gave her his shy smile. "You look lovely, as well."

"I thought I might attempt to be presentable if I'm to die."

Nikolai's smile wilted. Vika bit the inside of her cheek. So much for witty banter saving this night.

"Do you know why we were summoned?" Nikolai asked. He didn't sit in any of the chairs, and the guard did not command him to.

Vika shook her head. "I haven't a clue."

An interior door burst open at that moment—Vika and Nikolai must have been in an antechamber of some sort—and the tsar strode out. Vika's stomach again leaped to her throat. Nikolai gripped the back of a chair and appeared equally ill. But somehow, they both managed to curtsy and bow to the tsar.

"Rise," he said. Then he waved his guard out of the room. When the soldier had shut the door firmly behind them, he said, "This is not about the Game, enchanters, so you can stop looking like cattle going to slaughter."

Oh, thank heavens. Vika exhaled. Although the image of cattle going to slaughter stuck with her. It might not be tonight, but it would be some night (or day) not too far away.

"The tsarina is unwell," the tsar continued, "and she and I need to go to the South, to the restorative weather of the Sea of Azov. But I fear she will not survive a weeks-long carriage ride. Therefore, I need your help."

Nikolai bowed his head. "Your Imperial Majesty, I am happy to be of service. I can enchant your coach to carry you there faster."

The tsar grunted. He turned to Vika. "And you? Can you do any better?"

Vika bristled. Was this part of the competition, or was it not? The tsar had claimed it was not technically part of the Game. So why did it still seem as if she and Nikolai were being pitted against each other?

And yet this was what Vika had always wanted. To use her magic for the tsar. Perhaps she could heal the tsarina.

But, no. From what Pasha had told her on the island, the tsarina's condition was far more dire than anything Vika had worked on before. Mending the broken bones and stomachaches of animals was nothing compared to healing a sickness that even doctors could not cure. And Vika did not want to make a mistake. What if she made the tsarina worse? What if she killed her?

But the tsar hadn't asked Vika and Nikolai to cure the tsarina. He'd asked them to get her to the Sea of Azov.

"I can evanesce—magically transfer—you and the tsarina, Your Imperial Majesty," Vika said. But she didn't look at Nikolai. She didn't want to see if she'd upset him by showing him up.

"You can do that?" The tsar raised his brows.

"Yes, Your Imperial Majesty."

"Will it hurt the tsarina?"

"I . . ." Vika wasn't sure. She'd only evanesced someone else once. And really, she'd only ever evanesced herself twice, if she didn't count the two-foot experiment at Preobrazhensky Creek when she was younger. Blazes, what had she just committed herself to?

"No," Nikolai said, his tone steady. "It will not hurt the tsarina when Vika evanesces her. It's mildly disorienting, but not painful." Nikolai glanced over at Vika and gave her a subtle nod.

She felt the tug at her chest again, that connection to him, and she smiled. He wasn't angry that her solution to the tsar's problem was better. He supported her. Vika stood taller. Nikolai's confidence in her shored up her own.

"Very well then," the tsar said. "I shall make arrangements so the rest of our belongings will follow by coach, but the tsarina and I will leave tonight."

The tsar marched to the door that led to the hall and

300

flung it open. He gave orders to the guards stationed outside. A minute later, he strode back into the room, straight past Vika and Nikolai, and walked through the other, interior door into a different room.

"I suppose everyone will just think they left in the night for a romantic rendezvous," Nikolai said quietly.

Vika flushed. Not at the thought of the tsar and tsarina running away together, but at the sudden fantasy of her and Nikolai, escaping the city and the Game for their own secret tryst. She remembered what it felt like even just holding his hand in the steppe dream, how keenly aware she'd been of every single point at which his glove had pressed into hers. How her skin had tingled beneath the satin. How her composure had dissolved to jelly.

Now she looked up to find Nikolai watching her, and the heat rose in her cheeks again. He couldn't know what she was thinking, could he?

He smiled, then looked away.

Oh, mercy.

Soft coughing came from the room inside. Then, a minute later, the tsar reappeared, his countenance much softened, with the tsarina clutching his arm. They were quite a picture, him in his formal military uniform with his brow knitted tight with worry, and her in her white nightgown, smiling kindly but looking anything but regal. Vika pulled herself together to refocus on the task at hand. Scandalous thoughts about other enchanters would have to wait.

"I am sorry to trouble you at this hour," the tsarina said to Vika and Nikolai. "But Alexander said you could help me."

Alexander. How humanizing to hear the tsar referred to by his name. For the first time, Vika saw him as simply another person, not the heaven-appointed ruler of an empire, and not the final arbiter of the Game.

"Yes, Your Imperial Majesty," Vika said. "I believe I can help."

"Are you a doctor?"

Vika shook her head at this gentle, frail woman who had thought Vika's snowy gown at the ball had been a mere illusion of fabric. "No, Your Imperial Majesty. I am not a doctor."

"My dear," the tsar said, "these two are enchanters. They work with magic."

"Magic?"

He squeezed her hand. "Yes. Magic. It's real."

The tsarina's eyes widened, and Vika could see Pasha in her expression. That innocent wonderment at the existence of "otherness" in their previously ordinary world.

"I am going to evanesce you to the Sea of Azov," Vika said.

"Oh, my. What does that mean? And . . . right now?"

"It means I will magically transport you there, whenever you are ready."

"What do you need me to do?" the tsarina asked. "How will it feel?"

"You don't need to do anything," the tsar said. "Correct?" He directed the question at both Vika and Nikolai.

Nikolai stepped forward. "Your Imperial Majesty, do you like champagne?"

She smiled up at him. "I do."

"Well, evanescing is a bit like being transformed into champagne. Vika's magic will turn you into tiny bubbles, and you will fly through the air, a bit giddy and a great deal effervescent, all the way to the sea. And then when you arrive, you'll morph from bubbles back to yourself again, with the tsar by your side."

The tsarina smiled even brighter. "I rather like the idea of being champagne." She turned to Vika. "All right. I am ready."

"Your Imperial Majesty, just one thing, if I may . . . ," Nikolai said.

The tsarina nodded.

He flicked his wrist and transformed her nightgown into a burgundy traveling dress. A thick mink coat appeared as well and settled on her shoulders.

The tsarina gasped, but clapped her hands, delighted. "I should have thought to change. How silly to travel in a nightgown."

Nikolai dipped his head and smiled. "Even evanescing ought to be done in style, Your Imperial Majesty."

She smiled back kindly at him. "Indeed." She turned to Vika. "I believe Alexander and I are truly ready now."

The tsar nodded, himself pulling on a fur-lined greatcoat.

Vika glanced at Nikolai. Again, he gave her his subtle nod, his confidence. She turned to the tsar and tsarina.

One breath. Two breaths. Three . . .

And she evanesced the tsar and tsarina out of the Winter Palace, all the way to the sea.

CHAPTER FORTY-SEVEN

Sergei cried out from his bed. Galina dropped the armload of firewood she was moving near the fireplace—with nothing else to do in Siberia, and with Sergei indisposed, she had begun finding solace in the daily chores of their household—and rushed to his side.

His forehead beaded with sweat, and his black eyes were open but seemed not to see her. "Galina . . ."

"Shh, *mon frère*." She dipped a nearby washcloth in a basin of water and dabbed it on his head. "I'm right here."

"Something happened. There's no more." Delirium tinged his whisper.

The composure Galina had been trying to keep fell from her face. Her jaw tightened. "No more what?"

"No more of me left." He rolled toward the sound of her voice, his eyes still unseeing. "Tell Vika the truth about who I am. Who she is. And tell her I loved her."

Galina dropped the washcloth back in the basin. "Sergei, no."

"I am finished."

"No! I shall write to the tsar. I'll request that he declare a winner and end the Game. You will recover."

"Hm?" Sergei grunted.

"You'll get better."

But he ignored her. It was as if his ears were failing him, as well. "Tell Vika I am proud of her. And not to be upset at me for the bracelet, and for not telling her about me, or about her mother. I did it all because I love her."

"Sergei . . ."

His eyes drifted closed. Then they flitted open again, only to droop and fly open once more.

"Please don't go," Galina whispered.

"Sing to me," he said.

She swallowed the dread lodged in her throat, and she began to sing his lullaby. Her voice carried out from the cabin across the fields of snow.

> *Na ulitse dozhdik,*
> *S vedra polivaet,*
> *S vedra polivaet,*
> *Zemlyu pribivaet.*

Sergei sighed when she finished, and she tucked the sheets tightly around him. "Sing again," he said.

So Galina did.

At the end of the song, Sergei let out a low moan. Buzzards screeched outside. And then the light in Sergei's eyes snuffed out.

Her brother was gone.

She buckled on the bed beside him and cradled him in her arms. And for the first time since their father died, Galina cried.

CHAPTER FORTY-EIGHT

The night was shaded in midnight blue, and quietude kissed the air. Moonlight shimmered upon Saint Petersburg's streets, and sleepy ripples rolled through its canals.

There was no one out at this hour but the two enchanters. Nikolai smiled as Vika's footfalls on the cobblestones fell into sync with his. Unintentional and yet so inevitable.

After the tsar and tsarina had gone, he and Vika had taken a winding path through the city. Neither of them spoke, but they were both content with having no real destination at all. The Game was still upon them, of course, but the restlessness, the disquiet it normally inspired, had lifted, at least for now.

Nikolai watched as Vika moved beside him, impossibly light, impossibly strong. She had evanesced two entire people to the southern edge of the empire. She was a marvel. She was magic itself.

She glanced over at him and smiled.

If only tonight could stretch on forever, Nikolai thought.

But suddenly, Vika gasped. She grabbed onto the leather bracelet around her wrist. Her knees gave way beneath her, and she collapsed.

It was so fast, Nikolai didn't have time to catch her. Her head slammed into the cobblestones. If not for the embankment, she would have tumbled into the canal.

Nikolai rushed forward. "Vika, are you all right?"

But she didn't move or even murmur. She lay limp on the ground with one arm hanging over the embankment, her fingers dangling over the canal. Nikolai's own heart pounded as he reached to take her pulse.

It was there. Stuttering, like a broken metronome, but there. Barely.

Thank the heavens.

He scooped her up and cradled her against his body, and for a moment her magic, albeit weak, meshed with his, and he felt again that hot jolt like their connection at Pasha's ball. And then, as quickly as it had come, it was gone, and Vika was just an unconscious girl in his arms.

Nikolai held her tighter. "It'll be fine," he said, both to Vika and to himself, as he hurried toward the Zakrevsky house, which was only a few blocks away. "Everything will be fine."

But that was a lie, for there was nothing about him and Vika that would ever be fine. What a fool he'd been to think tonight could be any different.

When they arrived at his house, he charmed open the front door, hurled away all the protection charms he'd cast, and rushed her straight upstairs to his room. The door swung shut behind him.

"Vika," he whispered.

She didn't respond. Her head lolled over his arm. She was a rag doll.

He laid her down gently on his bed and covered her with a wool blanket. "Vika," he said, louder now. But still there was no response. He checked her pulse again. It stammered, but it was there.

He tried shaking her softly, careful not to jostle too hard. Nothing.

If only he could see inside her, like she could when she healed animals, then he could figure out what had gone wrong and how to fix it. He squeezed his eyes shut and tried. But he couldn't; it was all just a mass of red muscle and pink organs and crisscrossing veins. Living things were messy. It wasn't like seeing through the straight walls of a library at all.

He rubbed his eyes with the heels of his hands. *Think. If I can't use magic, then what? What would an ordinary person do?*

There was a girl who worked in the kitchen, one of Renata's friends, who constantly fainted. The cook kept smelling salts around to revive her.

Yes. Try that.

Nikolai opened his eyes and snapped his fingers. A silver vial of smelling salts appeared. He fumbled with the cap, and it clattered to the floor when he finally wrenched it off.

He wafted the salts under Vika's nose. "Wake up. Wake up. Wake up."

After a few passes, she stirred, and her eyes flickered open. "Nikolai?"

"I thought I'd lost you." He dropped onto the bed beside her. The knot in his chest unraveled.

"Where am I?"

"In my room. Thank goodness you're all right." This wasn't the death Vika's tea leaves had foretold. Nikolai threw the smelling salts onto his nightstand. He didn't care that they spilled.

"What happened?"

"You fainted."

"Oh." Vika's eyes fell closed. "Yes. I remember now." The red of her hair spread like blood against his white pillowcase.

It was so beautiful, and so . . . baleful. He had to touch it. His fingers reached out.

But her eyes opened again, and he stopped. He stuffed his hands beneath him and sat on them to restrain himself. "Are you all right?" he asked instead.

"I . . . I don't know. It felt like something latched onto me and sucked all my energy away. It happened so quickly." She passed her hands over her face and her torso, as if checking for abrasions. Her right hand circled her left wrist. "My bracelet. It's gone."

"What?" Nikolai whirled to his desk. Had something happened to both their gifts? He uncharmed the drawer and threw it open.

But his knife was still there in the hidden compartment. It seemed intact and untampered with. He slid his drawer shut again and charmed the lock. Then he turned back to Vika, who had drifted off again. "Vika," he whispered. "Was the bracelet enchanted? Did it have any special power?"

"I don't know."

"How could it have fallen off?" He remembered how tightly it had cinched to her wrist at Bolshebnoie Duplo.

And she'd been holding it when she collapsed by the canal.

"I don't know." Vika turned her head and coughed.

"I'm sorry. This isn't the time to interrogate you." He swirled his hand in the air, and a glass appeared in it. "Here. Water."

"Thank you." She managed to sit up and take a sip. Then she rested heavily against his headboard, as if even that small movement was too much work. "I haven't been this weary since the Game began. I feel . . . inadequate."

He looked again at her hair, and its fierceness—from the red down to the black stripe—seemed to represent everything she was. "You're anything but inadequate. You conjured an entire island. You evanesced the tsar and tsarina. Even now, your color is returning. You're not at all as weak as you think."

But as he said it, conflict again knotted in Nikolai's chest. For part of him wanted Vika weak enough so he could win the Game, but that part of him was rapidly losing ground to the part that wanted her to keep on fighting, to continue sparring with him.

And to the part of him that wanted to kiss her. That wanted to ask her to stay, to put out the candles and see what happened if the scars of two enchanters touched in the night.

The ground beneath him trembled at the thoughts. In fact, the entire room shifted. The paintings on his wall tilted. The glass of water spilled. Even the armoire moved several feet. Nikolai tried to clear his mind.

There are things more dangerous than a little magic, he thought.

Vika tensed on the bed, and he could sense a new shield

around her, stuttering. "What are you doing?" she whispered.

Nikolai shook his head, and the earth ceased its shaking. "I'm sorry. I was just thinking."

She scrutinized him for a second, then released the flimsy shield she'd cast around herself. "You have forceful thoughts."

Never had a statement been so true. Deuces, he wanted to kiss her. Touch her. More.

"Be careful," Vika said, still eyeing him from his bed. *His bed!*

"With what?" he managed to say without his voice pitching high or revealing too much. Or so he hoped.

"With thinking," she said.

Nikolai nodded. "I know." He turned away from her and tried to focus on the wall. On something plain and quotidian and not tantalizing at all. "Thinking can be a perilous sport."

CHAPTER FORTY-NINE

As soon as the sun rose, Aizhana heard the news of the tsar and tsarina's departure.

It would have been easier if the tsar had stayed put in the capital. It would have made killing him much simpler. However, the past eighteen years had been anything but simple, and Aizhana would not let a small bump in her plans derail her.

She stowed away on the caravan of luggage at the Winter Palace. She would follow the tsar and tsarina to the South. They would not foil her vengeance so easily.

CHAPTER FIFTY

Two days after Vika's uncharacteristic fainting incident, an envelope flew through the air and tapped its corner against her kitchen window. Vika leaped to open the glass pane and let the letter inside.

"What is it?" Ludmila asked.

The envelope was covered in frost, and the return address said only *Siberia*.

"It must be Father." Vika smiled so brightly, the muscles in her face ached.

"How do you know?"

"Who else in Siberia would charm a letter to me this way?"

What was inside? Where precisely *was* Sergei, and what had he been doing all this time? Vika tried to tear the envelope open, but her hands trembled, and her fingers acted as if they'd been reduced to useless sticks. She dropped the letter, and it skittered across the tiles, under the table.

Vika crawled to retrieve it. The talon-shaped table legs

seemed to stretch their claws at her. She scrambled to snatch the precious letter from their clutches.

When she had the envelope again, she tossed it into the air and flicked her middle finger and thumb at it. The wax seal broke, and the stationery inside slipped out and somersaulted down to Vika's hands. She unfolded it along its deep creases.

But the letter was not in Sergei's handwriting. It was something both harsher and more looping. Galina's.

The bottom dropped out from Vika's stomach.

Dear Vika,

We are not ordinarily to communicate with the enchanters during the Game, but in this instance, I believe the rules will permit it of me.

I am writing with the sad news that Sergei has passed. He wanted to let you know he was proud of you, and that he loved you as if you were his own.

Which brings me to another difficult point. On his deathbed, Sergei expressed his wish that I tell you the truth of your origins. He was not, in fact, your father. Like me, he was a mentor, and he found you on the face of a volcano, abandoned by a nymph. The identity of your father is unknown. But Sergei considered you his daughter until the end, and he wanted you to know he was sorry he deceived you. He had thought, perhaps wrongly, that it was for the best.

My brother's death is as much a shock to me as I am certain it will be to you. My apologies that this letter does not bear a happier report.

With condolences,
Galina Zakrevskaya

The letter tumbled to the floor. There was no magic to suspend it. Vika stood paralyzed in the center of the kitchen.

There were no thoughts.

Ludmila picked up the letter and read it, a fat tear rolling down her cheek as she finished. She placed her plump hands on Vika's shoulders and steered her to her bedroom.

"Sit," Ludmila commanded.

Vika did as she was told.

Ludmila collapsed on the bed beside her. The mattress heaved with her weight.

"Come here, my sunshine." She gathered Vika to her bosom. Vika did not resist.

There was nothing, nothing, nothing.

Nothing except Sergei being gone.

CHAPTER FIFTY-ONE

Nikolai sat restlessly at a table in the corner of the Imperial Library's public reading room. It had been a week since Vika evanesced the tsar and tsarina—and nearly two since Nikolai created the Dream Benches—but Vika still had not taken her fourth turn in the Game. So Nikolai tried to pass his time here in the library until his scar alerted him that it was his turn, but he fidgeted so much that another patron complained, and the librarian had to ask Nikolai to relocate.

Now he stared again at the words in a book of French poetry, but he couldn't make any sense of the verses. Why would a woman be compared to a carriage wheel? Or death to an otter in a creek? He considered going back to perusing the tomes on the occult throughout European history. They were soporific, but at least they seemed based in reality.

However, his thoughts wandered to Vika instead. At first, Nikolai had thought she needed time to recover after fainting by the canal. But then he remembered that she'd walked out of his house the other night almost her old self. She'd been a bit shaky, but nothing a little sleep wouldn't fix. After all, she was the girl who'd conjured an entire island after a night at Pasha's ball. She was not easily fazed.

Where was she? Even Ludmila's pumpkin was closed. Perhaps that was it, something had happened with Ludmila, and Vika had gone to help her. It made sense. (He'd conjured a few new stone birds—harmless ones—but they hadn't seen any sign of Vika, or Ludmila either.)

Nikolai pressed his fingers into his temples, so hard he actually drew blood from his skin. *You have to stop obsessing.* Having Vika in his bedroom had scrambled his brain. He needed to reassess his priorities again.

Forget how soft she was when you cradled her in your arms. Forget the way her hair smells like honeysuckle and cinnamon. Focus on the Game.

Nikolai scratched his fingernails down the sides of his face until they found their familiar place behind his neck. He stared blankly at the French poem below him and lowered his forehead to the pages, resting, ostensibly, on the library table.

He was still in that position when someone thrust a heavy book onto the table.

Nikolai started.

Pasha slid into the seat across from him. He wore his best—or worst, depending on opinion—disguise, that of an unkempt fisherman. He was unshaven and dressed in a rough tunic and trousers, so bedraggled he could have emerged straight from the bottom of the bay. It was certainly not the look of a tsesarevich. But it also was not the look of someone who would ordinarily frequent the Imperial

Library. A few patrons eyed Pasha with disdain.

"What are you doing here?" Nikolai whispered.

"Searching for you. You've been avoiding me again."

"No. I've only been . . . ill."

"But not too ill to read French poetry?" Pasha tilted his head to better see the slim volume on the table.

Nikolai flipped it closed. "On the contrary, the poetry made me only more ill."

Pasha smirked. "Regardless, I've tracked you down once again." He tapped the cover of the book he had brought. "This explains everything."

Nikolai glanced down at the book, and his stomach lurched, as if Pasha had brought the smell of fish past its prime into the library with him. *Russian Mystics and the Tsars.* "Where did you get that? And what do you mean it explains everything?"

"I've had it for a while, but you were so against me pursuing Vika and seemed . . . repulsed, almost, by the idea of magic that I hadn't shared the book with you. I didn't want you to think me a fool. But it really does explain everything—the enchantments around the city. The island. Vika."

Nikolai swallowed but didn't speak. Had Pasha finally caught up to Nikolai's deceit?

"I thought the charms around the city were merely amusements well timed with my birthday," Pasha said. "Oh, how vain I was! They *are* a game, but an ancient one: the Crown's Game."

Nikolai gripped the edge of the table as if the library were a ship heeling beneath him. His knuckles were bone white.

"Don't you want to know about the Crown's Game?" Pasha asked.

Nikolai shook his head.

"Well, I'll tell you anyway." Pasha began, in a low voice, to relay the details of the contest between enchanters. He started at the beginning, in the age of Rurik, and wound his way through a catalog of past Games, his eyes lightening and darkening as he recounted the history. Nikolai held the table even tighter.

Only when Pasha had finished did the color seep back into Nikolai's hands. Pasha had not mentioned Nikolai's involvement in the Game. Yet.

Pasha poked the *Russian Mystics* book. "Have you nothing to say? Nikolai! I've just informed you that there's an ancient contest of magic taking place in our midst, and that the girl I almost kissed is in the center of it and might die."

Nikolai groaned and brought his head back down to the incomprehensible French poem. "You almost kissed her?" he asked into the table. Jealousy blazed inside him. So much for trying not to think of Vika in that way. "When? Where?"

"On the island, soon after the benches appeared," Pasha said. "I tried to kiss her, but she told me she wasn't 'in a position to fall in love.'"

"What does that mean?"

"I don't know. But she promised I'd know if it changed."

Nikolai wanted to disappear into the table. "Why didn't you tell me?"

"Because you sleep too damn much and never come out with me anymore. But I'm telling you now, and you're flat on the table, falling asleep again." Pasha thumped his hand on the book.

Someone nearby shushed him, then made a fuss of standing up and relocating to a table much farther away.

"I'm not falling asleep," Nikolai muttered. It would have been impossible to. Pasha had (almost) kissed Vika. How could Nikolai have even thought he'd have a chance with her? Of course she would fall in love with Pasha. Pasha was the heir to an empire, and he was smart and dashing and could win a war with his smile. He was also not at risk of dying in the Game.

And that explained why she'd told Pasha she wasn't currently in a position to fall in love. She still didn't know how the Game would end. But if she won, then she *would* be in a position to fall in love. She would be Imperial Enchanter, and she would no longer fear commitment to Pasha, for she would know she could live happily ever after.

And Nikolai would be alone. No, dead. Exactly as his tea leaves had predicted.

Pasha knocked on Nikolai's head. "Then if you're not asleep, talk to me. You're my best friend. I think I love her, and she might die."

Nikolai peered up from the table. "You cannot love her. You hardly know her."

"If there were ever a girl a man could fall in love with without knowing, it would be Vika. I have to stop the other enchanter. Say you'll help me."

Were the library truly a ship, this would be the moment that it sank.

"Nikolai."

He shook his head.

"Say you'll help me."

Nikolai exhaled deeply. Why did Pasha have to get involved?

And yet, Nikolai had to respond. He couldn't hide against the table forever.

He pulled himself upright and charmed away the nausea and despair from his face, although it cost him what felt like the last of his integrity to do so. Instead, he put on the facade of being the same Nikolai he had always been, the practical one to Pasha's whimsy.

"I told you the first time we saw her, Pasha, that Vika is not the kind of girl you can give a glass slipper to and expect to turn into a princess. Likewise—assuming this Crown's Game is not mere legend—you cannot interfere. She wouldn't want you to."

"But perhaps in this instance—"

"No. She would not want your help. And regardless, you would be of no assistance. What would you do? Murder the other enchanter? For what other way is there to stop him?"

"I don't . . . I admit I didn't think it through quite that far." He tugged on his hair, and the fisherman's cap fell off.

Nikolai picked it up and tossed it back at him. "I'm right, you know."

Pasha turned the fisherman's cap in his hands.

"Let it go," Nikolai said, as much to Pasha as to himself. "Forget about trying to control the Game, and let it take its course. It will end how it needs to end."

Pasha frowned. "I wish there were something I could do to change it."

Nikolai closed his eyes. "Me, too, Pasha. Me, too."

CHAPTER FIFTY-TWO

Vika sat on the floor of the apartment and stared at the Imagination Box. She had brought it inside the flat after the ball, a rash and likely imprudent carryover from dancing with Nikolai, and it had been there ever since. And unlike the Masquerade Box, the Imagination Box's magic hadn't been extinguished. Vika hardly blinked as she looked at it.

One panel was covered with the word *Father* carved over and over, followed by the words *lies, lies, lies, lies, lies.*

Father, Father, Father, she thought.

I miss you, Father. I'm sorry, Father. I didn't know, Father. Lies, lies, lies.

I don't know my father. Or my mother. Was everything you ever told me a lie?

The other panel on the Imagination Box was covered with angry slashes, and the words *the Game* and *Galina* and *Nikolai* and *blame.*

It's your fault. Without you, without the Game, he'd still be alive. It's all your damn fault.

Vika growled through her tears. Then she reached out and touched the Imagination Box.

She obliterated the words with a single, violent swipe.

CHAPTER FIFTY-THREE

The bridge spanned the Fontanka River, composed of two stone arches with a wooden drawbridge in between. Four Doric pavilions housed the drawbridge mechanisms, and it was in the corner of one of these pavilions that Pasha stood, hiding. He'd grown out some of his blond stubble into a two-day-old beard, shadowed the rest of his face with a wide-brimmed hat, and donned a frayed coat over a common laborer's rough tunic and breeches. He'd even sewn lopsided patches onto the knees.

"Hello, Frenchie," Ludmila said as she approached the opposite side of the pavilion.

He peeked out from under the hat. A grin spread across his bearded face. "Why, if it isn't my Aphrodite of the pumpkin. How did you find me here?"

"A hunch."

"Ah, it was Ilya, wasn't it?" Ilya was the youngest member of Pasha's Guard, but the best one at guessing his whereabouts. "I'll have to be slyer to outwit him. Though he doesn't inform the rest of the Guard, which I appreciate."

"He thought you'd be watching the boats."

"Indeed. I'm trying to work out the inefficiencies in the water traffic around the city. There are times when there is too much traffic, and others when there is none at all. The delays cause all manner of problems, from spoiled goods to missed connections to accidents while the boats wait in the queue."

"Ah, and here I thought Ilya meant you were merely watching the boats as boys do when they dream of becoming sailors." Ludmila chuckled. "Don't you have a harbormaster whose job it is to manage this?"

"I do, and the tsar has asked me to meet with him several times, but he knows nothing except what's written on his timetables. But that's just paper. And reality isn't paper, is it?"

Ludmila shook her head.

"So I came to see the situation for myself. Also, I just like looking at boats and dreaming of becoming a sailor." Pasha flashed his famous smile. "But you did not seek me out to discuss river traffic. What can I do for you today, Madame Fanina?"

"It's about Vika."

Pasha inched closer to where Ludmila stood. "I've been wondering where she is. There haven't been any new enchantments in a fortnight. I thought perhaps it was because the festivities for my birthday had concluded."

Ludmila hung her head. "Vika's father passed away."

"Oh no." Pasha left the cover of the pavilion now and came out to the main part of the bridge.

"She received word two weeks ago. I haven't been able

to convince her to leave the flat."

Pasha continued to stand still and steady, as a tsesarevich should in the face of tragedy, even though he wished he could fly to Vika's apartment that very instant to gather her in his arms. "What can I do?" he asked Ludmila.

"Will you talk to her? Invite her for a walk, or do anything to take her mind off her father for a short while? I realize it's bold of me to ask, and you have the boats to observe—"

"No. I'm glad you came to me. I shall send a coach for her straightaway."

His carriage pulled up to the Winter Palace, hopefully with Vika in it. Pasha had returned home to shave and put on neater clothes, and to have pity on his Guard and actually inform them of his location and intentions. Now, as he passed Ilya in the courtyard, he patted him on the back and whispered, "The boats at Chernyshev Bridge. Well done. I'll best you next time." The guard laughed before he snapped his mouth closed and attempted to look stern again.

Pasha slipped into the carriage as soon as the coachman opened the door. Vika indeed sat inside, dressed in all black. She had even changed her hair so that it was no longer a single stripe of ebony, but an entire mantle of it. Her mien managed to darken even the white paneled walls and cream leather of the carriage. Good gracious, Ludmila had been right. This Vika was a different girl entirely.

"You requested my presence?" She hardly glanced up as Pasha slid onto the seat across from her.

"I heard you needed a change of scenery."

"The scenery in my room was fine."

"Ludmila said you've been staring at the face of an armoire with only an evil-looking rat as company. I don't think that qualifies as 'fine.'"

"His name is Poslannik."

"Pardon?"

"The rat. The rat's name is Poslannik. And he isn't evil."

"Ludmila is concerned about you."

The carriage started with a lurch, and the sound of horse's hooves—both those that led the carriage and those that belonged to the Guard—surrounded them.

"Where are we going?"

"I thought we might go for a ride in the country. I asked the coachman to take a scenic route to Tsarskoe Selo, my family's summer residence. No one is there now, so the gardens will be all yours. Perhaps the fresh air will do you good."

"My father is dead. Or the man I thought was my father. And my mother, whom I thought had died, apparently did not, but abandoned me instead. My entire life has been a lie. I doubt fresh air will do a thing to change that."

Pasha sat back in his seat and looked at her scowl. She was still beautiful, but with her expression as black as her hair, her beauty was of a fiercer kind. An almost frightening kind. After Vika's warnings about the danger of magic, Pasha wondered if he'd taken the recent enchantments too lightly, and if he'd fallen too easily under Vika's spell.

"I'm sorry." Vika sighed, and the furrow of her brow softened. "I appreciate you coming to see me. I shouldn't take my grief out on you."

"It's all right. It must have been quite a shock." His

concerns about her ferocity fell away. Instead, he wanted to protect her. But that was foolish. A girl like Vika didn't need protecting.

"I didn't even know he was sick," she said. "Father had gone away on a trip, and I simply assumed he was safe. He was so strong, I never imagined him otherwise."

Pasha wanted to cross the space between them and comfort her. But she would probably shift away. Wouldn't she? It was certainly a risk. But she'd come in the carriage. She could have declined. Pasha decided to take the chance.

He moved across the coach to the seat beside her, taking her hand. She startled and almost withdrew it, but then . . . she didn't. She leaned against him and rested her head on his shoulder instead.

A smile bloomed across Pasha's face. Even in her grief, Vika smelled sweet. Like flowers and warm spice. He tried not to move at all, so that she would stay nestled into his side.

"Father gave his entire life to me," Vika murmured. "But what was the point when he didn't survive long enough to . . ."

"To what?"

She shook her head against his shoulder. "I must make him proud. I can't let his death be in vain."

Pasha touched her arm gently. "I'm sure he was proud. It would be impossible not to be."

The roads grew rougher the farther they traveled from the center of Saint Petersburg, and the carriage bumped along the dirt. Soon, they were outside the city limits, and the scenery gave way to more space: fewer buildings, save for the small houses that sprinkled the landscape every now and then, and more fields and clusters of red- and gold-leaved trees. It was a good plan, Pasha thought, to head to Tsarskoe Selo. A walk through the gardens and woods really would do Vika good.

She didn't speak much. But Pasha was all right with that. She didn't need his words; she needed room to breathe.

He did not, of course, understand the full extent of her grief. But he knew the fear of it. He thought of the tsar and tsarina at the Sea of Azov. Pasha shuddered. *Mother will be all right. She'll recover. She'll return.*

As the carriage approached Tsarskoe Selo, Vika fell asleep against him, and Pasha was loath to wake her. Ludmila had told him of Vika's nightmares, the constant tossing and turning and unconscious wailing. So when the coachman slowed the carriage and inquired whether Pasha wished to stop, he commanded the coachman to continue onward. They would take a circuitous route around the nearby villages, then proceed slowly home to Saint Petersburg.

Pasha watched the countryside fly by. Occasionally, villagers would come out at the sound of the approaching horses, and when they saw the double-headed eagle on the carriage, they would fall to their knees in the grass and the dirt. Children chased after the coach. Gavriil tossed coins for them onto the road as the coach rambled away.

When they were almost back at the outskirts of Saint Petersburg, Vika's head rolled on Pasha's shoulder. He caught her gently before she slipped down, and he repositioned her so she could continue to sleep. For a moment, he thought about kissing her, maybe just on the top of her head as she slept. But then he scowled at himself for even thinking of doing it without her permission.

And then Vika's hair fell to the side and exposed her bare skin.

Pasha gasped. She writhed as something glowed orange on her collarbone. Two crossed wands, searingly bright as if they were the tip of a branding iron. Nearly invisible wisps of smoke floated up from the wands, and a faint hint of smoke that Pasha had not noticed before lingered in the air.

The wands were the same as the ones in his book.

So it really is true, he thought. And for a second, Pasha grinned as if he'd shot a hundred partridges in one day. Nikolai had not wanted to believe him, but Pasha had been right. For once, he'd known something Nikolai hadn't: the Crown's Game was real.

But then beside him, Vika gritted her teeth, and as the scar glowed brighter, she thrashed as if she were caught in the throes of a diabolical dream. How long had it been her turn—how long had it been burning—that it hurt her like that?

Reality rushed at Pasha, and he saw Vika through a whole new lens. One in which she was actually fragile. Because if the Crown's Game was real, it meant Vika truly could die at any moment.

He didn't want to lose her.

"I'll find a way to end the Game," Pasha said aloud. "I swear on my mother's throne, I will."

CHAPTER FIFTY-FOUR

The Magpie and the Fox was crowded as usual, but Nikolai had sent word earlier of Pasha's request to meet at the tavern, and Nursultan had reserved their table in the back. Nikolai arrived first—it happened on occasion when Pasha had to take an alternate route to evade his Guard—and Nikolai sipped on his beer while he waited.

He had just begun to take a bite of bread and smoked salmon when Pasha slipped into their booth. He was clean shaven this time, almost entirely himself but for the spectacles on his nose and the Wellington hat on his head. He promptly removed both as he settled into the darkness of their corner.

"I saw her today," Pasha said.

"Hello to you, too." Nikolai set down his bread and picked up the cold bottle of vodka Nursultan had left on the table. "Saw whom?"

"Vika. Her father passed away, and Ludmila asked me to comfort her. I took her on a carriage ride."

Nikolai paused mid-pour and missed the shot glass, and vodka spilled and dripped onto his trousers. He didn't move. Sergei had died? Was this why Vika hadn't taken her turn?

"When did it happen?" he asked. The calmness in his voice was 100 percent pretense.

"The drive?"

"No. Her father passing."

"A fortnight ago."

Exactly when Vika had fainted. And lost her bracelet. They had to be related. Nikolai poured a new shot of vodka for himself. He didn't even stop to pour one for Pasha or mumble a perfunctory toast; he just gulped it down and chased it with half a stein of beer.

"What's gotten into you?" Pasha said.

"Nothing."

Pasha shook his head, as if shrugging this off as another of Nikolai's brooding episodes. "I also confirmed she's part of the Crown's Game." Pasha pushed aside the platter of bread and fish and shoved his copy of *Russian Mystics and Tsars* onto the table. Did he carry that encyclopedia with him everywhere?

Nikolai considered drinking straight from the bottle. And yet he took Pasha's bait and asked the question he knew Pasha wanted him to ask. "How?"

Pasha flipped open the book to a page he had marked with a length of gold ribbon. There was an illustration of two wands crossed over each other. "Because the enchanters are branded with this when the Game begins. And when Vika fell asleep on me—"

"She fell asleep on you?" Nikolai clenched his fists, and the glasses began to rattle.

Pasha glanced up from the book. The glasses stopped shaking. He furrowed his brow. "Er, yes. She fell asleep on me in the carriage. She had her head on my shoulder, and when her hair moved, it exposed her collarbone. . . ."

Nikolai closed his eyes, as if doing so could undo everything Pasha was saying.

"And right there on her skin was this mark of the wands." He tapped the book. "Glowing orange and actually burning, no less."

Nikolai leaned against the high wooden back of the booth.

"Amazing and horrifying," Pasha said.

There was nothing but the noise from the tavern. Men singing a bawdy drinking song. Shouts to Nursultan to bring more pickles. A fistfight at one of the tables.

"Come now, Nikolai. You honestly have no comment? I spent the afternoon consoling the girl I'm in love with, and I confirmed that she might die as well. At least congratulate me on my detective work, or offer your condolences, I don't care. Something."

"I congratulate you on your sad lot."

"Oh, don't be such a curmudgeon." Pasha poured himself a shot of vodka and gulped it down. He bit off a chunk of bread to take off the vodka's astringent edge. "I thought you'd be more supportive. Or are you jealous? You're not interested in Vika, are you? You danced with her only once at the masquerade."

"I'm not jealous." Nikolai had lost track of how many lies he'd told Pasha by this point. He knew only that he was buried deep in them, and he was suffocating.

"I implore you again to help me stop the other enchanter.

You're resourceful. Surely you can think of some way out of the Crown's Game."

Nikolai squeezed his fists tighter. His nails dug into his palms. "I told you before. There is no way out."

"How can you be so sure? I've told you only the abridged version of the Game. There are many more details. There's so much you don't know."

"I already know too much, Pasha!" Nikolai picked up the vodka bottle and smashed it over the book. Glass shattered and flew across the table, several shards embedding themselves in Pasha's sleeve.

Pasha gasped. "What are you——"

But he stopped talking as the pieces of glass quivered, then slid across the table and back onto the book, where they reassembled themselves into the shape of a bottle. The shards in his arm wrenched themselves free and rejoined their glassy brethren. Even the liquid on the book cover converged into a small pool, then traveled up the side of the bottle in a clear stream before trickling back through the bottle's mouth and back inside.

He gaped at Nikolai.

Nikolai squinted at Pasha's arm. "I'm sorry. Did the glass cut you? Or is it only your sleeve?" There was concern in his words, strictly speaking, but his tone belied very little of it.

Pasha glanced down but was unable to speak.

"Just the sleeve then. Much easier." Nikolai's tone was more derisive than he'd intended to let on, but he couldn't shake it, because Pasha had pushed him too far. Nikolai snapped his fingers, and a needle and thread appeared. They dipped down to Pasha's shirt and began stitching the tears the broken glass had left.

"You're the other enchanter," Pasha whispered.

Nikolai kept his face an unfeeling mask. "I'm afraid so."

"You made the benches."

"And refaced Nevsky Prospect and conjured the Jack and ballerina. The Masquerade Box was mine as well."

"All this time . . ."

Nikolai sighed, and his mask dissolved. Now actual remorse began to flow. "I'm sorry I didn't tell you."

"You let me go on and on about the Crown's Game like a fool." Pasha stared at his sleeve, where the needle had finished its work, and a pair of scissors was snipping the extra thread.

Nikolai shook his head. "You're not a fool."

"But you made me out to be. I don't even know who you are."

"I'm the same person you've always known."

"No." Pasha rose from the booth. "You're not."

"Pasha."

"You've known this about yourself your entire life. And that means you've lied to me for the entirety of our friendship."

"It's only a small part of my identity. I'm so much more than this."

"Perhaps. But what else have you hidden from me?"

"Nothing!" Nikolai slapped the table.

"Did you befriend me for your own ambitions, to become closer to the tsar so you could win the Game?" Pasha's ordinarily angelic face contorted into something uglier. Something harsher. Something that looked like his father or his sister.

"No. I didn't even know the details of the Game until a month ago."

"Did you enjoy listening to me ramble about mysticism, then laugh behind my back?"

"I would never."

"And what about Vika? How will you finish the Game? Will you kill her so you can be victorious, so you can finally be somebody?"

"No! Pasha, what are you saying?" Nikolai jumped from his seat. "I could never hurt her, I love her, too."

"You what?" Pasha's mouth hung open.

Damn. Was it true? Renata had accused him of falling for Vika, but Nikolai hadn't fully admitted it to himself until now. Not actually being in love. The confession left him feeling both as if the floor had been pulled out from under him and, at the same time, made more firm.

The two boys glared at each other from opposite sides of the booth. Anywhere else, their argument would have attracted attention. But in the tavern, it was business as usual. At a nearby table, another bottle smashed against the wall and the men there began to yell.

"I love her, too," Nikolai said quietly as he sank back into his seat.

Pasha, however, did not sit. He towered over Nikolai. "So you lied to me about that as well."

Nikolai could do nothing but nod. He could argue that it was an omission, not a lie, but such technicalities shouldn't matter between friends. It was deception nonetheless. One of so many deceptions.

Pasha scowled. "You were the one who said I couldn't love Vika, because I hardly knew her. How is it possible, then, for *you* to love her? Do you know her so much better than I?"

"It's different. We're enchanters."

"And what is that supposed to mean? That you're somehow better than me because of it?"

"No! Just . . . we understand each other. There's no one else like us."

"So if we are only to fall in love with someone exactly like ourselves, I suppose that means I need to find a woman who is in line to inherit an empire, who has also been betrayed by her best friend."

Nikolai wilted on the table.

"I could have my Guard arrest you, you know. I could accuse you of kidnapping me tonight. I could have a firing squad on you by morning."

"I know you could."

"I could, but I won't, because in another version of this life, you were my best friend. And I wouldn't want *that* boy's blood on my hands."

"Pasha—"

"Why do you have to steal Vika?"

Nikolai sat up again. "What? I'm not. I said I love her, not that she loves me."

"She'd choose you over me, though. You've always had everything, and now you have to take Vika, too." Pasha stabbed a knife into the center of the loaf of bread.

Nikolai yanked the knife out. "How could you possibly believe that? You're the one who has everything. I'm an orphan with not a drop of noble blood in my veins and not a ruble or kopek to my name. All I have is my magic, and all that's going to lead me to is death."

"Not true. Do you not see what you have, Nikolai? You're better than everyone at everything, and you don't even try.

You're a better dancer, a better swordsman, a better scholar. Girls fall at your feet, and you don't seem to care. You excel at everything, whereas I'm only adequate. The only thing I've got is that I was born to be heir."

"You're more than that." Nikolai dropped the knife on the table.

"Tell that to my father. Or don't. He probably already likes you better than me anyway. After all, he's the judge of the Game, isn't he? So he knows all about you. He knows more about you than I do." Pasha jabbed at his book on the table.

"Please. Calm down. Let's be rational. I can explain."

"You've had years to explain. It's too late now. From this moment on, I want nothing to do with you or your kind. Keep your magic to yourself." He snatched the knife and stabbed it straight into the center of *Russian Mystics and the Tsars*. "And stay out of my life." Pasha glowered. Then he stormed toward the Magpie and the Fox's back door.

"Pasha, wait!"

But he didn't.

Nikolai buried his head in his hands. If only he'd told Pasha before. If only he hadn't listened to Galina about keeping his abilities secret. If only he hadn't been so afraid to tell his best friend about the Game.

But now it was done, and there was nothing Nikolai could do.

His tea leaves were right. He was alone. Again. Alone, alone, ad infinitum. Nikolai swilled the rest of the vodka— lukewarm now—directly from the bottle.

Then he slumped onto the table, his face next to the knife. He wanted the tea leaves to stop being right.

CHAPTER FIFTY-FIVE

Overnight, the leaves fell off all the trees, and the arctic wind blew in. Frost settled on bare branches, and birds made plans to migrate south. The canals iced over mid-color, and the fountain in the Neva froze in clear arcs of cold crystal. When the sun rose in the morning, its pale yellow rays were so weak, they couldn't even melt an icicle. Although it was only the middle of November, winter had arrived in Saint Petersburg.

But Vika didn't so much as shiver as she stood on the embankment of Ekaterinsky Canal. She was still upset at Sergei for lying to her about being her father. But more than that, she was now furious that he was no longer alive. As she stood outside the Zakrevsky house, Vika seethed, her magic hot and roiling through her veins.

"I hate you," she said, even though she was the only one on the street at this hour. "I hate you, Nikolai. I hate that you exist. If it weren't for you, I'd be the Imperial Enchanter. If it weren't for you, I wouldn't have to play this godforsaken Game. If it weren't for you, Sergei wouldn't be dead."

Vika lifted her hands. A hum filled the air, and the ground seemed to vibrate. From behind her, what at first appeared to be a snow flurry turned out to be a regiment of winter moths, bursting through the tree branches and beclouding the sky. From the dank crevices of Ekaterinsky Canal, an army of rats, slick with sludge and ice, emerged and scurried to Vika's feet. Poslannik led the charge.

"This is my fourth move," she said as a motley gang of feral cats slunk from the alleyways and crept up the front steps of the Zakrevsky home. Poslannik had spied through the windows for her and told her everything that was inside. She would destroy it all—Nikolai's precious clothes and his neat writing desk and the countess's ancestors' portraits on the walls. Her soldiers would scratch the gleaming banister and tear apart the Persian rugs and chew apart the strings of the piano. And all the while, she'd hold a shield around the house so Nikolai couldn't escape. So he'd have to watch his belongings and his home torn to pieces, before she caved the building in and killed him. All Vika wanted was an end to this monstrous Game. She would finish it once and for all.

Vika threw her arms wide in front of her, and the wind flung open the doors and windows of the Zakrevsky house. She circled her pinkie over her grimy troops so they would understand her commands, and then they flung themselves headlong inside, rushing into the dining room and the parlor, the kitchen in the basement, and the bedrooms upstairs belonging to Nikolai and the countess.

"Destroy and infest everything," Vika said. The rats tore into the pantry, gnawing apart too-precious croissants and breaking garish cups and saucers and countless wineglasses. The cats shredded the upholstery and sharpened their claws on baroque table legs.

And the moths flitted and crawled their way into Nikolai's armoire and began to eat holes in all his clothes. He would have nothing but rags left. A surge of wicked delight jolted through Vika. *How will you feel, Nikolai, without your dandy armor?*

But as soon as she thought it, she realized he wasn't inside. She couldn't feel the invisible string between them.

And then she remembered that tugging between them, that feeling that even though Nikolai was her opponent, he was also her other half. She remembered when she'd touched his sleeve at the masquerade, and how everything terrible between them had fallen away, leaving only the warm silk of his magic.

She remembered how Nikolai had looked at her when she lay vulnerable and faint on his bed. As if he'd wanted to kiss her. And how much she'd wanted him to.

Suddenly, the intoxication of Vika's fury collapsed. She felt the weight of the wrongness in her hands, which were still raised to the sky, and on her shoulders, in her gut, in her bones. It wasn't Nikolai's fault that Sergei was dead. Nikolai was as unwilling a participant in the Game as Vika was.

What am I doing?

Vika dropped her arms to her sides.

The crashing in the house suddenly ceased. The frantic energy around the Zakrevsky house stilled. The rats streamed down the front steps, confused, followed by the cats and a billow of moths. They disappeared into the dark interstices from which they'd come, as quickly as they'd arrived.

Vika waved a hand limply, and the windows and doors flapped shut. "I'm sorry," she whispered. Then she ran, as far away as she could, from Ekaterinsky Canal.

CHAPTER FIFTY-SIX

Nikolai staggered home, his head throbbing from drinking too much at the tavern last night, and from sleeping in a filthy alley in Sennaya Square afterward. He had also gotten into a fistfight with someone, for some forgotten slight, and he had a black eye and swollen knuckles to show for it. At least he'd refrained from using magic in the brawl.

He climbed the steps to the Zakrevsky house, wanting nothing but a hot bath to wash the last twelve hours away, only to find the front door unlocked.

Nikolai pushed it open and stepped into the foyer.

Galina's Persian rug had been reduced to tufts of red yarn. Chairs were broken and tables were overturned. The chandelier—imported from Venice—hung askew and was missing half its crystals.

And one of Nikolai's top hats lay halfway up the stairwell, trampled and holey, as if it had been nibbled through by vampire moths. Nikolai squeezed his eyes shut. "As if things couldn't get any worse."

And then his scar flared. The dull ache of it had been there since he woke, but he hadn't processed it through the skull-splitting headache and the black eye and the disoriented, clumsy walk back to Ekaterinsky Canal.

But now, Nikolai clutched his collar as he sagged against the gouged wall. If his scar was burning, then it wasn't an ordinary band of burglars who had been here. It was Vika.

Why this? And why now?

It wasn't the torn clothes and smashed vases that distressed him. Not really, anyhow. Nikolai had begun his life with nothing, and he could start afresh with nothing again. *But after everything that's passed between Vika and me . . .*

Nikolai shook his head. It was still a vicious game. And that reality ate away at him from the inside like turpentine.

The grandfather clock chimed, its pendulum swinging behind a cracked pane of glass. That clock was a Zakrevsky heirloom.

Galina would be hysterical over the damage. And she would likely blame Renata and the rest of the servants for not stopping the vandals.

I cannot let that happen.

Nikolai leaned his aching head against the wall. He allowed himself one more moment of despair. And then he snapped his fingers and began the painstaking process of trying to clean and mend what Vika had destroyed.

He could not fix everything.

CHAPTER FIFTY-SEVEN

The tsar had spent several days on horseback with his generals, inspecting the troops on the Crimean Peninsula. He had left Elizabeth to recover in Taganrog, a quaint town along the Sea of Azov, while he traveled here to get a handle on the fighting with the Ottomans. Now, having had more than enough of the harsh realities of war—the injured soldiers and constant threat of attack here reminded him again of the suffering his country had endured during Napoleon's onslaught—the tsar finally galloped back to camp for one more night's rest in his tent before he returned to Taganrog.

The stable boys led his horse away, and the guards outside his tent saluted. The tsar nodded to them and ducked into his tent, which contained not only a sumptuous mattress piled high with silk pillows and throws, but also an intricately brocaded armchair and footrest, a cherrywood desk, and a dining table inlaid with oyster shells.

An attendant awaited him. He bowed low to the ground.

"Good evening, Your Imperial Majesty. Would you like to read the letters that arrived for you today, or would you prefer to sup first?"

"Supper, please."

"Right away, Your Imperial Majesty." The attendant scurried out of the tent.

The tsar took off his belt and sword and sank into his armchair. He propped his boots on the footrest. The relief was instantaneous. Although he had spent most of the past few days on horseback, he had also spent significant time on foot, surveying the terrain. He looked forward to returning to the seaside with Elizabeth.

The front flap of the tent opened, and the tsar expected the smell of roast meat and stew to fill the air. Instead, the stench of rotting flesh penetrated the tent, and the tsar covered his nose and mouth with his sleeve and jumped up from his chair.

"What kind of supper did you—"

But it was not the cook or the attendant who stood at the tent's entrance. It was a stooped figure in a threadbare cloak, a hood draped over its head.

"Who are you? Guards!"

"Oh, it is no use calling for your guards, Alexander," the woman said. "They are, shall we say, indisposed."

He drew his sword from his belt, thankful it was still nearby. "Who are you? And how dare you address me solely by my first name?"

"I daresay I have quite earned that right." She tossed off her hood.

The tsar gasped. The woman was half mummy, half something else not quite human. "What are you?"

The ghoul clucked her tongue. "I am insulted. You first asked *who* I was, but now you shift to *what*? Poor manners, Alexander, even coming from you."

"Reveal your identity." He aimed the sword straight at her chest, but took another step back to inch away from the tentacles of fetor that curled out from her body.

The woman cackled, her voice gurgling at the same time, as if laughing despite choking on a cesspool of blood. "Do you not recognize me, Alexander? The rest of my face may have decayed—it was the cost of being buried underground for nearly two decades—but the eyes you will know."

He didn't want to look. What if this creature were a medusa, something that could turn him to stone or worse should he look upon it?

She slithered close to him. "Look at me!"

He flourished his sword. "Stay back or I will impale you, I swear on my life."

"Go ahead. Skewer me like a *zhauburek* kabob. See if it slows me down." She lunged at him. He plunged the blade straight through her belly. She laughed again and, unfazed, grabbed his chin, forcing him to meet her eyes.

They were golden, like glittering topaz, and there was something familiar in them that he couldn't quite place. For a moment, she held him in a trance. Then he got ahold of himself and wrenched away from her grip and her stink and, trembling, looked down at the sword protruding from her middle. "How? What?"

She pulled the blade out of her body and took several deep breaths. The blood that soaked her cloak began to fade, as if it seeped out of the cloth and back into her flesh.

Then she tossed the bloody sword with a clank onto the tent's floor.

"Y-y-you healed yourself."

"Do you remember me now?" Her mouth twisted in what might have been a smile, but appeared more a terrible grimace of rotten teeth.

The tsar took several more steps backward. If he could get close enough to the front of the tent, perhaps he could escape. "I don't believe it."

"Believe it, Alexander. It is I, Aizhana, your once beautiful, golden-eyed lover from the steppe. After you left with your army, I bore you a son. In fact, you have already met him. His name is Nikolai. But you may know him as Enchanter One."

CHAPTER FIFTY-EIGHT

Aizhana enjoyed watching the tsar wriggle under her revelation. She had been so young when she'd met him and so enthralled by his confidence and charm. Naively, she had believed his sweet words and allowed him to seduce her. She could still feel the sharp sting of betrayal when he left, not more than a month after he first took her to bed.

She had been ruined three times by him then, and another time since. His first offense: he took her virginity and left her spoiled, damaged goods to any boy in her village. His second offense: he left her with child, an unwed mother in the barren land of the steppe. His third offense: bearing his child nearly killed her. And his fourth and most recent offense: he accepted his own son into the Game and all but sentenced him to death.

So yes, Aizhana savored the tsar's current horror and fear. She still meant to kill him, of course, although, like a wildcat, she wanted to play with her food first. If not for the Game, she might have satisfied herself with informing him of the existence of another son. But since the tsar had crossed her one too many times and endangered not only her own life but also Nikolai's, he would have to pay.

The tsar ceased his attempt to escape from the tent. What was he thinking, anyway? There was no way he could run from her. He sagged onto the edge of his bed. "Nikolai Karimov is your son?" he asked.

"Yours, as well."

"Mine . . ."

"He does not yet know. But I shall tell him soon."

"He is the tsesarevich's best friend."

Aizhana clapped derisively and gave the tsar a wry, rotten smile. "Bravo, Alexander. You watched one of your sons grow up but did not even recognize the other when he was right there beside your chosen one. What a remarkable father you are."

"It's not my fault." He buried his head in his hands. "I could not have known."

"No, of course not. You were too busy bedding other women to keep track of the consequences."

"Is that what this is? A lover's revenge?"

Aizhana stalked closer to him. "Oh, no. It is so much more than that." She sat next to him on the bed—it was so similar to the bed on which she had lain with him, once upon a time—and placed her hands on either side of his face. He gagged at her breath.

She laughed and blew more of the rank air in his face, then smashed her lips against his. She forced her black tongue into his mouth, curling it and transferring the disease that flourished inside her into him. The tsar struggled but was no match for her, for she had imbibed the energy of

349

the half-dozen guards she had slaughtered outside his tent. She quivered in joy at forcing the prolonged kiss upon him. What an ironic end to a courtship that had also begun with a lingering kiss.

One of Aizhana's teeth broke off, so violently did she press herself against him. When she pulled back, the tooth tumbled from between their lips down to the floor.

The tsar stared at it in horror.

"Thank you, Alexander. That was the good-bye kiss I never had."

He scrubbed at his face with his sleeve. "I can end the Game, you know. I will punish you. I will declare Vika Andreyeva the winner."

"And murder your own son?"

The tsar shuddered.

"You will not declare the girl the winner. You will not be able to, for you shall not survive the journey back to Taganrog to inscribe the name of the winner onto the Scroll."

"I won't survive? What have you done?"

Aizhana shrugged. "Given you a parting gift, a token of my affection. However, you may not see it as such. You may see it as typhus."

The tsar clutched his mouth.

She laughed as she rose from the bed and strolled to the tent's entrance. "Good night, Alexander. May your eternal sleep be haunted by nightmares of your many sins."

The tsar sounded the alarm as soon as Aizhana swooped out of his tent. The remainder of his Guard rushed him into his carriage and onto the long road back to Taganrog. But fever and aches descended that night, with delirium following soon after. The journey back to the Sea of Azov was too far. By the time they arrived days later, Death was waiting at the bottom of the carriage steps. The tsar tumbled out of the carriage, and Death swung his scythe. It took the tsar's life just as he made it into the tsarina's arms.

Death took the tsarina soon afterward.

CHAPTER FIFTY-NINE

Pasha let his sister take his hand. They wore black from head to toe, and no one stopped them as they wandered through the Winter Palace. When they arrived in the massive hall, Yuliana pulled him through the hollow, deserted space, past the towering white columns and crystal chandeliers, until they reached the front of the room.

There on a dais stood a lone, empty chair, gilded in too much gold and upholstered in red, with the empire's gold double-headed eagle prominent for all to see. It was surrounded by yet more red and gold, including an even more ostentatious double-headed eagle displayed on the red wall behind the chair. This was the tsar's throne.

This was where Pasha would sit from now on.

But he didn't touch it. For he could still see his father there, dignified and majestic in full uniform, ambassadors and ministers bowing at his feet. He could see his mother enter the room, and his father rise to greet her and offer her this chair.

Then Pasha thought of everything else he'd lost. His best friend, who had lied and made him out to be a fool. And the girl he loved, who did not reciprocate, and who would probably pick the traitorous enchanter over him.

All this, while he stared at the throne.

But Yuliana had only so much patience. She pushed Pasha, and he collapsed into the chair. He winced as his arm touched the gold.

"You will be tsar," she said to him. "Whether you like it or not."

Pasha closed his eyes. He exhaled deeply as he sagged into the throne. Then he nodded. *I will be tsar. Because it's the only thing I have left.*

CHAPTER SIXTY

Nikolai stood outside the Winter Palace walls. Barriers had been set up in the snow, and the Guard was five men thick. If only he could evanesce, then he could get in to see Pasha. Not that Pasha would want to see him. Nikolai closed his eyes. He wished he could take back what he'd done and said, so he would be by Pasha's side now, acting as both pillar and best friend, as he ought to have been.

The streets of Saint Petersburg roiled like a sea of black. It seemed as if every citizen of the city had poured outdoors, draped in their mourning clothes and covered in sorrow. News of the tsar's death had traveled quickly from Taganrog earlier in the week, and just this morning, another messenger had come with an announcement that the tsarina's heart had failed, and she, too, had passed.

And so in Saint Petersburg, women wept openly and collapsed on the icy cobblestones. Men bowed their heads and occasionally dabbed their eyes with their handkerchiefs. The pews in the churches overflowed.

"What do you think is happening inside the palace?" Renata asked. She had insisted on accompanying Nikolai to Palace Square, even though he had wanted to be alone ever since Pasha lashed out at him two weeks ago at the Magpie and the Fox. Before news arrived of the tsar's death, Nikolai had attempted to apologize many times, waiting outside the palace and sending letters every day. But the Guard refused to admit him, and each of his messages was declined by the imperial secretary and returned to Nikolai unopened.

After the tsar's death, Pasha locked the palace down. Nikolai hadn't been able to think of anything but Pasha since then. He couldn't even focus on the Game, despite the fact that it felt as if the scar were about to char him straight through his skin to his collarbone.

"I haven't a clue what's happening in the palace," Nikolai said to Renata. "I imagine they are not only mourning but also making preparations for Pasha's coronation." Although it was widely accepted that Pasha would become the next tsar, his official coronation wouldn't take place until January, in Moscow. Tsars were always crowned in the old capital of Russia, but it took time to plan a coronation, especially an unexpected one. It was only the last day of November now. Nikolai slumped. He'd always thought he'd be one of the first invited when Pasha became tsar. Not so anymore.

"There is also a third item on the tsesarevich's agenda," a sharp but familiar woman's voice said behind them. Nikolai and Renata whipped around, and upon seeing Galina, Renata fell into a curtsy and almost tumbled into the snow.

Nikolai had a slightly better grasp of his composure and managed not to give away too much in his expression.

Still, he could see a hint of victory in Galina's eyes at having caught him by surprise.

"I thought you were exiled until the end of the Game," he said.

"As did I," she said. "But the Game's whirlwind brought me back. Which is fine by me. I tired of Siberia. It was too cold." Of course, she didn't mention her brother's death. How like Galina. And yet, there was something different about her since the last time Nikolai had seen her. She was thinner, and the lines on her face were more pronounced. Perhaps her brother's death *had* affected her in some way. Or perhaps it was just the black clothes, which were unflattering to her pale complexion.

"The tsesarevich has requested your presence," she said offhandedly, as if this were something that occurred on a regular basis. "Or is he the tsar now? No, I suppose not. He hasn't been made official."

"Pasha wants to see me?"

"Not for a hand of cards. Official business."

Nikolai crumbled inside. He had been so focused on his falling-out with Pasha, and then with the death of the tsar and tsarina, that he hadn't thought through the implications of the Game.

If Pasha was going to be tsar, then he would also inherit the role of final arbiter of the Game. He would be the one to decide if Vika and Nikolai lived or died.

CHAPTER SIXTY-ONE

Pasha strode down the hallway of the Winter Palace toward his mother's former audience room. They were the same chambers in which he'd caught his breath during the ball, but today's purpose would be far different. Then, he'd just been an heir, training for a seemingly distant future. But now that future had come. There would be no hiding to catch his breath today.

Yuliana marched beside him, and the Tsar's Guard followed close behind. That was another difference to which Pasha would have to grow accustomed. He'd kept on a couple of his own men—Gavriil, his captain, and Ilya, the one with a knack for sensing where Pasha went when he needed to get away—but otherwise, these guards were his father's men. It made it even more clear that Pasha's life had drastically changed.

"Are you ready?" Yuliana asked, tilting her head at the wooden chest that Ilya carried behind them. The Russe Quill and Scroll had come back to Saint Petersburg with the rest of their father's and mother's personal effects. Immediately, Yuliana had urged Pasha to conclude the Game. There was too much unrest in the empire, and their enemies would take advantage of the transition in the tsardom if Pasha was not strong. He needed an Imperial Enchanter now.

"I'm ready." Pasha smiled on the outside. But on the inside, he laughed cruelly—sadly—at himself. How could he ever be ready to sentence people to their deaths? Especially people he'd once loved? For that was what he was about to do: demand the end of the Game, and in so doing, command either Nikolai's or Vika's death. If only his heart were made of stone rather than quivering humanity.

Yuliana touched him gently on his sleeve, as if she knew his smile was mere deception. But of course she knew. She was his sister, who knew all his flaws. She was his strength where he was weak. "I will be right there beside you," Yuliana said. "Remember, this is for something greater than the two enchanters. This is for Russia."

Pasha swallowed and nodded. And as they continued their march down the hall, he repeated it to himself. *This is for Russia. This is no longer only about me.*

CHAPTER SIXTY-TWO

Vika arrived at the Winter Palace alone.

She had expected an opulent throne room, or perhaps a grand hall like the one that had hosted the masquerade. But instead, the guard escorted her to a small chamber with lilac walls and unembellished cream drapes, the room bare of furniture except for a desk and a few simple chairs. Vika relaxed a little. The unpretentious grace of the room seemed more like Pasha than a massive hall lined with red and gold and double-headed eagles along the walls.

Nikolai and Galina Zakrevskaya were already there. Neither of them sat, but rather stood several feet apart, as if it were unbearable for them to stand any closer together.

As Vika entered, Nikolai gave her a cursory bow. She had desecrated his home, and she knew she deserved not even a nod of acknowledgment. It was all she could do not to fly across the room and beg his forgiveness.

Then another guard entered the room. He cleared his

throat and announced, "The Tsesarevich Pavel Alexandrovich Romanov, and the Grand Princess Yuliana Alexandrovna Romanova."

As they all bowed and curtsied, Pasha marched in and stood behind the desk. He did not sit, and he didn't command them to sit either. The grand princess followed, although she halted on the side of the room and hovered by the window. Then a young guard appeared carrying a chest, the same one from the ceremony at Bolshebnoie Duplo. He set it down heavily on top of the desk. Their stiff formality would have suited an official throne room after all.

"You may all leave," Pasha said to the guards stationed around the room. He sounded less like himself and more like . . . his father. Vika shivered. The guards obeyed silently and closed the doors behind them. No doubt they positioned themselves immediately outside.

"I believe we all know why we're here." Pasha glanced at his sister, then pressed his fingers to the chest and lifted the lid. As he did so, the Russe Quill and Scroll floated out.

Vika noticed that Pasha did not look at her. It was as if he didn't know her either. Had she imagined the past two months? The dancing at the masquerade, the near kiss in the maple grove, the carriage ride after her father's death? Everyone had forsaken her.

"The Scroll is where the tsar declares a winner," Pasha continued. "Although I am not officially tsar, I will be soon, and I will need an Imperial Enchanter. But I would rather not have to choose between you. Therefore, I would like *you* to conclude the Game." He paused, as if waiting to see if anyone would interrupt him. As if testing out his new power. Vika had interrupted the tsar once upon a time, during the oath that seemed so long ago. But the sternness on Pasha's face frightened her more than the tsar ever had, perhaps because the austerity was so foreign to Pasha that Vika didn't know what it meant or what to expect. So she kept still and very quiet.

"I propose a classic duel to determine the winner," Pasha said.

"What do you mean, a classic duel?" Nikolai's eyes narrowed.

"A fight *à l'outrance*, to the death." Icicles hung off Pasha's voice. "A display of your skills in what this Game was supposed to be: a demonstration of which of you is better fit for the position of Imperial Enchanter. Who will help me strategize against the Ottomans? Who can put down the uprisings on the steppe? Who is not afraid to risk life to protect the empire?"

"You don't have to be a warmonger," Nikolai said.

"I am going to be tsar."

"The title doesn't matter." Nikolai took a step toward him. "It's what you do that defines you, Pasha."

The grand princess cleared her throat.

"You will address me as Your Imperial Highness," Pasha said to Nikolai. "And I will remind you that you are not my adviser yet. Don't get ahead of yourself, enchanter."

Vika gaped and looked from Pasha to Nikolai. She had thought they were best friends. Even Nikolai appeared stunned. What had happened between them? What had happened to *everyone*?

"What if we refuse to duel?" Vika asked, for now the world had gone completely upside down, and she could not resist speaking up any longer.

Pasha looked down at the empty chest. The Quill and Scroll still hovered next to him. The grand princess crossed her arms and nodded, as if encouraging her brother to carry through with something they had previously decided.

"My Guard has taken custody of your loved ones," Pasha said. "Ludmila Fanina and Renata Galygina have been placed under lock and key in an undisclosed location. They will be comfortable during the remainder of the Game, but should you not carry out my wishes, there shall be consequences. Your duel shall take place on the new island, beginning at dawn tomorrow."

"Pasha, no!" Vika said. "This isn't you!"

Pasha dragged his hand through his hair, catching himself only after he'd already mussed up half of his blond locks. He dropped his arms to his sides and stood with military rigidity.

"Perhaps it's not the Pasha of the past, but I have no choice. I am to be tsar. This is me now."

CHAPTER SIXTY-THREE

Galina braced herself. She had a feeling the Game's whirlwind would come for her again soon. The magic had only summoned her back to Saint Petersburg for the transition of the Game, but she would likely be exiled again shortly, for the same rules as before applied: she would not be permitted to assist her student.

The tsesarevich locked away the Russe Quill and Scroll and marched out of the room with the grand princess. Nikolai and Vika stood gawking after them, both immobile, as if the tsesarevich had confiscated their ability to move.

Galina whacked Nikolai on the back of his head. "Do not forget the gift I gave you."

He startled, then turned to her and huffed. "That is what you are thinking of, at a moment like this?"

"What else ought I be thinking of? The tsesarevich has made it clear that you are to execute a proper duel."

Nikolai scowled and looked away.

Galina shrugged. "And you, Vika. I hope you're happy

with the choices you made for all your previous plays. My brother gave his life to you through that bracelet." Any kindness Galina had felt toward the girl following Sergei's death had vanished. It was Vika's fault that Sergei had died. She should suffer some consequence.

"What?" Vika whipped around to face Galina.

"You didn't think you had suddenly gotten more powerful, did you? All that extra energy you must have felt came from my brother. You took and took from him until there was nothing left."

"No . . ."

"Oh, yes. He didn't simply die." Spit flew from Galina's mouth onto Vika's gown. "You killed him."

Vika looked as if all the blood in her veins had drained out, just like the life had drained out of Sergei. *Perfect*, Galina thought. *Let her despair do her in. Perhaps she'll simply lie down and lose the Game. She deserves it.*

Frigid air began to stir inside the room, and it merged into the tornado Galina had been expecting. She yelled over the churning of the wind, "You have all the training you need, Nikolai. Try not to make a mess of things. You ought to win."

Then the whirlwind enveloped Galina completely, blew open one of the windows, and rushed out into the winter cold. She hoped it was not carrying her back to Siberia.

CHAPTER SIXTY-FOUR

Vika fled as soon as the whirlwind had taken Galina away. She climbed out the open window onto the banks of the frozen river.

"Wait," Nikolai said, clambering out the window as well.

"Leave me be." Vika turned her back to him. She swirled her arm over her head, and a small blizzard appeared. It spat snow into Nikolai's eyes and pushed him back against the wall of the palace. Vika levitated, and a sleigh of ice formed beneath her.

"Vika, please. Wait."

But she either didn't hear him through the storm or she chose not to listen. She tapped on the sleigh, and it glided away on the surface of the river.

The blizzard pummeled Nikolai until she was gone from sight. As soon as the snowstorm vanished, Pasha's Guard appeared on the other side of the window.

"Hey, you! What are you doing there?" Two rough pairs of hands seized Nikolai by his collar and dragged him back inside. A thick layer of snow tumbled off his hair and coat onto the wooden floor below. The guards righted him and gave him a shove toward the door. "Make haste before we arrest you. The exit is that way."

Nikolai picked up his top hat, which had fallen off as he chased after Vika. He glanced back over his shoulder at the window, but the guards moved their hands to their swords in warning. He nodded and placed his hat back on his head, cold and wet from the now-melting snow, and trudged out of the room, down the hallway, and out into the square.

He bit his lip as he left. It might be the last time he walked through that door.

Nikolai stopped every so often on his walk home to steady himself on a streetlamp. The scar had been burning him, hotter and hotter, nearly unbearably, for the last two weeks as he contemplated his final turn in the Game. Vika had attacked him aggressively by ransacking the Zakrevsky house. Nikolai had needed time to calm down—to let it sink in that it was Vika's grief that had driven her to it, not hatred or real viciousness, he hoped—and to consider how he would respond.

Now, however, it was all moot. Pasha had changed the Game, and each scorching throb of Nikolai's scar served as a reminder that Renata's life was at risk. How could Pasha do this? It was bad enough that Nikolai and Vika might die, but to add Renata and Ludmila? It was as if Pasha's goodness had died when the tsar and tsarina did. Or maybe Nikolai had killed it by betraying him. Nikolai clutched the streetlamp tighter, although this time, it was as much from shame as from the pain of his scar.

Finally, the searing at his collarbone eased a bit, and although he was still sick with guilt, Nikolai released his grip on the streetlamp. But there was no relief, for at that moment, the stench of decay washed over him. He reached for his handkerchief and covered his nose.

"My apologies," a cloaked woman said as she crossed a small bridge over the nearby canal and approached him. "I need to speak with you, enchanter. Would you be able to cast a shield around yourself—or around me—to block the unpleasant smell, so that we may have a conversation?"

Nikolai started to respond but instead gagged into his handkerchief. It was as if the rot were crawling into his mouth. He waved his hand in front of the woman and formed an invisible bubble around her to contain the odor, not so much because of her request, but out of self-preservation. Only when he could breathe again did he register that this stranger had known he was an enchanter, and that, damn it, he had just performed magic in front of her without question. She had not even flinched.

"Thank you, Nikolai."

He took several steps away. "How do you know my name?"

"I know many things about you, perhaps even some you do not know yourself. Will you walk with me? I promise, you are safe."

"Tell me who you are."

"I will. That I also promise. But first, would you like to know who your father was?"

"My father?" Nikolai took a tentative step toward the woman.

She began to hobble down the street. "You inherited

from your father not only his broad shoulders and confidence, but also his adaptability. Despite his many flaws, he was quite skilled at adjusting himself to thrive through change. He would not have survived the war with Napoleon and all the other upheavals without it."

"I knew he was a soldier. But that is all that I knew."

The woman laughed, although it was more a shrill screech than a joyous chuckle. Nikolai cringed. "Your father was no mere soldier. He was a leader of men. Your father was the tsar."

Nikolai stopped in the middle of the street, in front of a small church. "Pardon?"

"You heard me right. Your friend the tsesarevich is your half brother."

"That's impossible."

"Is it? I think I ought to know. The tsar took me as his mistress during a monthlong visit to his army on the steppe. I was young and beautiful then, and we spent every night in his tent. Eight months after he left, I bore him a son, whom I named Nikolai."

"No." Every muscle in Nikolai's body tensed. It had to be a lie. What game was this old hag playing at?

"Oh, yes." She paused in front of the church's wooden doors, as if for dramatic effect. "In fact, since you are a year older than the tsesarevich, you could contend his right to be the next tsar. It's rumored the tsarina had her own affairs, as well, and it is reasonable to doubt whether the tsar was Pasha's father. *You* could be tsar, my darling. I've already been busy spreading gossip about the possibility around the city."

Nikolai clenched his fists. Then he snatched the invisible edge of the bubble surrounding the woman—he knew precisely where the edge was, for he had created it—and yanked her into the church. It was empty at this hour. He slammed her into the pews. She cackled.

"You could be arrested for treason," he whispered furiously. "*I* could be arrested for treason, simply for walking and talking with you. How dare you spew these lies."

The woman straightened her cloak and adjusted the hood over her head. Being hurled into the pew seemed to have had little impact on her.

"I don't know how you came to know my identity as an enchanter, but I could chain you to this bench for eternity if I so desired."

"I have no doubt. But you wouldn't do that to your mother, would you?"

"I have no mother. She died when I was born."

"I *almost* died. But I resurrected myself." The woman lifted the hood and let it fall to her shoulders.

Nikolai stumbled backward into another pew across the aisle. The woman looked as horrid as she had smelled before he contained her stench in the bubble. Her skin was yellowed and mummified in places, gray and sagging in others. Only her eyes glowed, wild with savagery.

God forgive me, Nikolai thought. *I've led the devil into Your sanctuary.*

"It is truly I. My name is Aizhana Karimova, and I was a faith healer on the steppe. The village thought I had died, but I actually lay in ante-death, the amorphous space between life and death. It took eighteen years, but I healed myself, leaching energy from the worms and maggots that squirmed over me. And when I emerged from ante-death, I went in search of the only thing that mattered: you."

Nikolai clutched a book of psalms that had been left in his pew. "It's not possible to rise from death."

Aizhana sighed, and all her audacity fell away. "It is when you are motivated by love." She frowned. Or what would have been a frown had the muscles of her face worked as they were supposed to, rather than pulling taut in some places and hanging loose in others. "But, my dear, why should you not believe in ante-death, simply because you did not know it exists? Healing is the business of transferring energy; resurrection is healing, but more ambitious. And there is nothing too ambitious for a mother separated from her son."

Nikolai remained in his pew, but his grip on the book of psalms eased. Just a fraction. It was nonsense, what she spoke of, and yet . . . it seemed possible that there could be a kernel of truth. Perhaps even more than a kernel.

She inched closer and opened her arms as if to embrace him.

"Stay back."

Her entire body slumped, but she did not try to advance farther. "I have been in the city a while now, but I did not feel worthy of you, Nikolai. I failed to protect you, and protection was my job as your mother. I could not face you until I felt I had been redeemed." Her face drooped. The skin near her mouth looked as if it might fall off her chin. It was a ghoul's rendition of regret.

"And are you redeemed now?"

Her eyes brightened. "I am."

"How?"

Now the skin near her mouth tightened, and she bared her rotten jaw in a monstrous, gap-toothed smile. "The villagers who neglected you have been punished. When I find Galina Zakrevskaya, she will feel my wrath as well. And the tsar . . . let us simply say his death was not accidental."

Nikolai clung to the psalter again. "You killed the tsar?"

"Believe me, he did not deserve to live."

"And the tsarina?" Nikolai's voice was hardly audible.

"She died of natural causes. She meant nothing to me."

If Nikolai hadn't already been sitting, he would have buckled onto the floor. His mother had come back from the dead. And she had murdered the tsar, who she claimed was his father.

He summoned the power to rise from the pew. "You may have been my mother in your past life, but not in your current reincarnation."

Aizhana's shriveled lips twisted with a sob. "But—"

"The bubble I've cast around you will remain to spare others from your fetor. But please leave Saint Petersburg. I do not wish your presence here."

"Nikolai." She whimpered. She attempted to stand. She fell back into the pew.

"I have charmed you to the bench. The spell will wear off in a few hours. Meanwhile, it may do you good to spend some time in this holy place. To think about what you've done."

"No! My son! I did everything for you. I love you, Nikolai."

But he strode out of the church without looking back. He had a mother who was a demon of the dead. He had a father who was actually dead. And he had a duel tomorrow, at the end of which either he or Vika would be dead.

Again, Renata's tea leaves were correct. Nikolai was born of Death, and Death would always follow him. The only question that remained was, would he also help usher in Death?

CHAPTER SIXTY-FIVE

In the evening, Vika woke in her bed on Ovchinin Island with her eyes nearly glued together from salt crust, and her mouth pasty and dry. Her flat in Saint Petersburg had been too quiet without Ludmila, and the city too big and impersonal. Vika had needed stillness and familiarity to sort through her thoughts, so she'd come home.

And cried and cried.

It was worse than after she'd first learned of Sergei's death. Then, she had been sad, but she'd also been furious. She'd been upset that he lied to her about her mother, and that he never dispelled her delusion that he was her real father. Her grief had been diluted by her sense of betrayal. It had taken time to come to terms with his untruths, and to understand that whether or not he was her biological father, he had cared for her and taught her everything he knew, and he'd been her father in everything but name.

However, unlike the letter about Sergei's death, Galina's accusation that Vika had been the one who took his life hit

Vika directly. There was no one else to blame. And so she cried.

But now she scraped the salt from her eyes. *It wasn't my fault*, Vika realized. *I couldn't have known and couldn't have stopped what happened.* Sergei had never taught her it was possible to channel energy as he had done. And it must have been his plan that when the Game began, he would sacrifice himself if he had to in order to help her. *Oh, Father.*

With this understanding, Vika rose from bed and cobbled together supper from the tins of fish in the cupboard and some old beets from the garden. Then she dived into her last few hours before the duel.

She did little in preparation for the duel itself. She figured that what she already knew would have to suffice; there was little else she could learn in these final hours. Besides, she wanted to save her strength.

Vika also had no inkling of what to expect from Nikolai. In fact, she had no clue about what to expect from herself. If he attacked, she would react. If he didn't, well . . . she did not know.

What Vika did do was tidy up the loose ends of her life. She made a list of all her valuables—there weren't many, but the contents of the chest buried under the valerian root (Father's "hiding spot") would be enough to last a comfortable lifetime—and left instructions that they were to go to Ludmila in the event Vika died. She also composed a letter to Ludmila and charmed both the list and the letter to self-destruct should Vika survive the Game, and to find their way to Ludmila if she did not.

After she'd run out of chores, Vika hiked into the forest to say good-bye to her longtime refuge. She climbed over icy logs and pushed her way through snow-covered shrubs until she reached Preobrazhensky Creek. It was frozen over, but she could still imagine its soft burbling, the fish glistening silver beneath its surface, and the frogs croaking their deep, vibrating songs on midsummer nights.

"Farewell," she whispered, and the wind between the trees stirred and carried her message through the woods.

Vika sat on a boulder on the creek's bank and touched the basalt pendant at her neck. Sergei had made her promise, long before the Game began, to remain his little Vikochka, no matter what the future would bring. Had she done that? Had she played the Game in a way that would've made Sergei proud? Or had she changed too much and lost herself?

"It would have been impossible not to change," Vika whispered. And as soon as she said it, she knew it was true, and she accepted it. But she didn't know if she would be able to accept becoming an outright murderer.

She sat in the forest for a long time, until the winter cold truly set in, and even the branches shivered. She rose from her rock to leave, perhaps forever. "Good-bye, my island. Thank you for everything." If she'd had any tears left, she might have wept.

As Vika returned to her cottage, the full moon glowed red in the sky. She thought of a saying Sergei had taught her when she was young.

White moon, angel moon.

Blood moon, demon moon.

She made haste and hurried inside.

At the stroke of midnight, as the calendar shifted to the date of the duel, a wolf howled at the red-black sky. It sounded like a funeral dirge.

CHAPTER SIXTY-SIX

The duel would begin as soon as the sun rose.

Pasha crawled across his bedroom and threw up in a vase.

He would not allow himself to get up from the floor.

CHAPTER SIXTY-SEVEN

At six o'clock in the morning, Nikolai stood on the banks of the Neva and looked out across the dark bay. In the distance, his lanterns lit up the island, but he knew there was no one there, for Pasha had declared it closed. Of course, if Nikolai had wanted to step foot on the island yesterday, he could have found a way. But he hadn't wanted to. Why visit the execution block where he might be scheduled to die?

Today, however, he had no choice. With one last glance over his shoulder, a farewell to the city he loved, Nikolai conjured a pair of skates and allowed them to carry him over the ice. It was a simple charm, one that wouldn't take too much from him before the duel commenced, and it would give him a few more moments of peace.

The calm was interrupted, though, by his scar, which scalded Nikolai's skin so unbearably, he clutched at his collarbone and his knees almost gave out. If Nikolai's skates hadn't been charmed, he would not have been able to continue across the frozen bay. So many times yesterday, he had thought of taking his turn in the Game simply to alleviate the pain of the wands on his skin. And yet, he had refrained, for it was his fifth and final move. He could not waste it. So he had had to bear the scar's searing.

He nearly crashed into the granite shore of the island. It had appeared too quickly. Perhaps his skates had glided faster than he anticipated. Perhaps he'd lost himself a little in the scorching wands. Or perhaps time had accelerated, the way it sometimes does when something dreadful is on the horizon. Regardless, Nikolai was at the island. The Game was upon him once again.

He clambered up the dock and changed his skates back into boots. He double-checked inside his coat that he had the knife Galina had given him, and then he began to walk straight to the center of the island. Here, the leaves were still green and the birds still sang in warm comfort, despite the winter that swirled in the bay and the river around it. The island was oblivious to its unhappy destiny.

Nikolai didn't know where, exactly, to go, but the main promenade seemed an appropriate choice, the kind of field of honor typically found in duels. It was shielded from view from the embankments of Saint Petersburg to give them privacy from nosy onlookers. There was enough space for the enchanters to fight. And it was tragically beautiful, a cruel and perfect place for one of them to die.

Pasha wanted them to fight a classic duel. But there was nothing classic about it. There would be no seconds to check Nikolai's and Vika's weapons—for how could anyone check a weapon he cannot see?—and there would be no attempt at reconciliation, for the duel was not instigated at Vika's or Nikolai's request. There would be no counting of paces, because Nikolai did not intend to shoot at Vika with a pistol. And there would be no witnesses.

Or would there be? Nikolai quickened his pace. Was it possible that Pasha intended to witness the grand finale? It seemed unlikely, but with this new version of Pasha, Nikolai could not be sure.

As Nikolai turned onto the promenade, he stumbled. There, among the flowers and the oaks, stood two iron cages. Renata and Ludmila were inside. Nikolai ran.

"Renata! Madame Fanina! Are you all right?"

Ludmila stretched from where she had been asleep on the ground. Renata, however, had been standing with her forehead pressed against the bars. She jumped at the sound of his voice.

"Nikolai!"

"What has Pasha done?"

Renata shook her head. "Not the tsesarevich. His sister. She's the one driving his decisions. She wants an Imperial Enchanter for him."

"Damn it, Yuliana," Nikolai muttered.

"What?" Renata pressed against the bars.

"Never mind, it's not important right now. I need to get you two out." He raised his arm.

"No, stop! Save your energy."

"I don't want you locked up like animals."

"The grand princess promised our safety if we remained in the cages."

"But why . . . Oh." Nikolai sagged against the bars. "She means to remind us to finish the Game quickly."

Renata cast her eyes downward and nodded.

Ludmila pulled herself up from the floor of her cell. "We

will try not to watch you fight. Think only of the silver lining. With us here, we are at least able to say good-bye."

"Good-bye?" Nikolai shook his head.

"Yes," Ludmila said. "Good-bye. Just in case."

At this, Renata took Nikolai's face in her hands and touched their foreheads together in the space between the bars.

"Nikolai . . ."

"Oh, Renata—"

"Don't say it."

But he had to. After all she had done for him. "You've been the best companion I could have hoped for on this strange journey. I could never thank you enough. Take care of Galina, all right? And if there's anything in my room that you want—"

"Stop." She shook her head against his. "I refuse to say good-bye. And I will not say good luck either, for there is neither good nor luck in this duel."

Nikolai nodded. She was, as she often was, right. Even in these last minutes.

"But I can't let you leave without this: I have said it before, and now I say it again—I love you. I loved you even before I knew of your magic, Nikolai, and I have loved you ever since. And I will continue to love you, no matter what you choose to do."

She leaned forward and pressed her mouth against his. Her lips parted, and there was such soft courage in her gesture, his lips parted, too.

She lingered, but eventually she pulled away. She caressed his cheek. And then she whispered one more time, "I love you. Now go. And don't forget to be *you*."

CHAPTER SIXTY-EIGHT

Vika arrived on an ice sleigh as the sun rose over the frozen horizon. She made her way toward the center of the island—it seemed the right place to start—and stepped onto the promenade just in time to see Nikolai kiss Renata.

Vika stopped mid-stride.

It took another moment for Vika to realize that next to where Renata and Nikolai gazed at each other, Ludmila stood locked in a cage. In fact, Vika had been so fixated on Renata's and Nikolai's lips, she hadn't noticed that Renata, too, was imprisoned.

"Ludmila!" Vika flew to the bars.

Nikolai leaped back from Renata's cell. "Vika . . . you're here."

She ignored him.

"Ludmila, who did this? We—*I*—have to set you free."

"Hush, sunshine." Ludmila stretched through the bars and patted Vika's arm. "Leave me be. The grand princess guaranteed our release at the conclusion of the duel."

"But you—"

"I'm fine. You must play the Game."

Vika shook the bars. But then her arms gave out and she pressed against the cage. "I'm sorry I never told you about the Game, Ludmila. I didn't want you to worry."

"I understand. I would have done the same."

"I'm even sorrier that you were swept up in it."

"No need for apologies, dear. Besides, there is no time." Ludmila pointed behind Vika. "The sun is rising."

Vika glanced over her shoulder. The sky had turned reddish orange, like a reverse image of the blood moon from the night. And with the sun hanging above the frozen water, the duel had officially begun.

It was Nikolai's move. Vika whirled around and pressed her back against Ludmila's cage so her friend would not be exposed.

"I won't strike when you're not looking," Nikolai said quietly. "And I propose we go elsewhere on the island. I think it better if Madame Fanina and Renata were not forced to watch. Meet me at Candlestick Point when you're finished saying your good-byes?"

Inside, Vika wilted, but outside, she merely nodded. No one before had called the peninsula at the northern tip of the island Candlestick Point, but she knew immediately what Nikolai meant. She had left Candlestick Point undeveloped when she created the island, hoping one of them would take advantage of the open space for an enchantment. Now it appeared it would be used as the field on which one of them died.

Nikolai bowed to both Vika and Ludmila. Renata squeezed his hand once more, and then he spun on his heel and strode away, as if he couldn't get away from the cages—and to Candlestick Point—fast enough. He didn't give even a passing glance to his benches.

"You should go, my dear," Ludmila said to Vika. "I hope for your sake it ends quickly."

"As do I. And I also wish it would never end." Vika's shoulders sagged.

Ludmila sighed and looped her arms around Vika, pulling her into the bars for an embrace. "I may not be your mother, but like Sergei, I have watched you grow, and I consider you my own. You are strong and smart, and however this Game ends, know that you will have done me and Sergei proud. You are a wonder, Vika. I'm blessed to have had you in my life." Ludmila sniffled, and Vika held her as tight as she could.

Then Ludmila released her and retreated into the middle of her cage. "Now go. Your fate awaits. I cannot keep you from it any longer."

Renata leaned against her bars. "Be brave," she said. "Both you and Nikolai."

Vika blinked back tears and nodded. Then she, like Nikolai, hurried away. She understood now that it was impossible to leave any other way.

He waited for her at the end of Candlestick Point, his back to her, looking out onto the unmoving bay. His dark figure cut against the dawn light, an ominous silhouette from his top hat down to the sharp toe of his boot. Vika's feet hardly touched the gravel as she approached, but they still stirred the air around her, and it was inconceivable that Nikolai would not have heard. Yet he did not acknowledge her until she was only a few yards away.

Nikolai turned to face her. The knife Galina had given him rested in his gloved hand.

Vika put up a double shield. Unlike Nikolai, she hadn't put on her gloves this morning, improper as that might be. They had never before impeded her magic, but she was not taking any chances today.

"How have you been?" he asked. "I haven't seen you in a while."

Vika narrowed her eyes. Was he actually trying to have a conversation, right here, right now? Or was it a deceptive ploy? She kept her distance. "You saw me yesterday in the palace."

"You ran away before we had a chance to talk. That hardly counts as seeing you."

"I did not run, I *glided* away in a sled. And I did not want to talk."

He gave her a wry smile. It might have been charming if it weren't for the dagger he twirled in his hands. "I missed you," he said. Then he corrected himself. "I missed your enchantments."

The image of him kissing Renata flashed in Vika's mind. "It was your move."

"I was waiting for inspiration. But then Pasha changed the Game, and I had to hold on to my turn." Nikolai clawed distractedly at the collar of his shirt, where the brand must have been searing into his skin. "But what I wanted to say, and did not get a chance to, was that I am sorry to hear about your father's passing."

Vika was dizzy with the conversation. Nikolai hadn't even mentioned that she'd destroyed all his possessions.

Were they enemies fighting a duel? Or were they friends making up for lost time? She didn't know whether to protect herself or open up to him. "Um, thank you. But it turns out Sergei was not my father."

"Oh . . . I'm sorry . . . that must have been quite a shock."

Shock is a mighty understatement.

Nikolai scuffed the heel of his boot on the gravel. "My father also died recently. Although I didn't know he was my father until after his death. Nearly the mirror opposite of your experience."

Vika blinked at Nikolai. "Oh. That's terrible. I'm sorry."

He shrugged. "I hardly knew him. But thank you." He looked at her and held her eyes. Vika thought she saw a flicker in his, a shape like a golden eagle, like an echo of their time together on the dream steppe. But then Nikolai looked down at his knife, and the memory of their shared moment evaporated into tense air.

The dagger gleamed. "I don't want to do this," he said.

"Then don't."

"It's the only way."

Vika jerked back to the reality of the Game. She checked her shields, and she began to pace along Candlestick Point, so as not to be too easy a target in a single static space. Who knew what that knife was capable of? Sergei's simple leather bracelet had been enough to drain his life. Surely Galina's gift would be equally as powerful, and likely much more vicious.

But Nikolai did not move to aim it at Vika.

"There's one more thing," he said.

"Yes?" Vika forced herself to continue walking. If only he would hurry and make his move. If he was going to kill her, she wanted him to end it now, before her own dread choked her.

"I love you," he said.

"What?"

He smiled sadly. "I was lost from the moment I saw you on Ovchinin Island. It took a long while for me to realize it, but it's true. I've spent my entire life scrambling to fit in and to change myself, Vika, but where I've belonged, and who I needed to be, has been right here the whole time. I love you."

Vika stood in one place, no longer pacing. "But . . . but you kissed Renata."

Nikolai shook his head. "She's only a friend."

"Are you sure?"

"I've never wanted anyone but you."

Vika gasped as the invisible string that connected them pulled taut. She wanted to let it reel her in, to pull her to Nikolai, and him to her. And yet . . . the dagger. "Then what is the knife for?"

"To end the Game." Nikolai gripped the handle, and sunlight glinted off the sharp edges of the blade.

Suddenly, it seemed as if the air grew thinner, and Vika's head swam as she tried to make sense of everything Nikolai was saying, everything Vika wanted him to say. And to *not* say. But she had to ask.

"You love me, so you're going to kill me?"

"I love you," Nikolai said, "so I want you to live."

"I don't underst—"

"Galina said this knife would never miss." He pointed the dagger at his chest. "This is my fifth move."

No, he couldn't mean to— "Nikolai! Stop!"

Vika lunged and threw a wave of magic at him.

But he was too quick. He thrust the knife deep into himself. It plunged up under his ribs on a direct path to his heart.

The violence of his act pierced through Vika, and she felt as if her heart, too, had been impaled. Her scream split the sky and shattered the morning's remains.

CHAPTER SIXTY-NINE

Nikolai was still standing. He didn't feel a thing, when he should have felt the blade slicing through muscle and grating against bone. When he should have been buckling in a pool of red. When Death was supposed to have come to claim him.

He looked down at himself. There was no knife in his hands. What? How?

And then he looked up at Vika, who had just screamed. Her eyes were wide, and a hilt protruded from her chest. Blood drenched the bodice of her dress.

"Nikolai . . . ," she gasped.

"Vika!" Unlike the night along the canal, he was quick enough this time to catch her before she hit the ground. He cradled her tenderly against his body. Her breathing was already shallow.

Galina had said the knife would not miss. So how . . . ?

Nikolai drew in a guillotine-sharp breath. Galina. The conniving, venomous harpy. She had known before Nikolai did that his weakness—his compassion for the tiger, for the lorises, for Vika—might lead him to attempt to end the Game by killing himself. So Galina had charmed the knife to hit the target she thought it ought to. Like she'd said, the knife would never miss.

"Vika. I'm so sorry. I didn't know . . . It was supposed to be me, not you."

She turned her head toward him, but her eyes were far away. Even the green in them seemed diluted.

He pressed his fingers to her throat and felt her pulse beneath her skin. The beat faltered. Then it recovered, but the rhythm was uneven.

What have I done, what have I done, what have I done?

"Vika, listen to me. I'll fix this. There must be some way to reverse it. You need to hold on. Hold on while I figure out how to right this."

She wheezed and more blood gushed from her wound.

I have to close it, Nikolai thought. But he had never done anything like it before. Galina had trained him as a master of mechanics. But what good was shipbuilding and fabric manipulating at a time like this? And the only way she had taught him to handle life was to end it. Damn her and her blasted tigers.

If only Vika could heal herself, like she did for the animals on her island. But she hadn't the strength. "Why can't I give you mine?" Nikolai let out a tortured wail.

But why couldn't he?

Sergei had channeled his energy into Vika. And Aizhana had taken life from other life. Nikolai didn't know how it was done, but the fact was, it *had* been done. And now it was his only hope. He would have to cobble together a way how.

"I don't know how to heal you, Vika, but I'm going to try to siphon some of my energy to you. And then . . . I don't know. Then I hope you'll have enough strength that you can heal yourself."

She didn't respond.

Nikolai squeezed his eyes shut for a second. "Please let this work." Then he opened them again and gritted his teeth.

Go. He tried to command his energy, in the same way he ordinarily directed his thoughts toward objects he wanted to move. *Go.*

He waved his hands. Nothing.

He pointed with his fingers. No response.

He even tried blowing energy out through his mouth, to no avail.

Go, go, go.

Vika's head drooped in his arms.

He propped her up and cradled her tighter, so close it was as if they were waltzing rather than dying. The panic rose in his chest; his own heartbeat accelerated to the speed of a mazurka.

And then . . . yes.

Like a dance. Like my enchantment at the masquerade.

But this time, instead of the rhythm of the orchestra, it would be the rhythm of Nikolai's own heart. And instead of charming Vika's feet to follow the tune of the mazurka, he would charm her stumbling pulse to follow his stronger one. Like any good dancer, he would lead her where he needed her to go.

Please work.

Nikolai closed his eyes. He focused on the steady beat of

his heart. *Ka-thump, ka-thump, ka-thump.* He charmed Vika's heart next, convincing himself it was the same as charming her feet, and he channeled the rhythm of his pulse like music into her veins.

Her heart tripped.

"Listen to the rhythm," he whispered. *Ka-thump, ka-thump, ka-thump.*

Her heart stumbled again.

No. Like this: *Ka-thump, ka-thump, ka-thump.*

There was a pause. And then hers went, *Ka-thump, ka-thump, ka-thump.* The raggedness of Vika's breath smoothed a little.

Yes. Nikolai kept his eyes closed. *Now, beat harder,* he urged, like a conductor asking his drummers to play louder. *Ka-THUMP, ka-THUMP, ka-THUMP.*

He felt her shift in his arms. *Ka-THUMP, ka-THUMP, ka-THUMP.*

The frigid wind whipped around him. It was like the snow flurry of Vika's dress in the ballroom, lifting their dancing to a frenzy. Nikolai harnessed the memory of that energy—the blistering tempo of the orchestra, the rapid movements of their feet—and propelled it into Vika's body.

She gasped and sat upright.

Nikolai linked his arms around her and pulled her close again. There was no telling what would happen if he lost the connection with her heart.

"Vika, listen. I'm going to extract the knife. But I don't know how to stanch the bleeding, so you'll have to do it. Can you manage?" He continued to listen to their rhythms as he spoke.

She blinked at him twice. Weakly.

It was all she could muster. He would have to take that as a yes.

"Don't worry. We can do this," he said, even though he wasn't sure if it was true. "I'll keep your heart strong."

Nikolai held her tight. Then he took a deep breath and wrenched the knife from her chest. He felt the sickening give of soft flesh as he did it, and it was only because he had to keep rhythm for Vika's heart that he didn't throw up.

As the blade came out, Vika shrieked, and the sound was a thousand banshees ripping Nikolai's soul apart. He trembled as he pinned down her arms to keep her from flailing. Vika's pulse stuttered, and a torrent of fresh blood surged from the wound.

We are not at Death's door, he told himself. *We are at Pasha's ball. Our feet are stamping and skipping, our hearts kicking and leaping.* "Remember the masquerade," he whispered into Vika's ear. "Remember how we danced."

Ka-THUMP, ka-THUMP, ka-THUMP.

Her heart reluctantly rejoined the mazurka.

She took in saw-toothed gulps of air. Her lungs were as fragile as the unlit paper lanterns in the sky. But Nikolai would not let her heart stop dancing.

And then he felt her tense against him, the muscles in her shoulders drawn back and growing strong. She doubled over again, then stretched out, twisted, and unwound. She moaned and cried. He held her tight as she carried out her work.

But soon Nikolai's arms began to quiver, and he was cold. So very, very cold. He had felt like this when he created the benches, and he knew he wouldn't last much longer. "Hurry . . . ," he whispered.

Vika took in a sharp inhale in response.

Now her heartbeat was solid, and his was flimsy, but still he continued to pour his energy into her. Her body kept contracting and writhing and contorting against his.

After what seemed an eternity, all her muscles relaxed. She collapsed against his neck and whispered, "I did it. I . . . I closed the wound." Her voice was her own again. "You can let go now, Nikolai."

His head was cloudy, and he didn't have the strength to unlink his arms from her. So he chose instead to open his eyes.

The knife was discarded by her side. She was alive.

But he felt as if he were not.

Vika sat up on her own. Then she let out a plaintive cry. "Nikolai." Her hand fluttered to her mouth. "Nikolai, what have you done?"

He shook his head. He didn't know.

He crumpled in a heap.

At least I die with her in my arms.

CHAPTER SEVENTY

The Russe Quill began to scratch on the Scroll. Pasha's stomach turned. He grabbed the vase again.

The Quill had written something else earlier in the morning, not long after dawn. But Pasha had not been able to muster the courage to look at it, to see what Nikolai's first play had been. He had lain on the floor instead, waiting for Vika to make a move.

The ensuing silence of the Quill had been too loud.

Now there was something new, and Pasha clenched his fists and forced himself to rise. Were they fighting, as Yuliana had told Pasha needed to be done? Or had Vika and Nikolai found a way around the rules of the Game? *Please let it be the latter. . . .*

But deep inside, Pasha knew there was no way out other than victory for one and death for the other.

He wrung his hands as he walked to his desk, dragging his feet to make the distance across the room longer. But he was there before he knew it. He hesitated before he picked up the parchment, looking around his bedroom for another excuse. Perhaps he ought to wait for Yuliana? But she was occupied with entertaining the English ambassador's wife, and if Pasha waited, she would only yell at him that if he was going to be tsar, he had better find the backbone soon to act like it.

So he reached for the Scroll, hands shaking. The parchment crinkled in his grasp. He didn't want to look, but there was nothing else to do.

1 December 1825: Winner—Vika Andreyeva

Pasha dropped his head to his hands and sobbed.

CHAPTER SEVENTY-ONE

One week after the end of the Game, Vika sat on the steppe bench and immersed herself in the dream. Soon, she would have to return to Saint Petersburg to take her post as Imperial Enchanter, but for now, she watched Nikolai's golden eagle fly over the barren plains. It was so unfair that his benches were still here when he wasn't. And yet, it was something. So she listened to the rustle of the dry grasses and felt the cool breeze on her face and remembered him.

Pasha had ordered an elaborate memorial service for Nikolai, but Vika hadn't attended. Despite Pasha's grief and his attempts to apologize for demanding the duel, Vika didn't want anything to do with him. At least not for now. Until he was officially installed as tsar and she had no choice but to serve him, Vika needed space. The wounds Pasha had inflicted were too deep and too raw.

There was another reason, however, that Vika hadn't wanted to attend Nikolai's memorial. It horrified her, but she was unable to cry for him. Perhaps she had used up all her tears before the duel. Perhaps the grief was so vast, mere tears could never be adequate. Or perhaps it was that something nagged at her, and she felt he wasn't entirely gone.

Nikolai had crumpled in her lap at the end of the Game. But instead of the wands bursting into flame and consuming him, as she'd expected, he'd disintegrated into nothing. As if, with all his energy drained, he'd simply ceased to exist. And because he did not exist, there was no scar to alight and burn. Then Vika's own scar had vanished from her skin. The Game had officially been won.

But even with Nikolai gone, there had remained a heaviness in the air, a lack of finality, as if his magic still lingered. It had been impossible to attend his memorial when it felt as if something of Nikolai was still there. Here.

The wind on the steppe whipped up, and the eagle soared on its gust. Behind Vika, someone pushed through the long grass. The footsteps on the hard-packed dirt were neither quiet nor particularly loud, as if the person could tread lighter but wanted to be sure Vika was not startled. She turned.

It was Pasha.

"I thought you might be here," he said. "I hope you don't mind me joining your dream."

Vika bit her lip, but she tilted her chin in greeting. "It isn't mine to keep."

He lifted his gaze up to the sky. For a second, it seemed as if the eagle turned its head at Pasha and glared. But then it was back to focusing on the ground. Vika probably imagined it.

"I miss him, too, you know," Pasha said.

The emptiness in Vika's chest echoed with Nikolai's absence. "It's no fault but your own," she said.

Pasha sighed heavily. "I know. Trust me, I know."

Vika looked at him then, really looked at him. His face was gaunt, his blue eyes almost gray and ringed with dark circles. His hair was irretrievable chaos. He was Pasha, if Pasha were a ghost.

"If I could take it back, I would," he said. "I was . . . *angry* that Nikolai hadn't told me he was an enchanter. And I was irrational with grief over my parents. Then Yuliana said I had to declare the duel, and she's so sure of everything while I am sure of nothing, so I listened. It's no excuse. I still made the decision. But I am acutely sorry for it. I didn't think it through."

"You didn't realize that if you demanded a duel to the death, one of us would die?"

Pasha shook his head. "I did, but I didn't. I was all emotion and reaction. I wasn't thinking."

Vika frowned. "I hope you clear your head before you become tsar."

"That's why I need you, Vika. I can't do this alone, or with only Yuliana by my side."

The look Vika cast him was so stony, it was worthy of the grand princess. "I'll be your Imperial Enchanter. I committed to it in my oath to your father."

"But you won't be there of your own accord."

In the distance, the eagle circled in the sky, then plummeted down toward the ground. A moment later, it flapped its mighty wings and emerged from the grass with a small animal drooping from its talons. The eagle rose into the air with its prey.

"Forgiveness doesn't come so easily," Vika said, as much to herself as to Pasha.

He smiled sadly. But he nodded. "I understand. But perhaps with time—"

"Perhaps."

He swallowed. "Right . . . Well . . . I'll leave you alone then. I shall see you after I return from my coronation."

Vika glanced at him. "I will be there in Moscow."

"You will?" The blue in Pasha's eyes flickered through the gray.

"Yes. To ensure no harm comes to you. I promised Father I would do my best to serve the empire, and that begins with the tsar."

"Oh . . . all right. I . . . I appreciate it."

Vika gave him a curt nod. "Good-bye, Your Imperial Highness."

He hesitated, as if he wanted to say more, but then bowed and retreated. There was a rustle through the grass as he awoke and exited the dream.

Vika closed her eyes and rubbed her face with her hands. If only the past could be undone.

But at least there was this. This dream where time was suspended. This bench bridging then and now.

Vika turned her focus back to the sky. But the eagle was gone, having successfully killed its prey. She squinted at the horizon, hoping to find it again. It would be with its *berkutchi*, its master.

They were difficult to see at first. But eventually, she made out a shadow at the mountain's base. The *berkutchi* sat atop his horse, the eagle perched regally on his arm. They were camouflaged in the shade.

Vika craned her neck and squinted harder. The outline of the rider sharpened. But it was not the profile of a burly Kazakh hunter, as Vika expected. It was instead the graceful silhouette of a gentleman, in a top hat.

She inhaled sharply.

The string at Vika's chest tugged at her. The shadow turned in her direction, as if he, too, had felt the pull. He paused for a moment when he saw her. But then he dipped his head, like their mutual presence was no surprise at all, and he raised his hat in a distant hello.

She was supposed to be invisible to the people in the dream.

Vika lifted her hand to wave, her heart pounding to the beat of a mazurka.

He was almost the same as he'd been at Bolshebnoie Duplo. Almost, because the shadow boy on the horse wasn't entirely there. Right now, he could only exist in this reverie.

But his silhouette was identical. Vika had been right that she could still feel his presence, and she could almost hear him in the wind, invoking the words he'd once written on her armoire:

Imagine, and it shall be.
There are no limits.

Vika smiled. Her magic was not alone.
The shadow was undeniably Nikolai.

AUTHOR'S NOTE

I first fell in love with Russian history and literature when I was in college. I had read Dostoevsky's *The Brothers Karamazov* in high school, and curiosity led me to the Slavic Languages and Literatures Department at Stanford. I'd only meant to take a class or two; instead, I graduated three years later with a bachelor's degree in the subject and an unabiding weakness for all things Russian (including the food!).

The Crown's Game is a work of historical fantasy set in an alternate Imperial Russia, but its foundation is based on true events and places. Much of the research for this book was actually done while I was in college, although inadvertently—little did I know then that my adoration of Tolstoy and my obsession with nineteenth-century Russia would one day lead to Vika and Nikolai.

I did, however, need to shore up on some historical details for *The Crown's Game*, for which I referenced my old textbooks as well as Orlando Figes's *Natasha's Dance* and Martha Brill Olcott's *The Kazakhs*.

An example of how I melded fact with fiction: Alexander I was the real tsar of the Russian Empire, from 1801 until 1825. He steered the country through much upheaval, including the Napoleonic Wars, and eventually brought about a period of relative peace to the empire.

It is undisputed that Alexander I had many affairs; he flaunted his mistresses openly, bringing them to court and even having children with them. He did, however, reconcile with the Tsarina Elizabeth near the end of his life, as well as find solace in mysticism, for which many questioned him, but the tsarina supported him. It was on a trip together to Taganrog, in an attempt to restore the tsarina to health, that Alexander died of typhus. Elizabeth soon followed (although I took some liberties with the dates of their passing), dying of a weak—some say broken—heart.

The Crown's Game diverges from actual history, though, in the story of the children borne by Alexander and Elizabeth. In reality, the tsar and tsarina had two girls, both of whom died in infancy. In *The Crown's Game*, however, their children are very much alive and grown, although they have a boy and a girl—Pasha and Yuliana—instead of two daughters.

Probably the most fun I had while doing research for *The Crown's Game* was investigating the profanity of the time. I turned to one of my professors at Stanford for help on this subject, and we have quite an amusing chain of emails discussing what Nikolai, Pasha, and Vika would or wouldn't have said. I also reread parts of *War and Peace* in an attempt to cull some of the aristocracy's exclamations from that period of time.

Many of the settings in *The Crown's Game* were inspired

by my trip to Russia in 2003, when I took a cruise along the Volga River from Moscow to Saint Petersburg. I remember seeing the shimmering wooden church on Kizhi Island and thinking it must have been constructed by magic—now it is indeed magical, as one of the locations in Nikolai's Dream Benches.

And, of course, there is Saint Petersburg . . . perhaps I love it because one of my dearest friends lives there, or perhaps it's because one can't help but fall for the beautiful capital. Most of Vika, Nikolai, and Pasha's Saint Petersburg is based on the actual city, from Ekaterinsky Canal to Nevsky Prospect, from the bronze statue of Peter the Great to the Winter Palace. The waterways and rivers are real as well, as is the Neva Bay and the many small islands linked by bridges and ferries that form the capital city.

However, both Vika's home, Ovchinin Island, and the new island she creates are figments of my imagination. I like to think, though, that they'd fit right in with the actual islands that dot the Neva Bay.

I do have to confess we took artistic license with the cover of *The Crown's Game*. The buildings in the crown would not have existed in 1825, but after many iterations, the team at Harper and I decided that this version best captured the essence of Vika and Nikolai's story. I hope the historians among my readers will forgive me this transgression.

As for whether the magic in *The Crown's Game* is real, well . . . that depends. Do you believe in what you cannot see?

ACKNOWLEDGMENTS

When I first came up with the idea for *The Crown's Game*, I emailed a few of my friends and said sheepishly, "So, hey, I started writing this crazy fantasy about two enchanters in a deadly duel who fall into impossible, bittersweet love, and it's all set in magical, Imperial Russia. . . ." I wasn't sure how they'd respond, but I was pretty sure it would involve good-natured laughing along the lines of, *There goes Evelyn on another nutty whim*. But instead, all three responded immediately and emphatically with, *YES. Yes, yes, yes, write it*. So thank you, Stacey Lee, Sean Byrne, and Jeanne Schriel, not only for your friendship over the years but also for telling me to chase this idea and make it real. *The Crown's Game* would not exist without you.

Thank you to my agent, Brianne Johnson, for loving Vika and Nikolai from page one, and for your gushiness and your sharp editorial insights and your mirrored Instagram pictures of your cat. Many thanks, too, to Cecilia de la Campa and Soumeya Roberts of Writers House, for bringing *The Crown's Game* overseas, and to Dana Spector at Paradigm Talent Agency for giving Vika and Nikolai a tour of Hollywood.

I cannot express enough gratitude to my brilliant and tireless editor, Kristin Rens, for helping me make this story bigger and brighter (and also darker) than I ever imagined possible. Kristin, you are the enchantress of publishing. Thank you to Alessandra Balzer and Donna Bray for championing *The Crown's Game* from the very start. To Joel Tippie and Alison Donalty for the breathtaking, perfect cover. To Kelsey Murphy, Jon Howard, Nellie Kurtzman, Caroline Sun, Megan Barlog, EpicReads, and the Harper sales team—I am so lucky to have you on my team.

Special thanks to Professor Richard Schupbach of Stanford University and his colleague Anna Bogomyakova for their expertise (and amusing emails) on nineteenth-century Russian swearwords. And to all my other professors and teachers at Stanford, for being there as I fell in love with Tolstoy and Dostoevsky and Russia's history.

This journey would not have been possible without the love, laughter, and wisdom from my writing family: Stacey Lee, Sara Raasch, Emily Martin, Sabaa Tahir, Monica Bustamante-Wagner, Tracy Edward Wymer, Anna Shinoda, Lara Perkins, Sean Byrne, Morgan Shamy, Hafsah Faizal, Dana Elmendorf, Elizabeth Briggs, Betsy Franco, Karen Akins, Karen Grunberg, and Puja Batra. I owe you an infinity of cookies. And ice cream.

Thank you to Denis Ovchinin, my Russian pen pal since we were teens. For you, Den, I created an entire island. I hope you like it.

Thank you to Kevin Hsu and Chanda Prescod-Weinstein

for your faith that one day, my words would become a real book.

To Dawn and Karl Ehrlich, thank you for always cheering me on.

Enormous thanks to the Tsar's Guard! Your enthusiasm and devotion have made this one heck of a year. The tsar could not have a better army in his service.

Eternal love to Andrew and Margaret Hsu, the very best parents a girl could ask for. Thank you for never setting a curfew, for letting me major in something as "impractical" as Russian literature and history, and for always encouraging my writing. I cannot wait to place this book—this real book!—in your hands. I love you more than you can ever know.

And last, but most important of all, thank you to Reese, for humoring me when my mind wandered to imperial Russia in the middle of breakfast, for spending weeks drawing a book cover for me, and for being proud of me and showering me with hugs and kisses. You are magic. You are the light of my life. And guess what? I love you!

Turn the page for a sneak peek at the sequel,
The Crown's Fate.

CHAPTER ONE

Vika Andreyeva was a confluence of minuscule bubbles, streaming through the wintry dusk. For a few moments, she gave herself up to the thrill of the magic, to the escape of evanescing. *I am the sky. I am the wind. I am freedom, unleashed.*

As soon as Vika rematerialized on the Kazakh steppe, though, solid reality replaced the joy of being everything, yet nearly nothing. She was here to work, to carry out an official assignment as Imperial Enchanter. She sighed.

Only half an hour earlier, she had appeared at the royal stables, where Grand Princess Yuliana Romanova had been grooming her horse. Or rather, a stable boy was grooming her horse, brushing its chestnut mane, while Yuliana pointed out every tiny knot.

The boy didn't see Vika appear in the corner of the farthest stall, but Yuliana's sharp eye missed nothing.

"Leave me," the grand princess said, shooing the stable boy away. He jumped and skittered off, well trained not to linger against Yuliana's wishes.

When he was gone, she turned to Vika and said, "Baroness Andreyeva, it would be preferable if you entered the room—or the stable—the proper way, by being admitted and announced by the guards. Like everyone else."

Vika cast Yuliana a sideways glance. "My apologies, Your Imperial Highness. It's just that, you see, I'm *not* 'like everyone else.'" She crossed her arms.

Yuliana huffed.

"I'm here because your messenger said you wished to see me?" Vika curtsied with more than a touch of sarcasm. Hay clung to the hem of her dress as she rose. She noticed but left it there. Vika had grown up in a forest; it seemed strange, almost, *not* to have bits of mud and leaves clinging to her.

Yuliana arched a brow at the hay. "I need you to do something."

No *How are you?* Or *Thank you for coming.* Not that Vika was surprised.

"What is it?"

"Manners, *s'il vous plaît*," Yuliana said.

Vika dipped her head and allowed it to bob down heavily. "Of course, Your Imperial Highness. I am at your service."

Yuliana rolled her eyes. "My brother and I need you to go to the Kazakh steppe."

"Pardon?" Vika jerked her head upright.

"Are you deaf now, too, along with being impertinent? I said, we need you to go to the Kazakh steppe. The last time Pasha was there, talk of another rebellion was underway. We need to find out if their plans have developed any further, but our traditional means of gathering intelligence via scouts is slow. However, *you* could evanesce to the steppe and come back all in the same day. We've never had information so fresh."

But Vika was hardly listening. She couldn't go. That was where Nikolai, Russia's only other enchanter, was from, and now he was gone because he'd lost the Crown's Game. . . .

How can I possibly walk through the steppe, as if it were just another place? Vika's heart stomped to the beat of a mazurka, painfully aware of the wrongness of each solitary move without Nikolai as her partner.

She shook her head. "I don't want to go. You can't send me there."

Yuliana had marched up to Vika, kicking hay in every direction. "I can, and I will. You're the Imperial Enchanter. Do your job."

Which was how Vika found herself on the steppe now. She gave herself another moment, not only to recover from evanescing—it always took a few seconds to get reoriented—but also to brace herself for facing this place that reminded her too much of what—*whom*—she'd lost only two weeks ago.

She took a very deep breath. *This is part of my duty. All my life, I've wanted nothing more than to be Imperial Enchanter, and this is what it entails. I can do this.* But it was a victory tinged with bittersweet.

She took another long inhale.

Before she left Saint Petersburg, Vika had transformed her appearance to blend in more easily with the Kazakhs, changing her hair from red to black, and her clothes from a puff-sleeved gown to a tunic-like *koilek*, a collared dress, and a heavy *shapan* overcoat made of sheepskin.

A few paces from the dark corner where she hid, the tented

marketplace bustled. There were tables piled high with nuts, and bins of spices. Stalls selling fur-lined boots, and others boasting silver jewelry, all intricately patterned and inlaid with red, orange, and blue stones. There was a table that specialized in all manner of dried fruit, and everywhere there were people, smiling and inspecting goods and bargaining.

A girl walked by, carrying a tray of enormous rounds of bread. They must have just come out of an oven, for their yeasty warmth filled the air. The smell, which reminded her of Ludmila Fanina's bakery at home, comforted Vika and pulled her out of her brooding.

Besides, brooding didn't suit Vika. It was more Nikolai's disposition than hers, and she was actually incapable of being melancholy for long before something inside her itched to move along. The one time she'd submerged herself in sorrow, after Father's passing, she'd come out of it more agitated than ever, and she'd nearly destroyed Nikolai's home in response, only to become mortified with regret halfway through. Vika would not make the mistake of wallowing again for too long. She clenched her fists and stashed away the swirl of emotions that surrounded her thoughts of Nikolai, as hard as putting away those feelings could be.

The bakery girl set down the tray at a stall a few yards away and began unloading the loaves onto the display. A crowd of women immediately surrounded the table, drawn to the fresh bread like garrulous seagulls to a picnic, and started yammering for the girl's attention.

Ludmila would love to try Kazakh bread.

Brilliant! Vika's eyes brightened. It would give her something to focus on other than Nikolai.

She conjured a few Kazakh coins in her palm. Then

she evanesced the money into the bakery girl's till and in exchange, evanesced a round of bread all the way back to Ovchinin Island, where both Vika and Ludmila Fanina lived. The loaf would arrive at Cinderella Bakery, Ludmila's shop, still warm and steamy. Vika sent a brief letter with the bread, even though she was quite sure Ludmila would know who'd sent it.

And now back to the task at hand.

Vika left the bakery stall and walked around the perimeter of the marketplace. The only flaw in Yuliana's plan was that unless the people were speaking Russian or French, Vika wouldn't understand what they were saying.

But why can't I?

Being the only remaining enchanter in Russia did mean Vika could ask more of the empire's magic, since she no longer had to share it. And she'd always been able to understand animals, like her albino messenger rat, Poslannik, by casting an enchantment over them. It had simply never occurred to her to translate another human language, because she'd needed only Russian, rudimentary French, and the speech of wolverines and foxes on Ovchinin Island.

As Vika walked, she began to conjure a dome, of sorts, to surround the entire marketplace. The enchantment began on the ground, like a shimmering veil of liquid crystal rising from the dirt. At least, that was how it appeared to her, for Vika could see the magic at work.

The enchantment trickled upward toward the sky, flowing as if it were not subject to the rules of gravity. It climbed the outside of the marketplace, then arched over the tops of the tents, enclosing the shoppers and vendors and their goods inside.

But not really. The dome wasn't solid; the people couldn't see it or feel it, and they could enter and exit as they pleased. Vika's magic would only capture the scene, and then she'd be able to take the enchantment back to Saint Petersburg to replay it for Yuliana and Pasha, who could walk through the memory dome as if they themselves had been here.

It also included an enchantment to allow Vika to understand Kazakh. Or an attempt at an enchantment like that, anyhow. If she could listen in, she could better root out whether there were any new developments in the region's unrest.

She smiled grimly at the marketplace before her. *I hope this works*, she thought, for if it did, she could capture scenes in other places, like the borders where the Russian and Ottoman empires chafed at each other. Such information would be invaluable.

She also hoped it failed, because spending the rest of her days alone, spying at the edges of the empire, would be no life at all.

The dome enchantment glistened lazily under the winter sun, its liquid crystal walls ebbing and flowing as the magic soaked up every word and action taking place within its confines. Vika picked up bits and pieces of the conversations. "Two pairs of boots . . ." "That's too expensive for a leg of lamb . . ." "But Aruzhan hates dried apricots—"

But then there was a lurch at the top of the dome, and Vika gasped as ripples stuttered over the surface of her enchantment, and a hole broke open into a jagged crack. Her power stumbled, as though the flow from Bolshebnoie Duplo—Russia's magical source—had suddenly been blocked. The sparks that normally danced through her fingertips were snuffed out.

What?

Her chest tightened, as if the air were being wrung from her lungs. The ripples threatened to build into something more, to cascade down the sides of the dome, undoing it all.

Vika opened her arms to the air, palms up, and labored to catch her breath while attempting to control the enchantment. She pulled on the magic that already existed, attempting to draw it up and over to patch the crack at the top of the dome. It was like tugging on fabric that was already stretched too tight; there wasn't enough of the magic to go around.

But then, as quickly as it had hitched, the power flowed smoothly through Vika again. She was almost certain it wasn't her doing—the magic had hardly budged when she pulled on it—but somehow, the ripples on the dome flattened into a serene surface, flowing over the crooked tear at the top to make it whole.

She dropped her arms by her sides, sweat beading on her forehead. What could have possibly caused a hitch like that in the magic? Her power had never faltered so completely before.

Fatigue suddenly trampled her, like being run down by a carriage pulled by half a dozen spooked horses.

And Vika laughed at herself, for in her head, she could hear what Ludmila would say, what she *had* been saying: *Too much work and not enough cookies. You need to take care of yourself, my sunshine. Rest and eat more sweets.*

Rest. Vika shook her head. There was no such thing as

rest for an Imperial Enchanter, certainly not one at Yuliana's constant command.

But that doesn't mean there can't be more cookies. Vika's stomach growled.

She evanesced a few more coins to the nearby bakery stall. A moment later, a *chakchak* cookie appeared in her palm, a cluster of fried dough piled together with syrup and walnut bits. Vika took a crunchy, honeyed bite.

She smiled. Popped the rest of the cookie into her mouth. And sent money for a handful more.

Being Imperial Enchanter wasn't all bad.

CHAPTER TWO

Once she finished capturing the scene on the steppe—and having heard nothing that would imply an immediate threat from the Kazakhs—Vika evanesced back to Saint Petersburg, to the banks of the frozen Neva River. Behind her, an enormous statue of the legendary tsar Peter the Great sat atop a bronze horse and watched over the capital he'd built, this glorious "Venice of the North." The city's bridges were dark at this hour, their holiday garlands that sparkled in the daytime now swallowed by the night, with only an occasional streetlamp casting ghostly halos upon the snow-covered cobblestones. And all the people of the city were fast asleep. All but Vika, of course.

To anyone else, midnight was silent. But to Vika, who could feel the elements as if they were a part of her soul, the darkness was full of sound. Water beneath the thick ice of the river, sluggish and near frozen, but still stirring. Winter moths flitting through the chilly air. Bare branches, bending in the wind.

She wouldn't be able to sleep for a while, if at all, not after spending the last few hours immersed in the steppe. Heavens, how she missed Nikolai. For a brief period of time during the Crown's Game, there had finally been someone else who could do what she could, who understood what it was like to be one—or two—of a kind, who knew who she truly was.

So instead of going home, Vika looked out at the frozen river in front of her, in the direction of the island she'd created during the Game. The people of Saint Petersburg had dubbed it Letniy Isle—Summer Island—for Vika had enchanted it as an eternally warm paradise.

But she shuddered as she remembered the end of the Game. Nikolai had attempted to kill himself, but the knife Galina gave him was charmed to "never miss," and by that, she'd meant "never miss the target that *Galina* intended." So when Nikolai plunged the dagger into himself, it had actually pierced through Vika. And to keep her from dying, he'd siphoned his own energy to her.

Vika closed her eyes as the echo of both Nikolai's and Father's deaths reverberated through her bones. Two incredibly important people had given their lives for her. She was unworthy of the sacrifice.

I would have stopped them if I'd known what they were doing.

But that was why neither had let her know.

The wind nipped more bitterly around her. Father was gone for good, but Nikolai . . . Well, she'd seen him—or a silhouette that looked like him—in the steppe dream. There was an entire series of enchanted park benches on Letniy Isle; a person need only sit on one of the Dream Benches and he or she would be whisked away into an illusion of Moscow,

Lake Baikal, Kostroma, or any of the other dozen places Nikolai had conjured. Each bench was a different dream.

Was Nikolai still there now, in the steppe dream? Vika had gone back every day since she'd seen him that single instance last week, but he had not reappeared. Yet the benches themselves still existed, which meant his magic hadn't been extinguished. Perhaps that meant Nikolai was still, somehow, alive, too.

Then again, Vika could feel the old magic inside the statue of Peter the Great behind her, and that had been created decades ago by an enchanter who'd died in the Napoleonic Wars.

But hopefully the shadow boy Vika had seen was a scrap of life that Nikolai had managed to hold on to for himself. Not quite enough to be real, but enough to be more than a dream.

"If you're still in the bench, I'll find a way to get you out and make you yourself again," Vika said.

As she uttered the promise, her chest constricted. But it wasn't the invisible string that tethered her to Nikolai as enchanters; this pull on her chest was a different sort.

Vika pressed her gloved hand to her left collarbone, where the scar of the Game's crossed wands had once burned.

Before the end of the Game, Nikolai had said he loved her.

It was possible Vika loved Nikolai, too.

But she didn't have much chance to contemplate her feelings, for behind her, heavy footsteps approached the statue of Peter the Great.

Vika's pulse sped up. Had someone seen her evanesce here? Ordinary people couldn't know about magic. A long

11

time ago, they had believed, and there had been witch hunts. Hysteria. Not to mention that the more people believed in magic, the more power Bolshebnoie Duplo generated, which in turn meant that enchanters were a greater threat to the tsar because they could possibly usurp him. It was why the Crown's Game and its oath had been conceived, to ensure that any enchanter would work *with* the tsar, not against him, and why common folk's belief in magic had to be suppressed.

After all she had survived, Vika didn't want to meet her end on a flaming pyre.

The footsteps drew closer. Vika darted away from the embankment and ducked behind the Thunder Stone, the massive slab of granite at the base of Peter the Great's statue.

A minute later, a young fisherman stumbled into view. He was singing.

No. Slurring.

Thank heavens, Vika thought as she relaxed against the Thunder Stone. *He probably didn't see me anyway, and even if he did, he won't remember in the morning.*

But then the boy reached the statue and stopped.

Oh, mercy, she thought. *Anyone but him.*

Vika lightened her steps as she inched around the Thunder Stone to a spot where he wouldn't see her.

Because he might have worn a fisherman's cap, but he was no ordinary drunk.

He was Pavel Alexandrovich Romanov—Pasha— tsesarevich and heir to Russia's throne.